1-2/9

Born in the Kingdom of Fife in 1960, Ian Rankin graduated from the University of Edinburgh in 1982, and then spent three years writing novels when he was supposed to be working towards a PhD in Scottish Literature. His first Rebus novel was published in 1987, and the Rebus books are now translated into thirty-six languages and are bestsellers worldwide. He is the recipient of four Crime Writers' Association Dagger Awards, including the prestigious Diamond Dagger in 2005, and in 2004 he won America's celebrated Edgar Award. A contributor to BBC2's *Newsnight Review*, he has also presented his own TV series, *Ian Rankin's Evil Thoughts*. Ian is a number-one bestselling author in the UK and has received the OBE for services to literature, opting to receive the prize in his home city of Edinburgh, where he lives with his partner and two sons.

You can discover more about the author at www.ianrankin.net

IN A HOUSE OF LIES

A missing private investigator is found, locked in a car hidden deep in the woods. Worse still — both for his family and the police — is that his body was in an area that had already been searched. Detective Inspector Siobhan Clarke is part of a new inquiry, combing through the mistakes of the original case. There were always suspicions over how the investigation was handled, and now — after a decade without answers — it's time for the truth. Every officer involved must be questioned, and it seems everyone on the case has something to hide, and everything to lose. But there is one man who knows where the trail may lead — and that it could be the end of him: John Rebus.

Books by Ian Rankin
Published by Ulverscroft:

WESTWIND
HIDE AND SEEK
THE HANGING GARDEN
DEAD SOULS
SET IN DARKNESS
KNOTS & CROSSES
FLESHMARKET CLOSE
THE FLOOD
THE NAMING OF THE DEAD
SAINTS OF THE SHADOW BIBLE
EVEN DOGS IN THE WILD
RATHER BE THE DEVIL

IAN RANKIN

IN A HOUSE
OF LIES

Complete and Unabridged

CHARNWOOD
Leicester

First published in Great Britain in 2018 by
Orion
London

First Charnwood Edition
published 2019
by arrangement with
The Orion Publishing Group Ltd
London

A catalogue record for this book is available
from the British Library.

ISBN 978–1–4448–4125–1

Published by
F. A. Thorpe (Publishing)
Anstey, Leicestershire

Set by Words & Graphics Ltd.
Anstey, Leicestershire
Printed and bound in Great Britain by
T. J. International Ltd., Padstow, Cornwall

This book is printed on acid-free paper

Tuesday

1

The car was found because Ginger was jealous of his friend Jimmy.

There were four of them in the woods that morning. It was the February break, no school for a few days. They'd taken their bikes as far as they could, then left them when the path became too overgrown, with roots and fallen branches suddenly forming a makeshift assault course. All four of them were eleven years old and in the same class. Ginger, Alan, Rick and Jimmy. Jimmy's bike was the most expensive — his stuff always was. Clothes, backpack, bike. His parents always bought the best. His bedroom was stuffed with game consoles and the latest releases. Which was why Ginger waited till Jimmy was standing at the very edge of the deep gully, sweating and panting after all that running and jumping they'd been doing, before giving him a shove. There wasn't much force to it. Ginger had intended that Jimmy would get a fright, maybe slide a few feet down the slope but be able to claw his way back without help while the rest of them laughed and watched and filmed. But the sides were steep and unstable, and Jimmy tumbled and skidded all the way down, falling into the mass of bracken, briar and nettles at the bottom.

'I didn't do it,' Ginger said, this being his default position in the classroom, the playground

3

and the house he shared with his parents and two sisters. Alan was cursing under his breath as he peered over the edge. Rick had a hold of the back of Alan's hoodie, as if fearing that Ginger wasn't yet finished.

'I didn't *do* it!' Ginger repeated more loudly.

All three of them watched as Jimmy got to his feet. He checked the backs of his hands for nettle stings, then his face, before reaching down for a severed branch.

'He's coming for you,' Alan teased Ginger.

But Jimmy was using the branch to prod at the bracken, swishing it aside as best he could until they could all see what was hidden there.

'Somebody dumped a car,' Jimmy called up to them.

'Cars get dumped all the time,' Rick commented. 'Are you okay to climb out of there?'

But Jimmy ignored him. He was moving around the car, doing his best to uncover it. The windows were still intact, but covered in a mossy film. He tugged his sleeve over his hand and started wiping.

The other boys looked at each other. Alan was the first to start scrambling down the gradient, Rick and Ginger following his lead.

'Anything worth taking?' Alan enquired. Jimmy's face was pressed to the glass. He tried the driver's-side door but it was jammed.

'I think it's a Polo,' Ginger muttered. Then, to clarify: 'The car, it's a VW Polo.'

Rick was rubbing moss across his palms. 'Nettles got me,' he complained.

Alan had circled to the passenger side and yanked the door open. The hinges creaked their resistance.

'Looks empty,' he said, climbing in. The key was in the ignition, so he turned it, but nothing happened. 'Dead,' he announced.

'Somebody nicked it and dumped it,' Ginger concluded, growing bored already and giving one wing a kick. Rick had unzipped his fly and was urinating against a clump of ferns.

'Piss is good for nettle stings,' Alan informed him, receiving a single raised finger in response.

Jimmy had gone to the back of the car and was pressing the release button for the boot. It opened an inch, then stuck.

'Help me out,' he commanded Ginger, the pair of them flinching as the rear window shattered. They turned towards Rick, who had thrown the stone and was now grinning as he brushed dirt from his hands.

'Fuck's sake!' Jimmy yelled.

'Let's get out of here,' Rick replied.

Ginger was peering through the hole in the glass. 'Something's in the back,' he announced, waiting until the others had joined him.

'Looks like a skeleton,' Alan offered.

'Must be a joke or something,' Rick said. 'Doesn't look real to me — does it look real to you?'

'What does a real one look like, Professor?' Jimmy shot back. He was taking photos with his phone. The others dug out their own phones so they could do the same.

'It's got hair,' Ginger said. 'Hair and a shirt.'

'We should hoof it,' Rick suggested. 'Leave it for someone else to find.' He turned away and started scrabbling up the slope. 'What are you waiting for?' he called back down to the others. Ginger and Alan were looking at one another, trying to decide. Then they heard Jimmy's voice and turned towards him. He had his phone pressed to his ear and was asking to be put through to the police.

2

Siobhan Clarke parked on the access road, behind a line of other official vehicles. A uniformed officer checked her warrant card before indicating the route into the woods. She opened the back of her Vauxhall Astra and swapped her shoes for a pair of wellingtons.

'Very wise,' the uniform said, studying his own mud-caked footwear.

'Not my first time,' Clarke informed him.

The back doors of the scene-of-crime van were open, a technician rummaging for something they needed.

'Is Haj in charge?' she asked, receiving a nod of confirmation. She gave a nod of her own and kept moving. Haj Atwal was as good a crime-scene manager as Police Scotland had. Clarke's phone vibrated in her hand. An 0131 number. There was just enough signal, so she answered.

'Hello?'

Silence at the other end. She checked the screen. *Call ended.* Clarke didn't recognise the number, but that didn't surprise her. Same thing had happened three times the previous day and a couple the day before that. Wrong number, she'd assumed, but now she was beginning to wonder. She passed four bikes. The boys had been taken by car to give their statements at a police station. Their bikes would be delivered later — as long as someone remembered.

It took her over five minutes to reach the gully. She heard the voices first, and then started to see the figures. A couple of thick ropes had been secured to nearby trees. One SOCO was climbing out of the gully, hauling himself up with effort, while another was using the adjacent rope to replace him.

'Survival of the fittest,' an officer next to Clarke muttered.

Peering over the edge, Clarke saw the car. Much of its camouflage had been removed. Photographs were being taken, the ground around the vehicle examined. Arc lamps were being assembled, hooked up to a portable generator — early afternoon, but the light was already fading.

'I'm guessing a doctor wasn't needed.'

'Not as such,' the officer commented. 'Pathologist's down there, though.'

Everyone in the gully wore the same white hooded overalls, but Clarke identified Deborah Quant. Quant saw her too, and gave a wave. The figure next to her seemed to ask who she was waving at, and when she replied, he held his hand up in greeting. A minute later, he was climbing out of the gully, making it look easy. He slid his hood back and held out a hand for Clarke to shake.

'I'm DCI Sutherland,' he said. 'But Graham will do. You're DI Clarke?'

'Siobhan,' Clarke said.

'And you're acquainted with our local pathologist.'

Clarke nodded. 'What do we know about the victim?'

'Malc. Deborah's unwilling to say how long he's been dead. Looks like there's some damage to the skull.'

Clarke made a show of studying their surroundings. 'Not an easy place to drive to.'

'I'm guessing it used to be a bit more accessible than it is now. We don't know if he was alive when he went into the gully or already trussed up in the boot.'

'How old is the car?'

'Not sure yet. Number plates have been removed. No sign of a tax disc, nothing in the glove box or the clothing. We'll give it to the lab and see what they say.'

'It's not some weird suicide?'

Sutherland shrugged. 'Deborah doesn't think the skull damage came from the crash. It's to the back of the head and points to a weapon rather than any other type of impact.'

'You said he was trussed?'

'Well, not exactly.' He got busy on his phone, turning the screen towards her. The photo showed the inside of the boot, a close-up of a pair of legs and feet. Grubby jeans, looking brittle with age, and white trainers that had begun to perish. The ankles were shackled by a pair of handcuffs. Clarke looked to Sutherland for an explanation, but all he could offer was a shrug.

★   ★   ★

The major incident team's office was based at Leith police station. Sutherland had said he would meet Clarke there.

'You know the place?' he had asked.

'I know it.'

She called her own office at Gayfield Square and explained that she would be elsewhere.

'Seconded to MIT,' DC Christine Esson commented. 'Don't think I'm not jealous.'

'I'll let you know how it goes.'

'Probably just need you to show them where they can get hot food and a drink.'

'Thanks for the vote of confidence, Christine.' Clarke hoped Esson could hear the smile. She ended the call and entered the MIT room. It was empty apart from some desks and chairs. This was the way things were now, thanks to the changes at Police Scotland — local CID reduced to a secondary role, a dedicated team parachuted in to run the show, a couple of rooms set aside for their use. Clarke didn't know Graham Sutherland but she had heard of him. She wondered why she was on his radar.

There was a noise behind her and she turned. Sutherland entered the room, eyes on her. He was tall, with an athletic build. Early fifties maybe. Short fair hair, a face that had caught the sun not too long ago, a gaze that said it wouldn't miss much. His charcoal two-button suit looked almost new, crisp white shirt, dark blue tie.

'Same as usual,' he commented, studying his surroundings. 'I'm betting the windows are stuck shut and half the sockets don't work.'

'Plus some of the desk drawers can be problematic.'

He offered her a quick smile. 'Rest of the team

will be here soon. Not sure you'll know any of them.'

'Which sort of begs a question, sir . . . '

'I said to call me Graham.'

'I mean, if you don't know the city, there are guides better qualified than me.' She had folded her arms. He met her gaze.

'I've heard good things about you, Siobhan. I can find my way around Edinburgh on my own, but I'm hoping you can help me find my way around this case. And besides . . . ' He broke off, swallowing what he'd been about to add.

'Besides?' she nudged him.

'I know you had a run-in with ACU. You're not the first and you won't be the last.' He took a step towards her, angling his head slightly. 'Way I look at it, cops are like family. ACU need reminding of that.'

'I'm not a charity case, Graham.'

He nodded slowly. Voices could be heard climbing the stairs. 'The real charity cases are about to walk through that door. We'll get the introductions out of the way and then start work — okay?'

'Okay.'

★   ★   ★

Clarke locked the lavatory door and sat down, tapping the names into her phone so she would remember them. There was another DI — Callum Reid. He had red hair and freckles and looked young enough to be Clarke's son. He'd come into the room holding a map, which he

11

had unfolded and pinned to the wall. It showed the woods and the villages and towns around them.

'This'll have to do till we can get hold of a whiteboard,' he had announced.

Sutherland had given Clarke a look to say this was entirely expected of Reid. *Mr Efficiency*, she typed into her phone next to his name. The two detective sergeants had the vague look of a comedy duo from 1970s TV. George Gamble was a portly figure in a three-piece check suit, all of it topped by a ruddy face and an unruly mop of hair. Tess Leighton was a good three inches taller than him and so thin Clarke wondered about anorexia. Her complexion was almost bleached, with dark hollows beneath her eyes. The two DCs on the other hand seemed like brother and sister. They were both fair-haired and of similar height and age, probably still in their mid-twenties. Phil Yeats introduced himself by specifying that his name was 'like the poet, not the wine lodge'.

'He never tires of explaining,' DC Emily Crowther added, shaking Clarke's hand.

The team had only recently come together, hand-picked by Sutherland, who himself hadn't led more than a handful of major investigations. As he'd explained this to Clarke, she had caught a subtext: *So don't let me down.* Then they had all gathered in front of the map, Callum Reid circling the woods with a thick black marker.

Having finished listing the names of her new colleagues as she sat in the toilet stall, Clarke tapped the edge of her phone against her chin.

At least now she knew why she had been brought in: to show ACU that cops stuck together. ACU: Police Scotland's Anti-Corruption Unit. They'd spent the best part of half a year trying to pin something on Clarke. They were finished with her now, but she reckoned they'd be back. She knew it rankled with them that they'd not got the result they wanted. *You're not the first and you won't be the last.* Sutherland had been telling her that he too had fallen foul of ACU at some point in the past. Was her secondment merely his way of sticking two fingers up at his old tormentors? She hoped not. He'd said he had heard good things about her. Bloody right, too — she was a good cop, a good detective, most of it learned the hard way.

Her phone started to thrum. Incoming call. This time a name came up instead of a number. She was half smiling as she answered.

'I was just thinking about you,' she said.

'Was it a Polo?' John Rebus sounded agitated.

'What?'

'The car in the woods. You need to check if it was a red Volkswagen Polo.'

'How do you know?'

'Radio says there was a body inside.'

Clarke's eyes narrowed. 'Are you telling me you think you know who it is?'

'I'm not saying it is, I'm saying it might be.'

'And you're going to tell me?'

There was a moment's silence. 'They've given you the case?'

'I'm attached to MIT.'

'Good for you. So you're down in Leith?' She

couldn't help but smile, and he seemed to sense it. 'See, I might be long retired, but the brain's still active.'

'The brain might be active, but you're not.'

'What's that supposed to mean?'

'Only one of us is the detective these days. So give me a name and I'll check it out.'

'I blame modern technology, you know.'

'For what?'

'The short memories your generation have. You've forgotten how to store information.'

'John . . . ' She sighed. 'Just tell me the name.'

'You've not even asked how I'm keeping.'

'I saw you last month.'

'Maybe my situation's deteriorated.'

'Has it?'

'Not so you'd notice.'

'That's good to hear.' She paused. 'John? You still there?'

'I'm on my way.'

'That's not how it — ' But Rebus had ended the call.

Clarke got up and unlocked the cubicle door, rinsing her hands before making her way back to the office. The team were trying to look busy while waiting for equipment and ancillary staff to arrive. Reid was stressing the need for a TV or monitor of some kind so they could keep an eye on the media's treatment of the story. Leighton was adding that someone should check social media, as a source of information and rumour. They were one desk short, so Yeats and Crowther were sharing. They didn't seem to mind, chatting among themselves until they noticed that

14

Graham Sutherland had finished the phone call he'd been on.

'Deborah Quant says we need a forensic anthropologist. She's contacting . . . ' he looked at the note he'd scribbled to himself, 'Aubrey Hamilton. Based in Dundee apparently.'

'But there'll be an autopsy?' Callum Reid asked. He was standing by his map as if to make sure no one else claimed ownership.

Sutherland nodded. 'With Hamilton assisting Professor Quant. Meantime, the kids' prints have been taken for purposes of elimination. I think Haj wants them terminated rather than eliminated — stomping all over his crime scene, leaving broken glass everywhere.'

'What do we make of the handcuffs?' George Gamble had removed his suit jacket and sat with his thumbs tucked into the pockets of his waistcoat.

'Good question.' Sutherland looked at each of them in turn. 'Any ideas?'

'They seem to be good quality,' Tess Leighton drawled. She sat very upright on her chair, like a disapproving Miss Jean Brodie.

'They're proper,' Sutherland agreed.

'Meaning police issue?'

'We don't know that yet.'

'But around the *ankles*,' Callum Reid said, shaking his head. 'Doesn't make sense.'

'Unless you want to stop someone running away,' Phil Yeats added.

Sutherland ran a finger thoughtfully down the bridge of his nose. 'Anything to add, Siobhan?'

Clarke cleared her throat. 'I've got a source

who thinks he might have a name for us.'

There was a sudden energy in the room. Reid forgot about his map and marched in Clarke's direction. 'Go on then,' he demanded.

'He wouldn't tell me.'

'Then let's go talk to him!' Reid looked towards Sutherland, expecting a nod or a word, but his boss's eyes were on Clarke.

'Who is it exactly you've been speaking to, Siobhan?'

'He's an ex-cop. Been retired a few years. And if I know him, he'll be turning up here in the next ten or fifteen minutes.'

'Feel like telling us a bit about him before that happens?'

'In ten or fifteen minutes?' Clarke gave a little snort. 'I doubt I'd be able to do him justice.'

Sutherland leaned back in his chair and folded his arms. 'Give it a try anyway.'

⋆   ⋆   ⋆

'They wouldn't let me past the front desk,' Rebus complained as Clarke led him up the stairs. 'Time was . . . '

Clarke stopped, turning to face him. 'Are you okay, John? I mean, really?'

'I've still got COPD, if that's what you're asking. It doesn't go away.'

'I know. It gets worse.'

'But somehow I'm still here.' Rebus stretched out his arms. 'Like the proverbial . . . '

'Bad penny? Bull in a china shop?'

'I think I was going to say 'ghost in the

16

machine' until I realised it's not exactly a proverb.' He paused, studying his surroundings. 'Just like old times.'

'*Nothing* like old times, John,' she cautioned him, starting up the stairs again. Rebus was breathing heavily by the time they reached the landing. He took a moment to compose himself, patting his pocket to check he had his inhaler.

'I kicked the cigarettes, once and for all,' he informed Clarke.

'And the booze?'

'Just the odd tincture, m'lud.' Pulling back his shoulders and fixing a look on his face that she recognised of old, he breezed past her into the room. Sutherland was already on his feet. He met Rebus in the middle of the floor and gripped his hand.

'Not every day you meet a legend,' he said.

'Me or you?' Rebus responded. Sutherland gave a half-smile before leading Rebus towards the waiting chair. Phil Yeats was leaning against the wall; it was his chair Rebus was settling on. Sutherland sat at his desk, hands clasped.

'Siobhan tells us you might have some information, John. We're grateful to you for coming in.'

'You might not be when you hear the name. It was 2006.' Rebus broke off and gestured towards Callum Reid. 'You'd have been in short pants, son.' Then, to Sutherland: 'Is it bring your kid to work week or something?'

'DI Reid is older than he looks.' Sutherland was still trying for levity, but Clarke could tell it wasn't going to last. His tone alerted Rebus, who scanned the room again. 'Short memories, like I was telling Siobhan. If I'm right, your car most likely belongs to Stuart Bloom.' He waited, watching as Sutherland's brow furrowed.

'I was still in Inverness in 2006,' the DCI eventually said.

'How about you, Siobhan?' Rebus held up a finger. 'Actually, I can help you there — you were on secondment in Fife. Three months, I think, which tied in almost exactly with the case.'

'The private investigator?' Clarke was nodding to herself. 'I remember us talking about it. He did a vanishing act.'

'That's the one,' Rebus said. 'Ringing any bells?' He looked around the room but was met by blank faces. Callum Reid, however, was already busy on his phone, starting a search of the name on the internet. The others realised what he was doing and followed suit. All except Sutherland, whose own phone had started buzzing. He pressed it to his ear.

'DCI Sutherland,' he said. His eyes were fixed on Rebus as he listened. Having thanked the caller, he waved his phone in Rebus's direction. 'Members of the public have been in touch. *Other* members of the public, I should say. Three of them gave the same name you just did.'

'Private investigator from Edinburgh,' Reid intoned, reading from his screen as he skimmed it. 'Disappeared in March of 2006. His partner was questioned — '

'Business partner?' Sutherland interrupted.

'Lover,' Rebus corrected him. 'Stuart Bloom

was gay. Boyfriend happened to be the son of a Glaswegian murder squad detective called Alex Shankley.'

'The boyfriend was a suspect?' Sutherland asked.

'No shortage of those,' Rebus stated. 'But when there's no sign of foul play and a body fails to turn up . . . '

Sutherland had risen from his chair and walked over to the map, studying it. Rebus joined him.

'Would those woods have been searched?' He watched Rebus give a slow nod.

'More than once, I think.'

Sutherland half turned towards him. 'And why is that?'

'Because of who owned them.'

'Spit it out, John,' Sutherland snapped, patience at an end.

'The man Stuart Bloom was working for. A film producer called Jackie Ness. Ness's house is the far side of the woods from the road.' Rebus peered at the map, eventually pressing his finger against a particular spot. 'There, more or less,' he said. 'And 'house' might be doing it a disservice — more like a mansion.'

'Ness still lives there?' Sutherland watched Rebus shrug. He turned towards the room. 'Get me that information,' he demanded of no one and everyone.

'A computer would be handy,' Phil Yeats said. 'My notebook's in the car. I could go fetch it.'

Sutherland nodded. Then, for Rebus's benefit: 'It's what laptops are called these days.'

19

'I know that,' Rebus retorted. 'So what happens now?'

Sutherland grew thoughtful. 'You worked the original inquiry. Be helpful to know what you know.'

'Always assuming,' Tess Leighton added, 'it really is this guy Bloom's car, *and* him in the boot.'

'We need to keep an open mind,' Sutherland agreed. 'But meantime, maybe John could give a statement, just to keep everything tidy. I'm assuming the paperwork is in storage somewhere?'

'CCU probably took most of it,' Rebus said casually, pretending to study the map.

'CCU?'

'I know it's called ACU these days, but it was the Counter-Corruption Unit in 2006. Wee history lesson might be needed for some of you. This was long before Police Scotland. We still had the eight regional forces then — '

'Why would CCU be involved, John?' Sutherland interrupted.

Rebus made show of thinking for a moment. 'Well,' he eventually said, 'we somehow managed to make a complete fucking mess of things. CCU was just the icing on the cake, so to speak.'

'He's not wrong,' Callum Reid said, eyes fixed on his phone, thumb busy. 'Bloom's family made over a dozen complaints during the inquiry and after. Just last year they were at it again.'

Rebus nodded slowly, eyes on Sutherland. 'Be a lot simpler if it turned out to be just about anyone in that car other than Stuart Bloom. Any

20

chance that it was a suicide?'

'I think we can pretty much rule that out. Someone covered the car with branches and bracken.'

'He might have done that before climbing into the boot, if he really didn't want to be found.'

George Gamble gave a gravelly chuckle. 'Ever come across a suicide handcuffed at the ankles?'

'Handcuffed?' Rebus looked from Sutherland to Siobhan Clarke and back again.

'I'm not sure we want that particular detail made public just yet.' Sutherland glared at Gamble.

'*Police* handcuffs?' Rebus pressed.

Sutherland held up a hand, palm towards Rebus. 'Let's not get ahead of ourselves. Maybe we should sit down and you can tell us the story.'

'Cup of tea wouldn't go amiss.'

Sutherland nodded and turned his attention to Clarke. 'Siobhan, you're the one with the local knowledge . . . '

'There's a café across the street. Probably the best option.'

Sutherland produced a twenty-pound note from his pocket and held it out for her to take.

'Hang on,' she complained. 'You want *me* to go?'

'I'm delegating,' he said with a sly look.

She snatched the note from him and walked over to Emily Crowther. 'Off you go then, DC Crowther.'

Crowther scowled and seemed reluctant to take the money, so Clarke placed it on the desk, sliding it towards her.

'Nicely delegated,' Rebus commented with a thin smile. Then, to Graham Sutherland: 'Where do you want me to start?'

3

A street of bungalows in Blackhall, quietly residential apart from drivers keen to avoid the adjacent — and busier — Queensferry Road. Rebus pushed open the wrought-iron gate. No sound from its hinges, the garden to either side of the flagstone path well tended. Two bins — one landfill, one garden waste — had already been placed on the pavement outside. None of the neighbours had got round to it yet. Rebus rang the doorbell and waited. The door was eventually opened by a man the same age as him, though he looked half a decade younger. Bill Rawlston had kept himself trim since retirement, and the eyes behind the half-moon spectacles retained their keen intelligence.

'John Rebus,' he said, a sombre look on his face as he studied Rebus from top to toe.

'Have you heard?'

Rawlston's mouth twitched. 'Of course I have. But nobody's saying it's him yet.'

'Only a matter of time.'

'Aye, I suppose so.' Rawlston gave a sigh and stepped back into the hall. 'You better come in then. Tea or something that bit stronger?'

'Tea will be fine.'

Rawlston glanced over his shoulder as he headed for the kitchen. 'First time I've known you to turn one down.'

'I seem to have picked up a wee dose of COPD.'

'What's that when it's at home?'

'Chronic obstructive pulmonary disease — known as emphysema in the old days.'

'Trust you to get something that has the word COP in it.'

'Aye, I feel like I drew a winning ticket there.'

'Well, I'm sorry all the same. Neither 'chronic' nor 'obstructive' sounds like a top prize.'

'How about you, Bill?' Rebus asked.

'Beth died last year. Smoked a pack a day all her adult life. Then she trips and hits her head and a blood clot gets her. Would you credit it?'

The kitchen was immaculate. Lunchtime's soup bowl and side plate had been washed and were sitting on the drainer. The plastic container the soup had been in had also been rinsed — there'd be a recycling bin outside the back door waiting to receive it.

'Sugar?' Rawlston asked. 'I can't remember.'

'Just milk, thanks.' Not that Rebus was planning on drinking the tea; he was awash with the stuff after his trip to Leith. But the making of the drinks had given him time to size up Bill Rawlston. And Rawlston, too, he knew, would have been using the time to do some thinking.

'Just through here,' Rawlston told his guest, handing over a mug and leading the way. The living room was small, a dining room off. Family photos, ornaments and a bookcase stocked with paperbacks and DVDs. Rebus made a show of studying the shelves.

'You don't hear much of Alistair MacLean

these days,' he commented.

'Probably a good reason for that. Sit down and tell me what's on your mind.'

There was an occasional table next to Rawlston's favoured armchair. Two remote controls and a phone, plus a spare pair of glasses. The colourful paintings on the walls probably reflected Beth's taste rather than her husband's. Rebus perched on the edge of the sofa, mug cupped in both hands.

'If it is him, it's likely a murder case. From the description of the body, he was probably already dead all the time we were looking for him.'

'The body was found in Poretoun Woods?'

Rebus nodded.

'We searched those woods, John, you know that. We had dozens of men . . . spent hundreds of hours . . . '

'I remember.'

Stuart Bloom had lived in Comely Bank, to the north of the city centre. The nearest police station to his home was the Lothian and Borders Police HQ on Fettes Avenue — colloquially known as 'the Big House' — so that was where they'd based the inquiry team, in two rooms usually used for meetings of the top brass. DCI Bill Rawlston had been put in charge, with Rebus and half a dozen other CID officers under him. At the first briefing, Rawlston had informed the group that this was his last year before retirement.

'You and me both,' Rebus had interrupted. Rawlston had locked eyes with him.

'So I want a result here. No slacking. No

tipping off the media. No back-stabbing. If you want to play politics, there's a parliament waiting for you down the road. Understood?'

But there had been slacking, and whispers to favoured journalists, and fronts stabbed when backs were not available. The team had never quite gelled, never become a family.

Rawlston placed his mug on the table next to him. 'Say it is him . . . '

'They'll open a murder inquiry,' Rebus stated. 'And the media will go digging out all the old stories, which our lot will already be looking at afresh. Then there's his family to consider.'

'They were at me again last year, did you hear?' Rawlston watched Rebus nod. 'As far as they're concerned, the whole thing was a conspiracy from the start, with us bang in the middle of it. Well, they finally got their official apology from the Big Chief.'

'Just before he was kicked into touch.'

'He said we'd behaved with 'institutional arrogance' in the way we dealt with all their bloody complaints. The nerve of the man . . . '

'Nobody ever proved we got the inquiry wrong, though,' Rebus felt it necessary to add. Then, when Rawlston said nothing: 'I seem to recall the mother was best described as feisty.'

Rawlston gave a hoot. 'We worked ourselves into the ground, and not one bit of thanks.'

'Quite the reverse, in fact.'

'I loved my job, John, but by the end, I was as relieved as hell to walk away.' Rawlston paused. 'How about you?'

'They had to drag me out. Even then, I went

back in for a while, working cold cases.'

'And now?'

Rebus exhaled. 'Washed up seems to be the general consensus.'

'So what brings you here?'

'Just thought you should know. There's a team already up and running. I spoke to them earlier, so now they know at least a bit of the story. But they'll be dusting off the case files, and at some point they'll interview the family . . . and the original inquiry team.' Rebus's voice died away.

'We're going to have to defend ourselves all over again.' Rawlston seemed to be staring at something beyond the living room walls. 'I think I knew from the start that it was one of those cases you take to the grave. In my case, sooner rather than later.'

Rebus took a moment to respond. 'How long have you got?'

'Six months to a year. I'm told I look as good as I ever did. I still exercise and eat my greens . . . take the various tablets.' Rawlston managed a wry smile. 'Never smoked in my life, but I spent thirty years married to someone who did. Would you credit it? And here's what's waiting for me at the end — all that old shite coming back to haunt me.' He looked at Rebus. 'You able to keep your ear to the ground, John? Let me know how it plays out?'

Rebus nodded. 'I reckon I can do that.'

'They're out to bury us, you know. They don't want the likes of us around. We smell of old days and old ways.'

'You said earlier about a conspiracy with us in the middle . . . ' Rebus had placed his untouched mug on the carpet and was rising to his feet. 'So what would you say if I told you the body in the car was wearing handcuffs?'

'Handcuffs?'

'Forensics will soon know if they were police issue. Doesn't mean they came from a cop, of course.'

'The Chuggabugs?'

Rebus gave a shrug. 'You ever hear from them?'

'They came to Beth's funeral. Didn't stay for the drinks, though.'

'Are they still on the force?'

'We didn't really speak.' Rawlston rose to his feet, straightening his shoulders and pulling back his head. But Rebus knew now, knew it was for show. The man was in pain, and the pain wasn't going anywhere.

'I was conscientious, John,' he said quietly. 'I did everything I could to the best of my abilities. Maybe that was never going to be enough for some people, but if there's anything you can do . . . anything to stop them flushing my reputation down the crapper . . . '

Rebus found himself nodding slowly, the two men locking eyes, knowing neither was being completely truthful at this meeting.

'Not just *your* reputation, Bill,' Rebus said, watching as Rawlston stepped in so close he feared for a moment that a hug was imminent. But there was a pat on the forearm instead.

'I'll see you out,' Bill Rawlston said quietly.

* * *

Having finally found a parking space for his Saab, Rebus was a few steps from his tenement on Arden Street when he heard a car door open behind him.

'Wondered when I'd be seeing you,' he said to Siobhan Clarke.

'Can I come up?'

'Brillo needs a walk.'

'Then I'll keep you company.'

He reached a hand out towards her, his keys dangling from one finger. 'His lead's hanging in the hall. Keech bags in the kitchen drawer beneath the kettle.'

She took the keys. 'What's the matter, old-timer — stairs too much for you?'

'Can't see the point when there are younger legs available.'

Clarke unlocked the tenement door and headed in. She was right, though — the two flights of unforgiving Edinburgh stairs were becoming a definite issue. More and more he'd have to pause at the first landing, maybe for a puff from the inhaler. He'd considered selling up and buying something at ground level, either a main-door flat or a bungalow. Maybe he still would.

Brillo was barking with excitement as Clarke led him back down to where the outside world with its plethora of sights and smells was waiting.

'The Meadows?' she guessed, attempting to hand the lead to Rebus.

'The Meadows it is,' he said, stuffing his hands

into his pockets and walking off.

'I'm not great with dogs,' Clarke cautioned, as Brillo strained against his leash.

'You're doing fine,' Rebus assured her. The sky was clear, the temperature not much above zero. A group of students passed them, swinging carrier bags filled with bottles.

'Your flat could do with a tidy,' Clarke stated.

'You were only supposed to go in the kitchen.'

'Your kitchen could do with a tidy,' she corrected herself.

'Are you offering?'

'I'm a bit busy these days. I just thought maybe with Deborah and everything . . . '

'Professor Quant and myself are taking a bit of a break.'

'Oh.'

'It's not that we fell out or anything. In fact, I should probably blame you.'

'Why?'

'For keeping her so busy.' Rebus paused. 'Your man Sutherland looks pretty useful.'

'No complaints so far.'

'Only day one, Siobhan — plenty fuck-ups ahead. What about the rest of his crew?'

'They seem fine.'

'Shouldn't you be with them right now, bonding over a few post-work drinks?'

'You know why I'm here, John.'

'Tell me.'

'I want to hear the whole story.'

'You don't think that's what I gave Sutherland?'

'First time for everything, I suppose.'

'I didn't lie, though, give me credit for that. Any progress since I left?'

'Not really.' She took a deep breath. 'So Stuart Bloom was a private eye, employed by a man called Jackie Ness to find out about a land deal. Ness had a long-time rivalry with another businessman called Adrian Brand . . . '

'Now *Sir* Adrian Brand.'

'Brand wanted a chunk of green-belt land so he could build a golf course; Ness reckoned the same land would be perfect for a film studio. He thought Brand might be lining pockets to clinch the deal, but he needed proof . . . '

'Enter Stuart Bloom.'

'Trained as a journalist, studied computers and how to hack into them. Was in a fairly open relationship with a lecturer called . . . '

'Derek Shankley.'

'Shankley's father Alex was Glasgow CID . . . '

'Murder squad to be precise.' They had reached Melville Drive. The Meadows lay before them, a large tree-edged playing field with the old infirmary and the university beyond it. Rebus reached down and unclipped Brillo's lead. The small, wiry dog bounded off. Clarke and Rebus stayed where they were, half watching as Brillo slowed and began nosing his territory.

'The night Bloom went missing,' Clarke continued, 'he'd just made a report to Jackie Ness at Ness's home.'

'The palatial Poretoun House,' Rebus agreed.

'Which happens to be next to Poretoun Woods. And it turns out those woods are where Bloom's body has been lying all these years.'

31

'If it's him.'

'If it's him,' Clarke conceded. 'Tess Leighton is putting in a late shift to check other missing persons from the period.' She turned her head towards him. 'And CCU became involved because . . . ?'

'For one thing, the family had complained we weren't putting in enough effort. They had the lover down as a suspect and thought we'd gone too easy on him.'

'Because of who his father was?'

'Alex Shankley was a hairy-arsed Glasgow cop. A man's man. Football on a Saturday, roast dinner on a Sunday. Spent his days chasing knife gangs and scumbags.' Rebus broke off.

'And ashamed of his son?'

'Maybe. I don't know. But word went around that it would be appreciated if we could try to keep mentions of Derek to a minimum. Wouldn't be so easy these days, but we had our fair share of friendly journalists back then.'

'Hang on, though. Bloom trained as a journalist. Wouldn't the press be keen to find out what had happened to one of their own?'

Rebus shrugged. 'He wasn't in the trade long enough to make friends.'

'Okay, so what about the meeting with Jackie Ness?'

'A regular update at the mansion. Bloom's instructions were to keep doing what he'd been doing.'

'And what had he been doing?'

'Asking around; buying a few drinks; accessing computers . . . '

'When he disappeared, you looked at *his* computer?'

'Not me personally, but the team did. He didn't have an office as such, worked out of his flat. Never found his laptop, though — or should I say 'notebook'. Didn't find his phone either. All we knew was, in the weeks after he disappeared, he didn't open any emails, didn't make any calls, and withdrew no money from a cashpoint.'

'Did you think he was dead?'

Rebus nodded. 'Fight with his lover; picked up the wrong stranger from a club; ended up in the wrong place at the wrong time.'

'Say he'd tried breaking into Adrian Brand's home, or maybe his office,' Clarke speculated.

'We interviewed everyone we could, most of them more than once. Wasn't as much CCTV back then, but even so, it was hard to just disappear into thin air. We were waiting for someone to talk, but no one did.'

'His parents are on their way here,' Clarke said with a sigh.

'From where?'

'They live near Dumfries these days.'

'You think they can make the identification?'

'More likely it'll be down to DNA. But Graham is asking Jackie Ness to look at the clothing. He was apparently the last person to see Bloom. Derek Shankley's being asked, too. You remember what Bloom was wearing the night he vanished?'

Rebus shook his head.

'According to the newspaper reports, a red check shirt, denim jacket and blue jeans — same gear we found on the body in the Polo.' She stared at him. 'I need to know what you're not telling me, John.'

'We've pretty much covered it.'

'I don't think so.'

'It's good to see you, Shiv. I just wish it didn't have to end like this.'

Her eyes widened slightly. 'Like what?'

Rebus nodded towards where Brillo had paused to squat. 'With you being the one who's got the keech bag.'

Clarke's phone started vibrating. She tried for a disappointed look as she handed Rebus the small black polythene bag. 'I'd better take this,' she said.

When Rebus returned with Brillo now back on his lead, he asked her who'd called.

'It's nothing,' she said, not managing to hide her exasperation.

'Doesn't sound like nothing.'

'I've had a few calls, 0131, but when I answer, they just hang up.'

'Not a number you recognise?' He watched as she shook her head. 'Tried phoning back?'

'One time. No answer.'

'It didn't go to an answering machine or anything?' Rebus gestured towards her phone. 'Give it another shot. Keep you busy while I walk over to that bin.'

By the time he'd dumped the bag, she was walking towards him.

'Someone picked up,' she explained. 'It's a phone box on the Canongate.'

'So who was on the other end?'

34

'Sounded like a tourist. Said they were just passing.'

'Bit of a mystery then. How many did you say you've had?'

'I don't know. Ten, twelve, something like that.'

'All from the same number?'

She checked her screen for recent calls. 'Two different numbers.'

'So check out the other one, maybe that'll give you the answer. That's what a detective would do, DI Clarke.' They shared a momentary smile, but then Rebus started coughing.

'Cold weather's a bugger,' he explained.

'You're doing okay, though?'

'Seem to have survived another winter. Annual spirometry test last week — lungs at seventy per cent.'

'Winter's not quite over yet — supposed to be snow on the way from Russia, maybe a lot of it.'

'A good reason to stay indoors.'

'You've dropped a bit of weight, that must be helping.'

'Who can afford food on a police pension? There *are* positives, though.'

'Such as?'

'If I catch an infection, it could be the death of me — the perfect excuse not to be sociable. Plus, I can't visit any big polluted cities like London.'

'You had plans to go there?'

'Not on your life.' Rebus's eyes shifted to Brillo. 'I know about ACU, by the way,' he admitted.

'How?'

'You're not the only cop I talk to. Why didn't you say?'

'What was there to say?'

'Jesus, Shiv, the number of times I was carpeted, I'm a walking encyclopedia on how to deal with those arseholes.'

'Maybe I wanted to do it on my terms rather than yours. Besides, it was no big deal. They were fishing, that was all, like CCU in the Stuart Bloom case.' She paused for a beat. 'Unless you and yours really *were* hiding something?'

'No comment, your honour.' They stood in silence for the better part of thirty seconds. A single night-time jogger was out; traffic was light; a couple of dogs had started a barking contest on nearby Bruntsfield Links, causing Brillo's ears to prick up.

'If you're not too scared of germs,' Rebus eventually said, 'we could go back to mine for a cup of coffee.'

But Clarke was shaking her head. 'I should be getting home. I'll probably see Deborah tomorrow; anything you want me to say to her?'

'Nothing I can't tell her myself.' Rebus paused. 'Just don't mention the kitchen.'

★   ★   ★

Clarke reasoned that Canongate was on her way home anyway, so she turned right at North Bridge and looked for phone boxes. A brace of them stood in front of a kilt shop, not far from John Knox's House. This was still tourist territory. She kept driving and found the street

36

getting quieter — seemingly darker, too — as she neared its foot, where the contemporary architecture of the Scottish Parliament faced off against the ancient scowl of the Palace of Holyrood directly across the road. Driving around the roundabout, she retraced her route. The kilt shop phone boxes were the only ones she'd seen, so she pulled her car in next to them and got out. Neither looked exactly enticing, their windows spattered and misted by the residue of flyers that had been only partially removed.

She took out her own phone and called the number. The ringing came from the box right next to her. She cancelled the call and yanked open the door. The aroma of urine was very faint, but still caught in her nostrils. She gave the interior a good look, including its floor, but saw nothing to interest her. Closing the door again, she tapped the second unknown number into her phone. Sure enough, the ringing this time came from the companion booth. Clarke looked up and down the street, craning her neck to check all the windows above street level. Her phone listed the dates and times of the various calls. Two in the early afternoon, most between seven and nine in the evening, one at midnight. Someone local? Using a public telephone so as to remain untraceable? It struck her as an old-fashioned solution. If you wanted to stay anonymous, you could do so on a mobile; you just had to withhold your number. But there were ways of getting past that. All police detectives knew as much. Was someone in trouble? Or had someone been given her number by mistake? Maybe they kept expecting a male voice at the other end. Or else it was some random crank. She'd even heard of automated calls, just checking that lines and systems were working. It could be anything.

There was a pub called McKenzie's across the road and she was tempted. But she had plenty of gin at home, plus the necessary tonic water and lemon. A man had emerged from the dimly lit interior to smoke a cigarette. She walked over to him and nodded a greeting.

'This your local?' she asked.

'Aye.'

'Ever noticed anyone using those phone boxes?' She pointed towards them.

He drew in some smoke and held it before exhaling. 'Who the hell uses a phone box these days?'

'Not everyone has a mobile.'

'You could have fooled me. You the police?'

'I might be.'

'So what's going on?'

'Just some nuisance calls.'

'Heavy breathing, you mean? Christ, that takes me back. Happened to my wife once. Years ago, mind.'

'What about the pub — any new faces turned up recently?'

'It's mostly Americans and Chinese, looking for coffee and something to eat. Place makes more money from meals than drink these days. Want me to keep my eyes peeled?'

'I'd appreciate it.' She found a business card in

her pocket. 'I'm based at Gayfield Square. They can always get a message to me.'

'Siobhan's a nice name,' he said, peering at the card.

'My parents thought so.'

'Can I buy you a drink, Siobhan?'

Clarke made show of scowling. 'What would your wife say?'

'She'd say, 'Robbie, I never knew you still had it in you.''

He was still chuckling as Clarke headed back to her car.

★   ★   ★

She drove the length of her street without finding a parking space, so ended up around the corner on a yellow line. There was a POLICE sign she could place on the dashboard, but it was, she knew from experience, an invitation to vandals, so instead she decided she'd remember to move the Astra before the wardens started their morning shift. A few late-night revellers were heading down Broughton Street with their fast-food containers, voices raucous with laughter. Music was pumping from one of the windows above her — but from the tenement opposite hers, praise be. There was someone sitting in a parked car. Their face had been illuminated by the screen of their phone, but the car interior was dark by the time Clarke found her key and unlocked her door. She made sure it clicked shut behind her.

The stairwell was well lit and uncluttered, no

mail waiting for her other than the usual advertising bumf. She climbed to her landing, unlocked the door to her flat and flicked on the hall light. She wondered what it would be like to be welcomed by Brillo or another dog. Nice to have something to come home to, maybe. In the kitchen, she filled the kettle. Rebus's own kitchen hadn't been that bad, she decided, noticing the dishes in her sink. While the water boiled, she headed through to the living room, pausing at the window. She could just make out the car below, its front driver's-side window illuminated again. She watched as the window slid down, a hand and wrist emerging, the phone pointed towards her tenement door. A single flash as a photograph was taken.

'What the hell?' Clarke muttered. She watched for a further moment, then stalked back into the hall, snatching up her keys and heading for the stairs. The car's engine was running by the time she hauled open the tenement door. Headlamps lit, wheels turning as it began to leave its parking spot. She couldn't make out the driver, no idea if they were male or female. As it pulled away, she stumbled over the kerb, taking a minute to right herself, by which time the car had turned into Broughton Street and was gone. No make, no number plate. She stared at the gap where the car had been, and decided to move her own.

'Silver lining, Siobhan,' she told herself, making for the corner.

Wednesday

4

The mortuary car park was almost full by the time Clarke arrived. She'd grabbed a coffee from her local café and carried it with her as she made for the staff entrance. Most of the attendants knew her and gave nods of welcome as she walked down the corridor. The autopsy suite was one floor up, so she climbed the stairs, opening the last door she came to. It led to the viewing area. There were two rows of benches, a glass panel separating the spectators from the room where the actual work was done. Sutherland's team had already gathered. They were concentrating on the ceiling-mounted loudspeaker as Professors Deborah Quant and Aubrey Hamilton discussed procedure. Both women wore regulation gowns, foot protectors, masks, caps and goggles. Quant was the taller, which was useful when they had their backs to the viewing room. Mortuary staff fussed around them with stainless-steel implements and bowls and various sizes of clear plastic specimen pouch. Scales had been fetched, though Clarke very much doubted there'd be anything in the way of vital organs to weigh. Graham Sutherland wasn't the only one to cast an envious eye at Clarke's coffee.

'What have I missed?' she asked.

'Clothing's in the process of being removed.' He handed a set of photographs to her. An identical set was being perused by one of the

43

mortuary technicians. They showed Stuart Bloom at various ages and in a range of poses. In one of the later ones, he appeared to be wearing the same jacket and shirt from the night he'd gone missing. Stepping closer to the glass, Clarke saw that the denim jacket and check shirt had been sliced cleanly in sections from the cadaver, though not without taking some skin in the process. What was left on the slab looked like a prop from a horror film. Tweezers were removing samples of hair, eyebrows and a fingernail, along with bits of glass from the shattered window.

'Apparently the wildlife have had a go at him down the years,' Sutherland commented.

'I thought the boot was closed, car windows intact?'

He looked at her. 'I mean bugs and the like. They smell decay, they're always going to find a way.'

Pathologist and anthropologist were now studying the skull, Quant circling the area of damage with her finger. They moved on to the jaw, examining the teeth.

'Dental records,' Clarke said. Sutherland nodded his agreement and turned towards George Gamble. While the other detectives were on their feet, Gamble had decided to stay seated, pudgy hands resting on thick knees.

'They're on their way,' Gamble obliged.

Sutherland's eyes met Clarke's. 'CCU agreed to release the case files. A couple of dozen boxes and about as many computer disks. It's all coming to us from the warehouse.'

'Joy of joys,' Tess Leighton drawled.

'Bit of reading for you, Tess,' Callum Reid said with a grin.

'For *all* of you,' Sutherland corrected him. 'Team effort, remember?'

Leighton wagged a finger at Reid, who gave a sniff and turned his attention back to the examination. The door swung open, a member of the mortuary team standing there in overalls and shin-high rubber boots.

'Could do with one of you in reception,' he said. 'They're threatening to gatecrash.'

'Who's 'they'?' Sutherland asked. Clarke reckoned she knew.

'The family?' She watched the assistant nod.

'And they've a reporter with them,' he added.

'Do the honours, Siobhan,' Sutherland said. 'We need one of them anyway for the DNA.'

'What do I tell them, though?'

Sutherland managed a shrug that didn't look wholly sympathetic. His attention was again on the autopsy, especially now that the ankles — still handcuffed — were being photographed, inspected, discussed.

Clarke tried not to let her feelings show as she made her exit, following the assistant to the public reception area. Another staff member was there, in white blouse and black trousers. She had risen from her desk and stood with arms stretched wide, as if to form a wall between the visitors and the stairs and corridors behind her. The assistant had melted away, leaving Clarke to walk to the receptionist's side.

'I'm Detective Inspector Clarke,' she announced, holding open her warrant card. This had the

45

desired effect — sometimes it did, sometimes it didn't. The visitors' attention shifted to her. She recognised Stuart Bloom's parents from the photographs of them online. They looked to be in their early sixties. The mother, Catherine, wore a well-cut black coat. Her hair was silver, cut short, suiting the shape of her face. Time and tide had not been so kind to her husband. He had a haunted look in the photographs, always very much leaving the speeches to his wife. Martin Bloom had been an accountant and possibly still was. His suit looked like he wore it most days with the same tightly knotted necktie. His hair needed a trim, and grey hairs sprouted from both ears.

'The family deserve to be told, DI Clarke. After all these years of police incompetence and cover-up . . . '

Clarke held up a hand as she studied the man who'd just spoken. He was probably still in his twenties, his face superficially like that of the Blooms' son Stuart. Yet Clarke knew Stuart had been an only child. The man realised something was needed from him.

'I'm Dougal Kelly. I'm a family friend.'

'And would you also happen to be a journalist, Mr Kelly?'

'I'm writing a book,' Kelly admitted. 'But that's neither here nor there.'

Clarke seemed wordlessly to agree. She had turned away from him to focus on the parents.

'Mr and Mrs Bloom, I know this is difficult, but right now we really don't have anything concrete we can share.'

'You could start by letting us see him,' Catherine Bloom blurted out, a tremor in her voice.

'That's not really possible until we have a positive identification.'

'You're telling us it might not be him?' Martin Bloom enquired quietly.

'Right now we don't know very much.'

'But you know *something*!' His wife's voice was rising again.

'Say it's not Stuart, and we let you view the body before the real family. You must see the distress that would cause.'

'How long until you know for certain?' Dougal Kelly asked.

'Not too long, I hope.' Clarke's eyes were still on the parents. 'If we could swab one of you for DNA. And maybe take a hair or two . . . '

'You can do that here?' the father asked.

'I'd think so.' Clarke turned to the receptionist, who was back in her seat, trying for invisibility. 'Okay if we use the waiting room while I check?'

'Of course.'

'And maybe rustle up a cup of tea or something?'

The receptionist nodded, picking up her phone.

'This way then,' Clarke said, leading them the few yards to the closed door.

'You seem to know this place well,' Kelly said, keeping his tone light.

Clarke gestured for them to go in. A few plastic chairs, a table covered in old magazines;

posters on the walls showing a field of sunflowers, a waterfall, a sunset. She sat down first, watching as they followed suit.

'Were you part of the original inquiry?' Kelly asked. Clarke shook her head.

'There better be *no one* from those days attached to this,' Catherine Bloom spat.

'Most of them are long retired,' her husband said, patting the back of her hand. 'DCI Rawlston and all that lot.'

'The Chuggabugs are still around!' his wife countered. Clarke thought she'd misheard.

'Chuggabugs?'

Dougal Kelly leaned forward. 'Too young for *Wacky Races*? Me too. Even in 2006 it was a relic, but that's the name they got.'

'Who?'

It was Catherine Bloom who answered. 'The cops working for Adrian Brand.'

'We only found out much later,' Kelly explained, 'that their colleagues called them that. Though not to their faces, I bet.' He saw he still had some work to do. 'Dastardly and Muttley? It was a TV cartoon. Same cars racing each other week after week. Dick Dastardly cheating and never seeing the benefit.'

'I've heard of it.'

'One of the cars was the Arkansas Chuggabug. A hillbilly driving and a bear as his passenger.'

'Okay . . . '

'And somehow Steele and Edwards got the nickname.'

A jolt of adrenalin shot through Clarke. She tried not to let it show. 'Steele and Edwards?'

48

'They were in Adrian Brand's pay,' Catherine Bloom interrupted. 'And no one thought *that* was suspicious? No one thought *that* was part of the conspiracy?'

Her husband had stopped patting her wrist and started rubbing it, but she snatched her hand away.

'I'm fine!' she barked, just as the receptionist put her head around the door.

'I need to know milk and sugar,' she announced with the falsest of smiles.

Clarke was on her feet and heading for the door. 'I'll just be a minute,' she explained. 'Forgot to check if we can do the DNA here.'

She retraced her steps to the car park, then stood there for a moment running a hand through her hair. Her phone was in her other hand, so she made the call. Rebus picked up almost immediately.

'Was it you that came up with the name for them?' she asked.

'And good morning to you, Siobhan. What name for who?'

'The Chuggalugs.'

There was silence for a moment. 'Chuggabugs,' he corrected her.

'Two cops called Steele and Edwards?'

'Thick as thieves, as the saying goes. Who have you been talking to?'

'Stuart Bloom's parents.'

'I wonder who told them.'

'They're with a writer called Dougal Kelly.'

'Never heard of him. Has my name come up?'

'Bill Rawlston's did. Next thing I know,

they're talking about Steele and Edwards and how they were in Adrian Brand's pocket.' She waited for a response but none came. 'Well, were they, John?'

'This might be better done face to face.'

'You know Steele and Edwards are still on the force, right?'

'I've not heard anything about them in years.'

'They're ACU, John. They were the ones who came after me.'

'Bloody hell — they were in uniform back then and unlikely to trouble an IQ test. They must know where the bodies are buried.'

'Not the subtlest phrasing under the circumstances.'

'I apologise. So the Chuggabugs went over to the dark side? Well, I suppose that makes as much sense as anything else these days. You at the mortuary?'

'Yes.'

'Seen Deborah?'

'Not to talk to. She's got Aubrey Hamilton with her.'

'The forensic anthropologist?'

'Yes.'

'A pretty good tag team. Maybe you'd best mention Steele and Edwards to your boss.'

'Why?'

'So he can pull them in for questioning, have a bit of fun with them.'

'You think I'd be that vindictive?'

'If not, I didn't teach you much.'

She found she could almost smile. 'I'll give it some thought.'

'Want to come dog-walking later? Let off some steam?'

'You mean keep you in the loop? How ethical would that be, do you think?'

'Throw me a bone here — keep me *and* Brillo happy.'

'I'll talk to you later, John.'

'Make sure you do.'

She ended the call and found that she'd walked all the way across the car park and out on to the Cowgate. When she turned round, she saw Graham Sutherland at an upstairs window, signalling for her to come back. She was trying not to blush as she retraced her steps.

⋆ ⋆ ⋆

Sutherland met her in the corridor outside the autopsy suite.

'What was that all about?' he asked.

'Just had to take a call,' Clarke answered. 'Plus, the Blooms want to know if we can do the DNA here.'

'Professor Quant is already on it. She's finished the preliminary examination. Professor Hamilton has a bit of work to do, and she wants to see for herself where the car was found.'

'Why?'

'Something to do with how the specific environment breaks down a human body. The jargon was a bit beyond me.' His stern look was beginning to soften. 'How are the parents?'

'She's frantic, he's more resigned. They seem

to be giving their story to a writer called Dougal Kelly.'

'Good luck to them.' Sutherland pushed his hands into his pockets. 'We're in limbo till we get the ID verified.'

'Doesn't stop us cracking on. Ninety per cent chance it's him. No other mispers from the time fit the description.'

Sutherland nodded. 'I suppose we can go through the old case notes while we're waiting. Maybe talk to a few people.'

'There's something I should probably tell you, sir. Two of the uniforms from the original inquiry are now ACU. They're the ones I recently locked horns with.'

Sutherland considered for a moment. 'Not a problem, is it?'

'Just thought you should know.'

'Is that what your call was about?'

'Sort of.'

'No secrets, Siobhan. Seems to me that's what was at the root of the original inquiry's problems.'

'Yes, sir.'

'Let's go back to using 'Graham' again, shall we?'

'Sir,' Clarke said, with a bow and a smile.

5

A visitor was waiting at the front desk of Leith police station. He was stocky and corkscrew-haired, with a pair of John Lennon-style glasses perched on his nose. Tweed jacket, chinos and an open-necked pink shirt.

'My name's Glenn Hazard,' he said, dishing out business cards. 'I'm here on behalf of Sir Adrian Brand.'

'You're in PR, Mr Hazard,' Sutherland said, having checked the card. 'Sir Adrian's one of your clients?'

Hazard nodded. 'The most important of my clients,' he clarified.

'And what brings you here today?'

'The story's already gone viral — you've found Stuart Bloom.' He sought each pair of eyes for confirmation.

'Not strictly true.'

'Well, the online community's latched on to it, so whether you have or not hardly matters.' He saw the look he was getting and backtracked. 'No, of course it matters. But my job is damage limitation. Sir Adrian has already had to deal with the fallout from when Bloom disappeared. It would be good to . . . control the flow of information and kill rumours before they get started.'

'What are you trying to say, Mr Hazard?'

'Poretoun Woods — they're owned by my client.'

'Jackie Ness sold them to Sir Adrian?' Clarke asked.

Hazard was shaking his head. He was about to start his answer when Sutherland interrupted.

'Best if you come upstairs, Mr Hazard. It'd be good to get this sorted out. Good for your client, I mean.'

The MIT room hadn't yet been aired and still smelled musty. One of the radiators hissed a constant complaint, and Callum Reid tried without success to open a window. Equipment had been unpacked, however — computers, a TV monitor, and a whiteboard perched on an easel — and it looked more like an inquiry hub than previously. Photos of Stuart Bloom and his partner Derek Shankley had been pinned up next to the map. Photocopies of newspaper reports from the 2006 investigation sat on each desk. Mugs and a kettle had appeared. Clarke looked towards Tess Leighton.

'You *were* busy last night,' she said.

'George helped, actually,' she replied.

Hazard settled on the chair that had been Rebus's the previous day. He looked the sort that would be hard to faze — probably a minimum requirement for working in public relations.

'Did you represent Sir Adrian back in the day?' Sutherland was asking as he got comfortable behind his desk.

'I wasn't in PR then,' Hazard replied.

'Interesting job, is it?'

'Every day a new challenge.'

'Bit like police work then.' Which was the end of the small talk. 'So Poretoun Woods are owned

54

by Sir Adrian Brand. Since when?'

'Just the past couple of years. They came with Poretoun House. He bought both from a hotelier called Jeff Sellers. Sellers had plans to turn the place into another hotel — boutique, five-star, you know the drill. I think the money ran out, so Sir Adrian stepped in. Snapped up a bargain, I believe.'

'Both house and woods used to belong to Jackie Ness,' Clarke said.

'Ness sold to Sellers.'

'Does he know your client's got hold of them?'

Hazard gave the thinnest of smiles. 'I'd imagine so, even though the actual owner is one of Sir Adrian's companies rather than Sir Adrian personally.'

'He's dusting off the golf course plan?'

'Not that I've heard. That was the other side of the city from Poretoun, you know — west rather than south-east.'

'There's still bad blood, though?'

'Maybe it would be more accurate to say both gentlemen have long memories. But that's really why I'm here. The media are going to have the proverbial field day. Stuart Bloom was snooping into Sir Adrian's affairs. Twelve years later he ends up dead on land owned by Sir Adrian. You can see how that's going to play, unless we manage the story with the utmost care.'

'We're not in the business of *managing* stories, Mr Hazard,' Sutherland stated. 'Back in the day, things might have been a lot cosier, but that was then and this is now.'

'You can't want to see an innocent man suffer,

his reputation damaged. I'm just saying that when you prepare your press releases and give your media briefings . . . '

'Keep your client's name out of it?'

'As far as possible, yes, to protect the innocent. I'd be more than happy to help your press office in the drafting of — '

'We might need to talk to Sir Adrian,' Clarke interrupted, walking to the side of Sutherland's desk so she was facing Hazard. 'Is Poretoun House our best bet?'

'He doesn't actually live there.'

'So who does?'

'I think it's empty. Sir Adrian has a house in Murrayfield.'

'So what are his plans for Poretoun House?'

Hazard offered a shrug.

'And just to get back to the subject,' Sutherland interrupted, 'why do you think the body was in those woods?'

Another shrug.

'Does your client have a theory?'

'From talking to him, I'd say he's always thought Jackie Ness must have fallen out with the PI and bumped him off. The woods would have been an easy place to hide the body. Half a mile of dirt track and no one around. It's certainly true that Ness had a temper on him. There are no end of stories about him — you can find most of them online.' Hazard paused and fixed Clarke with a look. 'If you do plan to interview Sir Adrian, you'll have to promise to do the same with Ness. It would look bad otherwise.'

'Thanks for the advice,' Sutherland said icily. His phone buzzed: incoming text. He read it and placed the phone on the desk in front of him. 'We're grateful to you for filling in a few blanks, Mr Hazard. Phil, will you see Mr Hazard out, please?'

Hazard looked reluctant, but Sutherland was already on his feet, extending a hand for the PR man to shake.

'If you need me for anything, anything at all . . . '

'We all have your card.' Sutherland nodded brusquely. He stayed on his feet as Yeats and Hazard left, then sought out Emily Crowther. 'Could you close the door, please, Emily? We should wait for Phil but we can fill him in when he gets back. Best do this right now.' He was leaning over his phone, dabbing at the screen. When it began to ring, he switched the speaker on.

'DCI Sutherland.' Clarke recognised Deborah Quant's voice. 'Thanks for getting back to me.'

'Team's all here, Professor,' Sutherland called out. 'We're ready to hear what you've got for us.'

'Whoever was babysitting the Blooms should have asked to see in the mother's bag. She'd packed half her son's life in there, including a copy of his dental records.'

Sutherland was gazing in Clarke's direction, but her eyes were fixed to the far wall as she concentrated on not letting colour flood her face.

'Looks like a positive match,' Quant was saying. 'We'll still do the DNA — belt and braces and all that. But both parents thought the hair

57

sample we showed them was probably Stuart's. Same goes for the photos of his clothing. No distinguishing features or tattoos, so that's pretty much what we've got.'

'Did you mention the handcuffs?'

'Absolutely not.'

'And cause of death?'

'Aubrey and I are pretty well agreed on that. Blunt object trauma. Hole in the back of the head is a couple of centimetres wide. Hammer maybe. Crowbar. We've taken samples to see if whatever it was has left any traces. After this length of time, I'm not hugely hopeful.'

'Thank you, Professor. Anything else we should know?'

'Aubrey wants to see where the car was found. She asked if your forensics team are still working there.'

'Car's gone to the lab.'

'Keep me informed of their progress. The floor of the boot will tell us if he was killed *in situ*. Professor Hamilton also says some interesting work is being done with soil these days. There's someone in Aberdeen might be useful.'

'How do you mean?'

'Mud on and in the car, bits of dirt ingrained in the tyres, that sort of thing. Might help you track where else it had been before it ended up in the gully.'

'I'll bear that in mind.'

'Ah . . . '

'What?'

'I can hear it in your voice — case hasn't been budgeted yet?'

'Not yet, no.'

'Well, I've no idea how much a soil expert costs these days, but I know money's tight. Having said which, I'm telling you the victim was Stuart Bloom, so the chiefs aren't going to want to be shown stinting.'

'You're a hundred per cent sure, Deborah?' Clarke asked.

'Hi, Siobhan. Thought I saw you in the viewing room. Let's say ninety-nine point nine.' Sutherland's phone was making a noise. 'Sounds like another caller trying to get through,' Deborah Quant said. 'You better take that. It's probably whoever's acting as chief constable this week.'

'News travels,' Sutherland said.

'Doesn't it just?'

Sutherland had picked up the phone, ending Quant's call and pressing the appliance to his ear.

'Yes, sir?' he said, making for the hallway. As he left the room, Yeats entered.

'What did I miss?' he enquired.

'Stick the kettle on and we'll tell you,' Tess Leighton replied.

6

Detective Inspector Malcolm Fox was chewing a pen at his desk. His feeling was, it made him look busy, like he was thinking great thoughts or working out a knotty problem. His computer screen showed that he was halfway through a memo on the reallocation of resources to Police Scotland's Major Crime Division. Around him, everything still felt new. Gartcosh was the site of the shiny high-tech Scottish Crime Campus, the nerve centre of Police Scotland. Forty miles west of the capital, it would always be another country to the Edinburgh-dwelling Fox.

The quiet hum of activity belied the fact that Police Scotland was in trouble. Then again, you never had to look too far to find a crisis of one sort or another. But the chief constable was on suspension while being investigated for various misdemeanours, as was one of his assistant chief constables, meaning that Fox's own boss, ACC Jennifer Lyon, was burdened by extra worries and workload. Despite all of which, there was little to keep Fox occupied. He had dropped heavy hints about a larger role, but Lyon had cautioned him to be patient. In relative terms, he'd only just got his feet under the desk. There was time enough ahead.

'Besides,' she'd added, 'climb too far up the ladder just now and you're liable to come across a rung that's been sawn through.'

Lyon had reckoned Fox's current task a promotion of sorts. If done well, it would get him noticed by those at the top. Everyone seemed to agree that policy was his strength. In other words, he was a desk jockey, good in meetings, presentable, happier with subordinate clauses than actual subordinates. Fox wanted to tell them: I've seen action, got my hands dirty in the past. He had even angled for a lateral move from Major Crime to Organised Crime and Counter-Terrorism, but Lyon had just given him a look. Lacking a chief constable, the deputy chief constable — who had been on the brink of retiring — was running the show but leaning heavily on Lyon for support, meaning she was often out of reach. Fox knew that big cases were effectively in limbo, awaiting decisions. His colleagues in Major Crime were anxious verging on mutinous, queuing up to gain the okay from Lyon over this or that course of action.

Which was why a couple of them sprang to their feet when Lyon stalked into the large open-plan office. A brushing motion with one hand told them this wasn't the time. Instead, Lyon was standing just over Fox's shoulder. Her hair was bottle-blonde and brittle, curving around the sides of her head as if to cocoon her face. In meetings, when she leaned forward, it covered her eyes, making her impossible to read. Now, Fox concentrated on her pale pink lips as she leaned in towards his left ear.

'A word outside, Malcolm.'

By the time he had got to his feet, she was already at the door. As Fox made to follow, he caught the looks from his colleagues. They wanted him to plead their cases. He gestured with his head, not quite a nod, straightened his tie and buttoned his suit jacket.

One feature of Gartcosh was its 'breakout areas'. Basically quiet, comfortable nooks where the various disciplines such as specialist crime, forensic science and the procurator fiscal could exchange information over a relatively relaxed coffee. The whole interior of the building felt like a high-security further education college. Lyon hadn't quite made it to her destination without interruption. Someone from HMRC's fraud unit was bending her ear, Lyon giving grim nods in the hope the man would take the hint.

'Sorry to interrupt,' Fox said as he approached. 'You said it was urgent, ma'am.'

Lyon tried for a disappointed look. 'Another time, Owen? Sorry about this.'

With a glower in Fox's direction, the HMRC man started to leave.

'I'll email you,' Lyon called out in assurance. Then, lowering her voice so only Fox could hear, 'Thanks for that. Let's sit down.'

They did, watching the ebb and flow of officers. One or two gave more than a passing glance, recognising Lyon and wondering who she was with. Lyon played with the lanyards hanging around her neck. Two passes: one a photo ID, the other giving keyless entry to the building's more secure sections.

'Is it something to do with the memo?' Fox nudged.

She shook her head. 'It's this Stuart Bloom

thing.' She saw his blank look. 'I thought you were in Professional Standards at the time?'

'When are we talking about?'

'Two thousand and six.'

'I joined the following year.'

'His family were still vocal then, and every year since.'

Fox was nodding. 'The private eye who went missing? Wasn't their original complaint dismissed?'

'And every one after. But now it looks like his body has turned up. Questions are going to be asked about how we missed it first time round. Some of the original team didn't exactly cover themselves in glory, from what I've been told.' She paused, her eyes finally meeting his. 'I want you to go take a look. You were in the Complaints, you'll maybe notice what shortcuts were taken. Anything from general sloppiness up to criminal conspiracy — there were always rumours and I'd like to see them quashed.'

'Wouldn't I be treading on the toes of the new inquiry?'

'Is that going to cause you to lose any sleep?'

'Not at all.' Fox reacted to her icy tone by sitting up a bit straighter. 'So I'd go through the original case files . . . '

'There's a bit more to it than that, Malcolm. The family always talked about it being a conspiracy, our lot colluding with the rich and the powerful, leaking stuff to the press to make sure the public saw only one side of the story.' She broke off, looking to left and right, checking she could not be overheard. All the same, she lowered her voice a little further. 'We're not releasing the information just yet, but the victim was handcuffed.'

'Police issue?' He watched as she gave the slightest of shrugs. 'You think cops were involved?'

'That's one of the things I want you to think about. Reporting back directly to me. I'll clear it with the officer in charge. The last thing we need right now is any more crap being tossed in our direction. Media and politicians have more or less scooped the latrine dry.' When she stopped speaking, Fox saw it suddenly in her eyes: the fatigue from having fought too many bouts, the hope that someone would deal with this and make it all go away.

'Leave it to me,' he said.

There was no nod of acknowledgement or smile of thanks. Lyon just got to her feet and strode off towards the relative safety of her own office. Fox sat for a moment longer, then took his phone out and checked the news. The body had been found in Poretoun Woods, south-east of Edinburgh. That meant the MIT's base would probably be Leith — there were only so many rooms across the country set aside for such operations. His eyes flickered over the story, taking in names and details. If Complaints had been involved, it would have been under the aegis of his predecessor, Ray Hungerford. Ray was still in the land of the living; Fox saw him at retirement parties and funerals. He checked his list of contacts, but there was no number for him.

Lowering the phone, he found himself staring at the door to the Major Crime office. They would be waiting for him to come back, ready for him to tell them he'd had a word with the boss. Instead of which, Fox stood up, pocketed his phone and headed in the direction of the outside world.

★   ★   ★

It took Fox only a few phone calls to track down Ray Hungerford. He was driving a black taxi these days, apparently, and Fox ordered the cab company to keep him where he was, on a rank on Lothian Road. The drive back into Edinburgh was slowed by roadworks on the M8 and one accident at the junction with a slip road. Fox kept the radio news on, but the media didn't have much as yet. He listened as Stuart Bloom's mother was interviewed. She implored anyone with information to come forward. Fox didn't doubt many would respond to her plea, the vast majority of them attention-seekers or cranks. Some would do it with the best intentions, swamping the inquiry before it had had a chance to establish itself. He couldn't see the major incident team welcoming him with anything other than impatience and irritation.

'Just like the old days in the Complaints,' he muttered to himself as the congestion ahead began to ease. Edinburgh loomed ahead, the castle on its raised volcanic platform visible for miles. Fox felt himself relax a little; he understood the city better than he did Gartcosh.

He knew how it worked.

There were three taxis lined up outside the Sheraton Hotel, but one had reversed to the very back of the rank, its flashers on, hire light switched off. Fox pulled up in front of it and got out of his car. As he neared the cab, its passenger-side window slid down.

'Keeping busy, Ray?' he enquired.

'You've put on a bit of weight, Malcolm.'

'Okay if we talk?'

'What about.'

'Maybe join me in the back?'

Hungerford kept the engine running so there'd be some heating inside the cab. He settled next to Fox and the two men exchanged a handshake.

'I've turned down three fares, you know,' Hungerford complained.

'I appreciate that. Pension not keeping you afloat?'

'It's my son's cab. I'm just in charge while he's on holiday. Gets me out of the house. You can't still be Complaints, surely?'

'Gartcosh these days, Major Crime.'

'The new Big House, eh?'

'They've got me looking at the Stuart Bloom case,' Fox revealed.

'That old chestnut. So it really is him in those woods?'

'Looks like. The original inquiry wasn't without its difficulties.'

Hungerford gave him a hard look. 'Are you working as a diplomat now or something? I was always a fan of plain speaking myself.'

'Okay then, the original case was pretty much a fuck-up from the start.'

'There was a good man in charge,' Hungerford countered. 'Never heard a bad word about Bill Rawlston.'

'The officers under him, though . . . ?'

Hungerford puckered his mouth. 'A prize collection of pricks, incompetents and chancers.'

'An assessment included in your report, I don't doubt?'

'There wasn't much of a report; everything was hearsay. A handful of officers probably were homophobic. Christ, it used to almost be mandatory. Friends of Bloom's from the gay scene were hauled in for questioning and not exactly treated with kid gloves. Meantime, you had a good cop in Glasgow who wanted his son kept out of it, even though that son had to be treated as a suspect.' Hungerford puffed out his cheeks and exhaled. 'The two moguls meantime . . . '

'Jackie Ness and Adrian Brand?'

Hungerford nodded. 'Usual cock-measuring going on there. They had lawyers crying foul at every opportunity, journalists eager to buy drinks for anyone who might have a story to tell . . . '

'Including officers from the investigation?'

'Undoubtedly. I dare say you've done something similar in your time; I know I have. Guy stands you a few nice malts, maybe you start to like him and decide he merits something in return. Some cops used to get off on it — the thrill of seeing a piece in the paper that they'd had a hand in.'

'Any names in particular.'

Hungerford considered for a few seconds. 'All this archaeology just because the body's been found?'

'High hiedyins want to be confident no zombies are going to start appearing among the skeletons.'

'And they've given it to you because you used to be Complaints?'

'That's about the size of it.'

Hungerford nodded while he contemplated. 'All we really did was dig into the case files and then ask a few questions. It was obvious that mistakes had been made, our own lot negligent or obstructive. Not for the first time, and by no means the last.'

'You made recommendations?'

'There were a couple of officers we could have come down hard on if we tried. Steele, one of them was called.'

'Let me guess — the other was Edwards.'

'You know them?'

'They work for ACU these days, based at Gartcosh.'

'Well, they were just uniforms back then, but playing all sorts of games.'

'Such as?'

'They had spare-time jobs, mostly as security. They'd even been part of Adrian Brand's bodyguard detail.'

'He needed bodyguards?'

'Rumours he'd taken money from an Irish gangster connected to the paramilitaries. There'd been a falling-out.'

'Nothing ever came of it?'

'Not that I know of. There was definitely something about Steele and Edwards, though — they owned top-of-the-line cars, took expensive holidays. Always the best clothes, designer watches . . . '

'All on a copper's salary.'

'But like I say, we never quite got to them.'

'Were they being protected?'

Hungerford offered a shrug. 'Brand bought tables at a lot of charity dinners, wined and dined his fair share of top brass and MPs.'

Fox grew thoughtful. 'And after you'd finished with the files . . . ?'

'They were sent to CCU for a look-see. Nothing came of that, so they went into storage. Whoever's in charge now, they'll probably be poring over them, don't you think?'

'If they're on the ball.'

'Not always the case, is it?' Hungerford chuckled.

'Steele and Edwards apart, anyone else of note?'

'Bloody hell, Malc, my memory's not what it was.' Hungerford rubbed his jaw. 'Mary Skelton — she was all right actually; bit of a looker and very pleasant with it. Doug Newsome — most you could say of him was he was lazy; didn't always write his reports up with a degree of rigour.' He paused and smiled. 'And then there was John Rebus, of course.'

Fox's mouth twitched. 'Why do you say 'of course'?'

'My time in Professional Standards, Rebus

69

was never far from a bollocking or a suspension. Did you never cross swords?'

'Rebus retired at the end of 2006. Well, sort of.'

'Sounds like you *have* come across him, though?'

'John Rebus has a way of turning up. Anything in particular blot his copybook on the Bloom case?'

'He was mates with the boyfriend's dad, a cop from Glasgow. Word was, they kept meeting for a quiet drink.'

'Which might not mean much in itself.'

'Unless information was being passed along. We never proved anything.'

Fox sat for a moment deep in thought, then he nodded slowly. 'Thanks for your time, Ray, I really appreciate it. It was good to catch up.'

'You know where I am if you need me again.' Hungerford had extended his hand, but not for the shake Fox was about to offer. The palm was upwards, stretched flat. He nodded towards the front of the cab, where the meter had been ticking throughout. 'Twenty-five fifty,' he said. Then, with a wink: 'Don't worry, I'll write you a receipt for thirty.'

7

The others had made their excuses after one drink, but Clarke and Sutherland stuck around for a second. He fetched her the tonic water she'd requested, along with a half of IPA to add to the pint he'd almost finished. The bar was about as upmarket as this part of Leith got, meaning cops could feel relatively safe there. All the same, they were seated at a corner table with a view of the door.

'Sure you don't want a gin in that?' Sutherland asked.

'Don't want to make a bad impression.'

'Two gins after work is hardly a disciplinary offence.' He chinked his glass against hers. 'Speaking of which . . . '

'How much do you know?'

'Just that ACU thought you were passing stories to a reporter pal.'

'I wasn't.'

'And also that you'd used a work computer to try getting the same reporter some information.'

'I was cleared.'

'Indeed you were, and you resent having been accused.'

'I was made to feel like I was a bad cop. I'm not.'

'These two ACU officers . . . ?'

'Steele and Edwards.'

Sutherland nodded. 'Do you hold a grudge against *them?*'

'No.'

'I think that's maybe a lie.'

'Depends how you define 'grudge'. Would I do them a favour in future? No. Would I want someone to attack them in a dark alley? No.'

'And if you saw them out having a drink, then climbing into the driving seat . . . ?'

'I'd phone it in like a shot.'

They both smiled, focusing on their drinks. Clarke leaned back, rolling her head, feeling the tension there.

'I remember,' Sutherland was saying, 'back in Inverness. There was a time-server none of us liked. He had a drink problem, but we covered for him where necessary. Day he retired, there was a party laid on in the canteen with more than a few refreshments. We all clapped and handed him the gift we'd bought, then watched and waved as he headed out to his car, ready to drive home. Traffic had been tipped off. He was stopped, lost his licence.'

'A sort of justice to that, I suppose.' Clarke sipped her drink. 'So did you grow up in Inverness?'

Sutherland nodded. 'Not much of an accent left, except when I visit family. I notice you're English.'

She shook her head. 'Born here; grew up there — I blame the parents. So where else have you been other than Inverness?'

'Aberdeen, Glasgow, even Skye for a while.'

'They have crime on Skye?'

'I like to think I eradicated it.' He made a little toast to himself. 'You ever been anywhere other than Edinburgh?'

'I was on secondment in Glenrothes when Stuart Bloom disappeared.'

'That was lucky — if you'd been attached to the case, you couldn't be on my team now. Conflict of interest, et cetera.'

Clarke nodded distractedly. 'So where do you live these days?' she eventually asked.

'Shettleston, in Glasgow.'

'Can you see Barlinnie from there?'

'More or less. How about you?'

'Five minutes from here. Just off Broughton Street.'

'On your own?' He watched her nod. 'Me too. Wasn't always the case, but you know how it is. I decided to marry my golf clubs instead. I don't suppose you play?'

'Do I look like a golfer?'

'I don't know — what does a golfer look like?'

'My idea of fresh air and exercise is the local café and paper shop.' Her phone buzzed. It was lying on the table to the side of her glass, so she could see that it was the call box again.

'Not answering?' Sutherland queried.

'It's not important.'

They waited for it to stop.

'I get the distinct feeling there's more to you than meets the eye, Detective Inspector Clarke.'

'Trust me, there really isn't.'

Sutherland thought for a moment, watching her from behind his raised glass. He smacked his lips when he lowered it. 'I know Tess has given the Bloom file a first pass, but would you like to take a look too?'

'Why?'

'Might be our friends Steele and Edwards will pop up there, something you could tuck away for future use.'

She stared at him. 'It was you who tipped off Traffic, wasn't it?' His left eyebrow was the only part of his face that moved. 'There's a prize if you tell me.'

'Okay, I'm intrigued.'

'A game of pitch 'n' putt at Bruntsfield Links.'

'An offer that's hard to refuse. But you might be wearing a wire, so . . . ' He maintained eye contact as he slowly but definitively nodded.

'Has to be on a warm day, mind,' Clarke cautioned.

'And how many of those does Edinburgh get?'

'We had one a couple of years back.'

They both started laughing.

★   ★   ★

The Meadows again, illuminated by the street lamps on Melville Drive.

The rain had stopped, but the grass was wet, the cold penetrating their shoes and chilling their toes. Rebus stood with hands in pockets, the collar of his overcoat up, while Clarke had pulled the hood of her waterproof jacket over her head. In front of them, Brillo was busy sniffing some invisible trail. It was like watching an infant take a line for a walk across a sheet of paper.

'He's determined,' Clarke admitted.

74

'Not to mention tireless — can't think who that reminds me of.'

'I wanted to ask you about Steele and Edwards. How dirty do you think they were back then?'

'You know that old saying — you need a lang spoon tae sup wi' the devil?'

'I thought that was Fifers.'

'Same thing. All you need to know is, that's what they were like. Kept everything to themselves. Always sat at a different table from everyone else, heads together. If they had a brain, it was a hundred per cent the property of Brian Steele. Grant Edwards had heft but not much else.'

'He's not changed much.'

'Well, you've had more recent dealings with them. But back then, none of us thought they would last too much longer in the force. They'd be up on a charge or else off to greener pastures.'

'Meaning what?'

'Steele owned a couple of executive cars, chauffeured bigwigs around. That's probably how he fell in with Adrian Brand. He always said police work was boring.'

'And Edwards?'

'Did some of the driving. Worked a lot of his free nights as a club doorman. Was said to have money in a car wash out near the Forth Bridge.'

'Did they try to influence the investigation?'

'At Brand's behest, you mean?' Rebus thought for a moment. 'Aye, maybe. They wouldn't have been above taking a few quid from him, either to keep him posted or else to make sure he wasn't given too much grief.'

'We had a visit today from Brand's PR man. He wants much the same.'

'I dare say he's not undercharging for his services either.' Rebus produced a lighter from his coat and flicked it until a flame appeared. 'Christ, I wish I still smoked.'

'Your lungs probably disagree.'

'Specialist wanted me to get an exercise bike — can you imagine?'

'Not really, no.'

'Me in the flat, pedalling away, going nowhere.'

A car had stopped on Melville Drive. They heard its door close and turned to watch as a dark figure approached.

'The prodigal returns,' Rebus announced. 'Or is it the swine that returns? I'm a bit rusty.'

'Hello to you too, John.' Malcolm Fox was gesturing towards the cigarette lighter. 'Thought you'd stopped.'

'This is just in case I decide to go out in a blaze of glory.'

Fox had leaned in towards Clarke to peck her on the cheek.

'Steady on,' Rebus chided him. 'We're not in bloody France.'

'How are you, Siobhan?'

She nodded in the affirmative. 'How about you, Malcolm?'

He nodded back before turning towards Rebus. 'I went to the Oxford Bar first off, but they said they hardly see you these days. I'm at the age where nothing should surprise me, but

I'll admit that nearly took my legs from under me.'

'Aye, they've had to announce a profits warning. Stock Exchange isn't happy. And speaking of happy ships, how are things at Gartcosh? Lost any more high hiedyins lately?'

'It's not exactly been plain sailing.'

'Latest allegations are all to do with bullying — hope none of that's been happening to you in the playground, Malc. We all know you're a sensitive soul. See, in my day we just took it on the chin.'

'Might explain why you ended up with so many bruises.'

Rebus stretched out his arms. 'Do you see any?'

Fox tapped a finger to his own head. 'In here, I mean.'

Rebus screwed his eyes shut. 'Well, despite the brain damage, let's see if I can still do a bit of mind-reading.' He pretended to cogitate. 'I see a skeleton in a car, a lot of media attention, and the top brass anxious about an old case and those who worked on it.' He opened his eyes again. 'And here you are.'

'You've not lost it.' Fox pretended to clap his hands.

'You're working at the Big House, you used to be Complaints, who else are they going to send to do their sniffing?' Rebus looked down to where Brillo was circling the new arrival. Fox bent at the waist and gave the dog a pat.

'Your name was mentioned in passing,' he admitted, straightening up again.

77

'How about Brian Steele and Grant Edwards?' Clarke asked.

'Them too.' Fox studied her. 'What's your interest, Siobhan?'

'I'm MIT.'

'Officer in charge?'

She shook her head. 'That's DCI Sutherland.'

'Siobhan has also,' Rebus said, 'had a bit of a run-in with ACU.'

'Meaning Steele and Edwards?'

'We used to call them the Chuggabugs,' Rebus commented.

Fox's eyes were still on Clarke. 'You've requisitioned the 2006 case notes?'

'Yes.'

'I need to take a look at them.'

'That's DCI Sutherland's call.'

'In point of fact, it's ACC Lyon's call, and I'm sure the message is on its way from her to your boss.'

'Isn't that nice, Siobhan?' Rebus drawled. 'You and Malcolm on a case again.'

'Actually,' Clarke parried, 'what *I'm* doing is investigating a murder.'

'That's true, Malcolm,' Rebus agreed, with the appearance of a sage nod. 'Whereas you're back to your old speciality of stirring the shit prior to slopping it over fellow officers, be they serving, retired or long buried. Must give you a nice warm glow.' He paused. 'You live in a bungalow, don't you?'

Fox frowned at the change of subject. 'Yes,' he eventually said.

Rebus nodded to himself. 'That's why I could

never live in one.' He had a sudden thought and turned his attention back to Clarke. 'Mind you, just say Malcolm *were* to find some dirt on the Chuggabugs — might not be a bad result.'

'Someone's going to have to explain that nickname to me,' Fox said.

'Cartoon characters,' Clarke obliged.

'Who recently had a go at Siobhan here,' Rebus added. 'Hence the appetite for a bit of dirt on them.'

'Thing to remember, John,' Fox cautioned, 'is that dirt has a way of spreading itself around.'

'So does pee,' Rebus responded, gesturing to where Brillo had cocked his leg against Malcolm Fox's ankle.

★   ★   ★

There was a space directly across the street from Clarke's tenement. Lucky, she thought. Then she wondered if it had maybe been in use until just before she got there. She remembered the car from the previous night. Exact same spot. Having locked the Astra, she looked up and down the street, but all the cars seemed to be empty. No sign of anyone loitering on the pavement either. As she approached the tenement, though, she saw there was something scrawled on the door. Big fat silver letters against the dark-blue paint. She took out her phone and switched on the torch function, though she had already made the words out. But she just wanted to be sure they said what she thought they did.

PIG SCUM LIVES HERE!!!

PIG SCUM OUT!!!

She scanned the rest of the door. It was pristine. But then she noticed the intercom. The same silver pen had been used to cover up her name. She took a paper tissue from her pocket and ran it over the ink. Not quite dry. Another look up and down the street before she slid her key into the lock. Once inside, she stood with her back to the door, waiting. But no one was hiding, no one coming down the stairs towards her. Her heart was racing as she climbed to her landing, checking the door to her flat. The graffiti artist hadn't come this far. Or if he had . . .

She unlocked the door and studied the hallway before walking in. Locking the door behind her, she crossed to the living room window, staring at the street and the windows opposite before closing the shutters and beginning to turn on the lights.

Thursday

8

There were TV cameras outside the police station on Queen Charlotte Street. Approaching, Siobhan Clarke saw Catherine Bloom giving an interview. Against her chest she held a blown-up photograph of her son. At her shoulder stood Dougal Kelly, making sure his JUSTICE FOR STUART sign was visible. Stuart's father stood well back from the action, watching his wife with what to Clarke looked like a mixture of pride and resignation. The campaign had been long and apparently tireless, but had taken its toll. Half a dozen print journalists were eavesdropping on the TV interview, holding up their phones to record the exchange. One of them gave a hopeful look towards Clarke, but she shook her head. She was barely inside the building when the text message arrived: *Meet later?* But cafés and wine bars with Laura Smith had been the start of Clarke's spot of bother with ACU. Smith was the only crime reporter left at the *Scotsman*, and the relationship had proved fruitful, Smith never overstepping the mark, never printing anything without first checking that Clarke was okay with it. But when she had started covering the suspensions of various officers at the top of the Police Scotland tree, ACU had come to demand who was leaking.

Truth was, Smith wouldn't even tell her good friend Siobhan Clarke.

Ignoring the text, Clarke climbed the stairs. She was a bit bleary, having spent half an hour the previous night removing as much of the graffiti on her tenement door as she could. She had checked it this morning — the words were still there, though they were faint. What would her neighbours think? Some knew she was a cop, some didn't. She would find a painter to cover it up with a couple of fresh coats, just as soon as she could stop yawning. Because that was another thing — around 1a.m., as she'd been drifting off to sleep, there'd been another call from the phone box on the Canongate.

'What do you want?' she'd snarled, listening as the line went dead.

'Nice of you to join us, DI Clarke.' The booming Glaswegian voice belonged to Detective Chief Superintendent Mark Mollison, divisional commander for Edinburgh. Clarke realised she should have expected a visit — especially when the media were in the vicinity. 'We've just been discussing when and where to hold the first press conference. Do you have any views?'

Clarke looked around the room. They were all there, making her the late arrival. Sutherland and Reid had positioned themselves next to the wall, with its spreading display of maps, photos and cuttings. The last of the computers had arrived, along with a free-standing printer. She realised that the noises she'd heard from the next door along were those of the final members of the support staff settling in.

'Not really, sir,' she managed to reply.

Mollison stood on his own in the centre of the room, hands clasped behind his back, rocking on his heels. He was well over six feet tall, with a face that was all burst veins leading to a nose that would not have disgraced Rudolph the reindeer.

'Apparently the spot where the car was found is being examined again this morning, and a team will carry out a detailed search of the woods — '

'Mr Mollison,' Sutherland interrupted, 'wonders if Poretoun Woods might make for an atmospheric backdrop.'

Clarke caught her boss's tone. 'I'm not entirely sure,' she ventured, 'that we have much to say to the media at this point in the inquiry.' She watched as Sutherland nodded his head in agreement.

'We certainly have information we *don't* want them getting,' Callum Reid added.

'The handcuffs?' Mollison guessed. 'Any news of those?'

'They're being studied in detail by Forensics today,' Sutherland informed him. 'All we know as of now is that they're an older model — in other words, not police issue at the time of Bloom's disappearance.'

'It'll come out eventually, you know — we need to have a strategy for managing it.'

'Absolutely.'

'No press conference today, though?'

'We could revisit the idea this afternoon, sir.'

Mollison tried not to look disappointed. 'Might as well get back to St Leonard's, then.

Wouldn't want to think I'm holding you back.' As he spoke, he threw a sideways glance towards Clarke. With a gesture of farewell to the rest of the team, he marched out of the office, his leather soles clacking their way back down the stairs. Shoulders began to relax; breaths were exhaled.

'One of you could have warned me,' Clarke complained.

'You've not given us your number,' Emily Crowther informed her.

'That's the first thing we should do then,' Sutherland decided. 'Everybody's contact details on a sheet of paper, pinned to the wall and copied into your phones.'

'Maybe a WhatsApp group, too?' Crowther suggested.

'If you think it useful.' Sutherland saw that Phil Yeats was heading towards the kettle. 'Coffee can wait, Phil,' he warned him.

'In Siobhan's case,' George Gamble commented, 'I'm not sure that's true. You must have kept her out past her bedtime, Graham.' There were smiles from behind the desks. Sutherland didn't join in but Clarke did — last thing she wanted was for the team to split into factions. While they copied their details on to the sheet of paper being passed around, she approached Sutherland. He had returned to his chair and was starting to type at his keyboard.

'Heard anything from Gartcosh?' she enquired.

'How did you know?'

'Malcolm Fox and me go back a ways. I

86

happened to bump into him last night.'

'So you *were* out late then?'

'Decided I'd better walk the pitch 'n' putt course, just to see what I've let myself in for.'

He gave a half-smile. 'Fox will be here soon. I informed everyone this morning. I've put Tess in charge of babysitting him. So if there's anything you think she should know in advance . . .'

Clarke nodded and walked over to Tess Leighton's desk.

'I've worked with Fox in the past,' she stated. 'He's good on detail, used to be in Complaints. He's thorough, maybe even a bit plodding.'

'Is he single, though?' George Gamble interrupted. 'That's what Tess is wondering.'

'Stick it, George,' Leighton rasped. Then, to Clarke: 'Any BO or bad breath? Farts and belches?'

'I think he'll pass those tests.'

'Puts him one up on George, then.'

'You forgetting something, Tess?' Gamble retorted. 'He worked for Complaints, meaning he got his jollies putting the boot into the likes of you and me. He might not smell, but that doesn't mean he doesn't stink.'

★ ★ ★

Jackie Ness's production company had an office in a shiny new glass-fronted development in Fountainbridge. Clarke and Emily Crowther had been dispatched to question him. During the drive, Crowther revealed that she had studied English literature at university, policing far from her first choice of career. She'd grown up in Fife and had a boyfriend who ran a bike shop on the edge of Dunfermline. They shared a house in the town and were planning to get married. She was starting to ask Clarke about herself when Clarke announced that they'd arrived.

Crowther was slim and blonde and probably fifteen years younger than her colleague. Knee-length skirt, sheer black tights, shoes with inch-high heels. She didn't quite look or act like an officer of the law, and Clarke began to get an inkling as to why Sutherland had chosen her for the task.

The company name was Locke Ness. On the wall behind the reception desk, the logo could be seen rising from the depths of a stretch of water.

'Clever,' Crowther said, which seemed to please the young receptionist.

'Mr Ness will be with you shortly,' she said.

'We did arrange a time,' Clarke told her firmly. 'If he wants to waste ours, maybe we can do this at the station instead.'

The receptionist's smile melted away. 'I'll ask,' she said, disappearing through a door. Crowther settled on the leather sofa while Clarke examined the shelf containing a handful of cheap-looking awards, and the wall-mounted posters for films such as *Zombies v Bravehearts* and *The Opium Eater Murders*. She had done a bit of reading up on the producer. He'd started by owning a string of video rental shops, then put money into low-budget horror films before moving to more mainstream releases. She wasn't aware of ever having watched any of his output.

The receptionist was back, followed by a man who was shrugging his arms back into the sleeves of his suit jacket.

'There's a restaurant next door,' he announced. 'I skipped breakfast, so why don't we go there? I'm Jackie Ness, by the way, in case you were wondering.' His eyes fell on Emily Crowther and he wagged a finger in her direction. 'The light loves you, did you know that? Catches your face just perfectly.' He turned to the receptionist. 'You agree, don't you, Estelle?' Then, to Clarke: 'The restaurant won't be busy, it's not lunchtime yet. There's a corner booth they normally keep for me. It's not like we're recording this or anything, is it? It's just background.'

'A better word might be 'preliminary',' Clarke told him. 'You're not under caution and you don't need a lawyer.'

'The amount they cost, praise be for that. And you are . . . ?'

'Detective Inspector Clarke. This is DC Crowther.'

He turned his attention back to Crowther. 'Just DC, or is there ever any AC?' Immediately he held up a hand. 'I know, I shouldn't have. Couldn't help it. Apologies et cetera.'

'Still living in the Betamax era, I see.'

Ness chose to ignore Clarke's rebuke. 'Half an hour,' he told the receptionist, already halfway to the exit.

'Longer if need be, Estelle,' Clarke cautioned, before following suit.

The restaurant served mostly burgers, and that

was what Ness ordered — albeit vegetarian — along with an Irn-Bru, while the two detectives stuck to coffee. He'd been right though: they were the only customers, and were directed to his favoured spot. Clarke and Crowther sat across from him and watched as he shrugged his way out of his jacket.

'Male menopause,' he explained. 'I'm always sweating or freezing.'

'Bit old for the menopause, no?' Clarke said.

'I was always told you're as young as the woman you feel.' He chuckled to himself. It never ceased to amaze Clarke that such specimens survived. She thought of the Loch Ness monster, the last of its kind.

'Is there a Locke to go with the Ness?' she enquired.

'Old business partner. We had a falling-out when he tried stiffing the taxman. The name makes people smile though, so I didn't bother changing it.'

'Anything in the pipeline just now?'

'There's *always* something in the pipeline. In fact, the pipeline's bunged up with treatments and pitches and great scripts that'll likely never get turned into films. Money just doesn't materialise most of the time.'

'Aren't you the one who supplies the money?'

'I *find* the money, and that's a whole different skill. Goalposts have shifted. In my early days it was DTV — direct to video. Now everything's digital. You've got kids making films on their mobile phones, editing them on their PCs, then chucking them on the internet. You've got

Amazon and Netflix. Everyone's streaming; DVDs and Blu-Ray sales are tanking. It's actually not the goal-posts that have shifted. It's like walking into a completely different game.'

'But you're surviving?'

'What else is there?'

He'd be in his early sixties, Clarke guessed, his hair silver but plentiful, his tan courtesy of a winter cruise or, more likely, a tanning booth. A good haircut, but his last shave had left a few grey hairs dotted about his round and shiny face. His teeth had been fixed, and he maintained the swagger necessary to his job, but his shirt hadn't been ironed and a button was missing, not quite hidden by the bright crimson tie.

Like his industry, Jackie Ness had seen better days.

'We're here to ask you a few questions about Stuart Bloom,' Clarke said, now the ice had been broken. 'He was working for you when he went missing.'

'It's a hellish thing. My first thought was the same as everybody else — lovers' tiff.'

'And when he failed to resurface?'

'Sometimes people just want to step off the grid. I did a film about it: quiet banking executive walks out on his family and becomes a vigilante.'

'How about your own relationship with Mr Bloom?'

'No problems there at all. He wasn't overcharging, seemed to be getting some good stuff . . . '

'Stuff on Adrian Brand?'

'Aka the Fucker.' His eyes moved between the two detectives. 'Pardon my French.'

'Did you ever suspect Brand might have known what was going on?'

'You mean did he have Stuart bumped off?' Ness's face creased in thought. 'It was always a possibility. Brand mixed with some ugly people. Stuart was getting close to proving it.'

'Something that could have put him in danger?'

'The cops at the time looked into it but didn't get far.' Ness broke off as his burger arrived. He picked it up and took a bite. He was still chewing as the drinks appeared. 'Help yourselves to a sweet potato fry,' he offered.

'What did you think,' Clarke asked, 'when the car was found in Poretoun Woods?'

He shook his head vigorously. 'Couldn't have been there all that time.'

'Why not?' Clarke waited while he swallowed and took a sip of the Irn-Bru.

'I used to film there. Not that exact spot maybe, but we were always in those woods. Anything vaguely medieval; anything to do with zombies or kids getting a scare.'

'The car was in a pretty deep gully, and well camouflaged.'

'I'm telling you I'd have noticed it. Added to which, those woods were a pet project of mine — them and the house. I spent a fortune restoring both.'

'How do you restore woodland?' Crowther asked, sounding genuinely curious.

'By planting rare and native species rather

than trees you grow as a crop. I had meetings with forestry experts, took on board everything they said.'

'You're saying you had a detailed knowledge of Poretoun Woods,' Clarke commented. Ness locked eyes with her above his burger.

'I know what you're getting at — means I'd have known about the gully and that it made a good hiding place. But why would I kill Stuart? He was a great guy, just doing his job and living for the weekend.'

'Weekends were special to him?'

'There was a club he liked in the New Town, somewhere just off Leith Street. Rogues, I think it was called. Him and Derek were regulars.'

'Derek Shankley, you mean? Did you ever meet him?'

'A couple of times. Never mentioned his dad was one of your lot. Apparently the father was none too happy about his son and Stuart.'

'How about you, Mr Ness?'

'I've no problem with gay people. Some of the best talent in my films were gay. Maybe not all of them totally out, back in the day, but that's how it was. Even now, plenty big names are still reluctant to step from the closet. I could give you a few that might surprise you.'

'Why did you sell Poretoun House?'

Ness's face darkened a little. 'Sunk too much of my own money into a film I thought was gold-plated. Then Billy — Billy Locke — had that run-in with HMRC and the company suddenly had penalties to pay.' He offered a shrug and dropped the remains of the burger back on to the wooden board it had arrived on. The small tin bucket of fries remained untouched. Ness stifled a belch.

'Why that particular spot, do you think?' Clarke asked.

'Maybe to put me in the frame. Stands to reason it was someone who knew my history with the woods.'

'But they're owned by your old rival these days.'

Ness's face darkened further. 'That was a kick in the teeth. Thought I was safe selling to Jeff Sellers. But then he goes and does a deal with Brand of all people. And you know why Brand did it?'

'Why?'

'To fuck with my head — excuse my French one more time. From what I hear, he's letting the house rot, and the woods too. Any invasive species, he lets it thrive. That's exactly what him and his kind are — an invasive species.'

'Meaning what?'

'Men like him are little more than pillagers and con artists. He'll say and do anything to get the land he wants, then build any old tat on it. I wanted that patch of green belt for Scotland's first film studio. It would have brought jobs and prestige. Brand wanted a golf course for his rich pals, and even then he'd have scaled it back to squeeze in more of his ticky-tacky houses.'

'Do the pair of you still butt heads?'

'I got tired of the lawyers' bills; wanted my life back. Plus, the longer Stuart stayed missing, the easier it was to read it as a message — lay off me and my business.'

Clarke took out her notebook and skimmed its pages, making show of finding her next question. 'Did you ever have dealings with a pair of men called Steele and Edwards?'

Ness gave a snort. 'They pulled my car over a few times to tell me I was speeding. I knew what was going on, though; Stuart had already warned me they were on Brand's payroll.'

'He had proof?'

'Why would he lie?'

'This was something he'd discovered in the course of his investigation?'

'Yes.'

'Did you ever make a formal complaint?'

He stared at her. 'Are you going to tell me it would have made a blind bit of difference?'

'Did Stuart Bloom have run-ins with them like you did?'

'He never said. The club did get busted a few times, though: cops looking for drugs, anyone underage, corrupt and depraved practices . . . Remember there was a spate of overdoses in the city around that time? That gave your lot the excuse.'

'Mr Bloom was never arrested in these raids?'

Ness tapped the side of his nose. 'Said he was smart enough not to be there those nights.'

'Are you suggesting he was tipped off?'

'His boyfriend's dad was a copper — put two and two together.' Ness poured the dregs of his can into his glass. Then he smiled. 'You know I used them in one of my films?'

'Who?'

'I had a crowd scene I couldn't afford, so I asked Stuart. Him and Derek rounded up a few of the guys they knew from Rogues. Now that I think of it, we filmed in the woods.'

'What was the film called?'

'*Zombies v Bravehearts*. Ever tried to make four zombies look like a horde?'

'Is that who Stuart and Derek played?'

Ness shook his head. 'They were queuing up to get into a kilt, stripped to the waist and painted blue. It was so cold that day, I could have saved the cost of make-up.'

'Is the film available anywhere?'

'I'm told copies fetch a small fortune online. Died a death when we first released it. There are clips on YouTube.'

'I'm guessing there'll be one somewhere in your office, though.'

'The only copy I have.'

'We'll bring it back, I promise.'

The low sun had shifted and was catching the side of Emily Crowther's face again.

'You really should consider acting,' Ness told her. 'Do you mind if I . . . ?' He produced a phone from his pocket and held it up to take a photo. But Clarke blocked the camera with her hand.

'No publicity,' she said. Looking crestfallen, Ness put the phone away again.

As they were leaving, he told the waiter he'd settle up at the end of the week. The waiter's look suggested he'd expected nothing else. With the DVD retrieved — in a plain black plastic box

96

— Clarke and Crowther headed back to Clarke's car.

'He could make you a star,' Clarke commented.

'Sleazy fucker that he is,' Crowther muttered in response. Clarke gave her a sideways glance. DC Emily Crowther had just gone up — way, way up — in her estimation, as had DCI Graham Sutherland. He'd known the way someone from the film world might react to a pretty face — and he'd been right.

'Why the interest in Steele and Edwards?' Crowther asked as Clarke signalled into traffic.

'They're ACU these days.'

'And you've just escaped ACU's clutches.' Crowther nodded her understanding.

'Graham told you?'

Another nod. 'You were exonerated, though?'

'Whiter than white,' Clarke said quietly, signalling to turn at the lights.

9

The first meeting between Malcolm Fox and Tess Leighton became an immediate battle of wills, which he ended up losing. The 2006 case files had been moved to a small, cold room down the corridor from the MIT office. Fox had argued that they should be returned to MIT.

'All due respect, Malcolm,' Leighton had drawled, 'we're running a murder inquiry in there.'

'I wouldn't get in the way.'

She had slid her eyes towards the stacks of boxes. 'You probably would, though. Easier to concentrate when you've got a whole room to yourself. I'm always around if you need me.'

Having said which, she had inched backwards to the door, closing it after her. An hour later, she'd stuck her head back into the room. 'We're making a cuppa,' she had informed him. 'How do you take it?'

'Just milk, thanks.'

'Settled in okay?'

'I'm freezing my arse off.'

'Mug of tea will sort you out.'

When she left, he made up his mind, trailing her to the MIT office and positioning himself against one of the radiators, palms pressed against it. Leighton was behind her desk, Phil Yeats busy at the kettle.

'Just till I've thawed out,' Fox explained to the room at large.

Graham Sutherland looked up from his computer. 'Making progress?'

'There's a lot to take in.'

'If you come across anything you think might be helpful to us . . . '

Fox nodded. 'You'll be the first to hear.'

'Meantime,' Sutherland said to his team, 'Aubrey Hamilton is heading to Poretoun Woods. Who's up for accompanying her? How about you, George?'

'I'd have to get some boots from somewhere.'

Sutherland shifted his attention to Callum Reid.

'Wouldn't I be more useful here?' Reid argued.

'I can do it if you like,' Fox chipped in. 'I wouldn't mind seeing the gully for myself.'

'You're not official, though, Malcolm.'

'I'll go,' Leighton said. 'Malcolm can tag along if he likes.' She shrugged as if to say: where's the harm?

'Don't leave me hanging, Tess,' Sutherland instructed. 'Hamilton finds anything, I want to know ASAP.'

Leighton nodded her understanding. She had lifted a carrier bag on to her desk and pulled out a pair of wellingtons. 'You got any?' she asked Fox.

'I'll manage,' he assured her.

Five minutes later, they were in Leighton's Corsa. She asked Fox about his work at Gartcosh, then whether he had found anything in the old files.

'You had a look at them before me,' he countered. 'What did you think?'

'I didn't like it that two officers had worked for Brand.'

'Steele and Edwards, you mean?'

'And the investigation really went out of its way to minimise mention of Derek Shankley, while still managing to focus on the victim's homosexuality. Lot of gay men pulled in for interview and held for longer than seems strictly necessary.'

'How about the family's complaints?'

'Thing to remember is, it was a misper. There were reasons to suspect foul play but no actual evidence of any kind — which didn't stop the parents expecting miracles.'

Fox nodded to himself. 'My boss told me the family's complaints had been dismissed — that's not quite the case, though. Police Scotland did end up apologising for the way we'd dealt with them.'

'Without admitting we'd got anything wrong.'

'I'm already seeing signs of sloppiness, Tess. It took over a week to get round to questioning Brand, for example. And nobody seems to have bothered even looking for CCTV footage from Bloom's neighbourhood or the route back into the city from Poretoun House.'

Leighton gave him an appraising glance. 'All of that from an hour's reading? I'm impressed.'

'It helped that you'd given it a go — the interesting stuff was all towards the top of the first box. I'm grateful for that.'

Leighton checked her sat nav. 'You never did get that tea,' she said. 'We could stop for a takeaway.'

'Maybe on the way back, but thanks for the thought.'

For the rest of the drive they discussed Police Scotland, politics and the state of the world, neither of them particularly willing to open up about their personal lives. But Fox reckoned it would happen; they were starting to get along.

★   ★   ★

Professor Hamilton had brought a male assistant with her. Fox hadn't met the forensic anthropologist before, but he knew her reputation. She was short, with brown hair cut in a fringe. She wore glasses, behind which the eyes remained sharply watchful. Blue and white crime-scene tape surrounded the perimeter of the gully. The ground had been disturbed, evidence of the fingertip search carried out the previous day. They'd tried uncovering the old track, the one the car must have used. There had been some success, though saplings and briars had replaced it at many points.

'Who'd have known there even was an access road?' Fox had asked as they trudged into the woods.

'Local farmers,' Leighton offered. 'Plus forestry staff, the woods' owner . . . '

'And anyone who bought an Ordnance Survey map,' Hamilton added. 'I got hold of one and it's still marked.'

'Nice to narrow things down,' Fox muttered as his shoes sank into the mulch of leaves.

A bored, cold-looking constable guarded the

crime scene. He wore a padded jacket and black gloves but seemed ready for a change of shift. He added their details to his clipboard and nodded towards the ropes that would allow them to negotiate the slope.

'Not that there's anything to see.'

No, because a farm tractor had been used to winch the VW Polo out, churning up the side of the gully in the process. Hamilton had already ducked under the tape and, ignoring the ropes, was cantering down the slope, her boots finding the necessary purchase.

'You a climber by any chance?' Leighton called down to her.

'Hill-walking,' Hamilton called back. 'But in Scotland that can often amount to the same thing.'

Leighton looked towards Fox. He shrugged to let her know he was happy enough where he was. To show willing, however, he began to circle the gully, noting more evidence of the painstaking search. Hamilton's assistant had joined her in the gully, having made the descent largely on his backside. The two of them began studying the pile of material that had been draped over the car.

'Uprooted rather than cut with a knife,' Hamilton eventually said, while her assistant photographed everything held up in front of him. She opened the folder she'd brought. There were dozens of crime-scene pictures inside, and she studied some of them closely, looking up from time to time to visualise the Polo. The SOCOs had bagged cigarette butts, rusty drinks cans, chocolate wrappers. They would be checked for prints and other identifiers. Hamilton scooped up some of the rich dark soil, crumbling it between her fingers. 'You can learn a lot from bugs,' she stated, her voice carrying without difficulty. 'Some insects frequent particular environments. And when it comes to man-made objects, those are prone to deteriorate at different rates, affected again by their environment.' She held up a photo of the Polo for them to see. 'I'm just not convinced,' she said, 'that this car lay in this gully for twelve years.'

'So how long was it here?' Fox called down to her.

'Not long enough for the amount of corrosion I'd expect to see.'

'Where was it before?'

'Could be the bugs will tell us. I still want a soil expert to examine it. I'm guessing we now have a budget?'

Leighton nodded.

'So I can talk to DCI Sutherland?'

'I'm sure he'll be amenable.'

'Then let's hope the person I want is available.'

Having done a circuit, Fox was back next to Leighton. 'Thoughts?' she asked him.

'I'll tell you what's uppermost in my mind right now, Tess.'

'What?'

He lifted one leg. 'I need to buy some new shoes.'

10

Sir Adrian Brand ran his empire from a vast Victorian house on Kinellan Road in Murrayfield. The gardens surrounding the property would have constituted a park in less desirable parts of the city. Sheltered beneath a car port sat a Bentley and a Tesla, the latter hooked up to its charging cable. When Clarke and Crowther rang the bell, the door was opened by Glenn Hazard.

'Nice to see you again,' Clarke told him, her tone giving the lie to her words.

'Sir Adrian is in the garden room,' Hazard replied. 'Though like me, he's wondering why you're wasting his time.'

'Because we get a kick out of it?'

He made an exasperated sound and led them across the vast hallway with its chandelier and polished parquet floor, through one door into a sitting room with what looked like a dining room off, then a set of glass doors into an airy conservatory filled with potted plants and wicker furniture. Brand sat pretending to read the *Financial Times*. He wore rimless glasses on an owl-like face. What hair he still had was slicked back across the top of his head and around his ears. His pale lemon shirt billowed, its top two buttons undone to expose tufts of silvered chest hair. While Jackie Ness's metal Rolex had looked fake, the gold one hanging loosely around Brand's thick wrist was almost certainly real.

Brand made a show of closing and folding his newspaper. His PR man had taken the chair to his right, leaving only a narrow sofa for Clarke and Crowther. The two women made space on it. The glass coffee table between them and Brand held a goblet emptied of fresh orange juice, a small pile of current affairs magazines, and an iPad showing a muted TV channel dedicated to Mammon.

'Thank you for seeing us at such short notice,' Clarke began.

Brand looked at her for the first time. 'You say that as if I had any choice in the matter.'

'I would imagine it's difficult to force you to do anything you don't want to do, Sir Adrian.'

His smile was as thin as the platinum chain around his neck. 'Well, I suppose I *was* curious. It's not every day a body turns up on land one happens to own.'

'Especially the body of someone you knew.'

'Sir Adrian never met Stuart Bloom,' Hazard snapped.

Clarke kept her focus on Brand. 'You knew who he was, though, knew the work he was engaged in for Jackie Ness?'

'This was all gone over at the time, Inspector.' Brand wafted a hand in front of him. 'I got wind that Ness had employed some sort of gumshoe. My people knew that someone had tried hacking into my computer system.'

'But you couldn't prove who it was?'

'I knew Ness was behind it; had my lawyers send a cease and desist notice.'

'You didn't go to the police?'

105

'I try as best I can to take care of my own affairs. And as you've said yourself, I had no proof of Ness's involvement.'

'You didn't think to confront Stuart Bloom?'

'No.'

'Or send an emissary to do it for you?'

Brand shifted a little. 'Again, no.'

'As part of our inquiry into Mr Bloom's murder, we'll be looking at original statements and interviews. Is there anything you said then that you might want to amend with the benefit of hindsight?'

'I told the truth, Inspector, just as I'm doing now.'

'As you say, the body was found on land you own — what do you think about that?'

'I've only recently acquired Poretoun Woods.'

'But all the same . . . '

Brand gave a shrug, the collar of his shirt rising as far as his ears. 'I feel sorry for his family, obviously, even though they've said some poisonous things about me in the past.'

'Libellous things,' Hazard corrected his employer. 'Over which Sir Adrian took no action.'

'That's unusual, isn't it?' The two men looked at Clarke. 'I mean, you've never been one to shy away from lawyers and lawsuits.'

'A man needs a hobby, Inspector.' Brand's smile showed a row of perfect teeth.

'The Bloom family felt you were being protected by the police, because of who you were.'

'They threw around all manner of wild

accusations. It was a Freemasons' plot, I was lining the chief constable's pockets — all of it absolute nonsense.'

'Do you still employ a chauffeur, sir?'

The change of tack didn't quite throw Brand. 'Not as such.'

'How about a bodyguard?'

'I often travel with Sir Adrian,' Hazard butted in. Brand turned to him.

'She means a *proper* bodyguard, Glenn. Ex-army, Krav Maga training.' Then, to Clarke: 'There's an agency I've been known to use on occasion, mostly for overseas trips.'

Clarke nodded slowly, pretending to digest this. 'Do you still have any dealings with Brian Steele and Grant Edwards?'

Brand's brow furrowed. 'Should I know those names?'

'They worked for you around the time Stuart Bloom disappeared, just in their free time — their day job was as police officers.'

'A lot of people have worked for me, Inspector.'

'They used to drive you around, act as muscle. I'm sure if you put your mind to it, you'll find you remember them.'

Brand eventually nodded. 'Steele and Edwards, yes. They were with me for a short time.'

'They were even the source of one of the Bloom family's complaints.'

'Were they?'

'Seeing how both of them were attached to the missing person inquiry. Possible conflict of interest, according to Catherine Bloom.'

'She came here, you know. More than once, actually. The gates were locked but she used the intercom, yelling at my wife.'

'Again, you didn't contact us?'

'She went away eventually. I felt sorry for her, never having had a son to lose.'

'Your wife isn't here today?'

'She'd have nothing to add. Cordelia has never taken an interest in my business.'

Hazard had leaned forward, elbows on knees, hands bunched into fists. 'You'll be asking questions of Jackie Ness, too, I trust? For the sake of parity?'

'We've just come from Mr Ness.' Clarke kept her eyes on Brand, whose own attention had drifted to stock-market listings on the TV channel. 'Any recent hostilities between the two of you?'

'Jackie Ness is living on past glories, such as they were,' Brand said without looking up. 'I've heard he's about two phone calls away from bankruptcy, and not for the first time.'

'You're saying he's no longer a rival?'

'Bastard's not big enough,' Glenn Hazard muttered.

Brand looked up from the screen, meeting Clarke's eyes. 'Jackie Ness is history,' he intoned.

'Why did you buy Poretoun House, Sir Adrian?'

'As an investment.'

'And how does leaving it to rot increase its value?'

Brand's eyes almost gleamed. 'It got to him, didn't it? He told you? I knew it would.'

108

'That's why you did it?'

'Cheap at half the price.' Brand appeared to notice Emily Crowther for the first time. 'Do you talk or are you just here for show?'

'I talk when I've got something to say,' Crowther offered. 'And as it happens, I *do* have something.'

'Yes?'

Crowther gestured towards the potted plants. 'You've got aphids. Quite a lot of them, actually.'

★   ★   ★

When the time came for them to leave, Hazard stayed on the doorstep, watching Clarke unlock the Astra and get behind the steering wheel, while Crowther climbed into the passenger side. Once the doors were closed and the engine started, Clarke asked Crowther what she thought.

'He was lying to us. You saw it too.'

Clarke nodded. 'About sending someone to talk to Stuart Bloom. Wonder who his PR was back then.'

'Wouldn't a lawyer be the more obvious choice?'

'Maybe . . . '

'You're thinking of those two uniforms, aren't you? Steele and Edwards?'

'Jackie Ness has already told us they harassed him. Wouldn't have been difficult for Brand to set them on Stuart Bloom.'

'Bloom knew of their relationship to Brand — he was the one who warned Ness.'

109

Clarke nodded slowly. 'Maybe Fox will find something in the archives.'

'Something that would earn him a drink?'

Clarke glanced towards Crowther. 'What are you saying?'

'Just the way you talk about him — you've obviously been close in the past.'

'Not *that* close.' Clarke paused. 'And when did I even talk about him?' Then she remembered. 'The briefing I gave Tess?'

'So I can tell her, then?'

'Tell her what?'

Crowther waved her phone from side to side. 'Tess sent me a text from Poretoun Woods. She's there with Fox. I get the feeling she likes him.'

'She's free to jump him any time she likes.' Clarke saw that Crowther had started composing a text. 'Maybe put it more diplomatically than that, though, eh?' She released the handbrake, watching Hazard's figure recede in the rear-view mirror. 'That was a good line about the aphids, by the way. You're into gardening?'

'You changing the subject?'

'Absolutely not. I was just wondering.'

'In truth, I probably wouldn't know an aphid if I saw one. But I reckon it'll have got him wondering.'

'Wondering and maybe even worrying,' Clarke agreed. The two detectives were chuckling as the gates opened automatically in front of them.

11

DCI Sutherland had gathered his team for a meeting. Fox stood by the door, waiting to be told to scram, but Sutherland seemed relaxed about his presence in the room.

'We need fresh interviews with everyone who was part of the inquiry last time round,' Sutherland said. 'We know that they might not always be willing. Some of Stuart Bloom's friends and associates felt they were treated with a lack of proper respect. So there may need to be an apology or two, a bit of mea culpa, but also some benign insistence.' He scanned the faces around them. 'We want to speak to every single one of them. It's been twelve years, so contact details will almost certainly have changed. I've requested extra staff to ease the burden, but we need to make a start as of right now.' He broke off. 'Are you listening, Siobhan?'

'Yes, sir.'

Fox noticed that half Clarke's attention was on her computer. She had plugged in a pair of earbuds but left one dangling. He slid around the periphery towards her. A film seemed to be playing on her screen.

'Tess,' Sutherland continued. 'News from the professor?'

'She can't be sure as yet how long the car was in the woods, but she doubts it was there all along.'

'Pathology tells us Stuart Bloom probably died ten or more years back, so where does that leave us?'

'It's definitely his car?' George Gamble asked.

'Serial number on the engine block confirms it. Doubtful he was murdered *in situ* — not enough blood and brain matter on the floor of the boot, according to Forensics. It's a miracle they can be so confident after all these years, but there you are. The two professors seem to agree — the way the body was positioned in the boot, the injured section of skull was towards the floor. Almost physically impossible to have hit someone while they were lying in that position and damage that particular section. Besides, putting someone in a boot and then hitting them? More probably it was done while he was standing up. Whacked from behind with an object as yet undecided.'

'And the handcuffs?' Phil Yeats asked.

'Standard issue for police officers in Scotland up until the millennium. Two metal links joining one cuff to its neighbour. By 2006 they'd been replaced by the Hiatt model — solid plastic moulding instead of the links. The Hiatts were stamped with serial numbers, meaning there's a record of who owned them. Alas, that wasn't true of the older model. Bear in mind, they could have been acquired from other sources. We're not saying these were definitively police handcuffs.'

'This place Rogues that Bloom used to go to.' Callum Reid nodded towards Clarke, who had reported on the meetings with Ness and Brand.

'Didn't happen to have a dungeon or anything, did it?'

'Doubtful, but worth checking,' Sutherland said. 'In fact, that's a good point: were there any S and M clubs operating in Edinburgh at the time? Or prostitutes specialising in bondage? Something to add to the list. DCS Mollison is keen for a press conference sooner rather than later; it'd be nice to have a bit of progress to report.' He noted that Gamble had his hand up. 'Yes, George?'

'We're not making the handcuffs public yet?'

'Why do you ask?'

'When it gets out — and it *will* get out — the family will start yelling police cover-up again.'

'In which case, we'd best try to find evidence one way or the other.' Sutherland scanned the room to ensure his words had sunk in. 'Now get busy.'

Clarke had noticed Fox standing behind her. She paused the film and turned to him.

'One of Jackie Ness's?' Fox guessed.

'Apparently Bloom and his boyfriend had walk-ons.'

Fox nodded towards the screen. 'Looks familiar.'

'It's Poretoun Woods. And filmed not long before Stuart's death.'

'Interesting. Good film?'

'As wooden as its setting.'

'Plot?'

'Scots and English readying to do battle, but up pop the undead. The enemies either join forces or get wiped out.'

'I quite like the sound of that.'

'It probably looked good on paper,' Clarke agreed. She noticed that both Crowther and Leighton were taking an interest in the conversation, so sent a quick scowl towards them. 'Any great revelations from the woods? You and Tess getting along okay?'

Fox gave her a quizzical look before replying. 'Professor Hamilton thinks car and body might have been elsewhere for the first few years. If we can pin down where and why.'

'Why it was moved, you mean?' Clarke nodded her agreement. 'But meantime, the focus is on a retread of the original inquiry.'

'Meaning officers as well as witnesses.'

'So we'll be questioning John?'

'Needs to be thorough, Siobhan.'

She nodded again. One of the admin staff was standing in the doorway.

'DI Fox?' she enquired. Fox turned to her.

'That's me.'

'You've a visitor downstairs.'

Fox thanked her and headed for the reception area. He didn't see anyone, but the desk officer pointed towards the door. 'They're out there,' he said. Fox stepped outside and looked to left and right. The TV cameras and reporters had gone. Standing at the corner, smoking a cigarette, was a figure he recognised. He drew in a sharp breath before heading towards the man.

'Hiya, Malc,' DS Brian Steele said. 'How's tricks?'

'We've not been properly introduced,' Fox responded.

'Maybe not, but you've seen me around Gartcosh and I've seen you. Major Crimes' gain is ACU's loss, if you ask me. Man of your experience, we could have made better use of you.' Steele was blowing smoke from his nose while studying the tip of the cigarette.

'What brings you here?' Fox demanded to know.

'Ach, I was just in the neighbourhood. I heard you'd been attached to the Bloom case, so I thought I'd say hello.'

'Without actually coming in?'

'That'll be happening soon, though, eh? A wee invitation to tell my side of the story. Me and Grant and everybody else who worked the case.'

'We can start right now if you like. Team's upstairs, and I'm sure I could lay my hands on some recording equipment.'

Steele exhaled more smoke, making sure it avoided Fox. The man was tall and broad with an unexceptional face and short black hair spiked with gel. 'Plenty of time for that, Malc. It was you I wanted to see.'

'Why?'

'Because we're on the same side. You were Complaints, I'm ACU. Neither of us likes dirty cops. I know you'll have heard some of the stories about me — bending the rules, pulling a few stunts. I'll bet similar things were said about you when you were Complaints. Nobody likes us, nobody trusts us, so they need their lies and rumours.'

'I'm not much clearer on why you're here.'

Steele took a step closer. 'Reopening the old

115

case is an opportunity for more lies, more mud-slinging. I'd just appreciate the odd update, confidentially. In return, I'll owe you one. Ask around, I'm a good friend to have.' He finished the cigarette and flicked it halfway across the road. 'And if you do need sacrificial lambs, I can give you those too. Skelton, Newsome, Rebus — take your pick.'

'None of them worked for Adrian Brand back then, though, did they?'

'Plenty cops had side jobs, Malc. It still happens, you know that. But when it came to policing, I gave one hundred per cent, same then as now. Many didn't do half as much.'

'Rebus?'

'More likely to be found in a pub than anywhere else. Half drunk or else hung-over. We covered for him, same as for Mary Skelton.'

'What did she do?'

'Her mum was sick; she kept nipping off to visit her. Except everybody knew it was a bloke she was seeing, afternoon delight and all that. I've never seen a woman more in heat.'

'And Newsome?'

'Doug Newsome was a waste of space. Half the interviews he said he'd done never happened, and the ones he did deign to do, he made stuff up when he transcribed them.'

Fox studied Steele. 'You were in the ranks at the time. Unusual for a uniform to know so much about the CID side of things.'

'I was conscientious. And I made friends. That's how you get ahead, Malc. It got me here, didn't it?' He smiled. 'So what do you say, a quick pint and a quiet chat now and again?' Steele broke off. 'What am I saying? You're a recovering alcoholic — apple juice is your thing, isn't it? When you're being sociable, I mean. Mostly you just like quiet nights at home in Oxgangs, when you're not keeping an eye on your sister, making sure her gambling habit's under control.' He was still smiling, but his eyes were as hard as marbles.

'You've done your research,' Fox conceded.

'It's how the world turns.'

'So tell me, what did you think when you heard Stuart Bloom had been found?'

'I thought it was an interesting location, especially if someone was trying to make sure we focused on Jackie Ness or Adrian Brand.'

'Were you one of the original search team?'

'In the woods?' Steele nodded. 'Only took us half a day, mind. The woods, the house and its grounds. More likely he'd met a bit of rough and been done in.'

'Did you visit Rogues at all?'

'Not then, no.'

'But other times?'

'We went in once or twice, acting on tip-offs. Drugs; underage kids.'

'Find anything?'

'Doesn't mean nothing was happening.'

'I'm guessing the tip-offs were anonymous?'

'Not every concerned citizen wants to stick their head above the parapet.' Steele was growing impatient. 'Sounds like I've already done my interview, doesn't it?'

'I doubt we've even scratched the surface.'

117

'My ears aren't picking up the warm sounds of a burgeoning friendship.'

'Nothing wrong with your hearing then.'

Steele looked down at the pavement between them. 'You've been known to hang around with John Rebus, Malc — is *he* a friend? Because he's probably got more to lose than most, you know.'

'How do you mean?'

'The boozing was the least of it. Bear that in mind when you bring him in for questioning. See, old cases can be like stripping wallpaper — you don't know what problems you're going to find beneath, kept hidden by the thinnest of coverings.' Steele held up his thumb and forefinger, so that a millimetre gap remained between them. 'I'm a hell of a friend to have, Malc, but I can be the exact opposite, too. Remember that.' He turned to leave, but then paused. 'Oh, and don't think of going running to your boss at Major Crime — Jen Lyon's got enough to deal with if the stories I hear are true.'

'What stories?'

'Bit of gardening leave coming her way. At this rate, you or me might be running the show before too long.'

He started to cross the road, and for the first time Fox noticed the large black Audi parked there. The driver's window slid down, giving him a clear view of Grant Edwards. Edwards was known for the perpetual smile he wore. His face was that of an oversized infant, almost cherubic. Fox got the feeling the man would have the same demeanour whether he was helping an old lady with her shopping or thumping someone in a bar fight. Interesting that he had stayed in the car, though. Steele had wanted to befriend Fox rather than intimidate him; that had been the plan. Besides which, Edwards wasn't known for either intellect or subtlety. Waiting in the car would have been Steele's decision. Fox sent a little wave of farewell in the Audi's direction as he headed back indoors.

★ ★ ★

Clarke had found two scenes where Stuart Bloom and Derek Shankley appeared as extras. Their job was to look fierce as they prepared for an imminent attack by the English, then scream and flee as the zombies appeared. The scenes seemed to have been shot in twilight, so it wasn't easy to pick them out from the other actors, but it helped that they always stood next to one another. When she watched for a third time, she thought she noted amusement in their eyes where fear should have been, as if they'd been sharing a joke between takes.

Always supposing the director bothered with more than one take.

Neither Bloom nor Shankley was listed in the closing credits. The director (and also co-writer) was Alexander Dupree. From an internet search Clarke knew that this was a pseudonym used by Jackie Ness to disguise how few people were involved behind the camera in his productions. Cheaply made, his films had still earned him substantial sums, at least until recently. If a thriller made it big at the international box office, a quick knock-off version courtesy of Locke Ness Productions would be in circulation within a matter of weeks. In interviews, Ness was particularly proud of this guerrilla approach. Get it out quick, and make sure both violence and at least partial nudity appear within the first ten minutes. 'Fear and desire,' he'd been quoted as saying, 'are what drive us. I just hold up a mirror so we can watch ourselves.'

From what she could glean from the nerds on the internet, the film had been made only a month prior to Bloom's disappearance. She supposed it was to Ness's credit that he hadn't tried to capitalise on the PI's newsworthiness at the time the film was released. Whenever he was asked by interviewers about Bloom's disappearance, he gave versions of the same answer: 'It would have been a great studio — great for film, great for Scotland. But that dream died.' She had mulled those words over. He was tying Stuart Bloom's disappearance to his own struggle with Adrian Brand. Without naming him, he was effectively *blaming* his rival.

Her phone buzzed: incoming call. She checked the name on the screen and slipped out of the office, pressing the phone to her ear as she closed the door.

'I've got nothing for you, Laura.'

'Okay,' Laura Smith said. 'But maybe I've got something for you.'

'What?'

'One of my colleagues doorstepped Alex Shankley this morning.'

'That was insensitive.'

120

'They'd actually gone looking for his son, but it was the dad who answered the knock.'

'Hang on, this was whose home?'

'Derek's. A tenement flat in Partick.'

'Okay.'

'Thing is, the father said they couldn't talk to the press until they'd spoken to you lot.'

'Very wise.'

'Siobhan, he was meaning today. That's why I'm back at my post.'

Clarke returned to the MIT office and crossed to the window, peering through a grubby pane down to Queen Charlotte Street. 'I don't see you,' she whispered, Graham Sutherland being within earshot.

'I'm round the corner. Probably explains why Malcolm Fox didn't clock me.'

'Hang on a sec ... ' Clarke left the office again and headed to the small room set aside for Fox and the box files. He was seated beside Tess Leighton, the pair of them deep in discussion, heads close. Clarke retreated along the corridor.

'When was this?'

'Not five minutes ago. He was meeting someone.'

'Who?'

'When you got in that spot of bother, you weren't the only one. It was the same guy who grilled me.'

'Brian Steele?'

'With his shadow parked up nearby.'

'Steele and Edwards were *here*?'

'For a friendly chinwag with Fox. He hasn't mentioned it?'

'He's not seen me to speak to.'

'What's ACU's involvement with all of this, Siobhan?'

'No comment.'

'Something's being hushed up, something about the crime scene.'

'Is it?'

'Come on, Siobhan. I wouldn't be doing my job if I didn't know.'

'And what is it you think you know, Laura?'

'Well, the handcuffs, for one thing.'

Clarke pressed her lips together for a moment. 'So now you know why ACU are involved — someone's leaking. If I had to guess, I'd say someone in the lab or on the scene-of-crime team.'

'Could be anybody really, couldn't it?'

'If you go public, ACU will think it's me again.'

'I know. That's one reason I'm waiting.'

'The other being?'

'You obviously don't want it known about. Makes me think you're scared it'll either frighten someone off or else people will jump to the wrong conclusion.' Clarke stayed silent. 'Steele and Edwards were in uniform when the Bloom case happened. Did they happen to work on it, Siobhan?'

'I can't discuss that. What will you do about the handcuffs?'

'It'll break sooner or later.'

'Can you give us a day or two?'

'Maybe.'

'You're right, Laura. If you're the one with the

exclusive, ACU will come for me.'

'Which is why I'll probably give it to someone else, let them grab the glory.'

'You'd do that?'

'Saves us both a bit of grief, don't you think?'

'Thanks, Laura.'

'That last mess with ACU, I do feel just a little bit responsible, you know.'

'Consider the slate wiped.' Clarke ended the call and watched as two men were led up the stairs and told to wait at the door to the MIT room. The elder of the two looked resolute, the younger hesitant.

Derek Shankley and his father.

12

The interview room at Leith police station. Clarke and Sutherland one side of the table, father and son the other. Four mugs of tea. Two sugars for Alex Shankley and the exact same for Derek.

'Thank you for making the effort, sir,' Sutherland told the retired detective.

'It was Derek's idea.'

The slight change in the son's face gave the lie to this. Derek Shankley wore a black leather biker jacket over a white T-shirt. Fashion, Clarke reckoned, would always win out over comfort. He looked cold, the jacket zipped almost to his neck. He had studs in both earlobes and a shaved head. Though clean-shaven, he had kept traces of his sideburns. His father had a chiselled face, but was slightly stooped, the years having taken their toll.

'You not recording this?' Alex Shankley asked.

'Unless one of you is here to confess?' Sutherland's smile told them he was joking.

'We're here to save you the trouble of making us come. It's hellish news about Stuart and we want to give you our thoughts.'

'Yes, I should have said . . . ' Sutherland turned his attention to Derek. 'We really are very sorry about Stuart.'

Derek nodded solemnly. He hadn't aged much since the days of *Zombies v Bravehearts*. Clarke wondered what his secret was.

'I was just watching you, Derek,' she said conversationally. 'The film you were in with Stuart.'

He almost snorted. 'Weren't we terrible?'

'You looked to be enjoying yourselves, though.'

'Well, you know what it's like on film sets.'

'Actually, I don't.'

'We want to know how we can help the inquiry, DCI Sutherland,' Derek's father interrupted, placing his hands flat against the table. 'We want Stuart's killer brought to justice.'

Sutherland nodded thoughtfully. 'Have you had much to do with Stuart's family, Mr Shankley?'

'Not much.'

'Yes, that's what they said. Sent your condolences?'

Shankley made a show of clearing his throat. 'I don't have their address.'

Clarke watched as Derek raised an eyebrow — his father had just lied again.

'Derek didn't have much to do with the family after Stuart's disappearance,' Sutherland commented.

'What have they been saying?' the father snapped.

'That they tried contacting him but he wasn't very communicative.'

'They never really liked me,' Derek conceded. 'I thought they blamed me.'

'Blamed you how?'

'In their eyes, Stuart might have been running from me.'

'Why would he have done that?'

125

'He wouldn't.' Derek's eyes were glazing with the beginning of tears.

'No tension between the two of you? No arguments?'

Derek looked to Clarke. 'You saw us in that film — what do you think?'

'Like I said, you were enjoying yourselves.'

'We always did.' He folded his arms as if to affirm the statement, the leather creaking.

'How about you, Mr Shankley?' Sutherland's focus was still on the older man. 'Did you have any issues with Stuart?'

'Absolutely not.'

'Quite comfortable with Derek's sexuality?'

'He's my son, isn't he? Of course I am.' It sounded a line that had been used many times before. Derek turned his head to look at his father. That makes three, Clarke reckoned. Three little white lies.

'Are you,' she asked Derek, 'still in touch with friends from those days? Friends Stuart would have known?'

'Some, yes.'

'It's just that we're compiling a list of people we need to speak to. If you could help us with addresses or phone numbers . . . '

'Sure. I've no classes today.'

'You still teach media studies?' Clarke watched him nod. 'And are there jobs waiting for your students at the end of the course?'

'Not as many as there were, and the ones that are there often don't pay. They're supposed to be working for the contacts they'll make, for the good of their CV, or because the internship's so wonderful why would they ever want paying to be part of it?' He rolled his eyes while Clarke turned from son to father.

'There's something I need to put to you, Mr Shankley. It concerns Rogues nightclub.'

'What about it?'

'It was subject to several visits by police officers. Unscheduled visits. But never when your son and Stuart were there.'

'What are you trying to say?'

'Just that you were a detective, sir, with friends everywhere, I'm guessing.'

Alex Shankley shifted his gaze from Clarke to Sutherland. 'I don't see what any of this has to do with Stuart's murder.' Sutherland seemed to agree, his eyes on Clarke.

'Perhaps Derek could step outside for a moment,' she said. The son looked to his father, who nodded his agreement. Clarke waited until Derek was on the other side of the door.

'There's something I'd like to share with you, but it would have to be in confidence. It's something you might well find useful, because it'll help you prepare yourself.'

'And in exchange?' Alex Shankley asked.

'You'll answer a question I'm going to put to you.'

Shankley weighed up his response. 'Very well,' he eventually said.

Clarke moistened her lips. 'Stuart's ankles were handcuffed together. Police-issue handcuffs most probably. We're keeping that to ourselves at present, so please don't go sharing, even with Derek.'

Shankley nodded his understanding. 'Public will think it was a cop, and I was a cop.'

'Now you'll be prepared,' Clarke stated.

Shankley nodded again. 'So ask me your question.'

'Did someone let you know whenever a police raid was due to be carried out at Rogues?'

'How would it have looked, a murder squad man's son being hauled into the back of a police van?'

'Is that a yes?'

'It is.'

'The person who told you, they had to be on the inside, somebody local.'

'You've already had your question, DI Clarke. You've got me feeling like a bloody snitch, but that's as much of my soul as you're having.' He leaned back in his chair and folded his arms. For the first time, Clarke saw the son reflected in the father.

'You didn't kill Stuart Bloom, did you, Mr Shankley?' Sutherland asked.

'No, I didn't.'

'And you didn't order or otherwise facilitate his death?'

'No.'

'Happen to keep any old pairs of handcuffs in the house?' Sutherland watched Shankley nod. 'Any of them gone AWOL down the years?'

'Definitely not.'

'Sure about that?'

Shankley gazed towards the door. 'It nearly destroyed Derek, you know. For a few months he was almost suicidal. Even now . . . ' He shook his head and sighed. 'Took me a long time to understand how much they really cared for one another.'

'Your wife . . . ?' Clarke asked.

'Died when Derek was young.'

'You brought him up by yourself?'

'Family helped.'

'Which is why it's interesting you've never felt able to contact Stuart's family.'

Shankley glowered at the two detectives across from him. 'Did you hear the things they said about us? About hard-working cops like you and me? When Stuart went missing, his mum phoned me day and night — CID and home. She never gave it a rest, said I should be shouting from the rooftops, talking to all those bloody journalists.'

'And now your son is teaching the next generation,' Clarke commented.

The man snorted. Sutherland shifted on his seat.

'You will,' he said, 'check the situation with those handcuffs, won't you?'

Shankley slapped the table with the flat of his hand. 'I've told you I had nothing to do with it.'

'And you've no inkling who did?'

'None.'

'Then we're probably done here.' Sutherland made to rise to his feet.

'But we may need to talk to you again, sir,' Clarke cautioned. 'And in the meantime, while Derek's here, it would be good to get those contacts from him.'

'If he's willing, that's fine. He might not know

everyone, though. If he can't give you a number or he doesn't know a name, don't read anything into it.' Shankley paused, stabbing a finger into the air between the two detectives. 'Don't forget, I know how you think. And I know how wrong that thinking can sometimes be. I've always stuck up for the force and I always will — but I *know*.'

'Don't judge us by the past, Mr Shankley,' Clarke said. 'Trust me, we've learned a lot from the cock-ups and cosy conspiracies of your generation.'

⋆ ⋆ ⋆

That evening, after just the one drink with Graham Sutherland, Clarke stood in front of Rebus's tenement and pressed his buzzer, leaning in towards the intercom.

'Yes?' his voice crackled.

'I looked for you on the Meadows.'

'Already done.' The door sounded to let her know it had been unlocked. She climbed the two flights. Rebus was waiting on the landing, Brillo at his side, tail wagging. 'Can I just say, Siobhan, that a woman of your age should have better things to do with her evenings.'

'Thought I was supposed to keep you in the loop.'

'A phone call would suffice.' She followed him down the long hallway into the kitchen.

'You've tidied,' she commented.

'Cut to the quick by your critique. Coffee or gin?'

'Actually I'm fine.'

He lifted a box of tea bags. 'Turmeric. Guess who from?'

'A certain pathologist?'

'She thinks I want to live forever.' He took a bottle of IPA from the worktop and opened it. They went into the living room, where a CD was playing. Rebus turned it down a notch.

'Is that classical?'

'Arvo Pärt.'

'Our pathologist friend again?'

'Music to soothe the fevered brow.' He sank into his chair. 'How's it all going, anyway?'

'Malcolm's settled in.'

'He's good at that.'

'He had a couple of visitors today — the Chuggabugs.'

'Sounds about right. They'll be checking their arses are covered.'

'You think Malcolm will roll over for them?'

'It won't be like that, Shiv. They'll doubtless have something to offer. Maybe they dug up some dirt on him. Our Malcolm's not half as shiny as he looks, remember.' Rebus swallowed a mouthful of beer. 'Anything else?'

'I sat and watched one of Ness's films — *Zombies v Bravehearts*. Stuart Bloom and Derek Shankley were extras. This was after I'd interviewed both Ness and Brand. Can't say I was enamoured of either — Ness might stab you in the back, but Brand's as likely to do it while looking you in the eye. Meantime, the forensic anthropologist reckons the car might not have lain in that spot throughout.'

131

'Good news for those of us on the original search team.'

Clarke nodded from her corner of the sofa. Brillo had settled by her feet, curled into a ball. 'Means there was maybe nothing in those woods for you to miss,' she agreed.

In the silence that followed, Rebus kept his eyes on her. 'Any time you're ready,' he said.

'Ready?'

'To say what you came here to say.'

She stiffened her back. 'Derek Shankley turned up at Leith along with his father. Definitely the father's idea, but it got me thinking.'

'That's because you're a detective.'

'See, Jackie Ness had hinted at something. Police raids on a club Stuart Bloom and Derek Shankley frequented.'

'Rogues?'

Clarke nodded. 'Stuart and Derek were never there, which could just be coincidence, of course.'

'But Ness didn't think so?'

'If you ask me, Bloom had maybe bragged about it, or at least let something slip.'

'That they were forewarned?' She nodded again, her eyes on his. 'And you think maybe it was the dad who tipped them the wink?'

'He admitted as much.'

'But he was Glasgow-based.'

'So there had to be someone else right here in Edinburgh.' She paused for a beat. 'Did you happen to know Alex Shankley back in the day, John?'

132

Rebus gave a thin smile. 'You know what the job's like, Siobhan. Gangs, drugs, acts of violence . . . there are webs and connections and chains. Murder squads have always pooled and shared.'

'Alex Shankley was a friend?'

'We did one another a few favours, just now and then.' Rebus had risen again to stand by the uncurtained window. 'Even before I had Brillo, I'd often walk down to the Meadows of an evening. Late, after the pubs had shut. I'd stand there in the middle of it all, listening to the night. You can hear the city, you know. If you train your ears. But hearing it isn't always enough.'

'Did Alex Shankley ask for your help when Stuart Bloom went missing?'

'You know damned fine he did — he wanted his son's name kept out of it. I spoke to a few of the seasoned hacks, made my case . . . '

'Promised them favours if they complied?'

'Quid pro quo, Siobhan — just like you and Laura Smith. Not so many laptop warriors back then; it was easier to manage the way news got out, the words used and the ones left unsaid. Christ, was it only twelve years ago? Seems like a different age.'

'The handcuffs, John.'

Rebus shook his head. 'It wasn't Alex Shankley. He'd worked murders half his life. He would know handcuffs were going to scream police involvement.'

'Would the Chuggabugs have known the same?'

'Up to a point.' He returned to his chair and sat down, the bottle clutched in his hand. 'Isn't it more likely those cuffs are there to send us on a wild goose chase? The cuffs and the gully both.'

'Why tie the ankles rather than the wrists?'

'I refer you to my previous answer.' Rebus dug a pack of gum from his pocket and held it up. 'Every time I feel like smoking, I'm supposed to chew one of these little bastards instead. From experience, however, they make the beer taste weird.' Having said which, he drained the bottle before sliding a lozenge of gum into his mouth.

'How many are you on?' Clarke asked, watching him chew.

'Twenty a day — is that the definition of irony or what?'

'I'm not sure.' Clarke's smile was fleeting. 'John, if it gets out you were jeopardising police operations . . . '

'By warning two young men to stay out of a club?'

'Nothing was ever found in those raids. Doesn't that sound to you like word got around?'

'Or else the club was squeaky clean. There'd been a bad consignment, a few kids OD'ing, one of them dying. That's what the raids were for — not just at Rogues but across the city. For a while, the dealers kept their heads down, job done.' Rebus grew thoughtful, his chewing slowing. 'You think ACU have an inkling about me and Alex Shankley?'

'I've no idea.'

'Malcolm hasn't said?'

'He doesn't know I know about the meeting.'

'And how *do* you know?'

'Sources.'

'Would that be Laura again?' Rebus gave a half-smile. 'Steele and Edwards were assigned to at least a couple of the Rogues visits in the months before Bloom disappeared. Then they worked the misper case. Could be they found out I was friends with Alex Shankley, joined the dots and then tucked it away for future use.'

Clarke picked up the thread. 'They also know that you, me and Malcolm are friends, so they tell him that if he does them a favour, they won't use the information.'

'Hearsay rather than information,' Rebus felt the need to qualify.

'All the same . . . '

'Aye.' Rebus raised the empty bottle towards her. 'Well, here's to you, Siobhan. Your visit's fair cheered up an old man.'

'Sorry about that.' Rebus had picked up his phone and was tapping away at it with one finger. 'Who are you messaging?'

'Malcolm, of course. I'm letting him know: if they want to come at me, let them come.'

'He'll wonder how you know.'

'It'll be more evidence of my almost supernatural powers.' Rebus pressed send, then gave Clarke an almighty wink.

13

She was on Clerk Street when her phone sounded. The call box again. She pressed her foot to the accelerator. Canongate was only a couple of minutes away. Maybe when she didn't answer they would stick around and try again. She signalled right, saw the two call boxes in front of her and cursed under her breath — no sign of anyone. She drove on for fifty yards, examining the few pedestrians, not recognising any faces. The street was quiet, so she managed a U-turn, heading back to the call boxes. There were plenty of narrow routes leading off Canongate. Her anonymous caller could have vanished down any one of them. She noticed that her smoking friend was back outside McKenzie's, so she parked and got out. He recognised her and jutted his chin by way of greeting.

'All right?'

She sought his name, pointed at him. 'Robbie, right?'

He pointed back. 'Siobhan.'

'I had another call, Robbie, not more than five minutes ago.'

'I've only just stepped out.'

'I don't suppose you passed anyone going in?'

'Didn't notice.'

'Meaning they might have?'

He offered a shrug, and then a cigarette.

'Don't smoke,' Clarke told him. 'I'll maybe see you inside.' She yanked open the door.

The place was busy and noisy. Thumping music, Sky Sports on the various muted TVs. Mostly a young crowd, maybe students, voices raised in raucous competition with the bass line. A row of older regulars stood at the bar, inured to everything around them, a collie asleep on the floor next to a stool and a dish of drinking water. The bar itself was well-enough lit, but there were shadowy booths and alcoves, which Clarke explored as she pretended to weave her way to the toilets. The toilets themselves were down a flight of stairs, and she paused for a moment halfway, wondering if anyone might emerge. No one did, so she headed back up. Another sweep of the bar and its clients. She was about to leave when a head rose from behind the counter. The barman had obviously been into the cellar, emerging through a trapdoor. He was passing bottles of spirits to a colleague. Clarke knew she knew him from somewhere. Had she been in here before? She didn't think so. Had he maybe worked one of the city's many other bars? It was possible.

She was pushing open the door as Robbie the smoker made to come indoors again.

'Not staying?' he asked.

'Maybe next time,' she replied.

She got into her car and sat there, thinking hard. Late thirties, early forties, thick black hair and sideburns tapering to a point. Tattooed arms, hooded eyes, stubble. Romany? She had an image of him wandering through woodland, a

137

guitar strapped across him. Hang on . . . Yes, because the last time she'd seen him he'd worn a black leather waistcoat over a white T-shirt and she'd thought the same. Where, though? In a courtroom. Not the accused. Not giving evidence. A tattooed arm draped around a woman's shoulders.

And then she knew.

He was Ellis Meikle's uncle, brother of Ellis's father. Comforting Ellis's mother at the end of the trial after her son was sentenced. Sentenced to life for murder.

'Ellis Meikle,' Clarke intoned, head turned to gaze at McKenzie's. Then she started the car and headed home, on autopilot all the way.

Friday

14

Morris Gerald Cafferty lived in a penthouse duplex in the Quarter-mile development, just across the Meadows from Rebus's tenement. Rebus tied Brillo up at the entrance and pressed the bell. A camera lens was above it. Rebus got in close, knowing his face would be filling a small monitor somewhere upstairs.

'Yes?' Cafferty's voice enquired.

'Got a minute?'

'Just barely.' But Rebus was buzzed in anyway. He took the lift. Last time he'd been there, Cafferty's gangland rival Darryl Christie had been only a few minutes ahead of him, armed and looking to take Cafferty out. But Cafferty had prevailed and Christie was serving time, meaning Edinburgh belonged to Cafferty now, and this was his eyrie, protected by CCTV and concierges.

He'd left the apartment door open, so Rebus went in. The short corridor led to a large open-plan space. Cafferty was pouring coffee from a cafetière.

'I forget how you take it.'

'Just as it comes.'

'No sugar?'

'No sugar.'

'Men our age, we have to look after ourselves.' Cafferty handed over the plain white mug and gave Rebus an inspection. 'Not too bad for a man with a debilitating condition.'

'You look okay too, more's the pity.'

Cafferty looked better than okay, actually. Winning back Edinburgh had taken years off him. He'd always had heft, but he seemed to have a renewed spring in his step.

'There's a gym practically opposite,' he explained, patting his stomach. 'I go when I can. You still got that bloody mutt?'

'He's parked outside. Stand on your terrace some nights and you'll see us just by Jawbone Walk. I take it business is good?'

'Nobody drinks the way they used to. Licensed trade is always a battle.'

'And the minicabs? Car wash? Flat rentals?'

'I see you're still keeping au fait.'

'I hear that place you took over from Darryl Christie is struggling, though.'

'The Devil's Dram?' Cafferty shrugged. 'Good times and bad, John. I'm thinking of changing the focus from whisky to gin.'

'I'm guessing you'd never part with it — not after what you went through to win it.'

'Ever been to see Darryl?'

Rebus shook his head. 'How about you?'

'I did try once but he knocked me back.'

'Weren't you afraid that once you walked into the Bar-L they'd lock the doors and not let you out again?'

'Legitimate businessman, John. That's what the judge said at the trial.'

'Aye, and like you, I could hear the inverted commas.'

'Tone of voice isn't what gets written down,

though.' The two of them were standing a few feet apart. Time was, they'd already have been weighing up the trading of physical blows, but now that each was afraid of the cost of losing, words would have to suffice. Cafferty was gesturing to a corner of the room behind Rebus, where the TV was showing a morning news channel. He'd turned the sound down, so they could see Catherine Bloom but not hear her.

'She's enjoying it too much,' Cafferty commented. 'All this attention, she thinks it gives her life meaning.'

'She's fought for years.'

'Years she could have been spending on herself. The woman's hollowed out, John. Don't tell me you can't see it.' Cafferty had pulled out one of the shiny steel chairs from beneath the glass-topped dining table. He perched there, waiting until Rebus took the seat opposite. 'I'm assuming she's why you're here.'

'Why else?'

Cafferty smiled, pleased to have been proved right. 'Murder inquiry means looking at the old case. Old case was one of yours. But like I said to you at the time, I had nothing to do with any of it.'

'I'm wondering what happened to Conor Maloney.'

Cafferty held out a hand. 'Pass me your phone and I'll show you how to use Google.'

'I've looked at Google. He seems to have gone walkabout.'

'Right enough, last I heard, he was taking a lot of cruises. Tax exile sort of thing.'

'When was that?'

'Four, five years ago. Conor might have overstepped the mark.'

'How so?'

'Trying to make friends in South America. Plenty drugs and money there, but they don't play games. He wasn't to their liking.'

'So he's on the run?'

'Taxman might be after him, but I've not heard that the Colombians are — or the gardai, come to that. He's just keeping his head down, enjoying a well-earned retirement.'

'He severed his links to Adrian Brand?'

'Conor liked the idea of a golf course, maybe a whole string of them, but it was only a passing notion.'

'Would he have liked learning that a private investigator was sniffing around?'

'You asked me that at the time, John.'

'But now Bloom's body has turned up . . . '

'Not my concern.'

'The thing I remember about our interview back then is how you tried to deflect attention on to an Aberdeen crime family — the Bartollis. If we'd gone after them, that would have suited you just fine.'

Cafferty smiled at the memory. 'Can't blame a man for trying. How's the coffee?'

'A bit weak, like your answers.'

'It's decaf. Better for the blood pressure. I can add a tot of something stronger, if you like.'

'I'll survive.'

'I don't doubt that.' Cafferty ran a hand over his shaven head. It was shaped like a bowling ball, with folds of fat at the nape of the neck. Nicks and bits of scar tissue evidence of the knocks he'd taken, all the way back to childhood. In gangs from his early teens, working his way up, learning and staying lucky and toughening his hide. There were probably points in his life where he could have turned to left or right, but he hadn't taken them. He'd vanquished his rivals, done some time, and now sat in his penthouse, alone and probably still dissatisfied. Rebus couldn't help thinking of his own tenement flat, and those night-time walks, and the solitariness, part of his mind always on his shadow self, Morris Gerald Cafferty.

'Will they want to talk to me, do you think?' Cafferty was asking.

'They might.'

'Who's in charge, anyone I know?'

'A DCI called Graham Sutherland.'

'From Inverness originally?'

'I don't know.'

Cafferty was nodding to himself. 'Pretty sure that's him. He's just a name to me though — no run-ins to speak of.'

'Siobhan Clarke's on the team, too.'

'Always a pleasure to do business with Siobhan. Is she still going out with Malcolm Fox?'

'They were never an item.'

'I heard otherwise.'

'If you paid for that, you might want a refund.'

'And Fox is still at Gartcosh?'

'Have you tried Google?'

'Touché, John.' Cafferty smiled again, scratching at his jawline. 'They probably will want to

145

talk to me. I told you back then, I put money into one of Jackie Ness's films.' Cafferty watched Rebus nod. 'It was actually Billy Locke who asked me. Billy was Ness's partner in the business. He was looking for new angels — that was what he called us. You got treated to a good dinner and he gave you his spiel, and you either got out your chequebook or you didn't.'

'A chequebook?' Rebus sounded sceptical.

'You're right — I was always strictly cash. Not that I put in much, and I got it back with interest. They asked me if I wanted my name added to the credits, but I said no.'

'Why?'

'By the time it came out, Stuart Bloom had gone missing.'

'You didn't want anyone making the connection?'

'There wasn't any connection, but you're right — wouldn't have stopped people trying.'

'Which film was this?'

'Some zombie flick with kilts and claymores.'

'Siobhan Clarke just watched the DVD of that. You know Bloom actually appears in it? Him and his boyfriend both.'

'News to me. I've probably got a copy here somewhere.'

Rebus looked towards the TV. There was no DVD player. 'Nothing to play it on, though.'

'Why would I? It was a pile of shite.'

'Did Ness ever ask you for help other than financial?'

'Against Adrian Brand, you mean? Like I said back then, I had nothing to do with that.'

'Doesn't quite answer my question.'

'Maybe he asked and maybe I said no.'

'You were scared of Conor Maloney?'

Cafferty gave a snort. 'You know me better than that, John.'

'If that golf course had gone ahead, with Maloney and his paramilitary money involved, wouldn't that have been seen as the first step?'

'Towards him pushing into Edinburgh?' Cafferty brushed the notion aside.

'How did Maloney get friendly with Brand anyway?'

'Some golf course in Ireland. They both owned a share. Country club type thing, that's what Brand wanted to bring to Scotland.'

'How did it feel when he went to Maloney rather than you?'

'It's ancient history, John. An archive's the place for it.'

'How *did* you feel, though? If not threatened exactly, then maybe pissed off at the snub, at the lack of respect it showed?'

Cafferty made a show of yawning. 'I'm beginning to think it's too early in the day for decaf, and way too late in the day for this little chat.' He pushed back his chair and rose slowly to his full height. 'Besides, I've got things to do, and you've probably got a dog to walk.'

On the TV, Catherine Bloom was no longer making her speech. Instead, aerial footage of Poretoun Woods was playing, with an old photograph of Stuart Bloom in the top right corner of the screen.

'Ness wanted me to buy that place, you know,'

147

Cafferty commented. 'Sticking point was, I had to carry on with the upgrading of both house and woods. He had it all planned out, and I had to sign up to every last bit of it.'

'So you've been to Poretoun House?'

'Not since it was sold.'

'And the woods, too?'

'Just the one day — I watched a bit of the filming. The acting wasn't up to much, but give Jackie his due, he always found some very pretty faces to point his camera at.'

'I know — we interviewed a slew of them.'

'Not with enough rigour to keep Madam Bloom happy.' Cafferty's eyes were on the TV again, though the story had changed to politics. 'One thing I see the new inquiry's keeping to itself,' he mused.

'What's that?'

'Bloom was wearing handcuffs.'

'And how could you possibly know that?'

Cafferty fixed Rebus with a look. 'Some of us are still in the game, John. Police issue, were they?'

'They're still being tested. Who have you got on the inside?'

'More to the point, how come *you* know about the handcuffs? Siobhan been whispering in your ear? That counts as a leak, I'd say, especially when the person she's leaking to was part of the original case and might yet be a suspect.'

'Handcuffs could have come from anywhere. I dare say you or your pal Maloney would have known where to find some.'

'Few quid to the right cop,' Cafferty agreed.

'Plenty of them on the take in 2006. Then there are people like your old boss Bill Rawlston — good friend of Adrian Brand's back in the day, used to be on his table at the odd charity event. Not forgetting the deceased's boyfriend's dad — a pal of yours, I seem to remember.'

'Anyone else you want to add?'

Cafferty pretended to think. Rebus decided not to wait for a reply.

'Brian Steele and Grant Edwards,' he stated. 'They did a bit of work for Brand — and for you.'

'For me?'

Rebus nodded, his eyes locked on Cafferty's. 'Don't think I don't know.'

'And what is it you think you know?'

'You met with Conor Maloney one time, not long before Stuart Bloom went missing. Took Steele and Edwards along as muscle.'

'Just Steele, actually.' Cafferty thought for a moment. 'Your pal in Glasgow CID? Makes sense they'd have Maloney on their radar.'

'From the moment his plane touched down in Glasgow,' Rebus acknowledged. 'Steele was in uniform back then, which means he'd have carried handcuffs as a matter of course.'

'The day he was with me, he was in a nice sharp suit — I remember being a bit narked because he almost put my own tailoring to shame.'

'What did you tell Maloney about Stuart Bloom?'

Cafferty shook his head. 'You really think this is going to work? Siobhan won't fall for it, and neither will anyone else. It's you and yours they'll be focused on, and rightly so. You're selling dodgy merch, John — frankly, I'm a bit embarrassed for you. But it does make me wonder how desperate you are . . . and whose tracks you're trying to cover. Take a bit of advice — you're not a well man. It's time you adjusted to that reality and tried to relax and enjoy yourself rather than knocking your pan out with all this stuff.'

Rebus rose to his feet. 'Thing is, this *is* me relaxed and enjoying myself. You, on the other hand . . . '

'What?'

Rebus gestured towards Cafferty's forehead. 'Vein in your temple there started beating out a tattoo five minutes ago — and that means my work here is done.'

Cafferty stayed seated as Rebus headed for the door. Only after it had closed did he press a finger to his temple. Rebus was right, he could feel the pulse there, and he wasn't entirely sure any length of gym workout would cure it.

15

Rebus hadn't been to Poretoun Woods since the early days of the misper inquiry. It seemed to him a bit less managed, its natural wildness taking hold. The track into the woods was easily identified thanks to the many visits by police and other professionals. Deep ruts showed where a tractor had towed the VW to a waiting trailer. One marked police car indicated that some poor sod was still on guard duty — to what end, Rebus couldn't say. The crunch of twigs and leaves underfoot signalled his arrival, giving the uniform time to lever himself up from the tree he'd been resting against.

'At ease, son,' Rebus said. 'I'm just having a look, that's all.'

'Off limits to the public,' the constable stated.

'I'm attached to the inquiry.'

'Then how come I wasn't told you were coming?'

'They've got too much on their plate at Leith as it is,' Rebus improvised. 'Sorry to have to tell you, but you're not their highest priority.'

His tone seemed to reassure the constable. Rebus reckoned the lad would have been in primary school twelve years back. The acne on both cheeks had probably bothered him since soon after.

'No point me asking if you've seen anything unusual?'

'A few gawpers from the village,' the officer confided. 'Couple of reporters. All they want is a photo of where it happened, even if it didn't happen here.'

Rebus studied him. 'You've heard, then?'

The uniform nodded. 'Car might have been transported here with the deceased in it.'

Rebus was peering over the crime-scene tape down into the gully.

'There's a rope if you want a closer look.'

'Son, do I look in any shape to do that?' Rebus raised a finger. 'And by the way, don't feel you need to answer.'

'Nothing down there anyway,' the constable conceded.

Rebus was looking around him. All he saw were trees. No way of knowing if he'd walked past here during the search. He'd been CID anyway, a sightseer while the uniforms covered the ground, armed with sticks and keen eyes. He recalled that a flooded quarry a few miles away had also been visited by divers with air tanks and powerful torches. Then there'd been the disused mines just south of Bonnyrigg. Photos of the missing man had been placed in shop windows, tied to lamp posts, pushed through letter boxes, while back in the CID office Bloom's phone records were being checked, his emails scoured for clues. Dozens upon dozens of interviews, because the longer he stayed missing, the more apparent it became that his vanishing act was not voluntary, and probably no accident. So they'd hauled in both Jackie Ness and Adrian Brand for a proper grilling, then the boyfriend. Hours of questions, all of it leading them in circles. Bill Rawlston had been old school, zeroed straight in on what he called Bloom's 'lifestyle', code for his sexuality. According to Derek Shankley, theirs had been a monogamous relationship, 'apart from the odd snog, obviously'. Snogs at private parties held in friends' homes; snogs on the dance floor at Rogues.

'The partner doesn't always know, though,' was all Rawlston said about that.

Brand and Ness had arrived for their meets with CID phalanxed by lawyers; Derek Shankley had taken his dad. Or, more likely, the dad had insisted on tagging along. Of course Rebus had known Alex Shankley. Shankley was an expert on Glasgow gangs and gangsters; Rebus knew more about their Edinburgh equivalents than anyone in the city. Information had been traded down the years. A tip-off about a summit; a request for surveillance; titbits learned from phone taps. Old-school cooperation, at the end of which a bottle of whisky would be sent as thanks and gratefully received.

'I worked the original case,' Rebus told the constable, in explanation for his long silence.

'I heard there were some issues.'

'If by issues you mean fuck-ups . . . ' Rebus, hands stuffed into his coat pockets, gave a shrug. 'Let's be generous and say we just took a few wrong turns. How much longer are you going to be out here?'

'This is supposed to be the last day. Tape comes down in the morning.'

The months would pass, Rebus knew, and

people would start to forget. Or else they'd walk the woods not having known in the first place. He wondered at the efficacy of dusting off people's memories, all those individuals interviewed first time round. Details would have evaporated, moments blurred. The human mind wasn't exactly a reliable witness at the best of times. Taking a final look into the gully, he spotted a green wreath against one of the steep sides, not quite at the bottom.

'The parents,' the constable explained. 'Yesterday morning, before my shift started.'

Rebus nodded slowly and started the long walk back to his car.

He didn't drive far, coming off the track on to a muddy tarmacked B road. A couple of left turns and he was at the gates to Poretoun House. The gates were closed, no sign of a bell or anything. A padlocked chain. When Rebus pushed, there was just enough give for him to squeeze through the gap — security obviously not much of an issue.

'That's what losing a few pounds does for you, John,' he said to himself. Twenty pounds actually. First time he'd gone to the Oxford Bar after shedding it, they'd asked if he had long to live. He'd been forced to tell them it wasn't cancer. No, not cancer, but he was buggered if he was going to let COPD have him without a fight. One of the other patients at the respiratory clinic had used a phrase — 'managed decline' — and it had stuck with Rebus. To him, it seemed to sum up his whole life since retirement, and maybe even before.

154

'Cheery bastard today,' he muttered as he walked.

The driveway was overgrown, the gravel surface green with weeds and moss. The house itself soon appeared, looking forlorn. He remembered visiting it to question Jackie Ness, in a huge and overly ornate living room. Mary Skelton had been with him; it was one of those rare days when she seemed able to focus on her job rather than her sleeping arrangements. Not that they'd lingered at Poretoun House. It had been a follow-up; they were there to take receipt of printed communications between Ness and the misper. Rebus remembered the film memorabilia, the posters and props. The hallway had become a repository for lighting rigs, rails filled with costumes, camera tripods. Had anyone thought to mention that Stuart Bloom had appeared in one of Ness's films? Had Ness himself or maybe Derek Shankley said something? If so, whoever they'd told hadn't thought it worth recording. The family really had earned their eventual begrudged and belated apology.

'Utter shambles,' Rebus said to himself.

He did a circuit of the building's exterior. Lawns that had stopped being tended to. A broken window pane, boarded up. Foliage sprouting from gutters and downpipes. No sign of life. He crouched by the front door, peering through the letter box. The hall was dusty and empty. No sign of any mail on the floor. Most of the windows had been shuttered, upstairs and down. But he found one where the shutters didn't quite meet and pressed his nose to the

155

glass. The living room was devoid of furniture, cracks appearing in its stuccoed ceiling. Didn't seem to him that anyone was even bothering to heat the place. Turning away from the house, he had a clear view towards the woods. The last time anyone had seen Stuart Bloom alive, he'd been driving away in his Polo.

'He was headed home,' Jackie Ness had told the inquiry.

Yes, because Derek Shankley was preparing an evening meal for them, wine open, music playing, the end of another long week for them both. Of course, they only had Ness's word for it that Bloom had left the meeting alive. The house had been searched and forensically examined, despite Ness's complaints. Outbuildings had been checked, as had the woods beyond. Not that there was any good reason to suspect the producer.

It was just that they didn't have much else.

Rebus returned to his Saab. It spluttered as it started, reminding him that it wasn't getting any younger. He patted the steering wheel in sympathy, mouthed the phrase 'managed decline' and drove the half-mile to the village of Poretoun, which basically consisted, now as then, of a single thoroughfare (imaginatively named Main Street). There had been two pubs, but only one survived. The hardware shop, bank and post office had also gone. The café Rebus remembered dropping into for a memorable black pudding roll still had its signage, but was closed and available to let. There was a convenience store, a solitary shopper emerging from it with a carrier bag. Rebus parked and pushed open its door.

'Just want some gum,' he told the Asian woman behind the counter. He found the Airwaves and picked up a pack, then a second for luck.

'You're trying to stop smoking,' she commented. Then, seeing from his look that she was correct: 'Takes one to know one. Have you tried vaping?'

'The technology defeated me.'

'Well, gum will rot your teeth but not your lungs.' She rang up the items. There was a small pile of that day's *Evening News* on the counter, so he took one, looking at the headlines on the front. There was a colour photo of Catherine Bloom and the promise of an exclusive interview inside.

'I must look up 'exclusive' when I get home,' he said. 'Can't be many people she's not spoken to.'

'Can you blame her, though? The way the authorities have treated that family is inexcusable.'

'We're only human,' Rebus said, accepting his change and making his exit. He crossed to the pub and stepped inside. It felt welcoming, with a log-burning stove and thick tartan carpet. Spotting the coffee machine, he ordered an Americano and slid on to a bar stool. A middle-aged couple sat at a corner table, conversing quietly. Another regular was engrossed in his crossword. Rebus placed the *Evening News* on the counter.

157

'Hellish, isn't it?' the barman said, nodding towards the photo of Catherine Bloom.

'Aye,' Rebus agreed.

'Have you been to the woods, then?' Rebus met the barman's eyes. 'You're not local and a lot of people have been dropping in here either before or after. They're taking the tape down tomorrow, I hear.'

'Reckon that'll spoil the tourist trade?' Rebus enquired, stony-faced.

'A sale is a sale, even if it's only coffee. I always reckoned that film guy had something to do with it.'

'Oh aye?'

'Orgies and everything, he used to film them. That was the rumour anyway.'

'News to me.'

'The woods have always had that atmosphere about them — did you not feel it? Back in the day when he owned them, there'd be blood spattered around. People said he was sacrificing chickens or something.'

'They must have been disappointed when they learned it was food colouring from his horror films.'

The barman studied him. 'You know a lot about it.'

'I worked the original inquiry. Even popped in here a few times.'

'I only started here later. Used to work for the competition.'

'Why did it close?'

'Things change, I suppose. Landlord retired and couldn't find anyone to take it on.' He looked around him. 'I give this place six months and it'll go the same way. Trade's dying, same as the village.'

'Christ's sake, Tam,' the regular said, looking up from his newspaper. 'You're like a broken record.' Then, eyes turning to Rebus: 'I remember you, though. You used to drink a pint of heavy.'

'That's some memory you've got.'

'To be honest, it was always going to be fifty-fifty. Back then, heavy and lager were what the place sold. Now it's flavoured vodka and beer in overpriced bottles, to attract a younger crowd that would rather be anywhere but here. As for all that shite about Jackie Ness and Poretoun Woods . . . ' The man shook his head. 'My son was an extra on some of his films. An orgy would have been just fine by him, but there was never a whiff of any of that. Long, miserable days, cheese sandwiches and as little pay as Ness thought he could get away with. Girls got a bit extra if they had to do nude, but the lads didn't.' He glowered at the barman. 'You saw one or two of those films, Tam. A flash of tit was as racy as it got.' He rolled his eyes and focused on his crossword again.

'What does your son do now?' Rebus asked.

'He took over his uncle's farm. Loved it ever since he was a kid. He's selling up now, though, getting out before Brexit hits. Whole thing's a bloody joke at our expense — and some around here even voted for it.'

The barman pursed his lips and busied himself with what few empty glasses there were,

159

while Rebus took a sip of coffee. It was bitter and lukewarm, which seemed to fit in with the way the village was changing.

'Will someone take on the farm?' he asked.

'Not as a going concern. It's going to be houses. Posh ones for folk with good jobs in Edinburgh or retirees from south of the border.'

'Wouldn't be anything to do with Sir Adrian Brand, would it?'

'It would.'

'I've just been to Poretoun House.'

'It's criminal what he's done to that place.'

'On the other hand,' the barman interrupted, 'all those new houses might be good for business.'

'Only if you add ciabatta to the bar menu,' Rebus said, pushing away his cup. 'And better coffee to go with it.'

16

Graham Sutherland and Callum Reid were in the interview room with Bill Rawlston. When Clarke asked why, George Gamble told her Rawlston had been at the heart of the original inquiry. Maybe he could point them in the right direction, offer shortcuts or share his instinct regarding motives and most likely suspects.

Meantime, the budget would allow for the soil analysis and whatever forensic tests the handcuffs and car interior required. The process was already under way.

Derek Shankley had managed another half-day away from teaching and was seated next to Phil Yeats, going through names and phone numbers. Clarke gave him a little smile of encouragement and headed along the corridor to the room where Fox and Leighton sat surrounded by the contents of the box files.

'Mind if I have a word, Malcolm?' she asked.

'Sure.' He got up and followed her back into the under-lit corridor with its flaking cream-painted walls.

'Making progress?' she asked. He shrugged a response. 'Is your deal with Steele and Edwards that you share it with them first? I know you talked to them yesterday.'

'I wondered how John knew. You saw them from the window?'

'Something like that.'

161

'You're lying. If you'd been watching, you'd know it was only Steele I spoke to — Edwards stayed in the car. And to answer your question, I told him precisely nothing.'

'Best keep it that way.'

'You think they might be up to their necks?'

'Anyone who could lay their hands on a pair of handcuffs is a suspect.'

'Always supposing the two are connected.'

She stared at him. 'Can we agree that it's at least highly likely?'

'I'm just trying to keep an open mind, Siobhan. That's something the original inquiry seemed to lack. From early on, there were just the two options — it was because he was gay, or it was because of his job.' Fox nodded towards the MIT room. 'You've got one of the chief suspects in there right now. He's either helping, or else pretending to.'

'We've actually got two *witnesses* in the building, Malcolm. Which one is it you're marking as a suspect?'

'The boyfriend. Not that I think he did it.'

Clarke folded her arms. 'What did Steele want with you?'

Fox took a deep breath. 'Just as you said, to be kept apprised.'

'You know you can't help them.'

Fox nodded slowly. 'But I need to appear to be. They reckon they can stick John's head in a noose otherwise.'

'You think you can convince them you're on their side?'

'I'll do my best. They played the Complaints

162

and ACU card — joined at the hip as we fight the good fight.' He paused. 'I know you have a bit of history with them.'

'So I know what utter bastards they can be. Be careful, Malcolm.'

'I get the feeling there's something you're not telling me.'

She gave a thin smile by way of reply, patted the lapel of his suit jacket and returned to the MIT room. Derek Shankley was taking a break, standing with a mug of tea by one of the windows. She walked over to him.

'How's it going?'

He managed a half-smile. 'Okay.'

'I'm assuming you'd managed to move on with your life. Now this comes crashing down on you.'

He had removed his leather jacket — it was draped over the chair at Yeats's desk. Different T-shirt from the previous day, black this time, tight-fitting. His body was toned, his stone-washed denims low-slung.

'You're right,' he said quietly. 'Instead of sleeping, I keep replaying our time together. We were friends as much as lovers; liked the same things, the same food . . . '

'When I watched the two of you in that zombie film, I could tell — you definitely looked like you had fun together, could hardly keep the grins off your faces.'

His smile broadened at the memory. 'That might have been the hash, mind you.' He froze, fixing her with a look.

'Relax,' she reassured him. 'What's said at the

163

kettle stays at the kettle.'

'Temperature was zero that day,' he went on. 'You could see your breath in the air. One of the crew said as much, asked if zombies breathed. Said how could they when their lungs would be shrivelled up. And there we were painted blue and trying to dodge them.' He paused. 'Actually, I just mentioned it to . . . ' He nodded towards Phil Yeats, who was checking texts on his phone.

'DC Yeats,' Clarke reminded him.

'I was telling him a few of us from Rogues worked as extras, but so did the teenagers from the local village. Talk about a culture clash — they saw us as some exotic species. One or two might even have wanted us extinct.'

'It came to blows?'

'Just a bit of name-calling, usually to our backs.' Shankley paused, rubbing one hand tentatively up and down a bare arm. 'It's not why Stuart was killed.'

'Sure about that?'

'Fairly sure.'

'Well then, speaking of Rogues . . . ' Clarke lowered her voice, moving a couple of inches closer to him. 'We know your dad tipped you off if a raid was coming. Do you know who it was that told him?'

Shankley shook his head.

'Sure about that?' She watched him nod. 'Well, let's keep all that to ourselves, eh? It's *definitely* got nothing to do with what happened to Stuart.' She waited for her words to sink in, then lightened her tone. 'Pretty dreadful films, weren't they?'

164

'Made by good people, though. The sound guy, the make-up girl, all that lot. They were lovely. Stuart and me used to go for a drink with the director of photography. He knew a hell of a lot more about filming than Jackie Ness. Told us stories about people he'd worked with, big names some of them. Plenty of gossip, too. Stuart learned a lot from him.'

'In what way?'

'How to photograph certain situations. You know, like if the light's poor or from a distance.'

'Useful in Stuart's line of work.'

'Same with the sound engineer — Stuart talked to him about taping stuff.'

'Eavesdropping, you mean?'

'Phone calls and stuff, yes. Plus meetings where there's a lot of background noise.'

'Have you given DC Yeats their names?'

'He hasn't asked.'

'Maybe you could give them to me, then. Are you still in touch?'

Shankley wrinkled his face. 'Not since Stuart vanished. I mean, they phoned to say how sorry they were and all that.'

'And their names . . . ?'

'Colin and Joe. I don't remember their surnames.'

Clarke led him to her desk, hitting play on the DVD and fast-forwarding to the end credits.

'Colin Speke and Joseph Madden,' she said, reading from the screen.

'Must be,' he agreed.

'They'd have been questioned during the original inquiry?'

'I guess.' She looked at him and he shrugged. 'Nobody asked me about them specifically.'

'Well I'm asking now: could Stuart have used their expertise on the job he was doing for Jackie Ness?'

Shankley furrowed his brow as if straining to remember. 'The three of them put their heads together a few times,' he conceded. 'Do you think it's important?'

'Probably not,' Clarke said with a reassuring smile, having realised she was talking to a civilian — and a witness at that — rather than a colleague. 'We just need to make sure we've covered everything we can. You still got their phone numbers or any way of contacting them?'

'Not really.'

'You're not Facebook friends with them or anything?'

Shankley shook his head, crestfallen that he was disappointing her.

'Don't worry about it,' she said. From behind his desk, Yeats was staring at them. 'Break time's over, I think, Derek. But remember what I said about those tip-offs.'

★   ★   ★

Leith police station had no car park, so Clarke had been forced to leave her Astra next to Leith Links. She got in behind the steering wheel and took out her phone. Gayfield Square was probably a five-minute drive at most, and she'd been considering it right up until the moment she made the call. DC Christine Esson picked up straight away.

'Hello, stranger,' Esson said by way of greeting.

'Are you in the office, Christine?'

'Somehow we're coping without you.'

'Sorry I've not been in touch. It's all been slightly hectic. Everything okay?'

'Sat in court four hours yesterday only for the trial to be postponed. Thank God for Candy Crush.'

'Are you busy today?'

'What do you need?'

'The Ellis Meikle case.'

'What about it?'

'Do you remember the uncle's name?'

'The one with the tattoos?'

'Yes.'

'It was Darian or Damian or something, wasn't it?'

'Dallas,' Clarke stated. 'That's what it was.'

'Why do you want to know?'

'He had a record, right?'

'He'd been in a few scraps.'

'Would his details be on file?'

'What's going on, Siobhan?'

'I'm sure it's nothing. I just wanted a word with him.'

'It'll all have been archived. Want me to retrieve it?'

'Only if you have time.' A car had drawn up alongside Clarke's. 'I'll talk to you later, Christine,' she said, ending the call. She lowered her window; Rebus was doing the same.

'Fancy bumping into you,' he called out across the gap.

'What are you doing here, John?'

'I was just going to blag a mug of tea. How about you?'

'I work here, remember?'

But Rebus gestured with his head towards the station. 'In actual fact, you work over *there*. But for some reason you've had to squirrel yourself away in your car to make or take a phone call. All very mysterious.'

'Maybe I was about to drive somewhere.'

Rebus gave a look that told her the lie was a disappointment to him.

'Okay,' she admitted. 'It's to do with the phone calls.'

'The ones from the call box?'

'It's opposite a bar on Canongate called McKenzie's. Ellis Meikle's uncle works there.'

'Ellis Meikle being . . . ?'

'A couple of months back he was found guilty of killing his girlfriend.'

Rebus nodded. 'Teenager? Restalrig?'

'Chaotic family life, et cetera, et cetera. Drink and drugs and hormones and jealousy.'

Rebus nodded again. 'And now his family are hassling the lead detective? Want me to have a quiet word — or even a fairly noisy one?'

'I'll take care of it. Now why are you really here?'

'Have you seen Malcolm?'

'I had a word with him about his little chat with Brian Steele. For what it's worth, I get the feeling Malcolm only wants to protect you.'

168

'Meaning the Chuggabugs have something on me?'

'John, every officer who ever worked with you has *something* on you.'

'Fair point.' Rebus tried for a look of contrition but failed. 'You got any means of contacting them?'

'You'd be wiser to steer clear.'

'I've always valued your advice, Siobhan.' He paused. 'Do you, though?'

'No.'

'But Malcolm would, right?'

'Take a telling, John, just this once.' When he didn't respond, she gave a deep sigh, rubbing at her temples. 'I could really do without all this right now.'

'Because you've got other fish to fry?'

'Stuart Bloom might have had a professional arrangement with a cameraman and sound recordist who worked for Ness.'

'Meaning what?'

'They helped him when it came to stuff like taping conversations and filming meetings.'

'Really?'

'It's what Derek Shankley says.'

'And this was just before Stuart disappeared?'

'I'm not sure yet. Sounds like it's coming as a surprise to you.'

'It is.'

'Derek says no one on the original inquiry thought to ask.'

'He could have volunteered the information anyway.'

'Yes, he could. But he didn't. I think his

feelings were hurt. You had him down as one of the main suspects. Plus you were managing to intimidate any friends of his you questioned.'

'My heart bleeds.'

'Do you remember questioning them at all — Colin Speke and Joe Madden?'

'Not personally. If anyone did, it'll be in the case notes.'

'Unless Mary Skelton or Doug Newsome got sloppy . . . '

'There is that,' Rebus conceded. 'Speke and Madden, you're going to talk to them?'

'If I can find them, yes.'

'Well, in the meantime, maybe I can cheer you up.'

She looked at him. 'How?'

'By telling you something you don't know.'

'Try me.'

'Big Ger Cafferty put some money into that zombies film.'

'Old news.'

'But he also spent a day watching it being made — at Poretoun Woods. What's more, Ness tried selling those woods to him later on.'

'You've been speaking to Cafferty.' It was statement rather than question.

'He passes along his regards.'

'You'd love to tie him into this, wouldn't you?'

'Of course.'

'You don't think it'll happen, though?'

'A man can dream, can't he? At the very least you could pull him in for a few questions, steal an hour or two from his day. It's new information, Siobhan.'

'I'll add it to the list.'

'You sound tired. You should take a break — nice wee drive to Gayfield Square for a look at the Meikle file.' She saw that he was smiling a teasing smile. 'I'm good, aren't I?' he said. 'And with you gone, I can have that parking space.'

17

Fox came out into the reception area.

'What can I do for you, John?' he asked.

'Maybe we could go upstairs and discuss it.' Rebus's eyes darted to where the officer behind the desk was pretending not to be interested.

'Best if we don't — conflict of interest and all that.'

Rebus pretended to consider this. 'You're keeping busy, then? No time for any of those old episodes of *Wacky Races?*'

Fox glared at him and gave a theatrical sigh. 'On you come, then.'

He led the way up the staircase. 'The pair of you need to be very careful,' he said. 'Only way Siobhan could have known about my meeting with Steele is if one of the media hanging around outside decided to tell her. My guess is, there's only one candidate who would have been able to put names to faces.'

'Laura Smith,' Rebus stated. Then, when Fox nodded: 'I just need a way to get in touch with Steele and Edwards.'

'Why?'

'Don't worry, Malcolm, collusion hadn't crossed my mind. Just been a while since I spoke to them.'

'Aye, right.' Fox had stopped outside the MIT office. He turned to face Rebus, arms folded. Rebus made a show of peering towards the room.

172

'I'm parched, if you're offering.'

'There's a café round the corner.'

Rebus studied him. 'Found anything in those files, Malcolm, anything I should be worried about?'

'See, that's precisely why you can't be here.'

The door to the interview room opened, three bodies emerging: Sutherland and Reid ushering Bill Rawlston out ahead of them.

'All right, Bill?' Rebus asked casually. 'Did they torture a confession out of you?'

Rawlston shook Rebus's hand. 'I believe the phrase is: every courtesy was extended. Have they got you up next, John?'

'Always happy to help the police with their enquiries.'

'Maybe once we're done with Mr Rawlston,' Sutherland said. 'This is by way of a tea break. He's not feeling quite one hundred per cent.'

'Sorry to hear that.'

'Just a bit of a cold.' The look Rawlston gave Rebus indicated that he didn't want anything said about his cancer.

'We were headed the same way,' Rebus commented, opening the door and gesturing for Rawlston to enter the MIT office ahead of him. 'Might not be enough mugs, mind . . . '

Sutherland gave Fox a questioning look, to which Fox had no ready answer. Rebus was playing host, adding a tea bag to a mug, switching on the kettle, asking Rawlston how he took it. Derek Shankley watched for a moment before rising to his feet and heading towards the throng of suits.

'I know you,' he said to Rebus.

'I questioned you,' Rebus agreed. 'Just the one time, I think. Obviously I made an impression.'

'Not a great one,' Shankley commented. 'But at least you didn't call me a poof to my face; you just looked like you might.'

'Different days now, Mr Shankley. I hope you're finding that out.'

Shankley scanned the room. 'Maybe,' he eventually conceded. His eyes went back to Bill Rawlston. 'You were in charge, weren't you? I saw you on TV.'

Rawlston nodded. Shankley moved his attention to Rebus and then back to Rawlston again.

'So two cops from the original inquiry are right here in the middle of the new one?'

'It's not how it looks,' Sutherland felt compelled to say. 'Mr Rawlston has been helping us with background — '

'And him?' Shankley pointed at Rebus.

'Well, yes . . . ' Sutherland turned towards Fox. 'Why *is* Mr Rebus here?'

'Don't go blaming DI Fox,' Rebus broke in. 'Front desk let me past. It was actually DI Clarke I was looking to speak to — nothing to do with this inquiry. DI Fox was trying to escort me off the premises when Mr Rawlston stopped to say hello.'

'Yet somehow,' Sutherland said, his irritation evident, 'here you are in MIT, making cups of tea like you own the place.'

'Guilty as charged.' Rebus sought out Bill Rawlston. 'I think they want you making your own brew.'

'Malcolm,' Sutherland said, 'see that Mr Rebus leaves the building, quick as his legs will carry him.'

'Yes, sir,' Fox said, placing a hand lightly on Rebus's forearm.

'I'm not being grilled today then?' Rebus made a show of confirming. 'Well, you know where to find me when you want me.'

He walked slowly back towards the doorway, taking in what he could. He responded to George Gamble's sneer with a wink, and heard a snatch of the phone call Phil Yeats was having with what sounded like the forensic lab at Howdenhall.

'No further forward with the handcuffs?' he asked Fox in a stage whisper.

'Don't suppose you lost a pair back then?'

'You know fine well, Malcolm, plenty cops hang on to at least one set.'

'Which neatly sidesteps my question.'

They were at the top of the stairs, the door closing behind them. Rebus stopped and turned to face Fox. 'You can thank me later,' he said.

'For what?'

'Lying about the front desk.'

'You know Sutherland will give them a roasting? And when they deny letting you in, he'll want me to explain myself.'

'You've got a bit of breathing space, though — use it wisely.'

'By concocting a story?'

'Or just tell him the truth — I wanted to speak to you about ACU and why they were waiting for you outside this very police station.' Rebus

175

paused. 'Not sure that would go down too well with your boss, but if that's the way you want to play it . . . ' He began to descend the staircase.

After a moment's pause, Fox followed. 'Why not just call Gartcosh, ask to be put through to the ACU office?' he asked.

'Would my call be logged?'

'Probably.'

'There's your answer then.'

'John, you have to realise that if you hold any kind of meeting with them, or even just speak on the phone, someone somewhere is going to wonder why.'

'And they'll see a conspiracy where none exists.' Rebus shoved at the door, exiting on to the pavement, Fox following close behind. Seagulls were raucous on the chimneypots opposite.

'The misper inquiry is riddled with holes,' Fox was saying. 'I've only had a couple of days with it and even I can see that. Tess Leighton knows, too. Notes were amended, dates and times are erroneous, officers not following up where they should, then covering their arses with more lies and half-truths. Plus, the investigation was far too cosy with the media — and not very sympathetic to Bloom's family or his circle of friends.'

'Human failings, Malcolm.' The two men were facing one another on the pavement, their feet only eighteen inches apart.

'Added to which,' Fox ploughed on, 'knowing their connection to Adrian Brand, your friends Steele and Edwards should never have been within fifty miles of that inquiry.'

'Ah, but we didn't know, not at the start.' Rebus slid a lozenge of gum from its packet and popped it into his mouth.

'It was up to them to come forward.'

'They did that, didn't they?'

'Not nearly soon enough. Jesus, John, this isn't rocket science.' Fox shook his head at Rebus's offer of gum. 'If I can see it, so can others. They won't all be on your side.'

'Do what you have to do, Malcolm. We're all grown-ups, we can deal with the consequences.'

'You're retired, though, John. You've not got as much to lose as some.'

Rebus nodded. 'Which is why the Chuggabugs are desperate to know where you're going with it. They've spent year after dirty year climbing to the giddy heights of ACU.' He puffed out his cheeks and exhaled menthol. 'I'd help if I could, you know that. If I had anything from back then, anything I could prove . . . '

'Is that the whole truth, John?'

Rebus gave a thin smile. 'Just keep digging, Malcolm. Maybe what you need is somewhere in those boxes, buried deep.' He paused. 'Now, I did say you owed me a favour.'

'Did you?'

'For covering your arse with Sutherland. Just Steele's number will do. I get the feeling Edwards has yet to progress to joined-up sentences, never mind joined-up thinking.'

Fox sighed, dug out his phone and got busy on the screen. Rebus's own phone let him know the information had been received. 'Buy you that

177

mug of tea?' he asked, gesturing towards the café on the opposite corner.

'I'd better get back in.' Fox seemed to hesitate. 'Is there any point in my warning you to tread carefully?'

'I always do, Malcolm. Plenty dog shit on the pavements around here.' Rebus gave a wave of the hand as he started walking towards his Saab.

18

Cafferty had several mobile phones on the go at any one time. He ditched numbers regularly, added and deleted accounts and providers. Same went for his email. The broadband in his duplex was extra-secure and checked fortnightly for attempted breaches. Even so, he preferred the old ways — face-to-face meetings in public places with plenty of background noise. The new technologies were fine — in many ways they had aided his various businesses — but you didn't learn about people from them, not the way you did when your eyes drilled into theirs, your senses alive to their gestures and tics. A bead of sweat; a quickening of the breathing; a nervous sniffle; the crossing and uncrossing of legs. He had never played poker but he knew he'd be good at it. His chief fear was there would always be someone better. He would end up annoyed, and needing some sort of payback.

When one of his phones rang, he checked to see which, and knew straight away who the caller was. He had only met Conor Maloney once, a summit of sorts held at a hotel near Glasgow airport. Maloney had booked the meeting room for a whole day. The receptionist had checked on her list to confirm that Cafferty — aka Mr Coleman — was there at the correct hour. Other appointments were listed, though Cafferty had no way of knowing whether they were merely a smokescreen. All he knew was, Maloney was booked on a flight back to Dublin that same afternoon.

Cafferty lifted the phone. 'You're a hard man to speak to,' he said by way of greeting.

'I'm a hard man full stop. What can I do for you, Morris?'

No one but his mother and a few school teachers had ever called Cafferty that; he suspected Maloney knew it, and used it to try to get a reaction from him.

'Where are you?' he asked.

'Now why would you want to know that?' The accent would always retain its soft Irish lilt, but there was gravel in there too. 'Let's just say I'm some place that requires a cold beer, and that beer's getting warm as we speak.'

'Stuart Bloom has turned up.'

'Fighting fit, I trust.'

'Dead in his car and wearing a set of handcuffs.'

'Handcuffs? So the boys in blue did away with him after all.' Cafferty stayed silent. 'Ah, come on now, Morris. Are we still playing that game? I told you twenty dozen times I had nothing to do with it.'

'Same as I told you it wasn't me. Doesn't mean one of us wasn't lying.'

'It's history, Morris. Leave it to the coppers.'

'They're dusting off the original missing person case.'

'And the best of Irish luck to them.'

'We both get a mention.'

'So bloody what?' Maloney held the phone

away from his face while he spoke to someone in what sounded like French. He was back a few seconds later. 'You and me did well to stay out of that little skirmish — end of.'

'Do you ever hear from your old friend Sir Adrian?'

'Not in a long time.'

'The story's all over the media; you know what that means.'

'It means we keep our heads down. Easier for me than you — I hear you came out of retirement.'

'I suppose that's true.'

'Hotels is where you want to be, not bars. Plenty money sloshing around.'

'Thanks for the advice.'

'Morris, I'm telling you, there's nothing to worry your pretty little head over. Everyone had an alibi that night, didn't they?'

'An alibi used to be an easy thing to arrange.'

'You're right about that. Bloody phones and CCTV these days, a man never knows who's watching him. Here, do you still use a computer?'

'On occasion.'

'And that advice I gave you?'

Cafferty glanced at the notebook sitting open on his desk. 'Sticky tape over the camera, don't worry.'

'Can't be too careful. And remember: the only way to ensure your phone can't be hacked is not to have a phone in the first place. Speaking of which, they've almost had enough time to trace this.'

'Who's they?'

'I'd be here all day if I started. Take good care of yourself, Morris. We're none of us getting any younger.'

The phone went dead. Number withheld, naturally. It had taken Cafferty five calls to get the message out that he wanted to speak. He wondered if Maloney had changed much from the stocky, bull-necked man he'd met. The demeanour had been cheery enough — the professional Irishman bit — but the eyes had remained serious as a stroke. Despite searching online, Cafferty hadn't found any photos of the man taken less than five years ago. When they'd met at the hotel, there'd just been the two of them, Maloney's two 'associates' waiting outside with Cafferty's own man. Then again, Cafferty's man had been an off-duty cop, so that evened things up a bit. There had been coffee and water and some biscuits and pastries, and a quiet chat about the feud between Brand and Ness, and how choosing sides might lead to 'awkwardness'. Wasn't it better to call a truce of sorts and focus on cooperation — Maloney and Cafferty seeking joint ventures rather than rivalry?

'Anything in particular?' Maloney had asked.

'There's a certain organisation in Aberdeen that's ripe to be put out to pasture . . . '

And Maloney had smiled, indicating that he'd known all along this was where their talk would lead.

Not that much had come of it; Aberdeen had dug in too deep, and Maloney hadn't liked it that there'd been bad drugs sold on Cafferty's patch, meaning increased police surveillance. Cafferty had protested that the drugs hadn't come from any of his guys, but it had been a hard story to sell to the Irishman. Either Cafferty bore the responsibility, or else he had competition in what was supposed to be a trade he controlled.

But there had been some dealings and exchanges with Maloney down the years, the two men remaining wary, never quite able to trust one another. One thing Cafferty felt confident about was that if Maloney had sensed the private eye as a threat, he wouldn't have blinked. And Bloom *had* begun to pose a threat, no doubt about that. His own reading at the time was that Bloom had been put under lock and key, maybe a safe house in Ireland — plenty of those left over from the Troubles. He'd be let go once the hint had been taken by Jackie Ness.

But no release had come.

And without a further face-to-face with Maloney, there was no way to know.

19

'I managed to condense it to thirty sheets of A4,' DC Christine Esson said as Clarke walked into the CID office in Gayfield Square. 'If you want more, I'll have to rustle everything up from storage. Mind telling me why it's suddenly bugging you?'

The office was small, just the four desks, one of them permanently vacant. Through the door was the even smaller inner sanctum belonging to DCI James Page. Clarke turned from that door to Esson.

'He's in a meeting at the Big House.'

'Which one?'

'Fettes.'

'I thought we'd stopped calling it that.' Clarke picked up the large manila envelope and eased the printed sheets from it. 'Where's Ronnie?'

'Called in sick.'

'You're home alone?'

'And somehow still managing to survive.'

Clarke sat down at her own desk, ignoring the pile of messages waiting there for her, the files rising to half the height of her computer.

'The last three days?' she complained.

'That's what happens if you're not here to flush it away.'

'A lovely image, thanks, Christine.'

'Any more flak from ACU?'

'Not exactly.'

'Meaning?'

Clarke looked up at her colleague. 'I'm just going to read this lot, if that's okay. Maybe chat later?'

Esson made a face and got back to work.

Ellis Meikle, aged seventeen, had been found guilty of the murder of his girlfriend. Her name was Kristen Halliday. They'd been an item since high school. Ellis had left at sixteen, no job, no prospects. Kristen had stayed on. Their social groups had begun to diverge. There were shouting matches, fuelled by cheap drink and whatever drugs were available.

Kristen had gone missing on a Wednesday afternoon. That night, her parents had turned up at the house Ellis shared with his mother and uncle. Kristen wasn't answering her phone. Had Ellis seen her? He had shaken his head, seemingly irritated at being dragged from his computer game. His mother and uncle had been drinking. The uncle wanted to round up a search party. Kristen's father said it wasn't his call to make. Tempers had flared. Kristen's mother wanted to phone the police. But Kristen had only been absent a few hours — nobody thought the police would be interested. They'd started ringing round her friends instead. One said that Kristen had been headed to the golf course to meet Ellis. Ellis was asked again: had he seen Kristen? Kristen's mother had made a lurch towards him, physically restrained by Ellis's mother, who had then been grabbed by Kristen's father, which brought the uncle back into the melee. The neighbours, alerted by all the noise, had started to arrive.

Things calmed down and a further bottle of vodka was opened. More phone calls, friends' doors knocked on. Just after dawn, a dog-walker had found the body on the golf course. Kristen lay in a bunker, lazily hidden beneath scooped sand, a single knife wound to her neck the cause of death. The police search team turned up the weapon sixteen hours later, in a patch of rough on a route leading from the bunker to the main road. It was an ordinary kitchen knife, four-inch blade, not particularly sharp. The wound was deep; it would have taken force, taken a certain rage.

The fingerprints on the handle were a match for Ellis Meikle. The last text received on Kristen's phone had been from Ellis, wanting her to meet him at the golf course.

The initial interviews were handled with sensitivity — Clarke knew because she'd been in attendance at three of them. It was her case. Her and Esson and Ronnie Ogilvie. The forensics were irrefutable: Kristen's blood on the knife and Meikle's prints. One thing they couldn't prove was where the knife had come from. Uncle Dallas was adamant none were missing from the kitchen in Restalrig. And how could he be so sure? Because he lived in the house, the house his brother Charles had moved out of, the house Ellis and his mother Seona shared. Charles Meikle meantime had got himself a flat in Causewayside, his daughter Billie going with him. Had the break-up been amicable? It had, mostly. No one was talking about a divorce.

They'd asked the kids who wanted to stay with who, and the kids had made up their own minds. Uncle Dallas had then begun calling round, and had eventually started staying over. He slept on the sofa apparently, Billie reluctant to let him have her room, even though it was vacant.

No funny business between Seona and her brother-in-law? The one time DC Ronnie Ogilvie had raised the notion with Uncle Dallas, they'd almost had to set phasers to stun. Dallas Meikle was ex-army; diagnosed with PTSD after a spell in Afghanistan. Electricity crackled just below his surface.

'You tried to organise a search?' Clarke had asked him.

'Ellis's lass was missing, of course I did.'

'It didn't strike you as odd that Ellis himself seemed quite relaxed?'

'We deal with stress in different ways — one thing I learned after the army.' He had run a hand down the tattoos on his neck. Clarke wondered if it was a tell of some kind, but she couldn't be sure.

The procurator fiscal's office saw nothing complex in the case. The source of the knife wasn't germane. The lack of blood on Ellis Meikle's clothing and shoes just meant he'd disposed of the ones he'd been wearing.

'He made a better job of it than he did with the knife,' Clarke had commented in one meeting, her words met with silence.

Trial. Guilty verdict. Murder rather than culpable homicide, though the defence counsel had pushed hard for the latter, love being a kind of madness, a rash act in the heat of a heightened moment.

No youth incarceration for Ellis Meikle — straight to HM Prison Edinburgh, meaning Saughton, not far from the Hearts ground where his dad had taken him to fortnightly football games, a tradition carried on since the separation.

Seona Meikle in tears as the trial ended. Dallas in a black leather waistcoat wrapping a protective arm around her, while her husband comforted their dumbstruck daughter. Clarke had bought the drinks for her team that evening. DCI Page had added fifty quid to the pot, meaning for them to have a meal, but in the end they'd made do with nachos — and a few more rounds of drinks.

What else were they supposed to do, sit in silence, their thoughts on the Halliday family and the Meikles? Plenty more work would be waiting for them the next morning. Ellis Meikle and the other players in the drama could be filed away and forgotten.

Now, seated at her desk in Gayfield Square, Clarke wondered about that. You couldn't let cases get to you. Yes, you had to treat everyone as a fellow human being, but you had to draw the line, not dwell on the suffering, the repercussions. You wouldn't be able to do the job otherwise. She'd seen colleagues weep on occasion — of course she had — and she'd seen them frustrated when a result failed to materialise. But you had to move on. You had to.

But that wasn't always what the families did.

There were copies of photos among the pages, and Clarke studied them. Ellis and Kristen together, shot with a phone at a party. Kristen sitting down to Christmas dinner with her family. Clarke remembered her parents, but had forgotten their names. Quietly distraught, shunning Dallas Meikle when he approached them outside the courtroom. More photos: the bunker, body *in situ;* the discarded knife; Ellis's cramped bedroom, its walls covered in posters advertising computer games; various items of his clothing.

No blood.

He had stayed silent throughout the majority of the interviews, answering 'yes' when asked if he'd done it. He wouldn't say why, wouldn't answer any of their other questions. Christine Esson got him talking about Scottish football, but hit a wall when she tried changing the subject.

When Clarke looked up from the file, Esson herself was standing there, arms folded, a defiant look on her face.

'Tell me,' she demanded.

'Ellis's uncle has been hassling me.'

'Hassling you how?'

'Phone calls for one thing.'

'What does he say?'

'Nothing — the phone goes dead every time I answer.'

'You sure it's him?'

'As near as can be. He works behind the bar at McKenzie's. It's across the street from the phone boxes where the calls originate.' Clarke offered a shrug. 'There was a car outside my flat, too. And stuff scrawled on the tenement door.'

'Make of car? Registration?'

'I'm a hopeless detective.'

'And you've not spoken to him?'

'I will. I just wanted to refresh my memory first.' She picked up the paperwork and let it fall again on to the desk.

'Families are never thrilled when you lock up their loved ones. Nephew and uncle were pretty close, as I recall.'

'The trial ended two months ago, though. Why's it taken him so long?'

'He's been festering?' Esson offered. 'Why did you give him your phone number?'

'I'm pretty sure I didn't.'

'You gave it to Seona, then?'

Clarke was shaking her head. 'I don't think so. More than likely I handed a card to Kristen's parents, but I can't see them passing it on to Ellis's uncle.'

'Probably not,' Esson agreed. 'Want me to come with you?'

'To see Dallas Meikle?' Clarke shook her head again. 'I think I can handle it.'

'Doesn't he have certain anger management issues?'

'I can handle it,' Clarke repeated with a little more force. 'Thanks for this, though.' She pressed a hand against the paperwork.

'At least it's a break from the body in the woods, eh?'

'Definitely,' Clarke agreed, hoping she sounded more confident than she felt.

'You don't need to go see him, you know. You could just report it.'

'I could.'

'But you'd rather do it all by yourself? That's a bad habit you've picked up, Siobhan — almost as if your old sparring partner is still at your shoulder.'

'John's been retired a long time, Christine.'

'So how come I still feel his presence?' Esson's eyes were drilling into Clarke's. 'How long since you last saw him?' she enquired.

Clarke thought for a moment, then checked her wristwatch.

'Thought so,' Esson said, returning to her desk with a weary shake of her head.

20

Harthill service station, just off the M8, almost equidistant between Edinburgh and Glasgow. Only time Rebus had used it was when visiting the nearby Shotts prison. He stayed on the access road, ignoring the petrol pumps and parking bays, and pulled in behind the black Audi. As he got out, he could hear the motorway traffic. There was an artic parked up not far away, its driver checking the tyres. Rebus stood beside the Audi. Steele was in the driver's seat, Edwards in the rear. They obviously wanted Rebus in the passenger seat but he slid in next to Edwards instead. That way he could keep an eye on both ACU officers.

'Relax, John,' Steele told him, 'this isn't *Goodfellas*.' His window had been lowered a couple of inches so he could flick ash from his cigarette out of it.

'It's been a while, Brian.'

'Thought we'd leave you in peace, now you're retired.' Steele met Rebus's eyes in the rear-view mirror. 'At least, I *thought* you'd retired. But you seem to hang around like the same bad smell.'

'Speaking of which, any chance of lowering that window a bit more?'

'You given up the coffin nails, John? Grant told me you had but I found it hard to believe.'

Out of the corner of his eye, Rebus saw that Edwards was smiling, not that that meant anything. Meantime, to make a point, Steele closed the window and kept smoking.

'I've got to ask,' Rebus said. 'When they culled CCU and re-branded it, how did you two manage to survive?'

'Aye, it was an ugly time,' Steele responded. 'All the complaints against CCU were made anonymously. *Anonymously*, John. Cowardly bastards wouldn't even put their heads above the parapet. Cops grassing up cops is ugly. We're supposed to be kin.'

'You didn't maybe join in, just to save your skins?'

Steele gave the slightest of snorts. 'Think what you want to think, John. All that matters is we're still standing.'

'You're quoting Elton John at me?'

'Thought it was apt — I hear Deborah Quant calls your prick 'Tiny Dancer'.'

There was a wheeze of laughter from Edwards. Rebus turned his head to face him. 'The only wee dancer around here is that brain cell of yours, birling around with no one to partner it.'

In the silence that followed, Rebus stuck a piece of gum in his mouth and started chewing, while Edwards just glowered.

'Bit of a surprise,' Steele eventually said, 'Stuart Bloom turning up like that.'

'Makes me wonder why he did,' Rebus replied. 'I mean, why now? The boffins don't think he was in that gully all those years, meaning at some point he was moved there.'

'Aye, that got us thinking, too.'

'I'm sure Grant here put the full force of his

193

intellect into it.' Rebus glanced towards Edwards again.

'So what have you told them at MIT, John?' Steele asked, flicking ash into an empty cigarette packet. 'I assume that's why you wanted to meet.'

'I've told them precisely nothing they didn't already know. For example, I've not mentioned your little jaunt playing bodyguard to Big Ger Cafferty.'

'I wasn't sure you knew about that. It was in my own time, if that matters at all.'

'Well remunerated, I'm sure. And he wanted you for your unique talents, I dare say, rather than so he could pump you for any gossip on Adrian Brand.'

'Mr Brand's name never came up.'

'But that's how he knew about you in the first place, the Brand connection?'

'None of this has anything to do with the Bloom case. I might as easily ask you about Cafferty; the two of you were pretty snug for a while. In fact, I hear you still see him, despite him never being far from Serious Crime's attention.' Steele turned his head to look at Rebus. 'You wouldn't have loaned him a pair of handcuffs, would you?'

'I was CID at the time, Brian; handcuffs were mostly used by uniforms, which is what both of you were.' Rebus watched as Steele reached into the glove box, pulling out a pair of old-fashioned metal cuffs.

'Still come in useful,' Steele said, trying to pass them to Rebus. Rebus kept his hands by his sides, and Steele laughed. 'You're scared I want your prints on them — we've gone from Mafia flick to conspiracy thriller. In fact, you might well have a point there — doesn't it strike you as a bit OTT? Not just the cuffs, but putting them round the ankles? It's like we're all supposed to take route one to the goal mouth — cops did it, and cops will take the fall. Me and Grant here, you and your boss Bill Rawlston. Not to mention Skelton, Newsome and the rest.

'But here's the thing, John.' He stubbed out his cigarette and twisted further in his seat so he was facing Rebus as directly as possible without doing himself an injury. 'Me and Grant, we always had that reputation, didn't we? Sailing a bit close to the wind. Skelton and Newsome were inept but not really players. Rawlston was lazy, just wanted a result he knew he wasn't going to get. As the weeks passed, it was all the same old ground being covered again. But you, John, well, you had a bit of a reputation, too. You'd worked some dirty cases, in Edinburgh and Glasgow both. That's how you got friendly with DI Alex Shankley, the father who didn't exactly agree with his son's sexuality, and wasn't keen on that son's partner being a private eye. All kinds of tensions there that were never explored because you kept putting up the barricades, all for the sake of your pal in Glasgow.' Steele paused. 'The same pal who probably kept you in the loop when Cafferty had that meeting with Conor Maloney. Think any of that'll stay unmentioned this time round? Think those tip-offs about raids on Rogues won't piss off your old comrades when they learn they came from you? Me and Grant here were on one or two of those raids, you know. You were setting us up to fall on our arses.'

'Is this ACU I'm talking to, or just two bent cops?'

'All I'm saying is, none of us has anything to gain by any of this getting out. I fully expect that Grant and me will end up at MIT, telling our side of the story. There are things we *could* tell, if we felt it was going badly for us. There'd maybe be a few good names and pensions lost along the way, even a prosecution or two. All those reports Newsome typed up of interviews that didn't actually happen . . . We might even find out who it was Mary Skelton was shagging. She died, by the way, three years back. You and her were pretty close, weren't you?'

'Not nearly close enough for an affair.'

'Maybe just a one-nighter, eh?' Steele returned to his original position, eyes on the rear-view. 'Then there's our old boss Rawlston — I hear he's not keeping well. Last thing he needs is to have all this dragged up again.'

'He's already been interviewed.'

'Doesn't mean they won't want to talk to him again. All those mistakes he presided over, all those cops under him who weren't doing their jobs.' Steele paused once more. 'I've always been the observant type. Grant, too. People underestimate him because he doesn't say much, but he sees and hears plenty.'

Rebus watched Edwards nod his agreement.

'We've worked our way up, John,' Steele went

196

on. 'Took a long time to get to ACU. Not too many more years and we'll be getting those pensions and heading off elsewhere. That's something we'll do our utmost to protect. Seems to me everyone who worked the case has something they want to keep safe or hidden. So tell me something, John — and I promise it won't go further than this car.'

'What?'

'Did you help Alex Shankley kill his son's boyfriend, or was it all his own work?'

'You'll have to do better than that, Steele.' Rebus pushed open the rear door and stepped out, leaning back into the car again. 'The most likely candidates haven't changed. I suspected it then and I'm thinking it now. In fact, I'm looking right at them.'

He slammed the door closed and stalked back to his Saab. He had almost reached it when he heard footsteps behind him. Edwards spun him round, slamming him into the Saab's bodywork, holding him there by his lapels while Steele took his own sweet time arriving. Rebus tried wrestling his way free, but the smiling grizzly was always going to win that bout. When he tried bringing his knee up into Edwards's groin, Edwards was prepared, twisting so Rebus connected with his upper thigh, then pressing his bulk harder against Rebus, until breathing became difficult. The driver of the articulated lorry leaned out of his window and called across to them; Steele brandished his warrant card and waved away the complaint. Something was hanging from his other hand. The handcuffs, Rebus realised. One of them snapped around his left wrist.

'No . . . ' he started to say, but too late. The other had been attached to the Saab's door handle.

'It's easy to hang on to old sets of cuffs,' Steele said. 'Problem is, the key's so fucking small you end up losing it.' His mouth was close to Rebus's left ear. 'You and your lot never had any time for us, back when we were in uniform. I heard the things you said, saw the gestures you made when you thought our backs were turned. I've never forgotten that. *Never* . . . '

Flecks of spittle hit Rebus's ear. Steele's leather heels ground against the asphalt as he turned and began to walk back to the Audi, Edwards following with a smirk. Rebus aimed a kick at his retreating leg but missed, swiping at air. He watched as the Audi headed off slowly in the direction of the carriageway. Waited a few minutes, in case it returned. Studied the ground, but Steele hadn't left the key there. The lorry driver was leaving too, without so much as a look in Rebus's direction. The metal was cutting into Rebus's wrist. He tried squeezing but was never going to spring himself that way. Instead, he lifted his phone from his pocket and eventually found the number he needed. Pressed the phone to his ear and listened as it was answered.

'Alex,' he said, 'I need a bit of a favour . . . '

*   *   *

After Alex Shankley had freed him, the two men headed into the cafeteria, bought a pot of tea

198

and a couple of caramel wafers and found a table by the window.

'Lucky the key fitted,' Shankley said.

'Don't you remember? Same key fitted most models.' Rebus rubbed at his reddened wrist. He had pocketed the cuffs.

'Why did they do it?'

'Steele and Edwards?' Rebus shook his head. 'You don't want to know.'

'Maybe I do, though. Is it tied to Stuart Bloom?'

'Sort of. Have you heard anything about the body?'

'Such as?'

'The ankles?' Rebus watched Shankley nod.

'It was mentioned at the interview. I notice it's not public knowledge.'

'Despite which, seems every bugger knows.' Rebus paused. 'Steele reckons you and me did it.'

'You and me?'

'He's got it into his head that we might have killed Bloom.'

'Steele's the one I warned you about? The one at the meeting between Cafferty and Maloney?'

'That's him.'

'He sounds like a shitbag.'

'No argument here.' Rebus slurped at his tea. 'You didn't, though, did you?'

'I didn't like the lad, John, but that's as far as it went. Christ, it was bad enough when Derek came out as gay. Looking back, I can see the guts that took, but you know yourself, cops weren't quite as touchy-feely back then. I knew I'd take

199

some stick, and that was the problem right there — it was me I was thinking of rather than Derek. Even so, it's one thing when your son tells you he's gay, but when you see them holding hands, a peck on the cheek . . . ' Shankley took a deep breath and released it. 'I wasn't comfortable, John, not at all comfortable. Then when Stuart turned out to be a private investigator . . . '

'You got more stick.'

'Boss had a few sharp words — if he got wind that I'd ever leaked anything to Stuart . . . ' Shankley made show of running a finger across his throat.

'You never did, though,' Rebus stated.

'I never did,' Shankley confirmed.

'Apart from the occasional warnings about Rogues, obviously.'

'Those were to Derek rather than Stuart.'

Rebus tilted his head in a show of agreement. 'Derek's going to be back under the microscope again — our lot and the media. Think he'll handle it okay?'

Shankley gave a confident nod. 'He's stronger these days — and he wants whoever did it caught. That's how I know he's got nothing to hide. For years he's mulled over what could have happened.'

'You're certain he doesn't know?'

'Same names keep coming up.'

'Brand and Ness?'

'I almost got tired of hearing them.' Shankley looked at Rebus. 'He didn't have anything good to say about the investigation either.'

'Our bedside manner could have been better,'

Rebus agreed. 'Having said which, you know yourself that we had to treat him as a suspect as well as a witness.'

'And now?'

'I don't sense any pointing of fingers.'

'Will you get into trouble, John?'

'Why should I?'

'Telling me about those raids; buying drinks for reporters so they'd lay off Derek . . . '

'All part of the service, Alex.'

'Will it come to light, though?'

'I doubt Police Scotland will want to make anything of it. They've got plenty wildfires they're busy fighting.'

'Seems the wrong word or look gets you accused of bullying. Wouldn't have happened in our day, John.'

'Might have been better if it had,' Rebus said ruefully, draining his cup.

21

The team briefing took place in the MIT room, Bill Rawlston and Derek Shankley both on their way home. Reid, Gamble, Leighton, Yeats and Crowther were seated. Clarke, having just made her report, was standing in front of Graham Sutherland's desk. Fox had slipped into the room and positioned himself just inside the door.

Sutherland was digesting what Clarke had just told them.

'Do we know the whereabouts of Madden and Speke?' he asked.

'If they're still working, it shouldn't be difficult,' Clarke said. 'Place to start would be Jackie Ness.'

'Except then we'd be tipping him off,' Callum Reid cautioned. Clarke noticed that he had been busy with his wall and whiteboard: thumbnail crime-scene photos added to the map; more details of players in the drama; even a small copy of the promotional poster for *Zombies v Bravehearts*. Now that the civilians had left, photos of the handcuffs had been brought out of hiding. Phil Yeats had circulated the list of names he'd compiled with Derek Shankley's help. It was lengthy and incomplete, and would tie up Yeats and maybe even Gamble for the next day or two. Fox and Leighton meantime had made progress with the case files without having much to add by way of new information or supposition. Madden and Speke, however, *were* new information, which was why Clarke sensed their boss was excited by it. The long working day was drawing to a close with too little otherwise to show for it.

'I want you to run with this, Siobhan' he announced. 'Emily can help. Find them and talk to them.' He turned towards Tess Leighton. 'They don't feature at all in the original inquiry?'

Leighton checked with Fox before shaking her head.

'One more screw-up to add to the growing list.' Sutherland rubbed his eyes.

'Any further news on the car or the handcuffs?' Fox asked from the back of the room.

'Hopefully tomorrow.' Sutherland checked the time on his phone. 'Let's give it another half-hour before calling it a day. If anyone wants to stay later, that's fine, too. But tired minds aren't much use to me, so make sure you take breaks as necessary. I'll be heading to the same pub as before. There'll be a drink behind the bar for each of you.' He picked up his phone and placed a call. 'But before all that, I'd better update DCS Mollison. He's planned a press conference in the morning, and an email update to go to media outlets tonight.' Pressing the phone to his ear, he turned away from the room, which was their cue to get back to work. Tess Leighton wandered over to the door and opened it, Fox following.

'She's taking the babysitting role seriously,' Crowther whispered to Clarke.

'More to it than that, you think?'

'I'd say he's her type.'

'And what type does Tess go for usually?'

'Sentient,' Crowther answered with a smile.

★ ★ ★

Clarke stayed for just the one drink with the team. Whenever cops got together, it was the usual slew of stories and anecdotes about stupid criminals, ineffective fiscals, cases won and lost. Then there were their fellow officers, the daft ones, the savvy ones, the ones who'd got locked out of their cars or inside a cell. Clarke kept the smile pinned to her face. She didn't mind really; such stories signalled their shared past and cemented their current status as a group, a gang. Fox told his fair share, and they accepted that he'd earned his place. Clarke wondered if Leighton had maybe dropped a hint to the others: he's okay, we can trust him. She definitely seemed to have relaxed around Fox, even leaning in towards his ear now and again to tell him something. They remonstrated when Clarke said she had to go. George Gamble was readying to get another round in.

'You'll be witnessing history, Siobhan,' Emily Crowther teased. 'George's wallet probably needs WD-40, it opens so seldom.'

'Just for that, I'm only getting you a half,' Gamble retorted.

But Clarke was already on her feet, sliding her arms into her coat. 'Please,' she said, 'nobody get breathalysed. If you need a designated driver,

Malcolm's your man . . . '

Fox was starting to remonstrate as Clarke left the pub. She walked back to her car and drove up Leith Walk, stopping and heading into an Italian restaurant just around the corner from Gayfield Square. Some stage musical was playing later at the Playhouse across the street and the place was busy, but the staff knew her and found the quietest table they could. She checked her phone while she ate: texts and emails, social media and news. She was trying to remember when she'd last read a book; time was, she'd have carried one with her. These days she was as likely to read them on a screen.

She paid up and got back in her car, continuing up the slope. The diversion was still in place as work continued on flattening the St James Centre and the offices around it. She remembered when it had been a shopping destination. Clothes and gifts and CDs. But she didn't recall a bookshop. As she crossed North Bridge, she looked to her right, admiring the view towards Castle Rock, illuminated against the night sky. Turning left at the lights, she was on Canongate and considering her options. It wasn't too cold out there, and parked cars were thin on the ground, meaning she might stand out if she stayed in the car. So she turned into a side street and found a space.

She had her phone in her hand as she walked past the two empty phone boxes. Twenty paces on, she paused to study a shop window. Then she crossed the road and passed McKenzie's, keeping on until she had reached the junction. Across the road and back down towards the phone boxes. It suddenly struck her: he might not even be working tonight. She could go in and see, but that might entail being recognised and scaring him off. So she ambled to the same shop window, then across the road and past the pub once more. Not too cold out? Had she really thought that? The chill was finding chinks in her armour at neck and wrist and ankle. Her breath clouded the air in front of her as she walked. A few more minutes and she would resort to plan B: her parked car.

She was crossing at the lights again when she saw a figure emerge from McKenzie's, making for the call boxes. She had her own phone in her hand as she picked up the pace. She was making as if to pass the figure in the first box when her phone vibrated. She placed it against the glass, causing him to turn his head towards her. It was Dallas Meikle, tattoos and all. He looked startled for a moment before regaining his equilibrium, replacing the receiver in its cradle and pushing open the door.

'Something you wanted to talk to me about, Mr Meikle?'

'How do you mean?'

'Stalking is a criminal offence, if you didn't know. Stalking a *police officer* can get you in even more trouble.'

'I was just calling a mate.' His eyes were everywhere but on hers.

'I just filmed you making that call,' she improvised. 'It went straight to *my* phone. I've got logs of all the other times, too. Well over a dozen of them, all made while you were working your shift. Then there are your visits to my flat, the graffiti on my door — your car was caught on CCTV.' She watched him accept the lie. 'No way you're not going to court,' she stressed.

Suddenly his eyes met hers. There was a fire in them. 'So how come you're not arresting me?'

'Maybe because I know who you are, which means I think you're hurting.'

'Hurt? You don't know the first thing about it.'

'This is because of Ellis, yes?'

'It's because you put a young kid in Saughton! Christ knows how he'll survive!'

'I wasn't the only detective who worked that case.'

'You're the one I remember, though. It was always your name in the papers.'

'Doesn't explain how you got your hands on my number.'

A humourless grin spread across Dallas Meikle's face. 'Maybe you're not as well-liked as you think, even among your own kind.'

Suddenly Clarke knew. 'A couple of ACU officers called Steele and Edwards?'

Who had just failed to get the result they wanted, and needed to feel they'd come away with something, no matter how petty.

'Phone number and address — I see you wiped the door clean.' The grin was still in place. 'Might need another visit.'

'Just try it.' The grin slipped slowly from Meikle's face. 'What did you hope to gain?' Clarke asked into the silence.

He considered for a moment before answering. 'I watched you lot in court. I saw what goes on behind the scenes. Little chats with the lawyers, because it's just a job to you. Going through the motions with a tidy salary at the end of each month and fuck the consequences. Ellis is a good kid; you treated him like he was something you'd stepped in.'

'I don't agree with that. Besides which, he confessed.'

Meikle was shaking his head. 'He told you he did it, but that's not the same thing. He couldn't lie to me when I asked him, so he just said nothing.'

'The evidence was put to the jury . . . '

'Fuck all of them, too. Let me tell you what they saw — they saw a kid from a broken home, no job and no college degree. They saw the picture your fiscal painted for them. They didn't see Ellis.' He seemed to be studying her, as if seeing her for the first time. 'I'm not saying you didn't do your job, any of you — I'm saying that was *all* you did.'

They were silent for a few moments. 'So what happens now?' Clarke asked. 'Do I have to change my phone number and move house?'

'Tell me this, do you ever give them a minute's thought, Ellis and all the others you've put inside?'

'It's not really . . . ' Clarke broke off. 'Maybe not as much as I could,' she conceded.

He took this in, nodding slowly, looking her up and down, his face softening. 'I really don't think he stands a chance in there, and I'm positive he didn't do it.'

Clarke had heard the words so many times from loved ones, friends, colleagues. She nodded slowly as an idea formed. 'Say I got someone to take another look — a fresh pair of eyes. Just to convince you we played fair.'

'But I don't think you did play fair, Inspector.'

She held up a finger. 'But if someone took another look . . . '

'What?'

'Would you go on the record with those names, the ones who gave you my number?'

'I suppose I might.'

'That's not quite good enough.'

He fixed her with a look. 'I'll have to think.'

'You do that — while I think about having you arrested.'

His mouth twitched. 'All right then, yes, as long as you convince me you've been thorough.'

'And meantime you'll stop the calls and visits and I won't press charges.'

She was waiting for him to nod his head in agreement, so he did, and when he looked down, he saw that her hand was waiting for him. He took it and shook, slow to release his grip.

'How do I know I can trust you?'

'You don't,' she answered, wresting her fingers free.

22

Rebus was in his kitchen when the call came: Bill Rawlston.

'Hiya, Bill,' he said, answering. 'How did the rest of the interview go?'

'Nothing I wasn't expecting.'

'Is that you done, do you think?'

'Unless you've heard anything to the contrary.'

'Maybe if you got your doctor to have a word, they wouldn't bother you any further.'

'I don't want anyone's pity, John. Sutherland phrased it perfectly — a result after all these years would taste all the sweeter.'

'He's got a way with words.'

'So you've nothing new to tell me?'

Rebus had placed the handcuffs on the worktop in front of him. He pushed them around with a finger as he spoke. 'Not really, Bill. It's been one of those days where not much happens.'

Apart from Cafferty, Poretoun Woods, house and village, Steele and Edwards, Alex Shankley . . .

'Well, keep me posted, eh?'

'Will do, Bill. And look after yourself.'

He ended the call only for another to replace it.

'Not interrupting anything?' Clarke asked him.

'Just my dinner.'

'Cordon bleu, I don't doubt.'

'Does microwaved stovies count?'

'Probably not.'

'Even with the addition of a coulis of brown sauce?'

'Listen, John, you've got cold case experience . . .'

'I've worked a few.'

'If I got you to do some digging on one that's still fairly fresh, it might give us some leverage with Steele and Edwards.'

'How?'

'They're the ones who gave my number to Ellis Meikle's uncle. My number *and* my home address.'

'No end to the spite in those bastards, is there?'

'They might end up getting their jotters if we make this work.'

'And all I have to do is take a look at the Meikle case.'

'Better still if you prove we put an innocent young man away.'

'Doesn't seem to me that would play too well for you. Funny thing is, when I read about how the uncle tried to start a search party, know what went through my mind?'

'What?'

'That's who did it — the uncle.'

'Bit odd that he'd want the case looked at again, if that were true.'

'I suppose. Then again, isn't he a short-fuse merchant? Could be he's not thinking straight.'

'He blames PTSD for the short fuse.'

'And Steele and Edwards gave Mr PTSD your address?'

'Yes.'

'He came to see you?'

'He scoped the place out, put up some graffiti so the neighbours would know they had a farmyard animal in the vicinity.'

'Bastard needs a kicking.'

'Maybe back in your day.'

'Don't piss about, Siobhan — you know how these things work. They always escalate.' He paused. 'Why don't you want to report it?'

'How do you think they've survived in ACU, John? They hear every rumour and bit of dirt . . .'

Rebus lifted the handcuffs, clutching them in his free hand. 'Meaning whoever you took it to, Steele would most likely have something on them?'

'It has to be more than my word against theirs. I need Dallas Meikle to tell his story.'

'And for that to happen, I have to take a look at the nephew's case?' Rebus thought for a moment. 'He really reckons the kid's innocent?'

'Seems that way.'

'He thinks or he knows? Is there something he's not telling you?'

'I don't know.' He listened to the pause as she considered this. 'Maybe,' she eventually conceded.

'We should take him out of the game, Shiv. He sounds dangerous.'

'I can handle him.'

'Got a taser tucked under your pillow?'

'Pepper spray,' she corrected him.

'Might help explain your love life.'

'Will you do it, John?'

'Of course I will. But if I don't get anywhere . . . ?'

'Then we won't have much choice, will we?'

'You mean we'll take Uncle Dallas out of the game?'

'Exactly.'

'I'll get started in the morning then.'

'Will it mean juggling your diary?'

'Don't worry about it. Just you concentrate on finding who killed Stuart Bloom.'

'Enjoy your stovies, John. I hope there's a helping left over for Brillo.'

'Night, Siobhan. And keep your hand on that pepper spray.'

Saturday/Sunday

23

Clarke and Crowther chose to work through the weekend, with the promise of at least one day's rest the following week. Not that they achieved very much, since both Joseph Madden and Colin Speke were out of the country, Madden finishing work on a TV documentary in Italy and Speke holidaying in Corfu. They'd be back by Tuesday, and both were based in Glasgow.

'That'll be our Tuesday evening then,' Clarke told her colleague.

'Oh, the glamour.'

With the office quiet — Callum Reid the only other masochist — they drank a lot of coffee and ate too many filled baguettes and chocolate digestives. Sutherland had a nephew's wedding in Dingwall, but phoned and texted half a dozen times both days for updates. Clarke, too, was keen for updates of her own. Christine Esson and Ronnie Ogilvie, the latter back from sick leave, had dropped off the Meikle case files at Rebus's flat. She'd told them everything — well, almost everything — and they'd been keen to help.

'Fair warning,' she'd told them. 'Could get you into trouble.'

But they'd insisted. 'If anyone asks,' Esson had joked, 'we'll pin the blame on you.'

'You better,' Clarke had replied in all seriousness.

Rebus had then phoned to say he'd commenced digging. 'Though half the stuff is on memory sticks — whatever happened to paper, ink and cassette tape?'

'Give us time, it'll all be kept in the Cloud, whatever that is. Good luck, John.'

'I should be thanking you — when you get to my age, the brain needs a bit of a workout . . . '

It had taken four messages from her before he'd told her to stop bugging him.

When I know, you'll know.

So she waited. Neither the soil expert nor the forensic lab was working a weekend shift. Crowther kept talking about what she'd do with her free Monday. Laundry and shopping, maybe a film or drinks with pals.

'How about you?'

'Much the same.' Clarke was trying to remember the last time she'd been to the cinema. The latest Star Wars instalment at the end of the previous year? Her phone pinged: incoming text. It was Fox, wondering how everything was going.

Personally or professionally? she texted back, though she already knew the answer.

I keep waiting for your boss to tell me I'm done and can go back to Gartcosh.

Clarke got busy on her screen: *Not his call, though, your boss's, no? If you want to hang with us, tell your boss there's more to find.*

There probably IS more to find. I'm just not sure I want to find it.

It's the weekend, Malcolm. Try to relax.

Buy you dinner?

Not this weekend. Thanks for the thought.
Why not ask Tess?
Maybe I will. You off Monday?
Feet well and truly up.
Which was a lie. She knew precisely what she'd be doing with her day off.

She'd be working.

★   ★   ★

Sunday late afternoon in Restalrig. Rebus didn't know this part of town well. He found the Meikle house easily enough, though, and the unloved park where the local teens hung out, when they weren't trying to procure cigarettes and booze from the grocer's nearby. Charles Meikle, Ellis's dad, had piqued Rebus's interest. Nobody had given him too much thought. He'd split up with his wife after a series of escalating arguments, arguments that had got physical, with Seona seeming to give back almost as good as she got — no police involved, no thought of pressing charges. He'd found himself a flat in Causewayside, his daughter Billie opting to go live with him. Meantime, Charles's brother Dallas, who had often had to keep the peace when things flared up between husband and wife — and between father and son — had moved into the family home.

From photos, Charles had got the looks and Dallas the muscles. Ex-army, PTSD — Rebus knew a bit about both, though he'd served in Northern Ireland in the days before PTSD was a thing the forces recognised. He'd lain awake plenty nights in the barracks, though, listening to the nightmares his fellow squaddies were suffering, knowing those same dreams might well be waiting for him if he allowed himself to relax. Coiled springs, the whole lot of them, overwound mechanisms constantly on the very edge of snapping. So yes, he reckoned he knew what Dallas Meikle was capable of — but what about his brother? They had evidence from the wife that Charles wasn't above raising his hand to his son, though never his daughter. In a city of short tempers, Restalrig made for a pretty good proving ground.

Rebus had stepped past a posse of kids and their bikes to get into the grocer's, where he bought more gum and tried to ask a few questions that weren't too obvious. The kids outside were just about to enter their teens. One or two of them had probably already driven a stolen car or trail bike at speed. It had become both sport and rite of passage in Edinburgh's poorer enclaves. You stole keys from a house and went for a drive, blood pumping. When you got bored or ran out of petrol, you wrote the car off or dumped the bike. Job done till tedium set in again.

Once upon a time, Cafferty and his men would have come along looking to recruit. They would cherry-pick the best, the sharpest, the most agile. These foot soldiers would transport drugs, learning the trade until they could afford to buy the cars and bikes they'd previously stolen. For all Rebus knew, it still worked that way. With Darryl Christie in jail, his network gone, there was no way of knowing how much Cafferty had taken over. Fox's lot at Serious Crimes didn't know, but then they were based half the country away. Police Scotland's process of centralisation meant a lot of local information-gathering either didn't happen or went ignored.

There were more bikes in the play park, and two kids kicking around a glass bottle that would shatter eventually. Seona Meikle's house was part of a terrace that had been given a facelift: freshly harled walls and new door and windows. Not too many keen gardeners, though, and a dumped car with four flat tyres and a notice on it that said POLICE AWARE. Rebus smiled at that. Back in the day, there would have been a beat cop who would have known every face, able to put a name to each. Not these days, not outside the Oor Wullie cartoon in the *Sunday Post* Rebus had just bought at the shop. The car being washed outside Seona Meikle's house looked nearly new. Rebus recognised the man soaping it. He walked over and gave a nod of greeting.

'All right?' Dallas Meikle responded.

'Nice car.'

'My brother's a mechanic — he'd give me pelters if I didn't treat it right.'

'That'll be your brother Charles? The one who used to live here?' Rebus watched for a reaction. There was a slight tensing of the forearms, but nothing else. 'My name's John Rebus,' he went on. I used to be CID. I'm giving DI Clarke a hand.'

'Oh aye?' Meikle was dressed in a white vest and oily denims.

'You like the odd tattoo then,' Rebus commented. 'Did you start when you were a soldier? I was army myself — never could stand needles, though.'

'This us forming a bond?' Meikle asked, pausing in his work. 'Old troopers together? I met more arseholes than amigos in my time in the forces.'

'I've no interest in us becoming pals,' Rebus shot back. 'You tried putting the frighteners on a good friend of mine. I had my way, you'd be facing a doing followed by a good long bit of jail time. Only thing you'd be soaping then would be your cellmate's hairy arse.'

'That right?'

'The bastards who gave you her number and address are just that — bastards. But they're clever with it. Tried huckling her, and when they got nowhere, they turned to you. Didn't really matter to them whether you just gave her a scare or a thumping. They knew damned well you'd do *something*.'

'This you telling me to back off? Bit late for that.'

'It's me telling you that I'm the one looking at Ellis's trial. If you want to have a go at anyone, I'm the one you want.'

Meikle was squeezing foamy water from the grey sponge. He gave a thin smile. 'Bet you thought you were a bit tasty back in the day, eh, old-timer? Nowadays I'd have you on the canvas before you could blink.'

'Try me.' Rebus pulled back his shoulders. 'I'll tear your head from your shoulders and use it to sponge off that graffiti you wrote.'

Meikle seemed to make up his mind, ignoring Rebus as he tossed the sponge back into the bucket. 'Ellis did this, you know,' he said. 'Cleaned the car, I mean. I'd give him a couple of quid. He'd save up to buy stuff for his computer. Time he spent on shoot-'em-ups, I was worried he might enlist.' He turned towards Rebus. 'Clarke told you what I think?'

'You don't think he did it, despite all those violent video games.'

Meikle gave a snort. 'Defence lawyer used that in her summing-up: a young man made momentarily violent by a world of violence. She mentioned me and my PTSD, Ellis's dad and his outbursts, even Seona, for standing up for herself. She was looking for a culpable homicide verdict, but the judge had other ideas.'

'Say for the sake of argument Ellis didn't do it, who else would you be looking at?'

Meikle stared at Rebus. 'Well, me, obviously — seems everyone thinks that's why I wanted to head the search party, so I could lead them anywhere but the right direction.'

'And why did you?'

'I can organise; I can get things started. Kristen's family were happy to wait for your lot to do something. Fuck that.'

'How did Ellis's prints get on the knife?'

'Maybe it was his knife; or he found it and tossed it.'

'Or he was there,' Rebus added. 'And he at least played a role.'

Dallas was shaking his head as the door

223

behind him opened and Seona Meikle stepped out.

'Who's this?' she called, her voice hoarse, a cigarette dangling from her fingers. Dyed blonde hair and too much make-up around the eyes; knee-length dress slightly too tight at the stomach.

'Nobody,' Dallas told her. 'He just drinks in McKenzie's.'

'You wanting a coffee or anything?'

'I'm nearly finished, and this bawheid's just leaving.' He lifted the pail and poured its contents over the bonnet of the car. 'I'm not as good at this as Ellis,' he told Rebus. 'Sorry I splashed your shoes.'

Rebus looked down at them, then back up at Meikle. 'Anything you think I should know?'

Meikle shrugged. 'Something happened at that bunker. Maybe Ellis was there and maybe he wasn't. Look a bit closer at Kristen and her family.' He took a step towards Rebus, the pail hanging from one hand. 'When they came to the house . . . well, what parent wouldn't want a search party? Your kid goes missing, you do anything and everything, no?'

Rebus found himself nodding.

'Something's not right. All the way through the trial, I could feel it.'

'I'm in the middle of going through the transcripts,' Rebus said.

'No you're not — you're pissing about in Restalrig, getting right up my fucking nose.' Dallas began to walk back towards the house. Watching him retreat, Rebus lifted his foot and

224

scraped some dirt from the sole on to the nearest gleaming chrome wheel rim. Then decided to continue his tour.

He checked no one had been at his Saab. Not that he thought it an obvious target: too old and unglamorous. He was chewing a fresh piece of gum as he headed to the park. Some people he'd passed — walking their dogs or fetching milk and papers — had nodded a greeting. It wasn't a bad area, he decided; it had just elements. That was the way they phrased it these days in Police Scotland.

Elements. Meaning a combination of feckless parenting, lack of opportunity, boredom and disenfranchisement. Rebus knew all the buzz words and he didn't necessarily disagree. But knowledge was one thing and politicians' words came cheap.

'Paedo.' The insult carried to him from across the park. He'd found a bench and settled with his *Sunday Post*. There were empty cans and takeaway cartons strewn around an overfilled bin next to him. A gull was pecking a hole in one of the cartons, seeking whatever was within.

Three kids were watching him. No way of knowing which one had called out. He gestured towards the three. Only one of them took up the challenge, pushing his bike with him as he approached.

'Fuck are you after?' the boy demanded to know.

'Ellis Meikle.'

'They put him away.'

'Did you know him?'

'Knew who he was.' The boy sniffed. His head was closely shaved, his teeth uneven.

'I wouldn't mind a chat with one or two of his mates. Reckon you could track them down?'

'What's it worth?'

'A fiver minimum.'

The boy gave a scowl. 'Fuck am I supposed to buy with that?'

'Name your price then.'

'Bottle of voddy. Payment up front.'

It was Rebus's turn to scowl. 'This is the gig economy, son. You get paid for results. Now what do you say . . . ?'

★　★　★

Three of them turned up, all older than Rebus's gofer. One stayed just long enough to tell Rebus he could 'get fucked', but the other two were happy to talk. Afterwards, Rebus paid off his gofer and both chatterboxes and headed towards the golf course. He kicked himself for not thinking to bring Brillo. Maybe he'd give him a long walk later, up to the grounds of the Astley Ainslie hospital. The bunker belonged to the seventh hole, just behind the green. Two bunkers sat side by side, but the steepest was the one where she'd been killed.

People were still out playing in the fading light, but Rebus knew he wasn't trespassing. This whole golf course was a magnet for Restalrig's young people, as he'd just been informed. There were copses where they could do drugs and have sex. They could ride their bikes — motorised and pedal — across the fairways at night when no one was around. Ellis and Kristen used to come here, with other friends or on their own. Ellis wasn't quite the loner he had seemed from the case files. He went to parties, drank and smoked dope. There were plenty of girlfriends in his past. Kristen had come as a surprise, though. She was loud and full of energy, and headed a coterie of other girls at her school. The feeling was, she could have done better than Ellis. Not that she was above getting into scrapes — playground fights; detentions; fallings-out with her parents. But for Ellis to do what he did . . . the boys told the same story: she must have driven him to it. Was she seeing anyone else behind his back? They didn't know. Did Ellis carry a knife? If so, he'd never shown it to anyone.

She must have driven him to it . . .

Ellis had texted her to meet him at the golf course. She had gone. And something had happened, Dallas Meikle was right about that — argument, confrontation or ambush? Rebus had asked the two boys about Kristen's parents. They were said to be quiet, weird, protective. Weird because they were churchgoers, though Kristen herself was lapsed. Protective because they often turned up in their car at parties and gatherings, ready to chauffeur their daughter home even when she'd not requested it.

'Gie'd her a total riddy,' one of the boys had told Rebus. 'One minute she's in a dark corner with Ellis, the next her maw's standing ower them shouting and yelling.'

Rebus wondered what a couple of God-fearing

227

folk had made of the arrangements at the Meikle household. Estranged parents, the uncle settling in, booze flowing, Ellis glued to his gaming screen. Did Rebus need to speak to them? Would they tell him anything? What would his excuse be for contacting them? He considered all this as he walked.

Bunches of flowers had been placed around the rim of the bunker. Those that had wilted had been repositioned at a distance and replaced by fresh ones. There were messages and photos, too, protected by plastic and polythene from the elements. Candles, an empty bottle of alcopop, a couple of small teddy bears. Rebus studied one of the photos of Kristen. It had been taken at the park. She had screwed up her face and was lifting her middle finger to the camera. Come on then, world, she seemed to be saying, let's see what you've got.

Several people had left copies of another photo, taken by the official school photographer. Kristen's long fair hair had been scooped up across her head, so that it draped down one shoulder. She was giving a pout and her lips were glossy. The top button of her blouse had been undone, her tie hanging loose. It looked recent, and Rebus guessed there'd be another copy in her parents' living room, even though they probably didn't approve of the way she'd chosen to present herself.

The case file had contained information on Kristen's various social media activities, Facebook and Snapchat and the rest. He'd read through the printout of her phone texts and emails. Her last text had been sent to a friend: *C u 18er E needs me*, accompanied by a winking emoji, its tongue protruding. E for Ellis, waiting for her at the golf course.

Some of her friends had given evidence in court. She had gone willingly, they'd said. No way she could have known what was to happen. No, she hadn't fallen out with Ellis. No, she wasn't seeing anyone else. No, nothing had happened at school of late, nothing out of the ordinary.

Ellis's day, too, had been as routine as any other, according to his mother: woke up late, went to the supermarket for her. Took his time, after running into some pals. In the meantime Billie had come to visit, sitting with her mum in the kitchen while Ellis retreated to his bedroom — with a couple of those same pals to start with. After they headed elsewhere, he stayed put, playing on his computer, headphones on, until he went out just after five. He said he was catching up with another friend, one with a brand-new console, but this was a lie — he had already texted Kristen.

'Why did he lie?' his mother had been asked.

She hadn't had an answer.

'Did he often keep secrets from you?'

'I don't think so.'

Rebus thought of Ellis Meikle, his side of the story yet to be told, sitting in a shared cell at Saughton, taking in the smells and sounds, wary and watchful. He stared down into the bunker and managed not to feel sorry for him.

24

Tess Leighton had put some make-up on, which ended up emphasising just how pale her skin's natural tone was. Fox had been relieved to see her order a starter and a main — polishing off both with the accompaniment of a large glass of Merlot. Not anorexic then. Just slender and maybe a touch anaemic. The restaurant was really more of a pub — the posher places he had tried to book were closed Sunday evenings. But the food had been fine, as predicted by the reviews he'd checked on TripAdvisor. He wore a jacket and chinos rather than a suit. No tie, shirt open at the neck. They'd discussed their neighbourhoods — Oxgangs in his case, Livingston in hers — and their upbringings. Both had been married once; neither had children. Leighton had two brothers, Fox a sister. He hadn't mentioned Jude's various problems, while Leighton had eventually admitted that one brother had had a bit of a breakdown. They both enjoyed reading, and country walks, and being police officers. She'd listened intently as he spoke of his days in the Complaints, then confessed that she'd always managed to stay out of trouble.

'No reports, no misdemeanours, no rebukes.'

'Probably makes you unique, Tess.'

She gave a small, non-committal shrug. 'Even Graham's had a run-in, you know,' she confided.

'With Professional Standards?'

'I think it went as far as ACU, except maybe it was CCU back then.'

'What did he do?' Fox placed his knife and fork on his plate, unable to finish the potatoes and carrots.

'I think it was his boss's retirement party — this was in his Inverness days. The boss accused Graham of getting him drunk, maybe even spiking his drinks, then getting Traffic to pull him over. Ended up banned from driving and blamed Graham for it.'

'The complaint was taken seriously?'

'All I know is he got a reprimand of some kind. Don't think he's been in trouble since.' She paused. 'Small beer compared to what went on in the Stuart Bloom case.'

Fox nodded, watching her.

'If you really wanted to,' she went on, 'you could do some damage to a lot of reputations.'

'I'm not Professional Standards these days, though, and I doubt ACU will want it when two of their own are front and centre.'

'I suppose not, though Steele and Edwards don't seem to have done much wrong. Rebus, Skelton and Newsome on the other hand . . . '

He nodded again. 'Listen to us,' he said with a smile that was only slightly forced. 'Even on a weekend we can't help talking shop.' They lapsed into silence as their plates were cleared. Neither had room for dessert, but they ordered coffee. Leighton watched their server head to the bar with their order, then turned her attention back to Fox.

'Was that your way of telling me to drop the subject, Malcolm?'

'I just don't want the mistakes of the past to interfere with the current inquiry.'

'That's it, is it? Rather than you trying to protect a friend?'

Fox considered his response. 'I've known John for a few years now. At one time, I wanted him kicked off the force.'

'But something changed your mind?'

Fox shrugged. 'It became academic when he retired.'

'For someone who's retired, he seems to spend a lot of time in police stations.'

'Only when there's a chance to cause maximum disruption.'

Her face broke into a smile. 'You do like him, don't you?'

He shrugged again. 'He's the kind of cop I could never be. He gets a kick out of taking risks.'

'You're not above taking risks yourself.' She leaned across the table on her elbows. 'You invited me out for dinner, after all.'

'The only risk there was that you'd say no.'

'Why would I have done that?' She leaned back again, plucking her napkin from her lap and announcing that she was going to 'the little girls' room'. He half rose from his chair as she left, then settled again. The server was hovering, having forgotten to ask if they'd be wanting a digestif, and how was the evening going?

'Just fine, thank you,' Fox said. He took his phone out, half minded to send Siobhan Clarke

232

a text. But then he thought better of it. Instead, he googled Livingston. When Leighton returned, he turned the screen towards her.

'You told me nothing much happens there,' he chided her. 'How could you forget you've got one of the biggest shopping malls in Scotland?'

Leighton pressed a finger to her lips. 'Don't want everyone knowing,' she stage-whispered. 'Bad enough as it is finding a parking space . . . '

The pair of them were laughing as their coffees arrived.

★ ★ ★

The sleek black Audi was blocking the driveway next to Fox's bungalow. Fox parked on the roadway behind it. As he got out, Grant Edwards emerged from the driver's side. Fox's first thought was: *Good job I didn't invite Tess back.* His second: *Would she have said yes?*

'Should you be out on your own?' he asked Edwards, making show of peering into the empty car. Edwards was dressed in a three-quarter-length black woollen coat. He slid his hands into his pockets. Fox was reminded of funeral person-nel, the kind who came with fake solemnity.

'Brian's busy elsewhere.'

'It talks!'

Edwards's mouth twitched. 'Only when there are no third-party witnesses.'

'How long you been waiting here?'

'Long enough to get annoyed. Our intelligence is you don't go out much — being a recovering alcoholic and everything.'

'Sorry to disappoint you.' Fox's hands went into his own pockets. He didn't have the other man's heft, but he was by no means insubstantial. He puffed out his chest a little and leaned back on his heels.

'Brian reckons he's due a report.'

'Brian is mistaken. He gets a report when there's something worth telling him.'

'How are you getting on with Sutherland's team?'

'Just dandy.'

'You sure about that? They know you were Complaints — I reckon they'll be sharpening the knives. You won't feel a thing till the first one slips in.' Edwards's grin spread a little wider.

'I'm not ashamed of having been Complaints.'

'Always hard to go back to CID, though. You know ACU's an option, once this is over — if it's over cleanly, I mean.'

'Your own names kept out of the story?' Fox nodded slowly. 'Steele made sure I understood.'

Edwards took a step nearer and dropped his voice. 'I'm not sure Brian really appreciates how close you and Siobhan Clarke were. But you'd be wise not to take her side against ours.'

'Do I need to take sides?'

'You might feel you do. I know you're not an item these days.'

'We never were.'

Edwards gave a slow shrug. 'How's she doing anyway?'

'DI Clarke?'

'Fitted into MIT okay? Giving it a hundred per cent?'

'What's it to you?'

'Sutherland needs a team that's focused — no distractions.'

'She's a good cop, Edwards.'

'Maybe, maybe not. Bit of a mouth on her, though.' Edwards's eyes narrowed to the merest slits. 'Do the right thing, DI Fox. Keep us happy.' He started to lower himself back into the driving seat, but paused halfway. 'Something tells me we wouldn't have to dig down very far to start uncovering *your* skeletons.'

Fox stood his ground until the Audi's rear lights vanished into the night. He got into his own car and sat there for a couple of minutes, hands wrapped around the steering wheel. Then he took several deep breaths, turned on the ignition and manoeuvred the vehicle into the driveway. It was only when he had locked it and was standing on his doorstep that he noticed he had a text waiting for him on his phone. It was from Tess Leighton, thanking him for a lovely evening. She had added a small x after her name. His smile was fleeting. What the hell had Edwards meant about Siobhan not giving it a hundred per cent?

Monday

25

On Monday morning, Clarke was on Rebus's doorstep at 8 a.m.

'I bring coffee and croissants,' she said into the intercom.

'That's the only reason I'm letting you in.'

She climbed the two flights. He had left the door ajar for her so she headed for the living room. The case files had been gutted. Sheets were stacked in a dozen separate piles, while Rebus's various jottings and notes were laid out next to his computer.

'You've been busy,' she said.

'Just don't touch anything.'

'You mean there's a system here?' She handed him a croissant and a Styrofoam cup.

'A system that makes perfect sense to me.' He dunked the croissant and sucked the coffee from it. 'Why aren't you at work?'

'Day off.'

'Then you should be in bed.'

'Whereas you look like you've been up for hours.' She tore off a chunk of croissant and gave it to Brillo.

'I reckon Dallas and Seona have to be an item,' Rebus stated.

'They say not.'

'But if they are, Ellis is bound to have known. The three of them under the same roof? Dallas tiptoeing up the creaky stairs of a night?'

'You've been in the house?'

Rebus shook his head. 'But I've visited plenty like it.'

'And if they *are* sleeping together?'

'Ellis might not have been happy about it. Maybe he sees his mum cheating on his dad, and gets the notion his own girlfriend might not be all sugar and spice.' Rebus lowered himself on to his armchair, still holding both coffee and croissant. 'He'd been hanging out with his mates that day; maybe one of them said something. He lied to his mum about where he was going. Seems to me that might not be the only lie coming out of that house. Then there's Kristen. Her pals say she hadn't said anything about splitting up from Ellis, but maybe she'd made up her mind. Her parents had told her often enough they thought she could do better. I'm wondering if she took up with Ellis *specifically* to piss off her God-fearing parents — hardly the basis for a strong and stable romance.'

Clarke frowned in concentration. 'Was any of that in the files?'

'Some of it I was told.'

'Who by?'

'A couple of lads who know Ellis.'

'So you *have* been to Restalrig?'

'Never said I hadn't. Bumped into the uncle while I was there. Another thing about Kristen, she liked to flirt — again, according to the word on the street. And when she was round at Ellis's house . . .'

'Her and Dallas?'

'He told her there was a drink waiting behind

240

the bar at McKenzie's for her.'

'He said that in front of Ellis?'

'According to the two lads.'

'She was only seventeen; she'd never have been served.'

'Sure.' Rebus bit into the croissant and chewed. Clarke had pulled out one of the dining table chairs and sat down. She sipped her coffee and gazed towards the piles of paper.

'So now we have Ellis jealous of his uncle?'

'Maybe.'

'I'm not sure this is what Dallas wants to hear.'

'He's come to the wrong place for fairy tales and happy endings.'

She nodded. 'So is that what I tell him?'

'He won't be thrilled.'

'Which means he won't give me Steele and Edwards.' She looked at Rebus. 'You've had no time at all, John. Maybe another few days?'

Rebus offered a shrug. 'I'm not sure how many more spadefuls are there, Shiv. Unless . . . '

She put her cup down. 'What?'

'A visit to the prisoner.'

'He won't talk to you.'

'A risk I'm willing to take.'

'Maybe if you took Dallas with you . . . ?'

But Rebus was shaking his head. 'Could mean me getting a story rather than *the* story.'

'Worth a shot,' Clarke eventually conceded. Her phone was vibrating. She dug it from her pocket. 'Got to take this,' she said. Then, pressing the phone to her ear: 'Yes, Graham?'

She listened for a moment. 'No, that's fine.

Absolutely. Yes, of course I'll come in. I can be there in twenty minutes.' After ending the call, she stared at the screen.

'I'm all for a bit of suspense,' Rebus nudged her.

'A potential break. Looks like my day off is buggered.'

'Spit it out then.'

'A fingerprint on the handcuffs. Well, a partial. It's fragile but it's there.'

'And do we know who it belongs to?'

She looked at him but didn't answer.

'Christ's sake, Siobhan, you can trust me not to blab!'

'I know I can. And it's Jackie Ness. The print seems a good match for Jackie Ness.'

'Well, well,' Rebus muttered, staring towards the window. 'Don't let me keep you then — not when you've justice to dispense.'

★ ★ ★

In the MIT office, Graham Sutherland was in conference with a fiscal depute. Clarke recognised the woman. Her name was Gillian Ramsay and Clarke had worked several previous cases with her. She was questioning Sutherland about the tests on the handcuffs. The partial had been identified because Ness had been fingerprinted during the original inquiry. Why? Because he had visited Bloom's flat, and even been given a lift in his car once. When they dusted the flat, and if they tracked down the car . . . well, the prints were useful. Weren't prints supposed to be expunged from the records after a time, though? It seemed these weren't.

'Defence counsel won't like that,' Ramsay said, making a note to herself.

'We're looking to see what else might be in the car; maybe a hair or something.'

'But DCI Sutherland, we already know that Mr Bloom gave Mr Ness a ride home one night. A hair left behind doesn't prove anything. Say the cuffs belonged to the victim, say they were lying there on the passenger seat and Mr Ness merely moved them?'

'Why would Bloom keep handcuffs in his car?'

'Wasn't his partner the son of a serving police officer? Could the partner have acquired them, perhaps to be used during role play in the bedroom?'

'I doubt it, but we can ask.'

'You certainly will ask. Meantime, I'm minded to advise that there's precious little here to form a serious criminal charge.'

'But we can still bring him in?'

'Of course. Accompanied by his solicitor and then asked some serious questions under caution, to be recorded for posterity.'

'But not charged?' Some of the air had escaped from Clarke's boss. He'd sounded elated on the phone. Now, the balloon had sunk back to earth. Ramsay was gathering together her things.

'Not quite yet,' she answered, rising to her feet.

After she'd left, there was silence in the room until Sutherland collected himself, clearing his throat. 'Forensic lab had the finger-print by close of play Friday. Sat on it all bloody weekend while they swanned off to watch the football or rugby and go for long afternoon rambles. Don't think I won't be taking that to DCS Mollison. But meantime, we do have a positive ID. It's not nothing — don't go thinking it is. Procurator fiscal needs everything to be watertight pre-trial. Means they're always sceptical. But this is something, and we need to run with it.' He looked to Clarke. 'What time do you think Ness gets to the office?'

'Probably not before ten.'

'So he'll be at home until nine thirty, nine forty? It's just gone nine now . . . ' He sought out Callum Reid. 'Take George with you. Go wait at his office.' To Clarke again: 'Is there a receptionist?' She nodded. 'If she gets in first, don't let her warn him. In fact, stay in the car till you see him.'

'What does he look like?' Gamble asked.

'Like that photo there.' Sutherland pointed to where Reid was standing, next to the map and the headshots. Reid tapped Ness's.

'He's actually changed a bit since then,' Clarke felt it necessary to qualify.

'Fine,' Sutherland said. 'George, you stay. Siobhan, go with Callum.' He saw the disappointment on Gamble's face. 'No need to be glum — if you're a good boy, I might let you sit in on the interview.' Then, switching his attention between Reid and Clarke: 'Why in God's name are you two still here?'

'We're not,' Reid said, grabbing his coat on his way to the door.

Detective Constable Christine Esson made her way out of Gayfield Square police station and looked both ways before crossing the road and climbing into Rebus's Saab.

'Still got this old thing, I see,' she said, closing the door.

'Are you talking to me or the car?'

Esson decided this was worth a smile. Her hair was short and dark; Rebus had always seen a resemblance to Audrey Hepburn, though Siobhan Clarke had never agreed.

'You didn't want to come in?' she asked him.

'Better if people don't start joining the dots.'

'You're making progress on Ellis Meikle?'

'There's a bit of expertise I'm lacking, Christine. I've looked at all the social media stuff, but it's really only Ellis's and Kristen's. I wouldn't mind knowing what was being said among their various friends — before the murder and after.'

'Just friends, or family members too?'

'The more the merrier.'

She puffed out her cheeks and expelled some air. 'It's a big ask.'

'Complicated, you mean?'

'Time-consuming,' she corrected him. 'In a perfect world, I'd maybe start a few fake accounts, friend all and sundry, wait for them to friend back, chat with them . . . ' She looked at him. 'It's weird, but people online will share stuff with strangers that they wouldn't say to their nearest and dearest.'

245

'Sounds like that might take a while.'

'It definitely would — weeks, maybe a lot longer.'

'So if that's not an option . . . ?'

'I'd just trawl where I can, butt into threads, add my tuppence worth. Might end up blocked or muted here and there, though. Plus a lot of kids use Snapchat, and those messages get wiped. And bear in mind they'll keep things private if they think it's sensitive . . . ' She paused, eyes still on him. 'Whereabouts in all of that did I start to lose you?'

'A sentence or two back.'

She smiled again. 'The good news is, this is something I can be doing in my free time. But it'd help if you gave me what you've got — accounts and user names for killer and victim; names of their various friends and family members . . . '

'I can email you all of that.'

'Not to my official account.' She took out her phone. 'I'm sending you my email address.' They waited until his own phone buzzed. 'Job done.'

'Thanks, Christine. Drinks on me when this is finished.'

She nodded slowly, her face darkening a little. 'We all worked damned hard on that case, John. We got the right result.'

'I don't doubt it.'

'Yet here you are looking for holes the family can take to an appeal. If you find any, there's omelette all over our faces.' She paused. 'On the other hand, I saw how ugly everything got between Siobhan and ACU. It's just funny that

246

to get at them, we end up messy too.'

'I'll help you clean up the kitchen after.'

'Oh aye? Bit of a speciality of yours?'

'I get the feeling someone's been talking.'

'Spilling the beans, you might say,' Esson commented, pushing open the door of the Saab and getting out.

26

All the way to the police station, Ness had asked what was going on. They'd been waiting for him outside the main entrance to Locke Ness Productions. In the car, they'd let him phone his PA. He'd said simply that he was held up and might not be in until the afternoon. Then he'd asked the two detectives again: what was going on?

'You got a solicitor?' Reid had answered. 'If not, one will be provided for you.'

They'd left him to stew in the interview room while his lawyer was summoned. Emily Crowther had taken him a weak cup of tea.

'Still thinks I could be in films,' she reported back. Sutherland meantime was as good as his word. Despite pleading looks from Clarke and Callum Reid, it was George Gamble who accompanied him into the interview room once the solicitor turned up. Phil Yeats had fetched the A/V equipment.

'Won't be new to you, Mr Ness,' he had commented.

'I'm happier on the other side of a camera, son,' Ness had replied. The room was stuffy, the heating having been turned up to maximum. Ness's jacket was over the back of his chair, and he had loosened an extra button on his shirt. The lawyer, Kelvin Brodie, was wise to such strategies, however, and asked them to either turn the radiator down or leave the door open.

'Don't want to abandon the interview over health and safety concerns, do we?'

Clarke knew Brodie from court appearances. She had expected Ness's solicitor to be the sort that specialised in business contracts, but Brodie was criminal law through and through. She was about to alert Sutherland to this when the door was closed from within, leaving her in the corridor along with the rest of the team.

Nothing much to do after that but wait.

Crowther had dug up a little more background on the DP and sound recordist, so they put their heads together in preparation for the following day. Fox and Leighton were in their own little empire, appearing in the MIT room only for coffee and tea top-ups.

'Heard from the Chuggabugs?' Clarke asked Fox when he approached her desk.

'No.'

'Going to tell them about the fingerprint?'

'I doubt I'll need to — they don't seem to lack sources.'

'Which is precisely why you should get in first. That way, you look keen. As you say, they'll find out sooner or later anyway.'

Fox nodded at the sense of this and went out to make the call while Clarke checked her own phone. Rebus had texted her to ask for an update, but she was ignoring him. Same went for Laura Smith, who was, in her own words, 'hearing jungle drums'. Which meant someone at the forensic lab had to have blabbed. Or maybe the fiscal's office. Or DCS Mollison had started spreading the news at Fettes or St Leonard's. No point really speculating, except that these days by the time a whisper reached the internet it had become an ill-intentioned and half-formed yelp, a yelp capable of spreading like the most virulent flu bug.

She thought of the pile of paper on Rebus's dining table, the one comprising social media messages to and from Ellis Meikle's various accounts, filled with young men's bravado. She knew there were porn clips and GIFs mixed in with it all, and demeaning commentary about local girls and their mothers. One of Ellis's friends had let Ellis know his mother Seona was 'pure MILF', leading others to chip in with thumbs up and thumbs down. How toxic would this culture eventually become? Clarke hoped she'd never find out, but as a detective, she feared she probably would.

Dallas Meikle's anonymous phone calls and graffiti had been innocent by comparison with some of the online abuse she had encountered. She wondered about that. Dallas could have sent anything to her mobile: images, texts, the lot. She reckoned he had known, however, that these would involve either a computer or a mobile phone on his part, and that those could always be traced back to their source. Maybe Steele and Edwards had given him the benefit of their wisdom.

'Wouldn't put it past them,' she muttered to herself.

After an hour and a half, Sutherland and Gamble emerged from the interview room and headed for the kettle, followed by the MIT team. Sutherland asked Yeats to go do guard duty outside the interview room door. Not that it was needed, but it would keep Ness on edge.

'He's having a confab with his lawyer,' Sutherland explained. 'And he's admitting nothing, says he's no idea how his print could have got on the cuffs, never seen them before.'

'Brodie meantime,' Gamble added, spooning coffee into a mug, 'wants to know how reliable the print can be after all this time. He went straight for the car and the fact Ness has never hidden that he was given a lift in it. So we'd expect to find his prints there for a start. His line is: Ness could have reached a hand down the side of his seat and touched the cuffs without realising.'

'He also,' Sutherland broke in, 'wants to know why we've kept an innocent man's prints on the database all these years.'

'Pretty much as the fiscal anticipated,' Clarke commented. 'Interesting that Ness went for a criminal lawyer, though — not everyone knows one.'

'Not everyone's been in a war with Sir Adrian Brand,' Sutherland said, stiffening his spine. 'Anyway, we're not done with him yet, not by a long chalk.'

'Juries love a bit of forensic evidence,' Emily Crowther stated. 'Let's not forget that.'

'Be nice to have something more than a partial fingerprint, though — I don't suppose the lab have come back to us in my absence?'

There were shakes of the head.

'I hope the soil expert's earning her fee,' Sutherland sighed.

There was a knock at the door. They turned to see Brodie standing there. 'Could my client trouble you for a sandwich or something? He's not had any breakfast.'

'The café does a reasonable BLT,' Clarke offered.

'My client is vegetarian.'

'LT it is then, always supposing they'll stoop to it.'

⋆ ⋆ ⋆

Jackie Ness was eventually released at 2.45 p.m. From around noon, Brodie had been complaining that they were going over the same old ground. A copy of the recording was handed over, while those in MIT who were keen got the chance to watch the interview courtesy of the copy they'd retained. Clarke studied Ness's body language; not that it was such a big deal these days. A lot of people knew the tricks, and she reckoned someone who had worked all his life with actors would know them better than most. Once the room had cooled down, he had buttoned his shirt and slipped his jacket back on, then sat without moving, hands clasped in his lap, face a mask, answering questions with the briefest possible responses and letting his solicitor do the bulk of the talking.

Sutherland was updating the fiscal's office by phone, while George Gamble stared into space. Clarke got the feeling he was rueing modern

252

policing methods and would have liked nothing better than to have beaten a confession out of the producer.

'We should take another look at the original interviews with Ness,' Callum Reid was telling Emily Crowther. 'We've only got his word for it that Stuart Bloom left Poretoun House alive. I know the place was checked over, but how thoroughly? Plus, crime-scene technology has moved on. I'm sure Sir Adrian would be happy to let us scope the place out. The story's beginning to come together.' He counted off on his fingers. 'Prints on the cuffs; Bloom last seen alive heading to a meet with Ness . . . ' He paused.

'I make that a total of two fingers, Callum,' Clarke interrupted.

'The car found in woodland owned by Ness at the time,' Crowther added. Clarke watched Reid hold up a third finger.

'Okay,' she conceded, 'but tell me this: what was Ness's motive?'

'Maybe they argued over Bloom's fee or something. Again, we only have Ness's word for it that everything was amicable between them. Could be he felt Bloom wasn't making enough progress, or was ripping him off. Come on, we've all seen it. People who've just killed someone don't exactly think rationally.'

'Which might also explain the handcuffs around the ankles,' Crowther added, earning a smile from Reid, as if this was an argument he could win with a show of hands.

'I'm not saying none of it happened that way,'

Clarke said. 'But proving it is something else.'

'We're missing a trick, though, if we don't factor in Poretoun House as the probable scene of crime.'

'Maybe.'

Reid was looking towards his boss, who was still on the phone. 'I'm going to press the case. If there's money in the pot for someone in a white coat to plop some mud under a microscope, surely we can get Scene of Crime to take their kit to Poretoun House.'

'Knock yourself out,' Clarke said.

★　★　★

The *Evening News*'s front page splashed on Jackie Ness's visit to Leith police station. There was a nice big photo of the producer as he made his way to a waiting taxi, Kelvin Brodie trying to hold a briefcase up to make the photographer's job more difficult. Rebus read the story — such as it was — through twice as he sat at a table in McKenzie's. If the media knew about the handcuffs, they weren't saying. The story was thin, but it would still shake Ness up. Rebus guessed there'd be reporters outside his home tonight, and his office in the morning. If there was guilt there, the cracks would start to appear, just so long as the media didn't tire of teasing their prey.

Rebus guessed that Fettes HQ had tipped the media off, or maybe it had been one of the MIT team. It had always been a game played between the cops and the journos. Yes, reporters could be a pain in the arse, but they were also immensely useful conduits. It saddened him that so much these days happened online, with every keyboard warrior suddenly a 'commentator' or 'pundit' or 'news-gatherer'. There was a lack of quality control. Anyone and everyone felt they had something to say and they weren't about to hold back. The public probably reckoned they were better informed than ever. They were, but not always by the truth.

Then again, had it been so different in Rebus's heyday? He'd tipped off journalists, fed them lies and half-truths when hoping to agitate a particular wasps' nest or unsettle a suspect or a witness. Stories had been planted and others suppressed. With the ear of as few as half a dozen reporters, you could control the story, or at least have a bloody good go at shaping it. When lied to, the media might snarl and spit, but they always came back for more. Nowadays, commentators lied to your face, feeding you pap from a spoon as if you were an infant. Twenty-four-hour news meant everyone wanted to be first with a story, even if it turned out to be wonky. A few of Rebus's old musical heroes had been reported online as having died, only for an apology to be issued later. He took nothing at face value now and required corroboration. Two sources, maybe even three before he believed anything the virtual world told him.

'What do you want?'

Rebus looked up from his paper. Dallas Meikle was standing there, having just arrived to start his shift.

'A minute of your time?' Rebus gestured to a free chair, but Meikle remained standing.

'Say what you have to say.'

'I need to talk with Ellis.'

'Why?'

'I just do.'

'He won't tell you anything.'

'But he'll see me if you ask him.'

'I suppose he might.'

'Will you do it?'

'He's no fan of the police.'

'In Saughton, I doubt that puts him in the minority. Besides, I'm just an old age pensioner.'

'I can't promise.'

'But you'll at least try?'

Dallas Meikle nodded, his eyes on Rebus. 'You're having doubts, aren't you? You're not as sure as you were that he did it?'

'He most likely did — that's something you might have to come to terms with. I'll have a better idea once I've seen him.'

'Even if he doesn't speak?'

'Things unsaid can still be important. Tell me, has he ever mentioned how he really felt about you moving in with him and his mum?'

'We talked it through.'

'You went there to make sure your brother behaved himself? Ever say to Ellis that it should have been *his* job?'

'I don't particularly mind if I fall out with Charles.'

'Better that than his son falling out with him?' Rebus nodded his understanding.

'We done here then?'

Rebus closed his newspaper. 'How well did you really know Kristen, Mr Meikle?' A small flame started to smoulder in Meikle's eyes. His lips stayed pursed. 'From what I've heard, she wasn't above flirting. Maybe it was just her nature, or to keep Ellis on his toes.'

'She never did with me.'

'But you knew the stories?'

'Kids these days aren't like my generation — or yours.'

'In some ways that's true, in others not so much.' Rebus got to his feet, folding the newspaper and stuffing it into his coat pocket. He handed Meikle a scrap of paper with his phone number on it. 'I'm going to visit Saughton tomorrow — if you can get word to Ellis, it would help. Get back to me after, and use your mobile rather than one of those phone boxes, eh?'

He exited the bar without looking back.

27

Brian Steele walked into the Devil's Dram with his girlfriend Rebecca on his arm. She had probably overdone it for this part of town — clinging floor-length emerald-green dress, slit up the side almost to her navel, and with a plunging neckline to boot. Her blonde hair fell in thick waves around her shoulders, and she wore three-inch stilettos. Not too much make-up — she really didn't need it — and just the right amount of high-end jewellery. As they had stepped from the cab, jaws had dropped, eyes lingering. The doormen knew Steele and held the door open for Rebecca.

'Everything okay, Shug?' he asked one of them, slipping a twenty into his palm.

'Fairly quiet, Brian.'

And then they were in. They'd been a couple of times before, including once under Darryl Christie's ownership. Steele liked all the theme stuff — devils and demons and imps scaling the walls and peering down from the dark red ceiling. There was usually a good DJ if you wanted to dance, and quiet booths if you'd rather sit and drink and eat. Steele had booked a table upstairs, overlooking the dance floor. Rebecca swayed to the rhythm as they climbed the glass staircase.

Once seated, Steele perused the whisky menu. It ran to eight pages, but he saw that more than a few offerings now had been scored through in black pen. Looking around, the place didn't seem quite as upmarket as it had once been: a corner of fraying carpet here, a broken light bulb there. There were fingerprints on the glossy table and the food menus were tacky to the touch.

After a long wait, a waiter dressed in red appeared, a bellboy's hat strapped to his head.

'No scallops tonight, I'm sorry to say,' he began. 'And no lobster or sea bass.'

Another waiter appeared behind him with a tray balanced on one outstretched hand.

'Compliments of the management,' he explained, placing flutes of champagne in front of them. Rebecca cooed, her eyes sparkling.

'And would management happen to be on the premises this evening?' Steele asked, receiving a nod in reply.

He sat back and studied the menu. After they'd ordered, Rebecca got busy on her phone, pouting for a selfie she could share with her circle. She began sending out texts with a dexterity that always amazed Steele, bearing in mind the length of her elaborate fingernails.

Rebecca owned a couple of nail bars in the city. Steele had helped with the seed money, but business was good. She complained sometimes that she had to pay higher wages than her competition, most of whom seemed to use labour from Vietnam or the Philippines. But she had plans for a third branch and a redesign of her flagship. Brains as well as beauty — about the only thing Steele didn't like about her was the incessant need to be on her bloody phone.

After their starters, a new waiter arrived at the top of the stairs and gestured towards Steele. He dabbed at his mouth with the napkin and told Rebecca he wouldn't be long.

Cafferty was waiting for him in a cordoned-off section of the basement bar. No music down here, other than piped lounge-style piano. Cafferty was on his own, arms stretched out along the back of a banquette.

'Take a pew, Brian,' he said.

'Rebecca's waiting upstairs,' Steele said as he sat opposite.

'I saw her. Christ knows what she sees in you, son.' Cafferty shook his head ruefully.

'Someone who shows her a good time, maybe.'

'Plenty of us could do that.' There was a whisky in front of Cafferty, and another waiting for Steele. He lifted the glass and sniffed.

'Highland Park 18,' Cafferty announced, lifting his own glass in a toast. Steele sipped and savoured, then nodded his appreciation.

'You do a good impression of a man who likes his malt,' Cafferty told him. 'But we know you prefer cooking lager, don't we?'

'I was brought up on cooking lager,' Steele confirmed.

'We all were, son, and look at us now.' Cafferty smiled and drained his glass, exhaling noisily as he replaced it on the table. 'But let's not keep the delightful Rebecca waiting, eh?'

Steele checked that the room was still empty. Even so, he leaned forward, lowering his voice a notch. 'Those cuffs I told you about? Turns out Jackie Ness left his prints on them.'

'That wasn't very clever of him. Who was it told you?'

'Malcolm Fox.'

'I know Fox — what's he got to do with anything?'

'Gartcosh have got him looking for fuck-ups in the original inquiry.'

'So he's at Leith, and feeding the juicy stuff back to you?' Cafferty digested this information. 'Do we know why Sutherland let Ness go?'

'Fiscal's yet to be convinced there's enough for a trial.'

'I'd say a fingerprint isn't a bad start, though.'

'Agreed.'

'A quick conviction would be nice for all concerned.'

'Trial's a trial — lot of stuff's bound to bubble to the surface.'

'Don't tell me you've got the jitters?' Cafferty's eyes were all but invisible in the dim light. He seemed to be made almost entirely of shadow.

'Nothing in the Bloom case to make *me* jittery,' Steele countered. He began to rise to his feet. 'Best get back upstairs . . .'

Cafferty's right hand descended like a guillotine and clamped around his wrist. 'You go when I say you can, Brian. Don't go getting above yourself. A fancy girlfriend and expensive threads don't hide the fact that you're just a cog — understood? Remember who's been your helping hand all these years, hauling you out of uniform and all the way to ACU.' He enunciated each letter slowly, showing teeth.

'I'm grateful, you know I am. When have I ever let you down?'

'Trust me, that's something you don't want to happen.' Cafferty slowly released his grip. 'You've not been interviewed yet?'

'No.'

'It'll happen, though. Make sure you've got your story straight — you and Edwards both.'

'No story to tell.'

'Rebus knows I took you with me to that meeting with Maloney.'

'So?'

'So what else do you think he might be keeping locked away inside that impressively thick skull of his?'

'The night Bloom disappeared, I was at the Police Club with my wife.'

'Remind me: your second wife or your third?'

'Second. We were there all evening, surrounded by dozens of witnesses.'

'And Edwards was there with you.' Cafferty sounded bored, having heard the story several times before. 'Adrian Brand was being driven to some golfing weekend at Gleneagles, and I was sitting on my arse at home with a couple of old chums. Alibis galore, in other words.'

'Not Ness, though — he didn't see another soul once Bloom had left. Made a few phone calls to do with his latest project, but that's about it. Bloom's boyfriend was back in Bloom's flat, allegedly, all by himself, getting the supper ready, and the boyfriend's murder squad father was at some amateur boxing bout in Glasgow.'

'Not everyone's covered,' Cafferty agreed.

'Just most of us — so there's nothing for us to worry about, no skeletons keeking out of closets.' He paused. 'Meaning we can all relax and enjoy ourselves. Now off you go before someone with a better suit and watch swoops down on Miss Nail Bar. What have you ordered anyway?'

'Pork belly.'

'Good choice. It's from my own piggery in Fife. Maybe we'll take a wee trip there some day.'

With a wave of one hand, Brian Steele was dismissed. Climbing back towards the light and the noise, he felt able to breathe again. Rebecca was holding her phone close to her face.

'Guess,' she said without looking up, 'how many men have tried buying me a drink in the last five minutes?'

'Lots,' Steele answered. Having placed the napkin back on his lap, the main courses arrived. But he was shaking his head. 'I've changed my mind,' he said. 'Bring me something else.'

The waiter looked startled. 'Anything in particular, sir?'

Steele picked up his flute and emptied it. 'Just so long as it hasn't come from one of Big Ger Cafferty's pigs,' he said.

★   ★   ★

Cafferty's office at the Devil's Dram was behind an inch-thick steel door with three locks and an alarm system. Only Cafferty himself had the means of opening the safe where the takings were kept. On nights when he wasn't around, his deputy would be driven to Quartermile accompanied by at least one of the doormen. The cash would be handed to Cafferty at his front door, along with the relevant paperwork. Of course, it was mostly credit and debit cards these days, plus contactless. Drinkers even paid using their smart watches. Cafferty preferred cash — it left less of a trail for HM Revenue and Customs to follow.

Most nights, he turned up at the club just before it closed, fixing the staff with a look that told them not to get up to any of the usual tricks. Not so much as a filched bottle of spirits or finessed tenner was going to leave the premises if Cafferty could help it. He also frowned on assignations with punters — next thing you knew, drinks were being offered on the house to people of no consequence. Only people he might have a use for merited the occasional freebie, people like Brian Steele. Cafferty knew that Steele loathed him and the feeling was entirely mutual. What the ACU man hated was that he belonged to Cafferty. As always, it had started with a few tiny tottering steps, but those steps had led Steele from a path that he was never going to find again.

Seated at his desk, Cafferty had started to replay the security footage from earlier in the evening. She was a looker, Rebecca. Cafferty knew her to speak to, of course; even had her phone number. He had paused the footage, zoomed in on the table. Steele had swapped the pork belly for a steak. Rebecca's choice was the salmon fillet. She'd be watching her weight, wanting always to look her very best. Cafferty thought about texting her to ask if she'd liked it, but by now she was probably in bed with Steele. So instead he turned from CCTV to internet, typing in Conor Maloney's name.

Maloney had remained a hobby. It irritated Cafferty that they could have become partners, had it not been for the private eye's disappearance and that bloody kid OD'ing on an Edinburgh street. With Maloney on board, Cafferty could probably have taken Aberdeen and Glasgow. Christ, maybe even Newcastle. And from there . . . who knew? Maloney probably hadn't been a paramilitary himself, content to negotiate with both sides. But the men around him had all come from that direction — sharp-witted and deadly. Yes, Cafferty could have used that, a whole trajectory lost to him. Instead of which, he had these meagre winnings from small-timers like Darryl Christie. It was nowhere near enough. Events had robbed him of the larger prize.

He kept clicking and searching. He knew Maloney's known aliases by heart, tried the same series of keywords. He had spent a small fortune down the years attempting to keep tabs on the bastard. He needed to know about Maloney. How much richer was he? What circles did he move in? Who did he rub shoulders with? Where in the world did he call home?

After a largely fruitless half-hour, he returned to the security footage, watching as Rebecca got to her feet, adjusting her tight dress. Steele was leading the way as the pair headed for the exit.

265

He didn't wait for her, didn't take her arm or hand as Cafferty would have done. He stopped for a word with the doormen, leaving her to wave down a taxi.

There was a knock at the door, so Cafferty closed the screen.

'What?' he barked.

The manager's head appeared around the door. 'About ready to lock up,' he explained. 'Want your car fetched?'

'I'll probably walk.' Cafferty checked one final time that the safe was locked, remembering for a moment another safe a long time back, one whose contents he had been keen to examine.

'Want me to tell Shug to hang around?'

'I'm not an invalid — I don't need a fucking carer!'

The manager's head disappeared again, the door closing. Cafferty had scared him. Cafferty could always scare him. And he liked that.

★ ★ ★

Rebus's eyes were stinging, reminding him of the days when he'd smoked, a stray puff catching him unawares. No smoking tonight, though, just too much time spent on the Meikle files. A desk lamp would have helped, but he didn't have one. He'd had the same CD on repeat, Van Morrison's *Moondance*, the volume turned down low. When he got up to switch it off, he felt his vertebrae click. Placed his fists either side of his spine and pushed. More clicks.

'Like a shagged-out record, John,' he told

himself. He'd allowed himself two beers, in between half a packet of gum. He had half a mind to call Deborah Quant for a chat, but it was gone midnight and she would be asleep. Peering from his window, he saw that a couple of flats opposite his still had their lights on; students probably. Marchmont had always been a student area, even back in the mists of time when his wife Rhona had persuaded him to buy there. She'd been a teacher and her feeling was that being around so many students would 'keep us young'.

Aye, right.

Not that he would have said that — not then. Or maybe he would; it was hard to remember the person he'd been, new to the city and new to the job.

He turned from the window and looked at the paperwork piled high on his dining table. He'd made pages of notes, each word capitalised so he'd be able to read it. His handwriting these days was a mess. But he knew the Meikle case now, knew it probably as well as anyone on Siobhan Clarke's original team. His phone had pinged earlier with a text from Dallas Meikle. Word had been got to Ellis that there was a visitor coming. A good night's sleep was now required; not that Rebus would get it. His mind was revved up as a result of all the reading. It would take more than another play of *Moondance* to switch off the motor. Meaning he might as well sit down at the table again for one last read-through. It was either that or wake up Brillo for an unneeded walk.

267

Switching from *Moondance* to *Solid Air*, Rebus went back to work.

Tuesday

28

At 11 a.m. on Tuesday, Emily Crowther phoned Clarke from Poretoun House. She was there with the scene-of-crime team, watching as they went about their business.

'You won't believe it,' she told Clarke. 'I'll send you a couple of pics, hang on . . .'

The line went dead and Clarke waited. She was in the MIT office, seated at her desk, on which sat a putter, nine iron, two tees and two golf balls. They'd been waiting for her that morning, a gift from Graham Sutherland. Across the room, the list Derek Shankley had helped compile was being gone through name by name, phone calls made, interviews arranged. Within a few seconds her phone pinged, alerting her to the photos. There were three of them. The SOCOs in their white overalls were taking the place apart, floor-boards removed, plaster scraped from the walls for analysis. Brand had insisted on being in attendance. In one photograph he had his own camera out, leaning down as Haj Atwal studied a section of floorboard. Clarke called Crowther.

'It's almost like he's enjoying it,' she commented. 'But have they found anything?'

'Not as far as I know. With a civilian in the room, Haj is being tight-lipped. What time do we leave for Glasgow?'

'Let's wait till after the rush hour. Six thirty should do it.'

'Might not be finished here by then. There are about twenty rooms covering three floors. The house is shagged but gorgeous. Why do you think he's letting us rip it up?'

'Because it's not really a house. It's two fingers raised in Jackie Ness's direction.'

'So the photos . . . ?'

'Doubtless winging their way to Ness as we speak.'

'Speaking of whom, any progress?'

'The car is being searched again, just in case we missed something.' Clarke saw that Graham Sutherland was getting to his feet. He was approaching the TV, seeking the remote so he could turn up the volume. 'Emily, I'm going to have to go . . . ' She ended the call. Sutherland was blocking her view of the screen. The volume was audible by the time she reached his side. The reporter was standing on the edge of Poretoun Woods.

'And after the questioning of film producer Jackie Ness and this morning's renewed search of his old home just the other side of these woods behind me, now comes the revelation that the victim, private investigator Stuart Bloom, was handcuffed at the ankles inside his recovered Volkswagen Polo. This was reported only moments ago by an internet-based news agency and has yet to be verified by ourselves, though police have made no denial.'

Sutherland made eye contact with Clarke. 'Because we've not been asked,' he growled.

'Press office should have warned us,' Clarke said. 'They must surely have known.'

272

Sutherland held out a hand towards her. 'Pass me that nine iron, would you? I want to put it through this bloody screen.'

Mobile phones had started ringing: her own and Sutherland's, plus the landlines not currently being used by Reid and Gamble. Tess Leighton appeared in the doorway, her own mobile pressed to her ear. Clarke nodded, then gestured towards the TV. Sutherland was muting the sound again. Fox had joined Leighton in the doorway. He raised an eyebrow in Clarke's direction: managed to blag one more day, he seemed to be telling her.

'Okay, people,' Sutherland intoned, 'we knew this moment would come. There's a press conference due this afternoon anyway, so we can deal with all the questions then. Or let DCS Mollison deal with them, at any rate . . . '

As if summoned by Sutherland's words, leather shoes could be heard climbing the stairs, Mollison's head appearing at the top. He strode into the room, face thunderous.

'We're just hearing it for ourselves right now, sir,' Sutherland said, raising a hand in apology.

'The family will be up to high doh,' Mollison snapped. 'As if they didn't have enough ammo against us as it is!'

And sure enough, the TV had switched from Poretoun Woods to Fettes HQ, Catherine Bloom positioned on the pavement just outside the gates, behind which stood a stern-looking uniformed officer, as if fearing invasion. As the camera moved position, Dougal Kelly sidled into view at Catherine's shoulder. Sutherland pressed the volume button again.

'We've always known,' Stuart Bloom's mother was saying, her voice trembling with emotion, 'that the police acted irresponsibly, lazily and almost certainly corruptly, protecting those who have against those who have not, and looking down on Stuart's family and circle of friends.' She paused for breath. If Clarke hadn't known better, she'd have said the woman had had media training. Then again, with Dougal Kelly in her corner, maybe she had. 'But now,' Catherine Bloom continued, 'we have evidence of potential involvement by the police in the crime itself and not just the cover-up. There needs to be an inquiry into the handling of this case, carried out by a police force from outside Scotland, and questions need to be asked at the highest level of government about what was known, what was brushed under the carpet, and *who* knew what.' She focused her gaze on the camera lens, speaking directly to the viewer. 'My son's callous murder must not have been in vain. I want justice; I want change; I want the guilty to be named, shamed and put behind bars — each and every one of them!'

The interview ended, cutting back to the studio and a visibly shaken newsreader. Sutherland cut the sound once more, hardly daring to meet Mollison's eyes.

'We need a chat in private,' Mollison said solemnly. Sutherland nodded and sought out Tess Leighton.

'Our room's at your disposal,' she quickly agreed. Sutherland led the way, Mollison at his heels. The office was quiet for a few moments, until George Gamble whistled softly.

'What happens now?' Phil Yeats asked.

'In public, not much,' Clarke guessed. 'Plenty of private bollockings, I dare say, and maybe additional staff and resources for us. But we still have a murder to solve, and stringing us up isn't going to help with that.'

'But everyone will expect us to focus on the investigating officers from the time.'

'And we're doing that anyway, aren't we?'

'What if we give the press Ness's fingerprint? Would that take the heat off?'

'The handcuffs are still handcuffs. We need to know how the hell they got there and whose they were to begin with.' Clarke ran a hand through her hair.

'It keeps getting messier, doesn't it?' Callum Reid asked. He was straightening his tie, as if in readiness — Sutherland dismissed to the changing room, him promoted to captain. Clarke gave him a stern look.

'I've survived messier,' she told him. 'This has a way to go yet.' More texts had started arriving on her phone. There was one from Laura Smith, so she opened it.

Buy you a bite? Usual spot 12.30?

Clarke tapped a one-word reply: *Fine.*

* * *

The café was on Leith Walk, almost equidistant between Leith and Gayfield Square police stations. It was run by an Italian family and specialised in toasted sandwiches so overfilled no one could finish them. The booths were cramped and the music cheesy. Clarke squeezed in across from Laura Smith and stared at the third member of their party.

'I've known Dougal a while,' Smith explained. 'We worked a night desk together some years back.'

Clarke gave Dougal Kelly a tight smile. 'Could you give us a minute? Maybe fetch a jug of water?'

He waited until Smith had nodded her agreement before heading for the counter.

'The handcuffs?' Clarke said quietly.

'I told you I'd give you a day or two. It was out there, Siobhan. Too many tongues had started wagging on your side of the fence.'

'How well do you really know this guy?' Clarke was staring at Kelly's back.

'The book he's writing won't be published till next year. And he definitely protects his sources.'

'He knows about the run-in we had with ACU?'

Smith nodded.

'And you brought him with you today because . . . ?'

'Just listen to what he has to say, okay?'

Kelly was returning with the pitcher and three glasses. 'All right if I sit down?' he asked. Clarke nodded, without managing to look welcoming. The owner was fetching his notepad. They ordered and he left, yelling instructions in the direction of the kitchen.

'Shouldn't you be stuck like glue to the

276

grieving mother?' Clarke asked Kelly.

'She's back in the hotel bedroom, digesting the news.'

'We still don't know where the cuffs came from,' Clarke stressed. Kelly just shrugged.

'One more piece of the jigsaw,' he commented. 'You have to admit, there's a picture emerging.'

'Unlike some, I don't jump to conclusions.' Clarke took a sip of water while Kelly sighed, gripping the rim of the table with both hands.

'I'll just say what I have to say, okay? The officers involved in the original inquiry — people like John Rebus, Mary Skelton, Douglas Newsome — they all fell down on the job. More than that; in some cases they broke the very laws they were honour-bound to uphold. I've got information on every single one of them.'

'Including a couple of uniforms called Steele and Edwards?'

Kelly couldn't meet her eyes. 'Not so much, no.'

Clarke gave a snort. 'That's because they're your source for all of this, yes? Happy to land everyone else in it just so long as they're protected?'

'I'm not saying they're whiter than white.'

'Trust me, that would be a tough sell around this table.'

'But Rawlston with his lazy assumption that there had to be a gay angle; Skelton bunking off half the time; Newsome altering statements; Rebus doing favours for Derek Shankley . . . ' He paused. 'You've not even started interviewing them, have you?'

'In Mary Skelton's case, that would require a spiritualist,' Clarke replied icily. 'In point of fact, we've already spoken with Rawlston and Rebus. And I'm sure Laura's let you know we've had a visit from Derek Shankley and his father, too. So if you're looking for evidence of sloppy policing or a cover-up, you need to try harder. And while you're doing that, we'll be doing our job, despite all the grief we're getting.'

'Can you really blame the family, after the way they've been treated?'

'All I know is, everyone on the team in Leith is working their damnedest, and media attention just gets in the way.'

'Catherine's hurting — her and Martin both.' Kelly paused and sighed. 'You know, all the time he was missing, they never once considered having Stuart declared dead. There was always that sliver of hope. For a while, Martin started drinking. He managed to kick it, but it nearly ended the marriage.'

'This'll all be going in your book, will it?'

'The family decide what goes in.'

'So it might not be the full story.' Clarke nodded to herself. 'Just another version.' She began to manoeuvre her way out of the booth and tossed a ten-pound note on to the tabletop. 'That should cover mine. Don't seem to have any appetite.'

'The Blooms could be useful to you, you know,' Kelly was saying. 'They have the ear of the media. Someone out there knows who killed Stuart and why. The longer this plays on TV and elsewhere, the more it might get to them.'

Clarke ignored him, waved an apology towards the frowning proprietor and yanked open the door. She was halfway across the pavement when Laura Smith emerged, clattering towards her on wedge heels.

'Siobhan . . .'

Clarke paused and waited. Smith glanced back at the window, where Kelly was watching.

'Sorry,' she said. 'I thought I was helping.'

'Me or him?'

The journalist tried for a look suggesting penitence. 'Let me make it up to you.'

'I'm listening.'

'A heads-up on a story we're running in the morning. It's about Sir Adrian Brand.'

'Yes?'

'You're out at Poretoun House, aren't you? Ripping the place apart from what I hear.'

'What's the story, Laura?'

'Just that Sir Adrian is friends with DCS Mollison. We've got pics of them at charity galas and out on the golf course.'

'So?' Clarke managed not to show that her heart had sunk a little. 'Have you asked DCS Mollison for a quote?'

'He's been hard to get hold of.'

'Since news of the handcuffs broke? Wonder why that could be, Laura.'

Smith scowled at Clarke's sarcasm. 'I'm a reporter, Siobhan. This is my job.'

'And did you find the story all on your own, or did you have a bit of help?' Clarke looked towards the window. Kelly was dabbing at his phone with both thumbs. 'He wants a friend inside MIT, and can give you something in return if you make an introduction?'

'A story's a story.'

'Not when it's being skewed. A game of golf? A charity night? Whoopee-fucking-do, Laura. You know as well as I do, it says everything and nothing, but that won't stop the conspiracy theorists lapping it up, especially when you add as a last line that DCS Mollison could not be reached for comment.'

'I couldn't get to him, but you can.'

Clarke raised both eyebrows. 'So you want me to do your job for you? Get him to talk to you? Dream on, sister.' She spun away and unlocked her car. She had already started the engine when Smith's fingernails tapped at the window. Clarke lowered it and Smith leaned in so they were face to face.

'Know how few of us are left out here in the wild, Siobhan? Journalists like me, we're an endangered species. It's all bloggers and social justice warriors and gossip hounds. How many of them can you put a name to? Maybe you better start trying, because soon they're going to be all that's left.'

Clarke watched her turn and head back inside, where her overfilled sandwich was waiting. Kelly had picked his up and was wondering where to start. Smith sat across from him. He spoke, she listened, then they both turned in Clarke's direction. She fixed her gaze on the windscreen in front of her and signalled to join the stream of traffic, ignoring the blaring horn of the taxi behind her.

29

Rebus hadn't been inside Saughton for a few years. His phone was confiscated and he had to go through an airport-style scanner. They even swabbed him to check for drugs. He explained about the inhaler and they asked upstairs before allowing him to hang on to it. And then he was in. The visitors' room was large and poorly heated, the tables busy with family members. Rebus was led towards Ellis Meikle. The young man sat rigid as a statue, jaw clenched, eyes fixed to the whitewashed stone wall over Rebus's shoulder after Rebus had seated himself on the red moulded-plastic chair.

'Thanks for seeing me,' he said.

'Thank Uncle Dallas,' Meikle muttered.

'You know why I'm here?'

'No.'

'Your uncle sort of asked me to take a look at the case. He says you shouldn't be in here.'

Meikle's eyes met Rebus's. 'They've got me in with the sex cases,' he stated. 'Say it's for my own protection.'

'They may be right. Won't have escaped your attention that this place is a jungle. Survival of the fittest and all that. Sex cases tend to be quieter, better-mannered.'

'I can look after myself.'

'Helps that you're a killer,' Rebus agreed. 'Killers always get a bit more respect.'

'I'm not a sex case, though. I shouldn't be in with them — it's embarrassing.'

'I can try to have a word . . . ' Rebus had been studying the young man. He was not yet quite an adult, his face a combination of the kid he had been and the man he was becoming. He still probably only needed a shave twice a week or so. He had defined cheekbones and thin shoulders, his prison-issue sweatshirt a size or two too large. He clasped his hands, pressing them across the top of his head, elbows jutting.

'Tell Uncle Dallas I did it. He knows I did.'

'If that's your story, there's not much anyone can do.' Rebus shrugged as if it meant very little to him one way or the other. 'But you know yourself that there are still questions and loose ends. The one thing that mystifies me is why you did it in the first place. Wasn't Kristen the love of your life?'

'What do you think?'

'I've seen the trial reports. She comes over like Princess Diana.' Rebus paused. 'Sorry, that's way before your time.'

'I know who you're talking about. Kristen wasn't exactly a princess, though.'

'No?'

Meikle shook his head slowly. Rebus waited, but no more words came.

'You finding your feet okay?' he enquired.

'Workshops and stuff, they keep us as busy as they can.'

'Not enough warders though; hours spent in your cell?'

The young man nodded again, slowly lowering

282

his arms and folding them.

'Do you see your mum and sister?'

'Once a week.'

'They doing okay?'

'What do you think?'

Rebus folded his own arms. An old trick. Copy the actions of the person opposite and they might begin to sense similarities rather than differences.

'You got kids?' Meikle asked into the silence.

'Grown-up daughter. I'm a grandad these days. Do you see your dad?'

'Not got a lot to say to him.'

'I hear you two used to like a bit of a dust-up.'

'Now and again,' the young man conceded.

'I'd have thought taking you to watch Hearts would have been punishment enough.'

This elicited a thin smile. 'You a Hibbie?'

'I'm agnostic.'

'What does that mean?'

'I try not to take sides.'

'So are you a cop or what?'

'Used to be. Retired now.'

'How do you know Uncle Dallas?'

'I'm not sure I really do. We're both ex-army, so there's that in common if nothing else. I've not met your dad yet, or your sister.'

'They've got fuck all to do with this!' Meikle's voice had risen a notch, his throat tightening.

'Easy, son,' Rebus cautioned. One of the warders was moving in their direction. Rebus waved him away. Ellis Meikle angled his body forward, elbows on the table. Rebus did the same.

'What's done is done,' Meikle said hoarsely.

'That why you were okay with me visiting?'

'Nobody can change what happened. I'm in here and that's all there is to it. Best you go tell Dallas that.'

'You wouldn't rather be outside, though? There might be something that could help you, something you've not told anyone. Mitigating factors, we call them.'

'Lawyer said the same thing — didn't do any good.'

'Keeping your mouth shut didn't exactly help your case, Ellis. Did something happen that day at home? Something that got your dander up, kept you seething all the way to the golf course? Did Kristen tell you something? Or your mum or Uncle Dallas? Had to be to your face — your phone was checked and there was nothing there. But this Jekyll and Hyde thing sometimes happens; a person's fine until they're not. Something changes them, and they go and do something, and then they're back to normal again.'

'Normal? You don't know us at all, do you?'

'Your family, you mean?' Rebus shook his head. 'I've talked to some of your mates, though, and they all gave me pretty much the same answer.'

'What?'

'She made you do it.'

'Kristen?'

Rebus nodded, maintaining eye contact. 'The not-quite-princess we didn't hear about at the trial.'

284

'I heard they made a shrine for her. Have you seen it?'

'At the bunker?' Rebus nodded again.

'It's still there after all these months . . . ' The young man nodded to himself. 'That's who she is then. It's all over the net so it must be true.'

'Plenty of shite on the internet, Ellis. I hardly ever use it and even I know that.' Rebus paused. 'Just do one thing for me — look me in the eye and tell me you did it.'

Meikle focused on him, unblinking. 'I did it,' he said.

Rebus found himself nodding once more, and puckering his lips as he did so.

'I think you're lying,' he commented.

'I stabbed her in the neck. She bled out on to the sand, her knees going from under her.'

'Then tell me why.'

Meikle blinked twice. 'What else was I going to do?' he said, rising to his feet as the warder appeared behind him.

'Time's up,' the warder announced.

Rebus got up from the table, watching as Ellis Meikle was led away. *What else was I going to do?* What the hell did that mean? The other visitors were saying their goodbyes to loved ones. As the prisoners headed one way, the visitors were escorted back down the corridor. A warder was waiting halfway, resting against a door. He stopped Rebus with a gesture.

'Got a minute?' he asked. Rebus watched as the corridor emptied.

'What's up?'

'Someone wants a word.' The warder pulled

open the door and Rebus stepped inside the prison library, a small room with half-filled shelves of well-used books. The door closed behind him, the warder staying outside. Rebus didn't see anyone at first. There was no one behind the desk. But then he heard a noise and half turned as a familiar face appeared from behind a stack. Darryl Christie had changed since his trial, his face puffy, skin sallow and with an unhealthy sheen to it. Warders as well as prisoners took on the same complexion eventually. A prison tan, it was called.

'Mr Rebus,' Christie said, holding out a hand for Rebus to shake.

'Thought you were in Barlinnie, Darryl.'

'They moved me. Closer to my family here. I can still pull a string or two when I want.'

'That how you knew I was here?'

Christie just smiled. 'Keeping out of mischief yourself?'

'Just barely.'

'I've been reading about the Bloom case. Going to be a few spankings there, eh?'

'You're well informed.'

Christie stretched his arms wide. 'The university of life.'

Rebus glanced towards the door. It remained closed. 'You seem to have made friends.'

'A few quid here and there keeps people sweet. So what brings you to this neck of the swamp?'

'Just visiting someone.'

'Ellis Meikle.'

'That's right.'

'Why, though?'

'I'm a friend of the family.'

'No you're not.'

'His uncle Dallas and me were in the army together.'

'Dallas Meikle? You're old enough to be his dad. Want to try spinning me another?'

Rebus thought for a moment. 'They've got him in with the sex offenders — would you be able to pull a string or two there?'

'I might.'

'Or keep an eye on the lad at least, make sure trouble doesn't find him?'

Christie took his time answering, pulling a book from a shelf and studying its jacket before returning it.

'Answer me this first — is Cafferty your bestie or your enemy?'

The scene played out suddenly in Rebus's memory: Cafferty's flat; Christie with a gun pointed at Rebus's face; knocked cold by the hammer Cafferty swung at him.

'He tried visiting you,' Rebus answered.

'To rub it in my face. He goes to *my* club every night, sits in *my* chair, orders *my* people around.' Christie's anger was growing, his whole body tensing. Rebus had shuffled back a few steps so he was close to the door. Christie had noticed.

'I'm not going to do anything to *you!* It's him I want.' He gestured towards a computer behind the reception desk. 'They let me use it for research. I know as much about Morris Gerald Cafferty as anyone — except maybe you, John. So tell me what I need to know — are you two bosom buddies or what?'

'I'd stick him in here if I could.'

Christie stabbed a finger in Rebus's direction, eyes glowing. 'You promise that? On your daughter's life?'

'You taking anything, Darryl?'

Christie snorted. 'Everyone in here's taking something. It's almost as rife as Barlinnie. The only thing you'll see more of than drugs is wagging tongues. Not much else to do but gossip. Plenty old-timers who've had dealings with Cafferty down the years. I maybe know things you don't.' He paused to lick his lips. 'Your lot have stopped targeting him, haven't they? No investigations, surveillance, phone taps? Nobody's paying a blind bit of attention, because Police Scotland has become one giant fucking psychiatric case.'

'DI Fox works at Gartcosh. I can ask him if Cafferty's being — '

'I'm telling you, Cafferty's been let off the hook. He's running the drugs, the brothels, the fences, the illegal immigrants. He's taking a cut from everyone and everywhere and nobody's doing anything to stop him.'

Rebus saw it in Christie's sunken eyes: Cafferty had become an obsession, an infatuation, almost to the point of madness.

'I'm out of the game, Darryl,' he reasoned. 'If you want Police Scotland to target Cafferty, give them what you've got.'

Christie shook his head. There was sweat beading on his forehead and he wiped it away. 'There's not enough — not in the here and now.

But then along comes Stuart Bloom . . . '

Rebus stared at him. 'You can tie Cafferty to Bloom?'

'There was a guy in here, one-time safe-breaker. Past it now, of course. He's back outside. Used to do jobs for Cafferty from the eighties on, was still with him in 2006. He knows a lot of what Cafferty was up to back then.' Christie was nodding to himself, eyes never leaving Rebus. 'You knew Cafferty then too, John — Larry mentioned you once or twice to people. Larry Huston. Name mean anything?'

'I think I remember it.'

'Get Larry to tell you what he knows.'

'Why don't I just hear it from you?'

Christie seemed to admit the reasonableness of this. 'Huston was out of here before I arrived, so it's all second- and third-hand — that's why it's better for him to tell you.' He took a step forward, then another, leaning in so his mouth was close to Rebus's ear. Rebus caught a blast of halitosis when he spoke.

'They're looking at pinning Bloom on you and yours. Wouldn't it be better all round if Cafferty took the fall?'

His fist passed Rebus's head and thumped once on the door. It opened immediately, the same warder standing there.

'Thanks, Bobby,' Christie said.

'No problem, Darryl.' Then, to Rebus: 'Let's go get you your phone.'

289

30

The team watched the press conference on the monitor in the MIT office. Mollison looked and sounded the part, parrying questions with professional aplomb while Graham Sutherland sat next to him, wriggling and twitching as if he would never get comfortable. When the cameras cut to the press pack, Clarke saw that Dougal Kelly had been allowed in and was seated next to Laura Smith, both of them recording the audio on their phones. More than one journalist wanted to know if the handcuffs were standard police issue and whether there were identifiers on them. Others asked about the questioning of Jackie Ness and the forensic team at Poretoun House. Mollison managed not to give much away while sounding as if he were being frank and open.

'It's a definite skill,' George Gamble commented.

'That's why he earns the big bucks,' Callum Reid added. Reid was watching like an avid student in a lecture theatre, Mollison the professor he wanted one day to become. Clarke shuffled further back to where Malcolm Fox was standing, at his favoured spot just by the door.

'I hear you took my advice,' she said in an undertone.

'Dinner with Tess, you mean?' He watched her nod. 'How did you know?'

'Word got around. So how did it go?'

'It was fine.'

'Did you happen to mention she was on the bench till I turned you down?' She saw his look and shook her head. 'Your secret's safe with me. But tell me, was it just dinner, or did things . . . ?'

'Just dinner,' Fox stated, giving her another look.

'You'll miss her when you're sent back to Gartcosh — any news on that front?'

'No.'

They watched as the press conference began to wind down. The media liaison office got busy handing out briefing notes, but there was sudden movement, Dougal Kelly confronting Sutherland and Mollison, phone held out in front of him like a microphone.

'You wouldn't take my question but I'm asking it anyway,' Kelly was shouting. 'Is it true that a fingerprint on the handcuffs has been identified as belonging to Jackie Ness? Why has this information been withheld from the family?'

'We're not at liberty to discuss — '

Mollison's words were drowned out by a barrage of questions from the room. Was that why Ness had been brought in for questioning and why his former home was being examined by a forensic team? Mollison's face had turned crimson, a mix of rage and embarrassment. He was waving away the questions with one hand and guiding Sutherland towards the exit with the other. The journalists were asking Kelly for more details, their recording devices thrust in his

291

direction. Was he sure? How did he know? Tess Leighton had turned away from the monitor and was making for Fox and Clarke.

'It was all going so well,' she commented.

'Mollison's going to be raging,' Fox added.

'With Graham bearing the brunt of it.'

'I dare say he'll share it around when he gets back.'

'Or before,' Callum Reid said, answering his phone. 'Yes, we saw,' he told Sutherland. 'All of us, yes.' He listened for a moment. 'We're wondering that ourselves. Should we pull Kelly in and ask him?' He listened again, shaking his head for the benefit of the room. 'You're right, probably wouldn't play well. But does that mean we shouldn't do it?' Another shake of the head. 'So when the phones start ringing, what do we say? 'Not a bloody thing',' he quoted, eyes on Clarke. 'Understood.' Clarke's own phone vibrated. An incoming text from Laura Smith: *I had no idea.* Well, of course. Kelly hadn't got the info from Laura. It had to be Steele and Edwards again. But could she say as much without it sounding as if she just wanted them stitched up?

Reid's call with Sutherland had finished. 'Ten minutes he'll be here,' he said.

'What should we do about Ness?' Fox enquired.

'How do you mean?'

'Press are going to be all over him again.'

'Not forgetting the Bloom family,' Leighton added. 'He's got a lot of grief coming his way.'

'Might be easier all round for him just to

292

confess,' George Gamble said from behind his desk while cracking his knuckles.

'Is protective custody an option?' Leighton asked. Callum Reid offered a shrug.

'Boss's decision rather than ours. I'd say he's going to have something else at the forefront of his mind, though.'

'Who leaked,' Fox said with a slow nod.

'Who leaked,' Callum Reid agreed.

★ ★ ★

There was still colour in Graham Sutherland's cheeks when he entered the office. His team waited in silence for him to speak. He eased himself on to the corner of his desk and folded his arms.

'Mollison is rightly furious. That was a hijacking, pure and simple. But like the best stunts, it got a result. That doesn't mean anything's changed. We still have plenty of work to do and that's what we need to focus on. Siobhan, you've got Glasgow this evening, yes?' He watched as she nodded. 'And you're taking Emily?'

'Once she's finished at Poretoun House, yes.'

'I dare say she'll have to barge her way through a few TV crews. Meantime, the line we're putting out is that enquiries are ongoing. No need to explain to the media that the fiscal doesn't reckon the fingerprint evidence will fly in court. Mrs Bloom wants a meeting with the chief constable. Mollison is what she'll get and he'll tell her as little as he can. The reporters will be champing at the bit, but again, that's not going to bother us unduly.' He paused for effect. 'What does bother *me* is that this was leaked in the first place. I know leaks can come from anywhere and plenty of people can be bought cheaply. I just hope to hell nobody points the finger our way.' His eyes met those of each of his team in turn, Fox included. 'And if they do, I trust I can say with hand on heart that I have every confidence in my officers.'

Having said his piece, he looked suddenly weary. Raising himself up, he rounded the desk and sat down.

'Mollison's going to be reporting directly to the chief. I doubt we'll be replaced — inquiry's too far along the tracks — but he raised it as a possibility, so I'm letting you know. Any questions?'

Fox cleared his throat. 'What do we do about Jackie Ness?'

Sutherland stared back at Fox. 'Jackie Ness?' he said. 'Quite frankly, Malcolm, and I say this with all sincerity — fuck him.'

31

The meeting was scheduled for a wine bar called the Savannah, off Sauchiehall Street. Clarke and Crowther arrived early — lighter traffic on the M8 than they'd feared, and the sat nav had proved equal to Glasgow's one-way system — and ordered food.

'What's quickest?' had been Clarke's question to their server. The answer had been Glasgow tapas. The large wooden platter took up half the table: haggis balls, potato wedges with tomato dip, gobbets of crusty bread, and miniature glazed sausages. They didn't talk much while they ate. On the drive west, Crowther had filled Clarke in on the search of Poretoun House. She'd arrived back in Leith just before five, the SOCOs having finished for the day at four. Attic and basement levels still to do.

'He seemed almost gleeful,' she had said, showing Clarke more photos on her phone of the search and Sir Adrian Brand.

'Was Glenn Hazard with him?'

'For about half an hour, mostly spent making calls and checking messages. Low boredom threshold, I think. He kept pestering me with questions about Jackie Ness.'

'You going back tomorrow?'

'Think I need to?'

'It's Graham's call. Maybe you could swap with Phil.'

It had then been Clarke's turn to give an update on the aftermath of the news conference. The press were camped outside Ness's home and office, but the man himself had wisely gone to ground.

'What about the family?'

'Madam Bloom's all over the news. Social media is a feeding frenzy.'

'We should charge Ness, don't you think?'

Clarke offered a shrug. 'Graham's having another word with the fiscal while the lab are trying to see if they can isolate any more partials on the cuffs.'

'And all while we ask ourselves the same question — who was it spilled the beans to Dougal Kelly?'

Clarke nodded without saying anything. Their plates had been cleared by the time the two men arrived. They looked around, spotted Clarke and Crowther and wandered over.

'I'm Joe Madden,' the taller of the two said.

'Colin Speke,' his companion added. Clarke and Crowther introduced themselves. Madden and Speke pulled out chairs and got comfortable. The bar was midweek quiet and Clarke had showed her ID when asking for the music to be turned down. Madden and Speke took off their identical quilted jackets.

'You know one another quite well?' Clarke asked.

'Aye, we've worked together a slew of times,' Madden said in a local accent.

'Live not too far apart either,' Speke added. 'So I offered Joe a lift here.'

'Explains why you walked in together,' Clarke said with a nod. Speke ordered an espresso and Madden a glass of red wine, Clarke and Crowther sticking to tap water.

'How was the holiday?' Clarke asked Speke.

'Fine, aye. My partner likes the heat; I go crispy after an hour.' He tugged up one sleeve of his jumper to show a reddened arm speckled with freckles.

'And Italy?' Clarke asked Madden.

'Sunshine can be a curse when you're filming,' he informed her. 'Getting the lighting right is a nightmare, and that's before the presenter starts squinting.'

'Well, we appreciate you taking the time to see us.'

'It's only taken you twelve years,' Speke said with a smile.

'Any reason you didn't come forward of your own volition?'

'To tell you what exactly?' Madden interrupted. 'That Stuart Bloom was an extra on a zombie film?'

Clarke sat back, mouth closed, running her tongue along her teeth.

Speke looked to his friend. 'The inspector here knows better, Joe.'

Madden's eyes were on Clarke. 'Well maybe if she tells us *what* it is she knows . . . '

The silence lay between them as the drinks order arrived. Madden's eyes stayed fixed on Clarke's throughout.

'I think we need to do this properly,' Emily Crowther interrupted, earning a slow nod of

297

agreement from Clarke.

'Meaning what?' Speke asked, the slightest of tremors appearing in his voice. He had started to lift his espresso cup but placed it back in its saucer untouched.

'Interview room at Leith police station, Edinburgh,' Clarke informed him. 'Questioned separately so we can make sure your versions add up. See, you've had a bit of time to think this over. Tonight you probably put your heads together for an hour or so, deciding how little you could get away with telling us. That wasn't terribly wise, as you're finding out. So: do we start again from the beginning, or do we have a patrol car take you to Edinburgh? Plenty cameras waiting for you there, Mr Madden, and you'll be the one squinting as you're led past them into the station.'

Clarke sat back and waited. Eventually Madden smiled.

'Can't blame us for trying, can you? Nobody wants mixed up in a murder.'

'That's not what it was, though. Stuart Bloom was a missing person in 2006. You knew him yet you didn't come forward.'

'We were waiting for the phone to ring,' Speke blurted out. 'You're right, we knew Stuart. We reckoned you'd be coming to talk to us.'

'But you never did,' Madden added. 'And the longer we waited, the more we wondered why not. If you'd found any mention of us, you'd have picked up the phone or knocked on our door. Reason that didn't happen was Stuart hadn't kept any record of us. Why? Because he was meticulous that way.' Madden tapped his forehead. 'He kept pretty much everything up here. That way, there was nothing for anyone to find if they came snooping — I don't mean the police, but people he was investigating. If they got wind of what he was up to, and sent their own investigator along for a nosy, or tried bugging his phone or getting into his computer . . . ' He tapped his forehead again, then raised his glass to his lips and sipped.

'We were scared,' Speke broke in.

'Not scared, Colin,' Madden corrected him. 'Just cautious.'

'So when he vanished, what did you think?' Clarke asked.

'That maybe someone had put the frighteners on him,' Madden speculated.

'There were dozens of possibilities,' Speke added. 'We heard the same rumours as everyone else.'

'Even wondered about the boyfriend,' Madden agreed. 'Say he'd killed him, maybe in a jealous rage. Well . . . son of a cop, his dad would have had a way of getting rid of the evidence.'

'And tonight,' Speke said, 'they're saying Stuart was handcuffed.'

'But with the only verifiable print that of Jackie Ness,' Clarke felt it necessary to qualify.

'I dare say your lot know how to make that happen, eh?' Madden drained his glass and smacked his lips, signalling towards the bar for a refill.

'You have a pretty jaundiced view of us,' Crowther stated. Madden looked towards Speke.

'Tell them.'

Speke shook his head furiously. Madden turned his attention back to the two detectives. 'Colin here used to go to Rogues. He saw exactly how jaundiced your lot are.'

Clarke was studying Speke. 'You're gay, Mr Speke?'

'I keep telling him that things have changed,' Madden continued, 'but he's still got one foot in the closet.' Speke had lifted the espresso cup and was trying to hide behind it. 'I blame the parents myself.'

'For what?' Clarke enquired.

'Dying before Colin could pluck up the courage to tell them.' He saw the look Crowther was giving him. 'Hetero as they come,' he told her, patting his chest with a palm.

'Were you at Rogues any of the times it was busted?' Clarke asked Speke. He shook his head and took a deep breath.

'Stuart always seemed to know in advance. He'd warn me off.'

'How do you think he knew?'

'I thought Derek was probably telling him.'

'And how did Derek know?'

'Well . . . ' Speke shrugged. 'His dad, no?'

'I wasn't so sure about that,' Madden offered. 'The guy who owned Rogues . . . ' He looked to his friend.

'Ralph Hanratty,' Speke obliged.

'I reckoned he had a cop or two in his pocket and they'd tip him the wink.'

Crowther and Clarke shared a look. They were trying to remember if Hanratty's name was on the list Derek Shankley had helped compile.

When Crowther slid her phone from her pocket, Clarke knew she'd be texting Phil Yeats.

'Can we move on,' Clarke said, 'to a few questions about your involvement in Stuart Bloom's business?'

Madden's fresh glass had arrived. He took a slurp. 'Is this because you don't like us asking you about cops in people's pockets and faking fingerprint evidence?'

'It's the reason we're having this meeting, Mr Madden,' Clarke corrected him. 'We've been told that you advised him in regard to surveillance techniques — '

'That's a bit of a stretch,' Colin Speke interrupted. 'Stuart just wanted to know what gear we used in certain situations.'

'He actually knew almost as much as we did,' Madden added.

'So you never went out with him on a job?'

'Maybe once or twice.'

Clarke looked at Madden. 'Go on,' she prompted him.

'Are we going to be in trouble?'

'Did you break the law?'

'I don't know.'

'Me neither, till I hear what you've got to say.'

Madden glanced at his friend, who put up no objection. He swallowed another mouthful of wine, almost finishing the glass; Clarke was beginning to wonder if he had a problem.

'We went out with him a few times so he could test bits and pieces of kit. A night-vision scope; special camera lenses; a few long-range mics.'

'Any location in particular?'

301

'There was a house in Murrayfield . . . '

'Owned by Sir Adrian Brand?' Clarke guessed. 'Surrounded by a high wall.'

Madden was nodding. 'That was the thing. Stuart was sure there'd be motion sensors that would floodlight the grounds, so the wall was as close as we could get. But that was only thirty feet or so from the back of the house.'

'With a clear view of the garden room?'

'You know the place?' Madden watched as Clarke nodded.

Speke cleared his throat. 'Stuart wanted to know about bugs, too, but I couldn't help him with that. He went to the internet instead, I think.'

'He bugged Brand's house?'

'House and office both was the plan.'

'Never carried out?'

Speke looked to Madden, who shrugged.

'How about computer hacking?' Clarke asked.

'Again, Stuart was a lot savvier than us.'

'But you knew he was hacking into Brand's computer?'

'I don't think he'd had any success. The tech wasn't as readily available. There was some software he needed but couldn't get his hands on.'

'Any other jaunts apart from Murrayfield?'

'Just Poretoun House.'

Clarke stared at Speke. 'Why there?' Speke shrugged and turned to Madden.

'I'm not sure Stuart trusted Jackie Ness,' Madden answered. 'With good cause, too — the man had tried stiffing us for money we were

302

owed; he did it to everybody if he thought he stood half a chance of getting away with it.'

'Was it the same procedure as Murrayfield?'

'Night vision; long-range mic,' Madden confirmed.

'What about bugs and computer hacking?'

'Of Jackie Ness?' Madden pondered this. 'Stuart never said anything.'

'Could money have become an issue between Stuart and his employer?' Clarke asked, receiving shrugs from both men in response.

'These little surveillance trips,' Crowther interrupted, having sent her text, 'did they throw up anything?'

This time the two men shook their heads simultaneously.

'You've wrung every last drop from us,' Madden said, draining his glass and waving it towards the bar.

Clarke handed over a business card to either man. 'We may have some follow-up questions. Any more foreign trips planned?'

They shook their heads again. Clarke got to her feet, Crowther following suit.

'Let me just . . . ' Clarke was reaching into her bag for some money but Madden waved her offer aside.

'You only drank tap water. This is on us.'

She thanked him and made for the door. 'They're paying,' she told the waitress, who was already on her way to the table with Madden's wine.

'Wish I'd had the steak now,' Crowther said as they stepped outside.

32

'This is nice,' Rebus said. He meant it, too. His own flat was usually scruffy, filled with accumulations of clutter. Deborah Quant's, on the other hand, was the epitome of order, each item carefully chosen and positioned, just a few books, a few knick-knacks. Each spacious wall held a solitary painting, which drew the eye towards the art. Her music came from an all-but-invisible Sonos system, and even her choices were tasteful. There were plenty of gadgets in her kitchen, but she had found cupboard space for them all, leaving the worktop largely empty. The flat was in a modern block in the Grange, walking distance from Rebus's home. Just the one niggle — Quant didn't want Brillo visiting. The dog's tail had started wagging, eyes at their most appealing, as he'd watched Rebus shrug into his good coat.

'Basket,' Rebus had ordered, trying not to feel guilty.

Quant had summoned him for a supper of pasta and fish, washed down with Pinot Grigio. Just a short interrogation about his health over the dining table, then the pristine white sofa for decaf coffee, a drop more wine, and music. The wall-mounted TV stayed off while they talked.

'Any news of the Bloom case?' Rebus enquired.

She made show of checking her watch. 'Only

took you seventy-five minutes, John — good going.'

'Is there, though?'

'The wheels of forensic anthropology grind slow, and apparently you can't hurry soil analysis. The lab in Aberdeen has a lot on its plate, so to speak, and a cold case murder isn't a top priority.' She lifted a finger. 'And if anyone asks, you didn't hear that from me.'

'Who's going to ask?'

'Have you not been questioned yet?'

'Not as such.'

'You will be, though.'

'If they get round to me. You know they got a fingerprint match from the cuffs?'

She nodded. 'The film producer.'

'He was questioned under caution.'

'And then released. I do watch the news, John.'

Rebus was thoughtful for a moment. Quant had tucked her legs under her and was holding her wine glass while cradling her head in her free hand, elbow propped on the arm of the sofa. Her long red hair had been drawn back from her face and was held by an elasticated band. She wore no make-up, well aware that she didn't need it. She looked a decade younger than her actual age and never seemed particularly fatigued despite her workload.

'I forget,' he asked casually. 'Did you do the autopsy on Kristen Halliday?'

'What's Kristen got to do with anything?'

'I was asked to dust off the case.'

'So you've looked at the files?' She watched

him nod. 'Therefore you know fine well I did the autopsy. What's this all about, John?'

'Ellis's uncle harbours a few doubts. He managed to persuade Siobhan that it was worth a fresh pair of eyes.'

'Every murderer's family doubts they could have done it.'

'But when you examined her . . . '

'She was stabbed in the neck. She bled out. Cause of death is all that was required from me.'

'You didn't pick up anything else from the body?'

'No recent intercourse. Traces of cannabis and vodka in her system. Not enough to make her incapable. No other marks such as bruising. Her clothes were bloodstained but otherwise clean.'

'No defensive wounds to the hands?'

'She knew her attacker, John. She was stabbed from the front by someone right-handed. They didn't creep up behind her or anything.'

'Just the one incision?'

'By a blade matching the one found discarded nearby with Ellis Meikle's prints on it.' Quant lifted her head, leaning towards him. 'Which might explain why he was found guilty.'

'We got prints from the handcuffs around Stuart Bloom's ankles too, yet Jackie Ness is still a free man.'

'Ness hasn't admitted anything; Meikle did.'

Rebus nodded distractedly. 'I went to see him this afternoon. He's in Saughton.'

'How's he doing?'

'A bit more talkative than at the trial.'

'I remember him when I was giving my

evidence. He kept his head bowed. I'm not sure he was really taking any of it in. We know he used drugs, drank too much, no job, broken family . . . '

'Just another statistic, eh?'

'You're beginning to have doubts,' Quant stated.

'I'm looking for the motive, Deb, and not really seeing one.'

'You know as well as I do, we don't always get that sort of closure. Plenty of killers don't know why they did it or else won't say.' She reached over and placed a hand on his knee. 'Cases are seldom a hundred per cent watertight. Ninety usually does it for the jury. Do you think Jackie Ness is going to get away with it?'

Rebus shrugged. 'If your forensic pals got a move on, I might know the answer to that.'

'Why did Siobhan bring the Meikle case to you?'

'She's snowed under.'

'And maybe she did it to keep you active?'

'Either that or out of her hair.'

'She must have dozens of cases like Meikle, though — does she have links to the uncle or something?'

'Sort of.'

'It's not just altruism then?'

'It seldom is.'

He watched as Quant tugged the band from her hair, shaking it loose so it fell across her shoulders and forehead.

'Are you staying?' she asked.

'I'd like to, but there's Brillo to think of.'

'You could walk him, then come back after.'

'I could.' His eyes scanned the room. 'I like it here.'

'The decor, the furnishings . . . ?'

'I think it's the fact you have a lift,' he joked, earning a cushion in the face.

33

Sir Adrian Brand and his wife Cordelia had been out for the evening - La Traviata, courtesy of Scottish Opera at the Festival Theatre. Parking was always problematic so they had taken a black cab. Afterwards, they managed a late supper at Ondine before heading home to Murrayfield. The cab dropped them at the gates.

'We'll walk,' Brand instructed the driver, handing over a twenty and telling him to keep the change. The cab started to move off as his wife glowered at him.

'It's only fifty yards,' he chided her, punching the code into the panel on the gatepost.

'But in heels,' she complained, lifting one leg for him to see.

'I'll carry you then,' he said with a smile as the gates began to swing open.

Neither of them had noticed the car parked across the street, or that someone had emerged from it and was striding towards them. Cordelia Brand caught a glimpse of the figure from the corner of her eye, and clutched her evening bag close to her chest.

'Adrian . . . ' she said.

Brand turned just as the fist was swinging towards him. It connected with the meat of his nose, blood splashing down his shirt front. A knee to the groin doubled him over, and a kick to the stomach put him on all fours. His wife was yelling for help, swiping at the assailant with her bag. He didn't seem to register her blows. Instead, he leaned down, grabbing Brand by the hair and pulling until his face angled upwards, tears streaming from the eyes.

'A man can only take so much,' Jackie Ness hissed, showing both rows of teeth. 'A lesson you should have learned by now.' He slammed Brand's forehead against the pavement, then straightened up and began walking back to his car. Cordelia Brand was torn between stopping him and helping her husband. Decision made, she fumbled in her bag for her phone.

★ ★ ★

It was 2 a.m. when Clarke got the call. She dressed and picked up her car keys. Jackie Ness's car had been pulled over on Melville Drive. He'd been placed under arrest and taken to St Leonard's police station. Sir Adrian Brand was at the Royal Infirmary, awaiting a scan. He seemed okay, but the doctors in A&E wanted to be sure. His wife had given a statement, along with a photo she had snapped with her phone of Ness's car leaving the scene, its number plate clearly visible. A statement had also been taken from Brand himself. Graham Sutherland was reading it as Clarke entered the MIT room in Leith. Callum Reid turned away from the kettle and handed Clarke a mug of instant.

'No milk, sorry,' he said. His hair was uncombed and his eyes were bleary. He wore a shirt and jacket but no tie. Sutherland, on the

310

other hand, looked immaculate. Clarke wondered if he slept upright in his clothes.

'I didn't bother disturbing anyone else's beauty sleep,' Sutherland said. 'Just thought my two DIs should be in the loop.'

'This is because of the Poretoun House search?' Clarke asked. Stupid question, but she was still half asleep.

'Mr Ness has been questioned by officers at St Leonard's, and that's the story he gave. Even showed them his phone. Over two dozen photos, sent to him by Sir Adrian Brand over a four-hour period. One of them is a selfie, Brand grinning while the work goes on behind him.'

'I'd probably have gone Tonto myself,' Reid commented. 'On top of the prints on the handcuffs and the media attention.'

'I dare say Professional Standards will want a word with us.'

'Not our fault he snapped,' Clarke felt it necessary to state. 'Has Ness put in a complaint?'

'He might, if his solicitor suggests it. Mitigating circumstances and all that.'

'Solicitor will say we should have known the reason Brand was on hand to take all those photos was to torment his old adversary.'

Callum Reid nodded his agreement and took a sip from his mug, wincing at its bitter contents.

'So what now?' Clarke asked.

'Lady Brand is at the hospital with her husband. I'd like you to go have a word, see what was said between the two men.'

'And then a chat with Ness?'

311

Sutherland looked at Clarke. 'Maybe tomorrow. He's being kept in the cells overnight. Chances are it'll be a sheriffs court appearance in the morning, a fine and another walk past the cameras and microphones.'

'After which we bring him back into custody?'

'Maybe. Meantime, go see what you can glean at A&E.'

Clarke's windscreen had already started frosting over again. They sat together and waited for the heater to do its job. Reid yawned and checked his phone for news. Clarke's own phone let her know she had a text. It was from Laura Smith.

Is it true about Ness and Brand?

Clarke texted back: *I'm not talking to you.* A reply came immediately.

Dougal didn't get the fingerprint story from me! My editor's raging I missed it! Can I phone you?

Instead of responding, Clarke released the handbrake and they headed to the hospital. No traffic on the roads apart from cabs. Clarke decided it was safe to ignore the odd red light, though Reid tutted theatrically every time she did it. He had brought his mug with him and she wished she had done the same.

'Professional Standards would be the icing on the cake,' he commented.

'That's the problem with this cake, Callum — it's all icing and no bloody filling.'

They made good time and parked near the doors to A&E, making sure emergency vehicles could get past. Two ambulances stood under the canopy, doors open. It was a busy night. There were eight or nine patients seated in reception and a couple of others on trolleys. Paramedics in green overalls chatted among themselves to the side of the reception desk. Clarke and Reid showed ID to the receptionist and were given a ward number. When they got there, Cordelia Brand was seated alone on a row of chairs, her bag on her knees, face ghostly, eyes staring. Clarke and Reid introduced themselves.

'He'll be admitted when they're done examining him,' Lady Brand said. 'There's a bed waiting, I think. But right now they're doing some sort of brain test. I'm sure he's fine. He's talking and everything, just hellish shaken.'

'You recognised the assailant?' Reid asked.

'Oh, it was Jackie Ness all right. Adrian had been laughing about him earlier in the evening. Sending him those photos — I told him it was childish behaviour. But how could we know where it would lead?'

'Had Ness contacted your husband at all? After the photos started arriving, I mean?'

'Not that I know of. There were just a couple of them, weren't there?'

'A couple of dozen actually,' Clarke corrected her. The woman's face tightened.

'Childish, as I say. But that doesn't excuse what happened.'

'Not at all,' Reid agreed.

'What did happen exactly?' Clarke enquired. 'Can you talk us through it?'

'If Adrian had let the driver take us up to the door, we'd have been safely inside before that

313

man could reach us. But no, we had to walk the length of the drive.' She showed them her shoes. 'In these, I ask you. But Adrian's mind was made up, so that was that. He was opening the gates when Ness walked over. He'd obviously been waiting in his car; for how long I can't say, but probably stewing all that time. I was warning Adrian — I thought it was a mugger — when the punch came. Adrian's nose was bleeding, and then a knee caught him in the groin area. There was another punch to the stomach, I think — no, a kick, a kick to the stomach. He was on the ground by then, but Ness yanked on his hair so Adrian was looking up at him. That's when he said it.'

'Said what?'

' "A man can only take so much. You should know that by now." '

'Those exact words?'

' "You should know that" or "you should have learned that" — something along those lines.'

Clarke jotted it down in her notebook.

'What do you think he meant?' Reid was asking. Cordelia Brand offered a shrug.

'The man's clearly lost his mind, wouldn't you say?'

A nurse had arrived through a set of swing doors. 'Another hour or so, I'm afraid,' she explained.

'Any chance we can talk to him?' Clarke asked, holding open her warrant card.

'Doubtful until morning. You'd have to ask the doctor.'

'Please don't go upsetting him,' Lady Brand

begged the two detectives. 'This will have bruised his ego as well as his face. He spars with his personal trainer, you know.'

'We can all get caught by a sucker punch,' Reid reassured her. The nurse was leaving. Lady Brand took her phone from her bag and showed them the photo of Ness's car.

'He should go to jail, but he won't,' she said.

'What makes you think that?'

'They're overcrowded as it is — all an assault merits these days is a slap on the wrist. I'm a prison visitor, so I know.'

'Saughton prison?' Clarke asked casually. Reid was giving her a questioning look, but she ignored him.

'Yes.'

'Ever encountered a teenager called Ellis Meikle?'

'He should be somewhere else, somewhere for younger prisoners. But then again, he *is* a murderer.'

'So you know him to speak to?'

The woman shook her head. 'Only by reputation — which is that he never says much, except to ask when he can have a games console. I don't think human life means as much to him as that other world he inhabits. Now if you'll excuse me, I think I'll go find a mirror so I can brush my hair and tidy my face. Need to look my best for Adrian when I see him.'

The two detectives watched her leave. She had good posture, her back ramrod straight. Clarke imagined her as a girl, books balanced on her head as she learned the necessary poise and refinement.

'What was all that about?' Reid asked as he checked his phone for messages.

'Just a case I worked on.'

'Do you keep tabs on all of them?'

Clarke didn't bother answering. She stared at the words she had jotted on her notepad. 'What do you make of Ness's outburst?'

'I'm not sure.' He put his phone away and stifled a yawn. 'So do we hang around here on the off chance of a word with the patient?'

'Depends how keen you are.'

'Bit of shut-eye wouldn't go amiss.'

'Hard to disagree. Bright and early at Leith, though?'

'Last one in buys elevenses.'

'You're on.'

★ ★ ★

Malcolm Fox was in his kitchen, hands wrapped around a mug of instant hot chocolate. He had slept fitfully, a couple of hours at most. Before bed, he had peered through his curtains, half expecting to see the black Audi parked across his driveway. Either that or Rebus's Saab. The further down he dug into the Bloom case, the more he found. Not hard facts as such, but hints and trails and links. Trace evidence, in a way. You looked for it at the scene of a crime, but that wasn't the only place you could find it. Rebus had been good, of course, one of the best — it was the reason Complaints had never been able to kick him off the force. But in covering up the flaws, mistakes and misdemeanours of others, he had left the faintest trace evidence of his own.

The question in Fox's mind was, what was he going to do about what he had found? In presenting his case, he would be showing himself at his best. Jennifer Lyon would take note; bosses even higher up the ladder would take note. He'd have established himself on a fast track to further promotion. That was what he wanted, wasn't it? Alternatively, he could take it to Steele and Edwards. They'd see to it he joined them at ACU. He'd spent some of his best years chasing down corruption within the force. At ACU he'd be using those skills again. And maybe in time he would even have enough evidence to send Steele and Edwards to court.

Which future awaited him? He stared at the skin forming on the surface of his drink and couldn't say.

Wednesday

34

In the morning, Sutherland dispatched Gamble and Crowther to question Sir Adrian Brand. He had been discharged and was back home, his eyes swollen and black from the punch he'd taken. His brain was fine, however, and his nose wasn't broken. The whole MIT room watched the TV screen as the security van carrying Jackie Ness arrived at the court building. Clarke caught sight of Laura Smith amongst the ranks of onlookers. Turning from the screen, she led Sutherland to one side.

'DCS Mollison just dodged a bullet,' she informed him. '*Scotsman* were going to run a story about how cosy he was with Sir Adrian. They pulled it after the fingerprint news and Ness's attack on Brand, but they'll find a use for it eventually.'

'How cosy?'

'Charity galas and golf outings — same as most of his predecessors.'

'I remember Bill Rawlston was one such.' Sutherland rubbed at his chin. 'Does Mollison know about this?'

'He was pretty busy yesterday as I remember.'

Sutherland nodded slowly. 'I'll warn him. Do I dare to ask how *you* know?'

'Old-school policing,' Clarke offered, keeping her face emotionless.

'I thought your run-in with ACU might have

taught you to use more caution in your dealings with our friends in the media.'

'I'm a slow learner.'

Sutherland managed a thin smile. 'Can't say I've seen any evidence of that.'

Over at Phil Yeats's desk, Clarke checked the list Derek Shankley had helped compile of Stuart Bloom's friends and associates. No sign of Madden and Speke, of course, but Ralph Hanratty's name was there, along with a phone number and a note: *2006/7??* Meaning, she reckoned, that Shankley hadn't been in touch with Hanratty since that time. She called the number anyway and got a recorded message telling her it was no longer in service, so she crossed to her own desk and did a Google search, smiling to herself: old-school policing. Hanratty, she learned within five minutes, had gone into the porn business: online only, it seemed. A subscription channel catering to all tastes. Some of the stuff had been too strong, and he'd ended up in court. Clarke wondered if Jackie Ness knew him; she doubted this was the time to ask.

Well, not the time to ask Ness, at any rate. Hanratty's home address, however, was on the database. She copied it into her phone and used the postcode to bring up a map. Eskbank, hard by Newbattle golf course. She realised Callum Reid was standing over her.

'Who is he?' Reid asked.

'Owner of Rogues back in the day. Now he sells porn.'

'Have we talked to him yet?'

322

'Doesn't look like.'

'Any particular reason he's suddenly of interest?'

'I heard a rumour he might have had a cop or two on his payroll.'

'I think we all know it was your friend Rebus who tipped off Bloom's boyfriend.'

'All the same . . . '

Reid picked up the list. 'Well, they all have to be questioned eventually. What order we do them in doesn't really matter. I hear that Doug Newsome is coming in later this morning and the ACU wankers this afternoon. We could slot this guy Hanratty in if you like.'

'Great,' Clarke said. 'Thanks.'

Reid made show of checking his watch. 'We do, of course, also have to make time for elevenses. Mine's a jam doughnut.'

'Thirty seconds you beat me by,' Clarke complained.

'First past the post, Siobhan — that's all that matters.'

★　★　★

'Does Larry Huston live here?'

The woman peered at Rebus from behind glasses that needed cleaning. She was in her forties and hadn't exercised in a while. Her hair either needed a wash or was already damp, and as it wasn't raining outside, Rebus suspected the former.

The house was on an estate of identical terraced properties, reminiscent of Restalrig. But

323

this was Murrayburn, across the city, yet another side of Edinburgh the tourists would never see.

'My name's John Rebus,' he said.

'Too old to be a rozzer, so what are you?'

'You're sharp,' Rebus told her. 'I used to be police. If Larry's in, you can tell him I'm here on behalf of Darryl Christie.'

The name meant something to her, though she tried not to let it show. She told Rebus to wait there and headed indoors. She was back half a minute later.

'In you come then. I'm his daughter, Brie, like the cheese — God knows why; him and my mum never even visited France, and the only cheese in the house was Co-op Cheddar. You wanting a drink?'

'I'm fine,' Rebus assured her. The living room was cramped, stuff everywhere — mugs and dirty plates, a clothes horse draped with laundry. Brie lifted a dozing black cat by the scruff of its neck, offering the chair to Rebus. Larry Huston sat in the chair opposite. It looked as frayed as its occupant. The spectacles must have been a two-for-one deal: Huston's were identical to his daughter's, right down to the smudges and smears.

'I'll take a cup, Brie,' he said.

'There's a surprise,' she snapped back, but she turned and left the room anyway. The brown wallpaper was starting to part company with the walls, and the floor-to-ceiling shelf unit would need a dust before any self-respecting skip would accept it.

'I know what you're thinking,' Huston rasped

from behind a cough. 'Proceeds of crime and all that . . . '

He'd be in his early seventies, hair scraped across the dome of his head, buttoned cardigan sagging, slippers split at the join between sole and upper. The room smelled faintly of urine — Rebus hoped it was the cat's. Huston's face was blotchy and his teeth stained by nicotine. He lit up while Rebus watched. Rebus was surprised to find he wasn't even remotely tempted, not that Huston was offering. He slid a hand into his pocket, just managing to stop himself bringing out a handkerchief to hold over his face. No way of knowing what germs were floating around; maybe the smoke would kill them.

'Christie still at the Bar-L?' Huston was asking.

'Transferred to Saughton.'

'Never met the lad, but I know who he is.'

'And *what* he is, I dare say,' Rebus offered. 'Sort you might have worked for once upon a time.'

'That was then, back when safe-cracking was a noble pursuit. Never any violence, you see, not on my part. Get me into an office or jeweller's and I could get you what it was you wanted.'

'How many times did you get caught?'

'Too many. Not always my own fault. Snitches played a part. Deals done when stuff was recovered. Suddenly everybody wants to talk and my name was always going to be mentioned, because I was never the sort to threaten retribution.' He paused, lost to memory, Rebus content to bide his time. Then: 'Ever heard of

Johnny Ramensky?'

'No.'

'Look him up in the history books. Most famous safe-breaker we ever produced. Gentle Johnny they called him, because he never used violence either. Turned war hero and got himself immortalised at the Commando Memorial. Like I say, a noble pursuit.'

'Is he rambling again?' Brie had shuffled into the room, bringing a mug of muddy-looking tea. She placed it on the arm of her father's chair. She seemed about to loiter, so Rebus asked if he could have just five minutes with Larry. Sniffing, she left again, closing the door with a bang.

'She's a good girl,' Huston said. 'Took me in when there was nowhere else. The boys at Saughton always teased me, said they knew I'd stashed some loot somewhere that would see me through to the end of my days. Fat chance. Wife got through every last bit of it while I was inside, then went and snuffed it before I could wring her neck.' He placed his smouldering cigarette on the edge of an ashtray and blew across the surface of the tea before taking a slurp.

'I wanted to ask you about Morris Gerald Cafferty,' Rebus said.

'Big Ger?'

'You did a few jobs for him.'

'Did I?'

'Darryl Christie says so.'

Huston digested this, weighing up his options. 'Well, what if I did?' he eventually asked.

'You knew Cafferty around 2006?'

'My memory's not what it was.'

326

'Darryl will be disappointed to hear that.'

'Not half as disappointed as Big Ger would be if I started shooting my mouth off. And last time I looked, Darryl was behind bars while Cafferty's walking around, meaning he could knock on my door any time he liked.'

Huston had grown so agitated, tea was sloshing on to one of his trouser legs. Rebus rose from his chair and stood over him. 'What is it you're scared of, Larry?'

And that was when he saw it — on the floor to one side of Huston's chair: an unkempt pile of recent newspapers, each open at the latest stories about the Stuart Bloom case. Rebus reached down and held one up in front of Huston's face.

'Why the interest, Larry? What is it you know?' He let the paper fall on to Huston's lap and placed both clenched fists against the arms of the chair, so that he towered over the man, blocking his view of the rest of the room. Huston's world now consisted of nothing but John Rebus.

'I'm not a cop these days,' Rebus intoned. 'I'm a civilian — old, washed up. But I know plenty who are still on the force and if I say the word, they'll come down on you hard. So you either tell me or you tell them. It doesn't go any further, you've my word on that. But if I have to bring in CID, you might end up back inside. Clean your glasses and look in a mirror, you'll see that would almost certainly be the death of you. So just for my own satisfaction — what do you know about Stuart Bloom?'

Huston's voice when he eventually spoke was

tremulous. 'This stays between us?'

'Absolutely.'

'How do I know I can trust you?'

'Because I'm giving you my word.'

Huston gave a long sigh and cleared his throat. 'The film guy had come to Big Ger, wanting a favour.'

'The film guy being . . . ?'

'Jackie Ness. He wanted to know if Big Ger knew anyone who could crack a safe. My name came up, so I met with the lad.'

'The lad being Stuart Bloom?'

Huston managed a weak nod. 'He wanted us to do an office belonging to Adrian Brand.'

'And did you?' Rebus had removed the mug from Huston's shaking hand, placing it on the carpet next to the newspapers. There was another nod. 'Just so I'm clear,' Rebus said quietly, 'with Stuart Bloom's assistance, you broke in and emptied the safe?'

'Yes.'

'Where was this exactly?'

'West End, just off Palmerston Place. Brand's company office at the time.'

'No alarm system?'

'The lad dealt with it and got me in, good as gold.'

'Cameras?'

'Aye, but we wore balaclavas and kept our traps shut.'

'And what did you take?'

Huston was shaking his head. 'I don't know.'

'You can do better than that, Larry.'

'I really can't. Once the safe was open, the lad

stepped in, stuffed everything into a bag he'd brought with him.'

'What sort of bag?'

'Just from a supermarket. White polythene.'

'You must have got a look, even for a few seconds?'

'Folders. I don't think there was anything except folders. No drugs, jewellery, cash. All I saw was cardboard files.'

'So what happened after?'

'I got paid.' The answer came with an accompanying shrug.

'You never saw Stuart Bloom again?'

'No.'

'What did Cafferty say?'

'I never saw him. I was picked up by your lot a week later for a factory I'd done a few months before. Got three years nine months. Big Ger sent a few quid to the house, but he never came to see me.'

'And when you got out?'

'I think he'd decided I was a liability. World was changing anyway — more sophisticated alarms and too much CCTV. Jewellers' shops were like Fort Knox.' He reached down to retrieve his mug. 'Got what you came for?'

'To be honest, I didn't know what I was going to get.' Rebus had wandered over to the window and was staring out at the row of houses opposite.

'It was bad enough when the lad went AWOL,' Huston mused, swapping teacup for cigarette, 'but then when they found him in his car . . .'

'You think it's why he was killed? The office break-in?'

'It happened two nights before he disappeared — what do you think?' He inhaled, exhaled, coughed again, eyes watering. 'And I'll tell you something else. Seemed to me it was all too easy. The safe was bog-standard, so much so I almost felt insulted — an old Sargent and Greenleaf, tumbler combination. Plus an alarm system that was a cinch to breach.'

'Meaning what?'

Huston gave another shrug. 'I thought at first it must be a trap. The lad wasn't exactly an expert — he said everything he knew about disarming an alarm he got from the internet — but he got us in there almost as if the place had been left unlocked and ready to plunder.'

Rebus thought for a moment. 'It was never reported, was it?'

'Not that I know of.'

'And this was just two nights before Stuart Bloom disappeared?'

Huston nodded slowly. 'Had to be Brand who got to him. I reckoned if the lad talked, I'd be in for a doing, too. That jail cell almost came as a relief.'

35

Seated kerbside in his Saab, Rebus called Siobhan Clarke.

'Not now, John,' were her first words.

'What's happened?'

'Ness ambushed Brand last night, didn't quite manage to break his nose.'

'Ambushed him why?'

'Brand was sending him photos of our SOCOs ripping up Poretoun House.'

'Fair play to him then.'

'I'm not sure the judge will agree. He's in court right now.'

'And Brand?'

'Home and recuperating.'

'You might need to question them both. I've just been talking to a peter who worked a job with Stuart Bloom.'

'A what?'

'Safe-blower — peter is what we used to call them.'

'Back in Dickensian times, you mean?'

'If that's your attitude . . . '

He heard her exhale. 'Sorry,' she said. 'Already been a long day. So this safe-blower . . . ?'

'Ness asked Cafferty if he knew anyone. Cafferty put him in touch with Larry Huston — that's the peter. Met with Stuart Bloom and helped him open the safe in Brand's office. According to Huston, they emptied the contents into a carrier bag and that's the last he saw of it. Nothing like that was in the car, right?'

'Right.'

'So we can add it to the missing laptop and mobile. And Siobhan, all this happened two nights before Bloom went AWOL.'

'Brand didn't report the break-in,' Clarke stated. 'It would have been in the file, wouldn't it?'

'I've certainly no memory of it.'

'So the night Bloom met with Jackie Ness, they'd have been discussing the break-in, maybe looking at whatever was in the safe?'

'I'd think so.'

'Understandable Ness never felt able to tell us that.' Clarke paused for a moment. 'John, dare I ask how you found this guy Huston?'

'I have my sources.'

'You want Cafferty, don't you? You want to be able to tie him to Bloom?'

Rebus gripped the steering wheel with his free hand. 'He *is* tied to Bloom! For one thing, he knew Jackie Ness, and for another, he knew the safe was going to be opened. Don't you think he'd be curious about its contents? Maybe stuff linking Brand to the Irish gangster?'

'Conor Maloney?'

'Information is power, Siobhan. Cafferty didn't just bludgeon his way to the top.' Rebus's eyes were on the house he'd just left. Brie Huston had pushed aside the net curtain in the living room and was watching him.

'So we need to bring in Huston as well as

332

everybody else?' Clarke asked without too much enthusiasm.

'Planes stacking overhead, are they?'

'One interview room may not be nearly enough. But give me Huston's address.'

Rebus reeled it off. Yes, he'd promised to keep the safe-blower out of it, but that had been just another little white lie.

'So who else is in the firing line today?' he asked Clarke as he started the ignition.

'Your old colleague Doug Newsome this morning; Steele and Edwards this afternoon. Plus we need to ask Ness about the attack on Brand — and Brand, too, come to think of it. Lady Brand tells us Ness said something like 'A man can take only so much — you should know that by now.''

'Interesting phrasing.'

'Then we've got Ralph Hanratty — he used to own Rogues. And that's just for starters.'

'Sounds like a perfect storm. Thing to remember is, every storm has a still centre. Find your way there and you'll crack the case.'

'Now he's giving me weather reports.'

Rebus could sense her tired smile. 'When you've spoken to Huston, will you bring Cafferty in?'

'We might.'

'Any chance of me tagging along?'

'No.'

'I still need to be questioned, you know — formally, I mean. Only chat I've had with you lot was back at the start, when you didn't even know who Stuart Bloom was.'

'So you're invited to make your statement and that just happens to coincide with Cafferty being in the building?'

'Bingo.'

'No promises, John.'

'I'm here when you need me, Shiv. And trust me, you *will* find that still centre.'

He ended the call and considered his options. By the time he reached Restalrig, it would be almost lunchtime, the local high school disgorging kids, friends of Ellis and Kristen among them. Local chip shop, bakery and corner store — that was where they'd congregate, and maybe the play park, too. Rebus got going, thinking of Darryl Christie. Cafferty being questioned — it wasn't much but it was a start. Would Christie keep his side of the bargain and make sure Ellis Meikle was kept safe?

And why was Rebus so anxious that he should?

★   ★   ★

Gamble and Yeats took the Doug Newsome interview, armed with information gleaned from Fox's trawl of the original case files. Fox didn't look particularly happy, despite the promise of a listen to the recording. Tess Leighton offered him half her Twix, but he shook his head. Jackie Ness meantime had been fined £250 and warned not to go within a hundred metres of Brand, his family, his home or place of work. He had left court into a maelstrom of media, only to be plucked out by Sutherland and Reid and taken

334

back to St Leonard's, solicitor in tow, to be asked about the words Lady Brand had heard him utter.

Afterwards, in the MIT room, Reid filled them all in. Basically, Ness had no recall of what he'd said. He had been pressed but could only shrug. It had been a moment of madness, the red mist descending — something the judge had taken into account when passing sentence.

'We might need to question him again,' Clarke interrupted, explaining about Larry Huston. 'And Sir Adrian, come to that.'

'So Bloom handed the contents of the safe to Jackie Ness?' Crowther asked.

'Or hung on to it,' Tess Leighton argued.

'Unless Cafferty got hold of it, of course,' Clarke added.

'It's a bloody good motive for murder,' Callum Reid agreed, brushing doughnut sugar from one trouser leg.

They all turned as Gamble and Yeats entered the room, Gamble handing a copy of the Newsome interview to Fox with the words 'Knock yourself out.'

'You will be shocked to hear,' Yeats told the room, 'that Mr Newsome reckons he did everything by the book. No faked records, no skipped interviews with suspects, no sleeping on the job. He did, however, have a few harsh words for Mary Skelton and John Rebus.'

'Did you ask him about Steele and Edwards?'

'Said he barely knew them. They were uniforms, well below his pay grade — his words, not mine. For what it's worth, his thinking at the time mirrored that of his boss — gay love triangle ends in tragedy. He took part in one of the raids on Rogues and didn't like what he saw. Proper little homophobe is our friend Newsome.'

Clarke's phone was vibrating in her pocket. She checked the screen and headed for the peace and quiet of the corridor.

'Mr Speke,' she said, answering. 'What can I do for you?'

'It's probably nothing, Inspector, but I was turning things over half the night and I remembered something. We shot a thriller for Jackie Ness a few weeks before *Zombies v Bravehearts*. It was supposed to be erotic; maybe it was to watch, but not to make. Female cop who jumps into bed with suspects and witnesses. That's how she gets them to talk. But one of them's a demon or some such nonsense and she ends up half demon and half angel.'

'Sounds riveting. What's your point?'

'For one scene, Jackie needed handcuffs. He asked if anyone could get hold of some. Ralph Hanratty had been talking about adding some manacles to one of the walls in Rogues — just for a laugh, you know? Manacles and chains and whatnot — not my scene, but Ralph wanted to try it for size.'

'He loaned you some handcuffs?'

'I'm positive they can't be the ones you found on Stuart. When I took them to Jackie, he thought they looked cheap. They *were* cheap; I'm not even sure they were proper metal.'

'So you handed them back to Hanratty?'

'I'm pretty sure I did. That's why I don't think

they can be the ones in the car.'

'What was the film called?'

'*Cops v Demons*, I think.'

'I should have guessed. Would you have a copy, Mr Speke?'

'Might have a DVD kicking about.'

'Could I send someone to pick it up?'

'If I can find it.'

'Might be helpful to have your fingerprints, too. Just for the process of elimination.'

'How do you mean?'

'We have unidentified partial prints on the handcuffs used to restrain Stuart Bloom. If they *did* turn out to be the ones Hanratty gave you . . .'

'I've got nothing to hide, Inspector.'

'Which is why I'm grateful for your cooperation. Was Mr Madden the cameraman on the shoot?'

'Yes.'

'Any notable extras among the cast? Stuart, maybe, or his friend Derek?'

'I don't remember.'

'Well, thanks for getting in touch.' Clarke ended the call. She was standing by the open doorway of the room commandeered by Fox and Leighton. Fox was seated in front of his computer, headphones on as he listened to the Newsome interview.

'Must be nice to have everything given to you on a plate,' she said, knowing he couldn't hear her. He was jotting in his notebook, a look of absolute concentration on his face. A dapper-looking man of around sixty was being led up the staircase by a constable. Ralph Hanratty, she presumed.

'Your timing is impeccable,' she told him, holding out her hand.

36

Hanratty was seated in the interview room, Tess Leighton across the table from him, when Clarke returned with his requested mug of black sugarless tea.

'Shabby chic,' was his summary of his surroundings. Hanratty himself was a peacock by comparison — tailored suit with crimson lining, white shirt and emerald-green tie, gleaming black brogues. His dark hair had had the grey taken out of it. There had maybe even been some cosmetic work done to his face. The skin looked tight, the eyes a little narrower than seemed completely natural. He had brushed a large folded handkerchief across the seat of his chair, and was now rubbing at the rim of the mug, prior to his lips touching it.

'You used to own Rogues, Mr Hanratty,' Clarke began. Leighton had opened a new notebook — identical to Fox's, Clarke noticed — and was ready with a ballpoint pen.

'That's correct.'

'You knew Stuart Bloom and Derek Shankley?'

'Socially? Not really.'

'They were regulars at your club, though?'

'Along with a few hundred other beautiful people.'

'What were your thoughts when Stuart went missing?'

Hanratty flicked a speck of dust from one trouser leg. 'I'm not sure I had any particular thoughts.'

'I've seen some photos of Rogues in its heyday — it was quite something.'

Hanratty smiled. 'It certainly was.'

'Must have been vexing that the authorities showed so much interest.'

'It went with the territory, my dear. The council were always trying to find us breaking noise limits; and as for the officers of the law . . . ' He rolled his eyes theatrically. 'Despite some of your own rank-and-file of the time being among my best customers.'

'Care to name any names, sir?'

'I'm not that type, dearie.'

'These raids, though — you were always warned in advance, no?'

'*Omertà*,' he said, miming running a zip across his mouth.

'That's not really acceptable in a murder inquiry, Mr Hanratty.'

'Well then, let's just say that the names have been erased from my memory. I met hundreds and hundreds of people; I can't be expected to remember them all.'

'But it's possible that some of the very officers who would raid your club were also part of your clientele?'

'It's possible.'

'We happen to know someone tipped you off, sir.'

'And you can prove that?' Hanratty smirked. 'Of course you can't. And none of it has any bearing on poor Stuart's death.'

'So why do you think he died?'

'I've not the faintest idea.' He gave Leighton a look. 'Make sure you record those words exactly as spoken.'

'You work as a porn merchant these days, is that right?' Clarke asked.

Another roll of the eyes. 'Online erotica,' he corrected her.

'DS Leighton here did a quick check of Companies House. Seems the other major shareholder in your business is William Locke — would that be the same Billy Locke who was co-owner of Locke Ness Productions?'

'It would.'

'So presumably you know Jackie Ness?'

'I know he needed good-looking people for his films, and sometimes found them at Rogues.'

'Mr Ness was one of your clients?'

'God, no. But word would get around that extras were needed for certain scenes. When you tell people they're going to be in a movie, they sign up gratefully, despite there being no fee, no expenses — sometimes not even a hot meal.' He paused. 'Though of course there were benefits.'

'What sort of benefits?'

'Let's just say people tended to be a bit glassy-eyed after.'

'You're talking about drugs?'

'Not unknown in the film industry.'

'Might explain why Stuart and Derek looked so giggly in the clip I watched. The biggest dealer in the city at that time would have been a man called Cafferty, is that right?'

341

'You tell me.'

'We know he was a friend of Jackie Ness's. Would he also have supplied your club, Mr Hanratty?'

'No illicit substances in Rogues, Inspector.' Hanratty held up both hands in a show of innocence.

'One young person died of an overdose, I believe . . . '

Hanratty wagged a finger. 'Be careful of libel. There was never any evidence those drugs came from anywhere near my club.'

'The victim *had* been to your club, though, as had the others who fell ill.' Clarke paused meaningfully. 'Bit of a coincidence, wouldn't you say?'

'World's full of coincidences,' Hanratty said blithely.

'Coincidences *and* connections,' Clarke stated. 'Tell me, did you ever appear in one of Ness's films yourself?'

'Never.'

'But you did help out on occasion. For example, Colin Speke asked if you had any handcuffs he could borrow.'

Hanratty glowered at her. 'Where are you going with this?'

'You know that Stuart Bloom was found with his ankles cuffed? Doesn't that strike you as a little . . . perverse?'

'I ran a club that was popular with the gay and lesbian community. I wasn't operating a fucking dungeon!'

'But you did toy with the idea, didn't you? A

342

little bit of mainstream bondage? That was why you were able to lend Speke the handcuffs for the film he was helping to make.'

'And I got them back, too!'

'Did you?' Clarke nodded to herself. 'Mr Speke couldn't quite remember. So what happened to them?'

'I've honestly no idea.'

'You kept them, threw them out, loaned them to someone else?'

Hanratty gave a hoot of laughter. 'This,' he said, 'is too fucking delicious. You'll do anything to throw people off the scent, won't you?'

'How do you mean, sir?'

'Handcuffs means police — everybody outside these four walls knows that. You get wind of a pair of toy fucking handcuffs that might have been within half a mile of Jackie Ness and his crew, and suddenly you think you just *might* be able to make a gullible public swallow the lie. Who will you leak it to, Inspector? See, you may have used the internet to find out all about me, but that works both ways. When poor Stuart's body was found, I began to devour the various news reports. And then your name came up, and you'd recently been in trouble for passing confidential information to a journalist at the *Scotsman*. You've been a naughty young lady, Detective Inspector Clarke. So *you* take your story to the papers and I'll take mine, and we'll see who's the more credible. Nobody *believes* you any more; nobody *trusts* you.'

He sat back, happy to close his mouth and let his words sink in. After a few moments of silence, he turned towards Leighton again.

'Need me to repeat any of that for you, sweetie?'

'I think I got it all,' Leighton said, tearing the sheet from her notebook and ripping it slowly and methodically to pieces in front of him.

37

Sir Adrian Brand had been questioned at home, in the same garden room where Clarke and Crowther had met him. Sutherland had taken Crowther with him, armed with the information on the break-in. This time Brand had his wife by his side, his hand held in hers, while Glenn Hazard stood at a distance, arms folded, ready to pounce whenever he didn't like the line of questioning.

'He flat out denied it,' Sutherland told Clarke when he called her immediately afterwards.

'He's lying.'

'You're sure this Huston character is reliable?'

'Gamble and Yeats are with him right now. Let's see what they say. Meantime, did you ask Brand about what Ness is supposed to have said to him?'

'He was a bit vague; says he's no reason to doubt his wife's version.'

'Why does he think Ness used those exact words?'

'He's no idea.'

'Lying again?'

'Not twelve hours ago he suffered a blow to the head. His wife is after a second opinion — private this time. She's worried the scan might have missed something.'

'If he pegs it, at least we can put Ness away for *something*.'

'Jesus, Siobhan, don't even say that.'

'Sorry, sir.' She gave Sutherland a brief update on the interview with Hanratty.

'Interesting about the handcuffs,' he concluded.

'I'm going to watch the DVD later. At this rate, I'm going to be an expert in lousy movies.'

'We all need a break, one way or another — either *in* the case or *from* the case.' He exhaled noisily from his nostrils. 'Hang on, I've got another call coming in. It's the lab, better take it. We'll be back there in ten minutes tops.'

Clarke put her phone back in her pocket. Tess Leighton was coming up the stairs towards her, having deposited Hanratty in a taxi.

'Quite the piece of work,' she commented.

'Nice touch with the notebook, though.'

'A page of doodles from earlier.'

'Well, I'd better let you get back to Malcolm. He'll be missing your company.'

Leighton gave her a look. 'It was just dinner, Siobhan.'

Clarke held up a hand. 'I didn't mean anything, Tess. I was just teasing. Forget I said it, okay?'

Leighton eventually nodded. Her eyes went over Clarke's shoulder. 'Talk of the devil,' she said. Both women watched as Malcolm Fox approached. He was holding his headphones and the memory stick with the Newsome audio.

'Singularly unenlightening,' he confessed. 'Thank God we've moved on from dinosaurs like that.'

'And like John Rebus, too?' Clarke enquired.

346

'John's old chum Newsome tries to take a dump on him. He's not shy about the friendship with Alex Shankley, the drinking, and the history with Cafferty.'

'Well, at least you have something to tell the Big House.'

Fox fixed her with a look. 'Don't worry, any report I make will focus on the facts rather than the fiction.'

'We were just being accused of doing the opposite,' Leighton informed him.

'Oh aye?'

They were interrupted by more footsteps on the stairs. Too soon for it to be Sutherland and Crowther, which could mean only one thing.

'Nice to see a welcoming committee,' Brian Steele said, Grant Edwards only a couple of steps behind him.

The Chuggabugs had arrived for their grilling.

★ ★ ★

Rebus had taken Brillo with him to Restalrig, figuring he looked less suspicious that way. And a few schoolkids did stop now and then to give the dog some attention, attention all too gratefully received. Brillo or no Brillo, however, he learned precious little to add to his store of knowledge about Ellis and Kristen. Darryl Christie had hinted that Cafferty was back in the dope business, always supposing he'd ever left it. Rebus had called Fox, asking for a name at the Organised Crime Unit. He'd then phoned Gartcosh and spoken with Fox's contact.

347

Cafferty was on their radar, of course he was, but they had no evidence and no surveillance operations against him currently under way. Nothing for it then but to phone the man himself. Cafferty picked up on the fifth or sixth ring.

'Hell do you want?' he demanded to know.

'You sound out of breath.'

'I'm at the gym. You should try it sometime. Might help you conquer those stairs of yours.'

'I'm enjoying a spot of exercise right now, actually, walking the gilded streets of Restalrig.'

'What the hell's in Restalrig?'

'It was Ellis Meikle's patch.'

'The kid who killed his girlfriend? I'm no further forward.'

'It's become a bit of a hobby, digging into old cases.'

'A solved case, though — where's the fun in that?'

'A few ends were left dangling. Maybe I can neaten them up.'

'And how am I supposed to help?'

'Ellis and Kristen both indulged recreation-ally . . . '

'Doesn't exactly put them in a minority round those parts.'

'Maybe so, but I'm wondering who the seller would have been. After all, who knows you better than your own dealer?'

'Sounds to me like you're clutching at straws rather than threads.'

'I have something to trade.'

'Oh aye?'

'If you think you can get me a meet . . . '

'Maybe you better tell me what you've got first.'

'I know about Larry Huston.'

'Now there's a name from the past.'

'Jackie Ness asked you if you knew anyone who could crack a safe. You gave him Larry Huston and Huston broke into Adrian Brand's office. Stuart Bloom took away everything they found.'

'So what?'

'So you might have wanted to know what was inside that safe. In any case, MIT are going to want a word. If they knew I'd just tipped you off, they'd buy me a ticket to Siberia.'

'They can ask me anything they like. I don't recall anybody reporting a break-in at the time.'

'Which only makes it all the more intriguing, no? What was it Brand didn't want anyone knowing had been taken from him?'

'Maybe you should go and ask him — once he's recovered from the thumping Ness gave him.'

'But meantime . . . '

'You in your car?'

'With my faithful mutt for company.'

'Keep an eye out for a text, then. It could take a while.'

But in fact it was less than ten minutes later when a message arrived. *Alley behind Singhs.*

Rebus walked with Brillo back to the corner shop where he'd bought the *Sunday Post* on his previous visit. The alley wasn't quite a dead end. A high fence separated it from a piece of waste ground at the back of a disused warehouse, the alley itself a dumping ground for discarded TVs and mattresses, at least one of which had been set alight at some point in the recent past. There were two large container bins, obviously belonging to the shop, although one of them, its lid missing, had become home to a trolley from a distant supermarket. A young man stood next to this bin, smoking, using it as an ashtray. He had his phone in his free hand and was texting with a dexterity Rebus could only marvel at. A black hoodie covered the youth's head and face. He wore faded denims and fashionable-looking trainers that were probably the envy of anyone who knew the brand and price tag.

'No names, no shit.' The voice was half muffled by the hood. Rebus realised there was a scarf under there too, wrapped around the face up to its nose. A BMX-style bike had been parked against the back wall of the shop, next to the solid metal delivery door. A security camera above had been draped with a polythene bag, rendering it useless.

'I couldn't care less about you,' Rebus replied, slipping a piece of gum into his mouth. He scooped a few dog biscuits from his pocket and dropped them at his feet to keep Brillo busy. 'I just want to know about Ellis and Kristen.'

'What's to know?'

'They bought from you.'

'Not much, not often.' The fingers were still busy. Rebus wanted to snatch the phone away and crush it underfoot, but he guessed that might conclude the meeting prematurely.

'What did you think of them?'

'I try not to think.'

'Maybe something you sold him sent him over the edge.'

The eyes met Rebus's momentarily. 'Don't fucking think so.'

'I hear weed's stronger these days than it used to be.'

The head was being shaken slowly but determinedly. Rebus shuffled his feet.

'So what were they like? You're about the same age, went to the same school?'

'Ellis was all right. Never talked much. Kristen was the one that wouldn't shut up. Probably talk to the mirror if no one else was there.'

'Was she seeing anyone apart from Ellis?'

'I told her she should have been seeing *me*. Didn't really mean it, though I wouldn't have said no to a quickie.'

'I hear she was the queen bee at school.'

'You heard right.'

'Meaning popular?'

'Well, she had her gang around her.'

'Not universally popular then?'

'Tongue like a blade. Didn't shy away from a scrap, either.'

'Fists and tongue — she ever use anything else?'

'A real blade, you mean?' Another shake of the head.

'How about Ellis?'

'Seemed to get all his aggression out playing those games of his. Maybe that's what you should be looking at — the effect of violent gaming on the teenage male brain. Me, I sell the antidote.'

'You reckon?'

'A smoke gets you the opposite of raging. Chilled and stilled and on top of the world.'

'Maybe I better buy some.'

'Maybe you should.' Rebus thought he could detect a smile beneath the black nylon scarf. 'One thing everybody will tell you about Kristen, she gave as good as she got.'

'Yes, I've been hearing that. The girls in her gang were a bit in awe of her.'

'Queen bee — you said it yourself. She could have had her pick of the drones, and for some reason she chose Ellis. If I didn't know better, I'd say he was just a hurdle she had to jump to get what she really wanted.'

'Ellis's uncle Dallas?'

There was a snort from beneath the hood. 'That fucking tattooed lady? No, I mean the one who was in front of him in the queue for looks.'

'Ellis's dad?'

'Recently separated, therefore fair game for a fair maiden who liked to play dirty. Such a shame she's not still around to play dirty with me.' He had finished with cigarette and phone both. Now he raised his head and studied Rebus properly. His eyes were beady and brown, forehead dotted with acne. Head probably shaved. Rebus had met dozens like him down the years.

'Gotta go,' the youth explained, reaching out a hand towards his bike.

'Bit of advice, son — get out while you can.

Days won't always be as good as this. You'll end up doing time, maybe not enough to compensate for the lives you've ruined, but a fair bit nonetheless. Right now you don't owe Cafferty anything, besides which he'll hand you to us on a platter if he ever needs something to trade.'

'He told me you weren't police.'

'I keep forgetting I'm not,' Rebus said, tugging at the lead and turning to leave.

38

Steele was the first interview, Edwards outside in the corridor on a chair. When they swapped places, Steele gave his colleague a wink. Edwards then went on to provide almost identical answers.

'Almost as if you'd rehearsed,' Clarke commented.

His fixed smile was unnerving. 'It was a long time ago, DI Clarke. You can't blame us for lapses of memory.'

'Precisely what your pal said.'

'And don't think we don't know there's an element of payback here where you're concerned, just because we did our job as ACU officers.'

Turning towards Crowther, Clarke cupped a hand to her ear. 'It's like there's an echo in here or something.' Then, to Edwards: 'How long did it take Steele to teach you to parrot all these lines? You've been in thrall to him for way too long, Edwards. He's going to fall eventually — and believe me, it will be a proper spectacle. Of course, he'll take you all the way down with him. In fact, if I know Steele, he'll see to it that you're the one who takes that plunge, with his hand on your back if need be.' She paused in the hope that her words might at least start to sink in. 'But meantime, let me ask you again. Did Adrian Brand get you to talk to Stuart Bloom at any point? Either to warn him off or to ask for the contents of his safe to be returned?'

'No.'

'And as far as you know, Brian Steele wasn't taxed with that job without your assistance?'

'No.'

'Any theories about the handcuffs?'

'No.'

Clarke made an exasperated sound and turned to Crowther again. 'Anything you want to add, DC Crowther?'

'I'm just wondering if Detective Constable Edwards was ever dropped on his head as a baby.'

Edwards's eyes drilled into Crowther's, but the smile stayed in place. 'You should mind your manners,' he warned her. Then, pointing a chubby finger in Clarke's direction: 'You also don't want to be hanging around with her. She's got her hand so deep in a certain reporter's pocket, she could probably fondle her arse.'

'Tell Steele to get a better script-writer for next time,' Clarke said. 'One who can do jokes at the very least.'

Afterwards, Steele put his arm around Edwards's shoulders as they walked back down the stairs, heads close together as they conferred. Clarke and Crowther stood at the top, watching. Neither man cast a backward glance.

'Wasn't that bad a line, actually,' Clarke admitted. 'If only more of our clothing had pockets . . .'

In the MIT room, Graham Sutherland was just finishing a phone call.

'Bloody soil results won't be in until tomorrow,' he said, not managing to hide his frustration. 'Lab has been all over the VW without finding anything new. Some of the vegetation that's grown through the chassis doesn't match what's growing in the gully, but it's just the usual bindweed and stuff that you'd find more or less anywhere in the lowlands. Means the car was sitting somewhere for a considerable period of time, long enough for the plant life to penetrate it from ground level.' He had walked to the whiteboard and was looking at the photos of the boot's interior. 'Mould, spores, moss and plenty of dead bugs.' He glanced towards Clarke. 'An episode of *CSI* would have wrapped this up by now.'

'Slightly bigger budget than us, I dare say.'

Sutherland just about managed a smile. 'Anything from the ACU interviews?'

'Just that they weren't thrilled I was the one asking the questions — so thanks for that, Graham.'

'Has that DVD arrived from Glasgow yet?'

'On its way here in a car.'

'If it *does* feature a similar set of hand-cuffs . . . '

She nodded. 'More questions for Jackie Ness. We need to ask him about the break-in anyway.'

'The break-in Sir Adrian says didn't happen?'

'Huston's sticking to his version.'

'Ness's lawyer is going to be far from thrilled if we bring his man back in again.'

'For about two minutes,' Clarke conceded. 'After which he'll be booking a nice skiing holiday paid for by his client's fees. Anyway, I really need to peruse the film first.' She watched Sutherland nod his agreement. 'There are also still a few interviews we've not done — I'm thinking of Cafferty, plus John Rebus.'

'What exactly is it you think Cafferty will tell us?'

'Sounds like he was closer to Jackie Ness than we thought. All we originally knew was that he'd put some money into Ness's business. Then it turned out he'd actually watched a day's filming. Now, he finds Larry Huston for Ness.'

'Fine,' Sutherland decided after a bit of thought. 'Bring him in.'

'And Rebus?'

'What's the one thing we've learned from putting questions to Steele and Edwards, Rawlston and Newsome?' Clarke couldn't think of an answer. 'Precisely,' Sutherland told her. 'I doubt John Rebus will be any different.'

★   ★   ★

'Been a while, Siobhan,' Cafferty said, settling into his chair in the interview room. Then, turning towards Emily Crowther: 'DI Clarke used to be one of our best customers at my club.' He dug some cards from his pocket and slid them towards Crowther. 'A few comps for you. The Devil's Dram, it's on Cowgate. Bring your friends — that's what Siobhan here used to do.'

'Back in the days before *you* owned it,' Clarke snapped back.

'Aye, you were happier when Darryl Christie

357

was in charge.' Cafferty folded his arms. He wore a shiny blue suit and a lemon-coloured shirt, open at the neck to display a profusion of silvered chest hair.

'We have a few questions about Larry Huston,' Clarke ploughed on.

'Am I supposed to know him?'

'He broke into a few safes for you back in the day.'

'Oh aye?'

'Including Adrian Brand's.'

'Is that right?'

'We have a statement from him.' Clarke pretended to study it for a moment. 'You'd been asked by Jackie Ness to find someone and you put him in touch with Huston.'

'And this is all a matter of record, is it? What does Jackie Ness say? Come to think of it, what does Sir Adrian say?' A smile was slowly spreading across Cafferty's face.

'I don't suppose you could put us in touch with Conor Maloney?'

'Name sounds Irish.'

Clarke gave a theatrical sigh. 'You can play as many games as you like, but you know we'll never stop digging.'

'Last I heard, Gartcosh had given up, fed up with their shovels hitting solid rock.'

'Whatever was in that safe might have been of interest to Conor Maloney. A couple of days later, Stuart Bloom had disappeared off the face of the earth. You're telling me there's no connection?'

. Cafferty turned his attention back to Crowther.

'Siobhan learned her shtick from John Rebus, but she'll never be quite his equal. Mind you, back when Rebus was on the force, interviews could end up a lot messier — blood to be wiped from the floor and the walls. Suspects tended to trip over their own feet and got suddenly clumsy around stairs. Nowadays you're all scared you'll end up on report.' His eyes were on Clarke again. 'Or being investigated by ACU.'

'Who found nothing,' Clarke felt obliged to reply.

'Nothing they could make stick,' Cafferty agreed. 'Just like you and this Larry Huston story — you're going to get nowhere with it. What are you going to do — charge me with being an accessory to a crime that never happened? Was it ever reported to the police? Did Brand ever put in an insurance claim?'

'Which is interesting in itself, don't you think? Maybe he was scared Maloney would find out about the theft. You knew, though, and maybe you passed the news along.'

'Why would I do that?'

'Just to be friendly with someone you thought could be useful to you.'

Cafferty shook his head. 'I don't blame you for trying, Siobhan, really I don't, but bringing me here was never going to get you anywhere. What's more, I think you always knew that, so why am I here? Rebus been whispering in your ear?'

'Has he been whispering in yours? Seems to me you knew we'd be coming for you and you knew why.'

'I've known the man longer than you have, Siobhan. We know he likes nothing better than playing both sides. It's as true now as it was back then.'

'What does that mean?'

Cafferty just shook his head again and began buttoning his suit jacket. 'We done here? You've wasted enough of my time to make me irritated, so you can report back to Rebus that there's that satisfaction at least.'

'Do you think Conor Maloney had anything to do with Stuart Bloom's death?' Clarke had risen from her chair at the same time as him, her eyes locked on to his.

'Maybe once upon a time I did,' Cafferty admitted after a moment.

'And now?'

'He'd have made it more public, to make sure everyone got the message. A bomb under the chassis, that sort of thing. Whatever else Maloney is, he's never been one for subtlety.'

'So who was it then? Was it Ness?'

'You tell me — you're supposed to be the detective here.' He turned the door handle and was gone.

Crowther rose slowly from her chair. 'Pretty good,' she commented.

Clarke looked at her. 'In what way?'

'He started out saying he didn't know anyone called Maloney, and by the end you had him stating that he didn't think Maloney was involved. And all without a drop of blood being shed.'

'Unless I make a dash for the stairs and give him a shove.'

They were smiling, albeit tiredly, as they left the airless room.

★ ★ ★

'Seen the vigil?' Malcolm Fox said. He was standing by the window of the MIT office, a mug cupped in both hands. Clarke and Crowther joined him. On the pavement opposite the police station stood Catherine Bloom and Dougal Kelly. They held JUSTICE FOR STUART BLOOM signs in front of them at chest height. There were no journalists, though a couple of pedestrians had stopped for selfies, and a white van tooted its horn in support as it passed.

'How long have they been there?'

'No idea.'

They watched as Cafferty crossed the street and started a conversation with them. He was nodding as he listened. Then he gestured towards the MIT room and all three raised their heads, Cafferty waving with one gloved hand. More talk, more nodding. He took money from his wallet and tried to press it into Catherine Bloom's hand, but she refused it. She accepted a hug, though, and Kelly a handshake, and then Cafferty was gone, walking in the direction of Constitution Street.

'I've seen everything now,' Fox muttered, turning towards Clarke, but she was already stalking towards the door. She took the stairs two at a time, yanking open the main door and striding across the two-lane road without looking right or left. Bloom and Kelly were stony-faced as she arrived in front of them.

'Know who that was?' Clarke said.

'A well-wisher,' Bloom said.

'Not even close. His name's Cafferty. Morris Gerald Cafferty. He's a gangster and a murderer. Drugs, people-trafficking, extortion — there's not much he's not tried his hand at. He was friends with Jackie Ness.' She fixed her gaze on Dougal Kelly. 'Name Larry Huston mean anything to you?' She waited until he'd shaken his head. 'He broke into Adrian Brand's office, taking Stuart with him. They robbed Brand's safe. This was just two days before Stuart vanished. And all down to Cafferty giving Huston's name to Jackie Ness.' She paused for a moment. 'Now, you can take that to the media — I've no way of stopping you. I just wanted you to know we're doing everything we can, while you are enjoying a chinwag with the worst of the worst. But do feel free to keep your eyes on us while your feet freeze. It won't distract us or slow us down a bit.'

'Why haven't you charged Ness with my son's murder?' Catherine Bloom exploded. 'Why are you so hell-bent on protecting him?'

'We're preparing a case.'

'He *is* the case! His fingerprint was on the handcuffs!'

'Obviously,' Kelly said, his voice conciliatory, 'the procurator fiscal doesn't think there's enough to take to trial.' His eyes were on Bloom, head angled slightly.

'It was Steele, wasn't it?' Clarke asked him.

'He told you the print belonged to Jackie Ness.'

Kelly turned his attention towards her. 'You really think I'd tell you?'

'That's why I'm asking.' Clarke gestured towards the police station. 'We can always chat in there if you'd prefer.'

'That sounds like a threat,' Catherine Bloom said, eyes reduced to slits. 'And all because Dougal exploded your cosy conspiracy of silence.'

'Mr Kelly's outburst helped push Jackie Ness over the edge.'

'Aye, and after attacking a man, he gets off with a fine — what's that if not evidence of you lot going easy on him?'

Clarke shook her head. 'Think what you like, Mrs Bloom.'

'I will, don't worry.'

Clarke was still shaking her head as she turned and crossed the road again. As she reached the far pavement, a horn sounded. She couldn't tell if it was a complaint aimed at her or a thumbs-up for the silent protest.

Ten minutes later, when she checked from the window, Bloom and Kelly were gone. Her phone rang, not a number she recognised. She answered anyway.

'It's me,' Dougal Kelly said. 'I put Catherine in a cab back to the hotel, told her I felt like walking.'

Clarke squeezed her eyes shut for a moment, feeling bone tired. 'None of what you're doing is helping. If your book is all that matters to you, fair enough, but if you care about the family, you'll make Catherine see sense. She needs to get her life back.'

'Stuart won't get his back.'

'Is it justice she wants or revenge?'

'She wants closure, I think. You know they can't even fix a date for the funeral until the fiscal releases the body, and that might not happen till after any trial. Twelve years they've been waiting.'

'Will a few more weeks or months really make such a difference?'

'Every day weighs on them.' Kelly sighed. 'Martin's started drinking again. Catherine's stopped speaking to him.'

'I'm sorry to hear that. Would it help if I said I really think we're getting close?'

'I'm not entirely sure Catherine would believe it.'

'I don't know if I believe it myself — but I keep saying it so I don't give up.'

'That story you told us about the safe in Brand's office . . . Would it be best kept out of the spotlight?'

'As of right this second, yes, probably.'

'Yet you blurted it out.'

'A moment of madness.'

There was silence on the line for a few moments. She could hear him walking past other pedestrians, buses rumbling close by. 'I'm sorry I spoiled your lunch with Laura,' he eventually said.

'You did a lot more than that, Dougal.'

'If you'd been in my shoes, you'd have asked about the fingerprint too.'

'Would I?'

'The way Ness reacted, doesn't that make him look like a guilty man?'

'Guilty of being pushed too far, maybe.'

'You really think he's innocent?'

'I'm trying to keep an open mind. It *was* Steele, wasn't it? He's been feeding you stories about the original inquiry, and now he's served up Jackie Ness for dessert.'

'I'll deny it in public.'

'Of course you will, but this is just between us.' She listened to his silence. 'For my own satisfaction.'

'Let me buy you another lunch.'

'Not a good idea.' She saw that someone from the front desk had arrived in the doorway, holding what looked like a glossy black DVD case.

'By way of apology,' Kelly was saying.

'I'll think about it,' Clarke told him, ending the call.

39

Rebus recognised her and got out of his car, locking it after him. Billie Meikle had a key out, ready to open the door to her tenement, but had paused to watch a group of students as they passed, probably heading home from the university. She was dressed in her school uniform and was toting a heavy-looking backpack.

'Billie?' Rebus said. 'Is your father at home? Can I come up and have a word?' She gave him a troubled look. 'I'm with the police,' he explained. 'Nothing to worry about, it won't take long.'

She didn't say anything, just pushed at the door and held it while he followed her inside.

'You moved schools, eh?' he asked as they climbed the stone stairs. He was praying the flat would be no more than a flight or two up. 'How's it working out?'

'It's great.' She had stopped at the first landing and was unlocking a red door with no name on it.

'You like living with your dad?' Rebus tried not to sound too breathless.

'Yeah.'

She was fourteen, her hair a mass of brown curls, falling over her forehead, half covering her eyes. Gawkiness would leave her soon, as would the puppy fat. She was already thinking of college, thinking of joining those students she had paused to study.

The flat was minimally furnished, not enough books to fill the single bookcase in the hall, the seating in the living room angled so that the vast flat-screen TV was the focus of attention.

'He'll be home soon,' she said.

'I'm happy to wait. Do you see much of your brother?'

Her cheeks reddened. 'Just the weekly visit.' She was shedding her outer coat and blazer, the backpack hitting the floor with a thump.

'I saw him yesterday,' Rebus told her. 'I'm fixing for him to have an easier time of it inside.'

She seemed uncertain what he meant but thanked him anyway. 'Do you want a coffee?'

'I'm fine,' Rebus said, settling on one of the chairs. 'You got homework to be getting on with?'

'Always.' She had hoisted the backpack onto the small round dining table and was emptying it. 'Maths, biology, geography, English . . . '

'Can't help you with any of those.'

She pretended an interest in a textbook while asking her next question: 'How was he?'

'Your brother's doing okay.'

'He doesn't like that he's in with . . . with people who . . . '

'That's one of the things I'm trying to change.'

'Why?' Now she looked at him, keen for knowledge.

'Because it's not right, I suppose.'

She considered this and nodded slowly in agreement.

'You visited your mum that day, didn't you? Did Ellis seem his usual self?'

'He was on his computer mostly. He had a couple of mates round.'

'But you popped into his room to say hello?'

'He didn't even take his headphones off — just a grunt and a wave.'

'And you hadn't heard anything about him and Kristen? Maybe breaking up or having a row?' Rebus watched her shake her head. 'Kristen was at your school, wasn't she — your old school, I mean?'

'Yes.'

'Did you know her? To hang out with?'

'She was three years above me.'

'I suppose at your age that seems quite a gap.'

'She had her own friends.'

'Did she ever visit here?'

Billie shook her head.

'Not even when Ellis was visiting?'

Another shake.

'So your dad didn't really know her, then?'

She spun towards him. 'What have they been saying?'

'Who's they?'

'All of them!'

'I didn't mean to upset you.' She had turned her face away from him again and was sifting through her books. 'You're right, though — I've been hearing that Kristen might have had a thing for your dad.'

'He wouldn't give her the time of day.'

'Just rumours, then.'

'It's revolting, you know — the stuff out there.

The stuff in here.' She was holding up her mobile phone.

'World's always been full of idiots, Billie, bullies and racists and the like. You just have to remember, a phone can't really hurt you.'

'Yes it can,' she replied quietly.

'Did you get messages about Kristen? About her and your dad?'

The sound of a lock turning, the front door opening.

'You home, duchess?' Charles Meikle called out.

'In here!'

The grin on Meikle's face disappeared when he saw there was a visitor.

'He's with the police,' Billie told him.

'Oh aye?' Meikle removed his blue parka. He wore overalls underneath. 'So can I see some identification?'

'I'm not actually a police officer,' Rebus explained. 'What I told Billie is that I'm working *with* them.'

'What on?'

'Your son's case.'

'He's in jail, if you hadn't noticed. Trying to pin something else on him, are you? Help massage your clear-up rate?'

Meikle's looks were almost worthy of Hollywood — chiselled face, brooding eyes, mop of black hair swept to one side, just the right amount of stubble. He'd had a few run-ins with the police in the past, but not since breaking up with his wife. According to the files, he'd been a car mechanic half his life, and, from what Rebus

369

had seen of the flat, was doing his best as a single parent.

'Just a few niggles that we'd like taken care of.'

'You don't think you've done enough damage?'

'He visited Ellis,' Billie interrupted. 'He's helping him.'

'What you have to remember, duchess, is that the police will lie to your face and then lie some more.'

'Billie's right, though,' Rebus said quietly.

Meikle just shook his head and disappeared across the hallway into the kitchen. Rebus followed and watched him fill the kettle from the tap. The place was immaculate, draining board and sink empty, surfaces wiped clean. He wondered: Billie's work or her father's?

'You still here?' Meikle asked.

'I know you and Ellis had a few differences down the years,' Rebus said, 'but did you get on okay with Kristen?'

'How do you mean?'

'Just wondering how well you knew her.'

Meikle stabbed a finger towards him. 'Shouldn't go listening to gossip, should you?'

'Billie says she never came round here.'

'That's right.'

'But you *had* met her?'

'When she was with Ellis, aye. At his mum's.'

'Things were okay between you and your ex-wife?'

'Yes.'

'Your brother wasn't an issue?'

'There's nothing going on between them.'

'And nothing between Dallas and Kristen?'

'More fucking lies,' Meikle muttered, shaking his head as he dropped a tea bag into a mug. 'Don't you sometimes think there's more shite out there than anything else?'

'Billie said much the same.'

'I told her she should ditch that phone, but she can't do it. They have to have them these days.' Meikle rested his knuckles against the worktop as he waited for the kettle to boil. 'Best thing I ever did was ask if she wanted to come live with me. Her old school was rubbish, grades dropping.' He paused. 'I'm doing everything I can, really I am.'

'I've seen no evidence to the contrary.'

'I've not always been a good dad — you're right that me and Ellis used to have a fair few ding-dongs. He's not a bad kid, though.'

'So what drove him to do it, Charles?'

'Did you try asking him?' Meikle watched Rebus give a slow nod. 'Aye, me too. But I don't think even *he* knows. At the trial, his lawyer tried putting the blame on us — Seona and me. Bad upbringing, bad parents . . . '

'She was doing her job, trying to get him a lesser sentence.'

'I know that. It still hurt, though.' He stared at Rebus. 'Is that all you've got, then? I was leching after my own son's girlfriend so he decides to top her?' He shook his head again. 'Jesus . . . '

'You don't visit Ellis, Mr Meikle — why is that?'

'He won't let me — don't think I haven't tried. I've had Billie practically beg him.' He pinched the bridge of his nose and screwed shut

371

his eyes for a moment. 'After the split, he took his mum's side, reckoned it was all my fault — maybe that was payback for all the rows I'd had with him. He's still my son, though; I still love him. I'd do anything for him, if he'd let me.'

Billie had been listening from the hall. She burst in and gave her father a hug. His eyes stayed closed as he stroked her hair. Father and daughter seemed close to tears, and Rebus suspected it was a regular occurrence. He retreated as quietly as he could and let himself out, standing on the landing for a minute or two while he considered what he had heard and seen.

And, most importantly of all, what he'd *not* seen.

40

Graham Sutherland walked into the MIT room with a face like thunder. He crossed to the window and stood there, hands in pockets, saying nothing. Clarke looked to Callum Reid, who just shrugged. Tess Leighton entered, closing the door after her, looking as though she'd been summoned. Eventually Sutherland turned round. When he fixed Siobhan Clarke with a look, she began to realise what was coming.

'You were seen yesterday,' he told her, working hard to keep his jaw from clenching, 'just prior to the press conference, in a café halfway up Leith Walk. You were with Dougal Kelly, is that right?'

'Him and Laura Smith, yes. Laura invited me — I'd no idea Kelly was going to be there.'

'Neverthless — '

'Ask her,' Clarke ploughed on. 'I was there about two minutes before I got the hump with Kelly and walked out.'

'Two minutes in which you discussed Jackie Ness's fingerprint?'

'Absolutely not. If I'd done that, Laura would have known too. She was as surprised as anyone when Kelly blurted it out at the press conference. I wouldn't have told *him*, I'd have told *her*! And who saw me anyway? Anyone with an axe to grind?'

'One of the admin staff.' Sutherland was about to say something else, but Clarke was already on her way. She flung open the door, stalked to the office next door and stared at the faces there, half hidden behind computer screens. Women mostly; civilians.

'Nobody likes a grass!' she yelled into the room, before marching back into MIT. Sutherland had moved to the middle of the floor. All eyes were on Clarke.

'Until recently,' she stated, her voice betraying the slightest tremble, 'people kept saying I was in Laura's pocket — so why would I give the Ness fingerprint to Dougal Kelly? Don't you see — it's Steele. It has to be.'

'Explain,' Sutherland said, folding his arms.

'I know how it looks.' Clarke held up her hands as if in surrender. 'But Steele and Edwards have been talking to Kelly, sharing gossip from the original inquiry, giving him dirt on practically everyone involved, except themselves.'

'You've got a bit of history with them,' Sutherland said.

'I know this looks like I want payback.'

'More to the point, can you prove it?'

'Not without Dougal Kelly.'

Sutherland thought for a moment. 'What was the meeting about anyway?'

'Laura's a mate. I thought it was just a catch-up.'

'What did Kelly want?'

'A contact on the inside, I think. We really didn't get very far.'

'Why not?'

'Because he wanted to talk about the team on the original inquiry and how they'd fallen down on the job.'

'You didn't want to hear that?'

'Not especially.'

'Because it might have meant hearing something unflattering about John Rebus?'

'Because,' Clarke countered, 'my focus is the current case, not what happened back then.'

Sutherland pursed his lips and stared at the floor, then raised his head and scanned the faces around him.

'Thoughts, people?'

There were shrugs, and twitches of mouths, and a clearing of the throat from George Gamble.

'Thanks for the vote of confidence,' Clarke said drily.

'Your reporter friend, she'll back up your story?' Sutherland asked.

'I'd hope so, since it happens to be the truth.'

'Then again, she's a mate — you said as much yourself — so she'd want to cover your back.'

'Am I being reprimanded? Kicked into touch?'

'Course of action yet to be decided.'

'Thanks a fucking bunch.' Clarke turned and started to leave.

'Where are you going?'

'Some fresh air — want someone shadowing me to make sure I don't get up to anything?' She waited for a response. When none came, she headed for the stairs.

$\star$ $\quad$ $\star$ $\quad$ $\star$

Rebus was driving through the city when Christine Esson called him.

'Bad time?' she asked.

'Bloody roadworks,' Rebus snarled. 'What can I do for you, Christine?'

'I've done what digging I can. Ended up using a few aliases, so I can keep monitoring the chat. This is by way of an interim report.'

'Fire away.'

'Kristen wasn't hugely popular among Ellis's friends. They all fancied her, but none of them actually liked her. Too stuck-up and too mouthy. Nothing to suggest she wasn't in love with Ellis, though, or was seeing anyone else. Her parents are a bit . . . '

'Religious?'

'Cold, I was going to say. After she died, they went deep and silent, their social media presence non-existent. Ellis's mum, on the other hand, went into overdrive. Anyone bad-mouthed her son, she hit back hard. Mostly Facebook and Twitter for her, a mix of Snapchat, Tumblr, Instagram, Flickr, Reddit and WhatsApp for everyone else.'

'Everyone else meaning . . . ?'

'Kristen and Ellis's peer group.'

'What about Ellis's sister?'

'She's online a fair amount. I tried saying hello to some of her friends, but I think they twigged. Not sure my 'voice' was right.'

'You're telling me you're not down with the kids?'

'Steady, Grandad.'

'Is she still in touch with pals from her old school?'

'Looks like.'

'But no trouble integrating at her new one?'

'Nope.'

'Her dad says her old school had been letting her down.'

'Can't help you there. But about her dad . . .'

'Yes?'

'I think I found traces of him on a dating site — he only seems to have the one email address and used his real name. Having left his wife, he seems to be in the market for a younger model.'

Rebus's brow furrowed. 'How young?'

'Nothing illegal — not that I can find. Late teens to late twenties.'

'How did you find out?'

'A tweet he sent to a mate he works with, thanking him for the tip. I scrolled back through the workmate's timeline.'

'He ever have dealings with Kristen?'

'Anything between them could have been deleted.'

'How about Kristen and Dallas?'

'Same goes. Sorry I can't be more helpful.'

'It's all helpful, Christine.'

'One other thing. There's always a fair bit of goading and sneering online, even between friends. One seems to have a go at Billie harder than the others. They go by the name Chizzy. I'm not sure Billie knows them, except online.'

'What sort of stuff are we talking about?'

'They'll comment on a photo, saying Billie's

looking fat or spotty — that sort of thing. Pretty harmless, and always accompanied by winking or laughing emojis. But it's the sort of thing a girl like Billie might take to heart.'

'Any idea who Chizzy might be?'

'Well that's the thing.' Esson paused. 'I'm thinking Billie's mother.'

'What?'

'I might be totally wrong, but it's just a couple of the things Chizzy says. She spells 'laughs' as l-a-f-z, for example. Seona Meikle does the same on her Facebook posts. I could be reading too much into it, of course.'

'Can we find out Chizzy's real identity?'

'We'd need someone a bit more technical. I'm strictly amateur hour.'

'What does that make me?' Rebus asked.

'Thing is, why would Seona be taunting her own daughter?'

'I'll need to think about that.'

'Want me to keep going?'

'If it's no bother.'

'I'm actually quite enjoying it.'

'Just so long as it doesn't cross the line into stalking.'

He heard her give a tut. 'Incidentally,' she said, 'I even decided to check your social media presence.'

'Oh aye? And?'

'There isn't one.'

'Did that come as a surprise?'

'Not in the least. But knowing how frugal you are . . . '

'Tell me.'

'You could FaceTime for free.'

'I'm still getting the hang of phones without wires, Christine — don't start bamboozling me.'

41

'Well,' Clarke said, 'I thought *Zombies v Bravehearts* was bad, but it was *Gregory's Girl* by comparison.' The end credits had finished and the DVD's main menu was showing on her TV screen. She was seated on the sofa next to Rebus. He had nodded off for a couple of minutes in the middle and missed absolutely nothing. She stepped over the dozing Brillo, crossed to her living room window and closed the curtains against the Edinburgh night.

'Looked like they shot some of it in Craigmillar,' Rebus said, popping open the empty DVD case. 'Must have saved a fortune, not needing make-up for the demons.'

'The two male leads were the same as in *Bravehearts*.'

'Neither seems to have become box office gold.'

'I googled them — they're not actors any more.'

'Were they ever?' Rebus poured the last dregs of his solitary bottle of IPA into the glass. Clarke had managed two gins before switching to tonic only. The evening had been her idea — the still centre Rebus had told her to find. A couple of microwaved ready meals followed by the film. She checked her copious notes.

'As for the female cop . . . procedure wasn't exactly her strong point.'

'I'd say the camera's interest was in the two strong points at the tips of her breasts.'

Clarke writhed in mock distaste. 'Fifteen minutes ten and twenty-six minutes forty,' she intoned. 'The two scenes where we see the handcuffs. Second one is the best.' She used the remote to skip through the film. 'Here we go.' After a few seconds, she hit the pause button. 'Nice close-up.'

The film's heroine had apprehended a thug after a chase and had him on the ground, pulling handcuffs from her belt and clamping them around the man's wrists.

'They look pretty real, don't they?' Rebus asked. 'The same kind we used back in the day?'

'They're not from a joke shop,' Clarke replied. 'If that's what you're asking.'

'So where *did* they come from?'

'Something we need to find out. We can't prove they're the same ones Bloom was wearing, though I'd swear they're the exact same model. Plus, say they *are* the same ones, the fact that they're in this film would explain how Ness's prints could have got on them.' Clarke was kneeling only a foot or so from the TV screen. She gestured towards it. 'It would help if we knew what happened to them after this.'

'Ness is the obvious person to ask.'

'Tomorrow for definite. Sorry you weren't there when we brought in Cafferty.' She returned to the sofa and lifted her glass.

'You're forgiven. I take it he gave you hee-haw?'

'He admitted knowing Conor Maloney, for what it's worth.'

'You could have FaceTimed me and let me listen.'

Clarke smiled. 'Suddenly you're an expert on FaceTime?'

'Since a few hours back, aye. Christine's been mentoring me.'

'Oh?'

'There's nothing I don't know about Ribbit, Pratchat and what have you.'

'Wonders never cease,' Clarke said with a smile. 'So you've got her checking Ellis's online history?'

'She's being a bit more thorough than that.'

'I'd best say thank you next time I see her, then.' She paused. 'So what else is happening with Ellis Meikle?'

'I've been on it all day.'

'Not just leaving it to Christine?'

'Perish the thought.'

'Any conclusions?'

'Just that you can tell Dallas Meikle you've earned his co-operation.'

'They were questioned today, too — Steele and Edwards.'

'Articulate and charming as ever?'

'Wouldn't it be wonderful if Ness had got the cuffs from one of them?'

'They didn't know Ness, though.'

'They knew Adrian Brand.'

'Yes, so why would they do anything for Brand's sworn enemy?'

Clarke didn't know the answer to that. 'I want

them hurt,' she said instead.

'Really? I'd never have guessed. Now can I have that second beer I made you promise not to hand over, no matter how much I begged?'

'Over my dead body,' Clarke said, rising to her feet. 'I'll make us a cup of tea instead.'

When she left the room, Rebus leaned down to give Brillo a rub.

'Nearly time to go home,' he explained as the dog raised his head. 'And Siobhan's going to have to vacuum this carpet by the look of it.' He raked his fingers across the floor, scooping up as much dog hair as he could, while thinking back to Charles Meikle's flat with its neat and tidy kitchen. The residue of oil on the mechanic's knuckles would have left marks on the worktop. Everyone left traces. The handcuffs were still on the TV screen. Police issue. CID or uniform, you'd know where to find some. Maybe, like Rebus, you kept a set at home as a memento. He'd checked a few nights back and they were still there in the drawer, a pair of the old chain-link design, along with the rudimentary key that accompanied them. There was other stuff in the drawer, too: a retractable steel baton and his old warrant card. He didn't doubt that the likes of Alex Shankley, Doug Newsome and even Bill Rawlston would have a drawer almost identical. And if one of those drawers was lacking an item, what did that prove?

'You okay with redbush?' Clarke was asking from the doorway.

'Not even tea's straightforward these days,'

Rebus pretended to complain. He followed her back into the kitchen. She had her back to him when she spoke.

'Thanks for coming over, John. I appreciate it.'

'After the day you've had? Least I could do.'

She half turned her head towards him, managing a thin smile. 'Do you think Graham will kick me off the team?'

'Question is, why hasn't he already?'

'To which the answer is . . . ?' She handed him a mug.

'Maybe he believes you. Maybe he even likes you.' Rebus offered a shrug. 'But if word gets to Mollison, it might be a different story. How are the rest of MIT handling it?'

'I'm not sure yet.' She leaned back against the worktop.

'Steele won't admit anything,' Rebus commented.

'I know.'

'But Dougal Kelly's got nothing to lose by telling MIT it wasn't you.'

'You think I should ask him?'

'Your call.'

'It'd mean owing him a favour.'

'Sod that. He wants a favour afterwards, he can go whistle.'

'Maybe I won't say that when I talk to him.'

'Best kept on a need-to-know basis,' Rebus agreed, taking a slurp of tea.

'How's the redbush?'

'It almost tastes like tea.' Rebus was eyeing the bottle of IPA visible on the worktop behind Clarke.

'Down, boy.'

Rebus turned his head towards the doorway, where Brillo was standing and watching.

'I wasn't talking to the dog,' Clarke said.

★ ★ ★

After Rebus and Brillo had gone, Clarke stood in her living room, ready to do the tidying. But instead she took a deep breath and called Dougal Kelly.

'Hi there,' he answered.

'My boss thinks I might be the source of the leak,' she said without preamble. 'My workmates are giving me looks behind my back and it's all your doing.'

'They know we had lunch?'

'In point of fact, we *didn't* have lunch, but I was spotted in the café with you, which amounts to the same thing. I need you to tell DCI Sutherland that you got the gen from elsewhere.'

'Are you really in trouble?'

'Will you talk to him?'

'I can probably do that.' He paused. 'I've been mulling over what you said about Brand's safe being broken into by Stuart and this guy Huston. I've persuaded Catherine we shouldn't go public with it just yet. But it raises a possibility, doesn't it? Stuart goes to Jackie Ness afterwards. Maybe he's holding back the contents of the safe; maybe he reckons whatever he found is worth a lot more than Ness has been paying him. They argue, and Ness ends up clobbering him.'

'We've found nothing at Poretoun House to suggest that.'

'Could have been outside, maybe as Stuart was getting back in his car.'

'I suppose,' Clarke admitted, rubbing at her eyes. She felt like she could sleep the clock around.

'You're exhausted,' Kelly said into the silence. 'Go grab some shut-eye. I'll talk to your boss first thing.'

'Will you tell him you got it from Steele and Edwards?'

'Probably not.' Kelly paused again, as if he'd been about to say something. Clarke felt cogs shifting in her head.

'Steele wanted us to meet, didn't he? He put the idea in your head — said I'd be prime candidate if you needed someone inside the investigation?'

'What if he did?'

'It means he's coming for me,' Clarke stated, pinching the bridge of her nose. 'And thanks to you, he's in with a shout.'

Thursday

42

'This is beginning to look a lot like harassment,' Kelvin Brodie said as he sat down with his client in the interview room. Sutherland and Clarke sat opposite, Clarke fiddling with the recording equipment. She reckoned her presence in the room was a message from the DCI to the rest of the team. Kelly had been as good as his word, according to Sutherland.

'So you believe me?' she had demanded to know, but all she'd got in return was a thin smile, no way of really reading it.

Jackie Ness looked pale and drawn, eyes bloodshot. His solicitor meantime wore an even more expensive-looking suit than previously and had a nervous energy about him, a parasite successfully locked on to its host. Ness had become big news, lifting Brodie's profile. The eventual outcome probably didn't matter — no such thing as bad publicity, as they said.

Not that the media interest seemed to be having that effect on Ness.

All four identified themselves for the record, and Clarke nodded to her boss that the gear was behaving itself. She then passed a set of photographs across the table. They'd been shot on her phone from the DVD and printed on to A4 paper. A bit grainier than she'd like, but fit for purpose.

'Do you recognise these, Mr Ness?'

It took a moment for the producer to rouse himself. 'They're handcuffs,' he eventually said.

'As used in your film *Cops v Demons*. I watched a copy last night.'

'If you say so.'

'The sound recordist on that film was Colin Speke, yes?'

'If you say so,' Ness repeated.

'Well, it's his name on the closing credits. You asked Mr Speke if he knew anyone who could lend you handcuffs for a couple of scenes. He fetched some from Rogues nightclub, courtesy of Ralph Hanratty. You weren't happy with them, though — does that ring any bells?'

'Maybe.'

'But these handcuffs . . . ' Clarke gestured towards the photos, which the solicitor was busying himself studying. 'These look like the real deal; very similar — maybe even identical — to the ones found attached to Stuart Bloom's ankles.' She paused to let that sink in. 'So what we're wondering is, what happened to them after you'd finished the shoot?'

Ness gave her the bleary look of someone who'd spent a night in a cell and not managed home since. 'Know how many plates I have to spin to get a film in the can? How am I supposed to remember a detail like that?'

'Even if it was to lead us to whoever killed Mr Bloom?'

'I'd help you if I could.' The producer shrugged. His shoulders were slouched, but Clarke wasn't completely convinced. She had to keep remembering that this was a man who'd spent his life around actors.

'Who sourced them then? You'd been asking around the crew and actors; someone must have come up with the goods?'

'Joe Madden maybe? No, not Joe . . . ' He arched his neck, staring towards the ceiling for inspiration. 'You're right about Colin — he brought along these flimsy bloody things, looked like they should have had pink fur wrapped around them. Sex shop crap . . . '

'Take your time,' Clarke said, as Kelvin Brodie checked his watch.

'I think we can take it that my client doesn't remember. Shall we move on?'

'Well then, there's the little matter of the break-in.' Clarke's eyes drilled into Ness's.

'Break-in where?' Brodie asked.

'At Adrian Brand's private office. Just a couple of nights before Stuart Bloom vanished.'

Sutherland had removed a typed sheet from a manila folder, studying it as though to refresh his memory without bothering to show it to either Brodie or his client.

'You had asked Morris Gerald Cafferty for help in finding a safe-breaker,' Clarke told Ness. 'I'm curious: was it your idea or Bloom's? Opening the safe, I mean? I don't suppose it matters. What's pertinent is that you put a man called Larry Huston in touch with Bloom, and the pair of them broke in and emptied the safe.'

'That's an extraordinary claim to make, DI Clarke.' Brodie was holding his hand out, but Sutherland wasn't about to relinquish the report. 'I'd be grateful to see your evidence.'

391

'We have a full statement from Mr Huston.'

'And a list of the items taken? Did this Huston fellow actually meet with my client, or only with Bloom? Is he perhaps a fantasist persuaded by you to concoct this frankly far-fetched tale?'

'He's a credible witness, Mr Brodie.'

Brodie turned towards Jackie Ness.

'Never happened,' Ness responded.

Clarke made show of raising an eyebrow. 'Cafferty says it did. Larry Huston says it did.'

'I've never heard of anyone called Huston and I only ever met Cafferty a couple of times, and only then because Billy Locke had got him to invest in one of my films.'

'*Zombies v Bravehearts?*'

'Yes.'

'He even watched you filming some of it in Poretoun Woods.'

'Did he?'

'He says he did.'

Ness offered another shrug. 'Know how many hangers-on there are on a film set? Everybody from the executive producer's nephew to some extra's boyfriend or girlfriend.' A light seemed to switch on behind his eyes. 'That's where the cuffs came from! I remember now. One of the extras had a mate who always seemed to be kicking around the place. Everybody liked him because he ... ' He broke off, eyes on his lawyer, then leaned in and whispered something.

'Unwise to hold anything back that could be germane to this inquiry,' Clarke said in warning.

Brodie mulled over what his client had just told him, then nodded. Ness turned his attention back to Clarke.

'He always had a bit of powder on him — powder and pills. I never touch the stuff, and I don't condone its use.'

Clarke thought back to her conversation with Hanratty, and the glittering onscreen eyes of Stuart Bloom and Derek Shankley. 'We already know there were drugs on set, Mr Ness. You're saying this individual was a dealer?'

'I never saw money change hands.'

'Presumably he wasn't giving them away for free, though?'

Sutherland cleared his throat. 'Do you happen to remember his name, Mr Ness?'

Ness puffed out his cheeks and expelled air noisily.

'Maybe you kept a list of everyone who visited the set?'

'I'm not Paramount Pictures. Security consisted of a question or two to anyone hanging around I didn't recognise.'

'But this man attended regularly, and you knew he was distributing drugs.' Clarke leaned forward a little. 'I find it hard to believe his name has slipped your memory. Did he ever play a role in one of your productions?'

'Might've been an extra, I suppose. I've an idea his mate was one of the zombies on *Bravehearts*, so he might've been too.'

'And his mate was . . . ?'

Another shrug. 'One of the locals.'

'Maybe a name for him, then?'

A slow shake of the head. 'I really am trying to help you here.'

'Did you ask him where he found the handcuffs?'

'I think I was just delighted they had a bit of heft to them. Sounded right, too — Colin said as much when we did this shot.' He tapped a finger against one of the photos, showing the cuffs around the actor's wrists.

'And after you'd finished with them . . . ?'

'Inspector,' Brodie said, fussing with his watch's leather wristband, 'are you going to present any evidence that the handcuffs photographed here are actually the ones used in the crime?'

'We're gathering information, Mr Brodie.'

'Admirable, I'm sure. But if they are the same, you must see that their appearance in one of my client's films would explain precisely why his partial fingerprint ended up on them.'

'I'm well aware of that.' Clarke's eyes were on Ness. 'If we could prove they're the same, it might save you from going to trial, Mr Ness.'

Ness snapped his fingers as if suddenly remembering. 'His first name was Gram.'

'Gram?'

'You know, like a gram of cocaine.'

'And Gram was the dealer rather than his friend the extra?' Ness nodded.

'But you don't know the friend's name?'

'Mr Ness is doing his level best here, Inspector,' Brodie interjected.

Clarke ignored him. 'This friend was an extra, Mr Ness? In *Bravehearts*? *Cops v Demons*? And

Gram might have been onscreen too?'

'I can't be sure.'

'It so happens I have both films here with me. Would you be willing to watch them and see if you *can* spot either man?'

Ness considered for a moment, then nodded slowly. 'Probably safer here than outside — if it's not the media stalking me, it's Stuart's bloody mother.'

'You'll want your solicitor present, of course.' Clarke turned her attention to Kelvin Brodie. Three hours of B movies played on a laptop with Jackie Ness for company. The look the lawyer gave her would, Clarke knew, warm her during many a long dark night.

43

Rebus sat in his Saab, watching the Meikle house, radio playing softly. After twenty minutes and half a pack of gum, Dallas Meikle emerged, getting into his car and driving off. Rebus locked the Saab, walked to the front door and rang the bell. Seona Meikle opened up, cigarette in hand. The look she gave him was the opposite of welcoming.

'Do I know you?' she rasped.

'I was here a few days back. You saw me chatting to Dallas.'

'He said you drank at McKenzie's, but that was pish. I can tell every time he lies.'

'Had a bit of experience, then?'

'Who are you and what do you want?'

'I'm ex-CID. I've been given the job of looking at your son's conviction. I'm assuming Dallas hasn't said anything.'

She took her time folding her arms, the cigarette hanging from a corner of her mouth. 'No,' she finally admitted.

'Well, Dallas was harassing one of the detectives on the case. She brought me in to help.'

'Help what?'

'Examine the evidence; dig down a bit deeper than maybe happened at the trial.'

'Trying to get him off, you mean?' Her eyes narrowed as the smoke hit them.

'Trying to establish what actually happened, and why.'

She shook her head. 'Bloody Dallas. I *knew* he couldn't let it rest.'

'You think your son did it, Mrs Meikle?'

'Who else?'

A fair question, but not one Rebus felt like answering. Instead, he slipped his hands into his pockets, keeping his stance casual. 'I've been studying some of the family's social media,' he said. 'Just working out relationships, stuff like that.'

'Is that legal?'

Rebus fixed her with a stare. 'I'm wondering why you call yourself Chizzy, Mrs Meikle.'

'Eh?'

'When you're pretending to be a pal of your daughter's. When you're having a bit of a snipe at her.'

'Go fuck yourself.' She had unfolded her arms and plucked the cigarette from her mouth.

'She won't be too happy when she finds out, I dare say.'

The woman had taken a step back and was starting to close the door on him.

'It's because she chose her father over you, isn't it? That's what's pisses you off.'

'Go fuck yourself,' she repeated.

'And now you don't even have Ellis,' Rebus pushed on. 'Just you and your brother-in-law, all nice and cosy. But not really cosy at all . . . '

His last words were called out to a door that had clicked shut. He leaned down and prised the letter box open, withdrawing his fingers rapidly as the cigarette was stubbed down towards them.

'Attempted assault, Mrs Meikle,' he called out, receiving in response the familiar refrain, this time from deeper inside the house. Seona Meikle was done with him.

★　★　★

'That went well,' Sutherland told Clarke when they returned to the MIT room. Clarke just nodded and told Phil Yeats to take a laptop and the two DVDs to the interview room. Seated behind her desk, she remembered a call she had to make. She found Derek Shankley's mobile number on the list next to her computer.

'Yes?' he answered.

'It's DI Clarke, phoning from Leith. I hope I'm not disturbing you?'

'I'm marking coursework.'

'I won't keep you. I was just wondering if the name Larry Huston meant anything to you?'

'Afraid not.'

'We think he helped Stuart break into Adrian Brand's office and steal from the safe there.'

'Really?' Shankley sounded bemused.

'Stuart probably met or spoke with Huston sometime before the break-in. The break-in itself happened just a couple of nights before his disappearance.'

'Stuart never really talked about work.'

'No?'

'He always said what I didn't know couldn't hurt me.'

'Two nights prior to his disappearance, were

you maybe waiting for him at his flat?'

'Let me think . . . Yes, probably.'

'He wouldn't have got back till late.'

'His line of work often took him out at night.'

'Having got the contents of the safe, I'd think he might be elated, a bit more than usual even?'

There was silence on the line while Shankley thought back. 'Yes, that's right,' he eventually said. 'He was quivering all over. Poured himself a whisky, which was unusual. I remember now. I thought he was feverish or something.'

'And he had a carrier bag with him?'

'Nothing out of the ordinary in that.'

'Not shopping, though; maybe something he was reluctant to show you?'

'Could be, I don't really recall. I know he stayed up late. I woke up when he came to bed. He seemed . . . a bit cast down. Maybe just tired, I thought. He was okay in the morning.'

'Did you see the bag after that time?'

'I don't think so . . . Is it important? Maybe it got taken in the break-in.'

Clarke felt her stomach lurch. 'What break-in?'

'A week after Stuart vanished, I got a call from a neighbour. Someone had kicked in his door.'

'What did they take?'

'Actually, I'm not sure they took anything. I mean, nothing I could identify as missing.'

'The bag?'

'I don't know if it was still there.'

'Why didn't you report this, Derek?'

'The neighbours beat me to it. Police were there by the time I arrived.'

'Which police?'

'The kind who wear uniforms and ask to see your ID.'

'Would that information have been passed to the squad investigating Stuart's disappearance?'

'How am I supposed to know that?'

'You're not,' Clarke conceded.

'Was there anything else, Inspector?'

'Just one thing. Stuart and you were extras in *Zombies v Bravehearts*. I saw you on the DVD, remember?'

'Yes.'

'I don't suppose the pair of you had taken anything? You seemed a bit . . . glassy.'

'Better that than wooden.'

'You're not going to get in trouble, Derek. I just need to know.'

'There was plenty of stuff on set, if that's what you're asking. Pills and weed mostly — coke for those who could afford it.'

'Supplied by a man called Gram?'

'Now that you mention it.'

'Ever know his surname?'

'Don't think so.'

'Could you describe him?'

'Just . . . really ordinary.'

'Local accent?'

'I think so.'

'Apparently he had a friend who might have been an extra alongside you.'

'I can't help. It was a few days, a long time ago, in a haze of whatever was on offer. Then when Stuart went missing . . . ' Shankley sighed. 'I'm sorry, I just don't remember.'

'If you do, you know where to find me.'

'Can you tell me what this has to do with Stuart's death?'

'Not at this exact moment. Goodbye, Mr Shankley.'

'Inspector?'

'Yes?

'Would it help to take a look at Stuart's flat?'

'What?'

'His parents hung on to it. I was allowed to clear out my stuff, but after that . . . '

'They've still got it?'

'According to Dougal Kelly.'

Clarke paused. 'I didn't realise you two knew each other.'

'He interviewed me for the book he's writing. Told me the place hasn't been touched in twelve years. Family never wanted Stuart declared dead — maybe Catherine thought he'd come back to it one day.'

'Could you get me the key?'

'Best if it's someone else who asks. I've been *persona non grata* ever since Stuart vanished.'

'Yet you'll be in the book?'

'Not if Catherine gets the final say. I really think the only reason she keeps Kelly around is that he's become a surrogate.'

'For Stuart, you mean?'

'You've noticed they look similar?'

'Maybe.'

'It's the eyes, the mannerisms . . . '

'I'll ask Kelly if he can get me the key.'

'I wouldn't mind tagging along — if that's okay. Just to refresh my memory.'

Kelvin Brodie was standing in the doorway, clearing his throat to announce his presence. 'I'll see what I can do,' Clarke told Shankley, ending the call. She walked towards the lawyer.

'Might have something for you,' he said.

Through in the interview room, the film had been paused. Jackie Ness was on his feet, leaning over the laptop screen, palms pressed to the desk.

'I'm pretty sure,' he said. 'Pretty sure.' He lifted one hand and touched first one face and then another. 'Those two there.'

Clarke peered at the screen. 'The zombies with their faces caked in mud and gore?'

'Real mud, fake gore.'

The eyes were just about discernible, but little else. Height and hair colour were almost impossible to guess.

'Will they be in other scenes?' Clarke asked.

'Look,' Brodie said impatiently, 'you've got your identification. I'm not sure what further gains will be made by — '

'It's a good film,' Jackie Ness broke in. 'I'd forgotten that. Still an hour to run.'

'And *Cops v Demons* after that,' Clarke reminded him. 'Another classic. So, please, do keep watching. Both of you.' And with a fixed smile for the benefit of the solicitor, she made her exit.

Next stop: Malcolm Fox's room. If anything, the mounds of paperwork around him had multiplied. He had loosened his tie and the top button of his shirt.

'Still here, then?' Clarke said.

'Managed to convince ACC Lyon I wasn't quite finished.'

'Murder inquiry, Malcolm. Got to be more exciting than pushing paperwork around a desk at Gartcosh.' She saw him sweep his eyes across the contents of the room and gave a smile. 'Different then,' she corrected herself. 'But tell me, with that big forensic brain of yours, anything in this lot about a break-in at Stuart Bloom's flat?'

'When?'

'Week after he disappeared. Neighbours phoned it in; our lot went out to have a look.'

Fox gave a frown of concentration. 'I'm pretty sure there's nothing here.'

'So much for joined-up thinking.'

'Nobody put two and two together?'

'Probably reckoned it was opportunist — guy's not at home, so the place is unguarded.'

'What did they take?'

'Derek Shankley reckons very little, if anything.'

'Any idea what it means?'

'Maybe that whatever they wanted wasn't there. Or it *was* there and they took it.'

'The contents of the safe?'

Clarke shrugged. 'From what Derek says, whatever was in that safe didn't exactly fire Stuart up.'

'But someone still wanted it back?'

'Or else didn't know it was worthless.' Clarke scanned the room again. 'Always supposing he didn't hand it over to Jackie Ness at their final meeting.'

'What does Ness say?'

'No break-in, ergo nothing to hand over. Where's your baby-sitter?'

'Tess reckons I'm one of you lot now.'

'Just the one dinner date so far?'

'We had a drink last night. It was meant to be a film, but nothing took our fancy.'

'I should have invited you round to mine for a DVD.'

'*Cops v Demons*?'

'The very same.'

'Did you glean anything?'

'Handcuffs very like the ones used on Stuart Bloom.'

'And?'

'We may have a lead on their supplier.'

'A cop?'

'No.'

'But they *are* police issue?'

'Of a certain vintage. Guy who provided them was a dope dealer.'

'Cafferty?'

'Why do you say that?'

'He ran the trade back then.'

'Except he'd gone quiet after those overdoses.' Clarke paused. 'So things are pretty hunky-dory with Tess, eh?'

'I'd say so.'

'She said anything about me?'

'I've reassured her you're one of the good guys.'

'What about the rest of the team?'

'They know that you and I go way back.'

'Meaning they're unlikely to open up to you?'

Clarke nodded her understanding.

'Sutherland's had a private word with each of them, though, according to Tess. He's on your side.'

'Might end up not being his call.'

Fox caught her meaning. 'ACU?'

'Heard anything from them lately?'

'Steele wanted to know how his interview had gone down with MIT.'

'Hope you told him: like a cup of cold sick.'

'I was maybe a bit more diplomatic.'

Clarke pressed her hand against the nearest tower of paper. '*Is* there enough in here to see someone put on a charge?'

'Almost certainly.'

'But not Steele and Edwards?'

'Probably not.'

'Skelton and Newsome?' She watched him nod slowly. 'Bill Rawlston?' He let his hand waver in front of him, meaning maybe. 'John Rebus?'

'Oh, John for definite.'

'Alerting Shankley to the raids on Rogues?'

'For starters, yes.'

'You mean there's a main course?'

'With cheese and petit fours to follow.'

'Going to let me peruse the menu?'

'I don't think you can afford the prices, DI Clarke.'

'My credit's no good?'

Fox sighed. 'John was trying his damnedest to tie Cafferty to Bloom's disappearance, even if it meant feeding lies and half-truths to a friendly journalist or two. He was hoping to flush

Cafferty out, I think. It didn't work, but one of the journalists ended up in hospital.'

'Cafferty's doing?'

'A street mugging. But reading between the lines, yes, Cafferty's doing. The reporter made a complaint about John. John denied everything.'

Clarke digested this. 'Cops and journalists, eh?' Her eyes were fixed on Fox's. 'It can lead to all manner of complications.'

The silence lay between them until Fox broke it. 'You know, don't you?'

'That it was you leaking to Laura Smith? Of course I know.' 'She told you?'

Clarke shook her head. 'Laura always protects her sources — we both know that. But you're forgetting that it was me who introduced you to her. Who the hell else was it going to be?'

Colour had risen to Fox's cheeks. 'I was so sorry ACU went after you.'

'Not sorry enough to own up.'

'No.'

Clarke shrugged. 'Steele and Edwards saw what they wanted to see. They knew I had a relationship with Laura. You were canny enough to keep yours well camouflaged. Then there was my history with John.'

'They were trying to get to him through you?'

She shook her head again. 'They want me *because* they've never managed to hook him.'

There was a further silence until Fox cleared his throat. 'We still pals, Shiv?'

'Unless you're bumping me for Tess Leighton — then again, maybe you see her as *more* than just a pal.'

'Time will tell. And meanwhile, if you need my help holding anyone's feet to the fire . . . '

'Flames are getting closer to Steele and Edwards,' Clarke stated, nodding slowly.

'Their kind usually has an extinguisher to hand.'

'They might find they've all been emptied.'

'By you?'

'By John and me,' she corrected him. 'I just hope we get to them before they get to me.' She fixed him with a stare. 'Remember to keep all this to yourself — just for a change.'

She was watching the colour rise to Malcolm Fox's cheeks once more when Graham Sutherland put his head round the door.

'Our presence is requested at St Leonard's,' he said.

'Mollison?' Clarke guessed.

'Mollison,' Sutherland confirmed.

44

DCS Mark Mollison was seated behind the world's tidiest desk in his office at St Leonard's police station. There were awards arranged on the windowsill behind him and others on the walls. Siobhan reckoned some probably dated back to schooldays. He'd even framed what looked like his university degree. He offered a seat to neither her nor Graham Sutherland. He'd had time to prepare the frown on his face and the hundred-yard stare.

'You had a meeting with this Kelly scumbag just before his outburst,' he said without preamble. 'A little warning would have been nice.'

'DI Clarke has assured me — ' Sutherland began, but Clarke took half a step forward, not quite shouldering him aside.

'Would I be wide of the mark if I guessed it was ACU who told you?' He didn't seem inclined to answer. 'With respect, think about how they could possibly know.'

'What is it you're saying?'

'I'm saying *they're* the ones who leaked to Dougal Kelly.'

'As part of a continuing vendetta against you?' Mollison smiled with half his mouth.

'I know it was them,' Clarke continued. 'And they knew I'd call them out on it, so they got their defence in first.'

'Did you or did you not meet with Kelly?'

'I didn't know he was going to be there.'

'So you just thought it would be you and Laura Smith — the same reporter who saw you become the focus of an ACU investigation lasting much of last year?'

'I didn't realise she was on some sort of blacklist — anyone else I'm not supposed to consort with?'

'Siobhan . . . ' Sutherland was giving her a warning.

'I note,' Mollison broke in, eyes on Sutherland, 'that none of this seems to be coming as a surprise to you, Graham.'

'DI Clarke volunteered the information, sir. She knew how it might look and wanted me to know.'

'You didn't see fit to pass the news along?'

'Apologies for that.'

'Our media office are apoplectic. They've got reporters demanding to know why we would talk to an incomer like Kelly and keep them in the dark.'

That figured, Clarke thought. With Mollison it was all about the public image.

'All I can say, sir,' Sutherland went on, 'is that I'm minded to accept DI Clarke's version of events. Someone leaked, but not her.'

'And keeping her on the case won't poison the atmosphere within MIT?'

'DI Clarke has earned our trust, sir.'

Clarke kept her eyes on the wall behind Mollison, her face betraying nothing.

Mollison stayed silent, then gave a sigh. 'ACU

are champing at the bit to open an investigation.'

'Surprise, surprise,' Clarke couldn't help muttering, earning her another hard stare.

'From what I've heard,' Mollison said icily, 'I can't see any reason for that investigation not to happen.'

'Except,' Sutherland broke in, 'that it would interfere with the inquiry, just as we've reached a critical point. And hasn't Police Scotland aired enough of its dirty laundry in public of late? Surely ACU can wait till the case is wrapped up?'

'When someone is drip-feeding evidence to outside parties?'

'No one from inside my team, sir.'

'Who else then? Who else does Kelly know? Who has he met with?' Mollison held up a thumb. 'He knows Laura Smith — and who is it *she* knows?' His eyes were on Clarke again.

'He knows ACU too,' she stated. 'They've been giving him tit-bits from the original inquiry, covering their arses by grassing up everyone else.'

'You can prove that, can you?'

'My word against theirs,' Clarke conceded. 'Right up to the point Dougal Kelly goes public with it.'

Mollison grew thoughtful again. 'Maybe ACU should be having a chat with Mr Kelly.'

'Oh aye, that'll go well.' Clarke just about succeeded in not rolling her eyes. Sutherland was squeezing her elbow with his fingers.

'Is there anything else, sir?' he enquired.

Mollison considered this, then made a

brushing motion with one hand.

'Thank you, sir,' Sutherland said. He gave Clarke the chance to say the same, but all she did was free herself from his grasp and open the door.

Outside, he puffed out his cheeks and exhaled.

'Thanks for sticking up for me,' Clarke said. 'Even if it did mean telling a few untruths.'

'I dare say it's not the first time Mollison's been lied to.'

'I don't want you getting in trouble on my account.'

'I'm only protecting that game of pitch 'n' putt you promised me. Besides, ACU do seem badly to want another crack at you.'

They had exited the station and were in its rear car park, where Clarke's Astra waited. Another unmarked car sat at the end of a line of patrol vehicles — the black Audi, its driver's-side window lowered, giving a view of Brian Steele.

'Speak of the devil,' Clarke commented. Then, to Sutherland: 'I need a word with him, and I'd rather you weren't a witness.'

'I'm a big boy, Siobhan.'

'Even so . . . ' She began to walk purposefully towards the Audi, leaning in towards it so she was face to face with Steele.

'DI Clarke,' he said with a sneer. 'What brings you here?'

'There's one thing you need to know,' she told him, her voice quiet but firm. 'When you come for me — *if* you try coming for me — don't think I won't be yelling from the rooftops who it really was who spoke to Dougal Kelly.'

'Would that be just before you jump?'

'Think I'd give you the satisfaction?'

'Your phone's ringing,' he said, gesturing towards her jacket pocket. Clarke dug the phone out and held it to her face. Her dentist. She waited for the call to ring out.

'Nothing urgent?'

'Just a wrong number.'

He tried for a solicitous look. 'Often get those, do you? Annoying, I'd guess.'

Clarke tried not to let her sense of satisfaction show. He'd fallen for it. As far as he was concerned, she was still being harassed by Dallas Meikle.

'You'd better go see your pal Mollison,' she told Steele. 'Press your case again.' She leaned further into the window. 'I'm ready for anything you bring, you smug, bent-as-a-paper-clip cock.'

She walked back to where Graham Sutherland was waiting. Behind her, she could hear Steele chuckling.

'Must have been a good joke,' Sutherland commented as she unlocked the car.

'An absolute killer,' Clarke agreed.

45

Rebus was parked outside the gates of Billie's school. He'd arrived early, which was just as well. Soon after, parents had started turning up, meaning the street was now lined with cars waiting to give lifts home. He was thinking about families and the lies they told each other. From the outside, it was hard to know what was happening behind their walls and curtained windows. Even once you'd crossed the threshold, there'd be secrets unshared. In an age of the internet and mobile phones, kids and their parents lived ever more separate lives, sharing confidences but also hiding bits of their true selves behind masks. It had been hard enough in the past to read people, but these days you had to push your way through so much that was fake and misleading. Modern policing fell into that trap, heading straight for technology — computers and CCTV — to replace old skills and the occasional inspired guess or piece of intuition.

A CD was playing quietly on the Saab's antiquated sound system, not Arvo Pärt this time but Brian Eno, another gift from Deborah Quant to help his 'mindfulness'. When she'd explained the concept to him, he'd argued that it was something he'd always done, that it used to be known simply as 'thinking'. He realised he needed to call her, fix another supper date — maybe even a sleepover. But meantime his

413

phone was buzzing.

'Hiya, Siobhan,' he said, answering. 'Any more flak to report?'

'Did you know that Stuart Bloom's flat was broken into a week after he disappeared?'

'No.'

'Another balls-up by the investigation. How about a drug dealer called Gram?'

'As in Gram Parsons?'

'What?'

'He was a musician, died young.'

'So it might have been a nickname?'

'Maybe this Gram guy was a fan of the original. He was a dealer?'

'To most of the people working on Jackie Ness's films.'

'I'd remember if that name had come up.'

'He's the one who supplied the handcuffs.'

Rebus thought for a moment. 'Cafferty's gang were in charge of the east coast back then. I doubt he'd have countenanced competition, no matter how minor-league.'

'I've been discussing that with Malcolm. It got me thinking. A deadly overdose practically on the doorstep of Rogues. We go in hard on the club, cracking down but finding nothing, because the club's been tipped off by you.'

'I'll deny that, of course,' Rebus broke in.

'But did you do it to save Stuart and Derek's bacon, or were you goading Cafferty? I mean, anybody those raids flushed out would likely have been selling on Cafferty's behalf.'

'You're over-thinking things, Shiv — remember the still centre?'

'You got a journalist put in hospital, John.'

Rebus gave his bottom lip a bit of a gnaw. 'Collateral damage,' he eventually said. 'Malcolm's good at digging, isn't he?'

'Yes, he is. Should I ask Cafferty about this Gram guy?'

Rebus thought for a moment. 'There's no other way of identifying him?'

'I suppose we could re-interview everyone who ever played a role behind or in front of the cameras in one of Ness's flicks.'

'I'm hearing a lack of enthusiasm.'

'I'm beginning to think this could have been wrapped up back in the day.'

'If we hadn't been such a bunch of lazy, useless, conniving bastards, you mean?'

'Something like that.'

'You're forgetting — we didn't have a body.'

'What you did have were two powerful businessmen, neither of whom you landed a glove on.'

'We lacked that little thing called evidence, Siobhan.'

He heard her give a long sigh. 'That was by no means the only thing you lacked, John,' she said, ending the call.

Rebus couldn't find it in him to feel slighted. She was right, after all. He had lied about not passing information to Alex Shankley. He'd lied, too, to cover Skelton and Rawlston's arses. He'd turned a blind eye to the manifest shortcomings of Newsome and the likes of Steele and Edwards. Instead, he'd made more frequent visits to various pubs, using alcohol to blur everything and make it all right. Less than a year till his retirement, he'd begun to fear that the job was just that — a job rather than a vocation. He couldn't solve every crime, and even if he did, crime would keep happening, so what was the point? Cafferty and the other bosses — the Starks in Glasgow, the Bartollis in Aberdeen — would go on and on. There would always be drugs and stabbings and domestics, and the odd person whose wiring wasn't right. People would always be rapacious and lustful, envious and angry. He had forgotten about the journalist, the one he'd zeroed in on because the kid was hungry and easy to manipulate, one of those reporters who got a buzz from hanging out with cops. After the beating, the kid had slunk off home to his parents. Rebus hoped he had flourished. Then again, so what if he hadn't? Rebus couldn't even put a name to him.

He chewed some gum and watched through the windscreen as the school began to disgorge its cargo at the end of another day. A trickle at first — the keenest to escape — and then a mass of gossiping, shrieking teenagers. Boys nudged and shoved each other, showing off for the girls, who tried their best to look bored or unimpressed. They were busy on their phones, or talking among themselves. So many of them, Rebus worried he might not see Billie.

But then she was there, to one side of a line of four. All girls, all her age. She carried the same backpack they all did. Short, tight skirts, black tights on spindly legs. She was animated, turning with a half-smile towards a lad who had flicked her curls. Her friends huddled as if to mark his effort out of ten. He didn't say anything, just returned to two of his own friends. There was so much energy emanating from the various groupings, Rebus could feel it as a physical force, pushing against him. He knew he was looking at the future, but also that the futures these various young people imagined for themselves might not work out the way they hoped. There'd be tears and traumas along the way, mistakes made, promises broken. Some would marry their sweethearts and live to regret it. Others would break apart. A few would trouble the police in later years. There'd be early deaths from disease and maybe even a suicide or two. Right now, none of that would seem feasible to them. They were alive in and of the moment — and that was all that mattered.

Watching Billie, he saw a girl who was relaxed and bright, and who had made friends. He thought of her father's words back in their kitchen: *Best thing I ever did was ask if she wanted to come live with me. Her old school was rubbish, grades dropping* . . . Yes, if your kid was unhappy, you'd want to change it. If their grades were falling and they were becoming sullen and withdrawn. Hard to imagine Billie like that now. She seemed almost to glow. They all did.

Having seen enough, Rebus picked up his phone and called Cafferty.

'You again,' Cafferty said.

'Me again,' Rebus confirmed.

'It was Christie, wasn't it? He's the one who gave you Larry Huston?'

'What makes you think that?'

'I hear I've become a bit of an obsession. Plus, Christie's just been moved to Saughton, and that was Huston's home from home. Lot of chat goes on in prisons, Rebus.'

'I wouldn't know.'

'Yes you fucking would. I hear you went to Saughton yourself. To see Ellis Meikle, I'm guessing. But along the way you had a little one-to-one with Mr Darryl Christie. If he can't get to me, he wants you to have a go. Fucking good luck with that.'

'I hope you're not threatening Larry Huston. Anything happens to him, there'd be no one but you in the frame.'

'Huston's a nobody. There was no break-in — go ask Sir Adrian.'

'You know damned fine that's already been done. Tell me this then: whatever happened to Gram?'

'Gram?'

Rebus spelled it for him. 'He was a drug dealer, so there's a better than even chance he was one of yours or on your radar.'

'I'm drawing a blank.'

'He sold to Jackie Ness's crew. I thought you visited the set?'

'Nobody was doing drugs while I was there.'

'No?'

'I think I'd have noticed. Got a description for this Gram?'

'Not yet.'

'Could you have heard wrong? Maybe Graeme with an e?'

'Spill.'

It took Cafferty all of ten seconds to make his mind up. 'The kid who OD'd, I looked into it. The name I kept hearing was Graeme. Used to deal a bit in places like Rogues. Made himself scarce after the kid died.'

'Where was he sourcing the stuff?'

'Aberdeen maybe.'

'I remember you trying that line with us at the time so we'd go after the Bartollis for you.'

'Aberdeen, Glasgow . . . wherever he got the stuff, it wasn't from me.'

'Didn't really matter, did it? It cost you Conor Maloney's friendship anyway.'

'How come you always know where to stick your pins in me?'

'Oh aye, you're hurting.'

There was a chuckle on the other end of the phone. Then it went dead.

46

Late afternoon in Leith. The MIT office had made room for two visitors. Aubrey Hamilton had brought the soil specialist from the James Hutton Institute in Aberdeen. The specialist's name was Professor Lee-Anne Inglis. She was in her early forties, with long brown hair, parted and tucked behind one ear. She had come armed with data. There were charts and the results of chemical analyses. She explained to the room about 'soil fingerprints' and the records she had compiled from hundreds upon hundreds of samples. A few crumbs on the sole of a shoe or embedded in a tyre could pinpoint where that shoe or tyre had recently been. Soil, vegetation, pollen — all were crucial. Something the size of a grain of rice could be as unique as a fingerprint.

'I used cross-matching first,' she explained, holding up one of her charts. 'Then gas chromatography and other tests.'

Chairs for her and Hamilton had been placed in the centre of the room, so that they were ringed by the MIT officers. Fox, with the rapt attention of a school swot, was studying the stapled sheets that had been handed out. Gamble, in contrast, had barely glanced at his before scratching his head and shrugging his shoulders in Phil Yeats's direction.

Graham Sutherland was perched on one corner of his desk, Callum Reid on another, while Leighton and Crowther stayed behind their own desks and Siobhan Clarke stood by the map on the far wall, arms folded, listening intently. Ness and Brodie were long gone. The initial spotting of the two extras had been the only one. She didn't know why the lawyer had looked so furious — he was bound to be billing Ness by the hour.

'You've got us a location for the car?' Sutherland nudged.

'Not a precise one, no,' Inglis intoned. 'That was why I was keen to give you the information in person. It's not for lack of effort.' She held up her own copy of the handout in support of this. 'But what I can say is that before it was in those woods, the car was on farmland of some kind.'

'Farmland?'

'The deposits show straw and animal manure below the loam and nettles picked up when it rolled down into the gully, the loam itself a good deal fresher. I'd say the car sat where you found it for no more than three years, and before that was in a field or a farm or a byre — the faecal matter is bovine. The soil type is from the Scottish lowlands, probably east coast rather than west. The sample was at least ten years old, maybe more.'

Clarke studied the map. 'So all you're asking us to do is search every farm in lowland Scotland?'

'For a car that's no longer even there,' Sutherland added.

'I'd suggest,' Inglis went on, ignoring their tone, 'the car was driven from the farmland to

421

the woods. The tyres had picked up bits of grit and stone found on tarmacked roads, but without the earlier deposits becoming dislodged.'

'Driven rather than transported there on the back of a flatbed?' Yeats asked. He looked around the room. 'Say it sat in a field for nine or ten years — battery would be flat; tyres, too. Oil, spark plugs . . . ' He shrugged.

'Someone from a garage would have had to get it going,' Gamble agreed.

'Someone with a bit of know-how anyway,' Yeats said.

Inglis had risen from her seat and approached the map, standing the other side of it from Clarke so they could all see. She found Poretoun Woods with her forefinger. 'Maybe a twenty-mile radius. A longer drive would have dislodged the deposits.'

'We can probably discount Edinburgh,' Clarke mused.

'I wouldn't,' Aubrey Hamilton piped up. 'Plenty green belt around the edges of the city, meaning farmland.'

'Am I allowed to say it's needle-in-a-haystack stuff?' George Gamble announced gruffly. 'What does it matter if the car was stuck in a field all those years?'

'Think that could happen without someone knowing?' Clarke enquired. 'We find where the car was kept, we've got ourselves someone who can tell us who put it there *and* who moved it again.' She looked to Sutherland for confirmation. He was nodding to himself slowly as he sifted through the handout.

'This is very useful, very useful,' he intoned quietly. To Clarke's ears, it sounded as if he was trying to convince himself.

★ ★ ★

By 5.50 p.m. they were back in what had become their usual bar, minus Reid and Yeats, who had appointments elsewhere. Between the departure of the two professors and knocking-off time, they had managed, by dint of an internet search, to find the name and phone number of the person they needed at the National Farmers' Union Scotland. But that person had gone home for the day, as had everyone else in the office.

'It can wait till morning,' Sutherland had said. 'I don't suppose the farms will have gone anywhere, and it's not as if we're going to be visiting any of them at dead of night.'

When Rebus texted, asking Clarke's whereabouts, she texted back. Not fifteen minutes later, he walked in.

'Perfect timing,' Sutherland said. 'I was just about to get in another round.'

'My shout,' Rebus insisted, pointing at each of them in turn until he'd amassed the order.

'I'll help carry,' Sutherland said, accompanying Rebus to the bar. He had removed his tie and loosened his shirt collar.

'How's it going?' Rebus asked him.

'Slow but steady.'

'Charges imminent?'

'Hope springs eternal. What brings you here anyway?'

'Just need a word with Siobhan.'

'And maybe with DI Fox too, eh? See if he's finished finding all the dirt from first time round.'

Rebus looked over to where Fox and Clarke were pretending to be chatting while actually much more interested in what might be being said at the bar.

'Fox has tried taking me down in the past,' Rebus commented. 'He never got very far.'

'How about Steele and Edwards — ever had any run-ins with them?'

'I have a sneaking suspicion they saw me as one of their own. If we got too close, no way of knowing who would leave the grubbier marks.'

'They seem to have led charmed lives.'

'Maybe not for much longer.' Rebus paused. 'Siobhan and I both know why you brought her in to MIT. She won't thank you for the knight-rescues-damsel scenario, but I do. It sent ACU a message, reinforced by the way you've stuck up for her since.'

'I get the feeling you think you might be about to send them another.'

Rebus handed two twenties to the barman.

'You think of her like a daughter, don't you?' Sutherland asked.

'I've got a daughter.'

'Maybe a favourite niece, then?'

'Another scenario she wouldn't thank you for,' Rebus said, hoisting two of the glasses and making his way to the table.

Eventually people started to drift off — home-ward bound or in search of food — until only

Rebus, Clarke and Fox were left.

'Here we are again,' Rebus commented, raising his glass in a toast. 'Almost like the old days.'

'But without the pints and nicotine,' Fox said. He was drinking sparkling apple juice, same as Rebus.

'I can appreciate,' Rebus went on, 'that while a civilian was present, nobody was ready to open up about the case. But now it's just the three of us . . .'

'How much do you know?' Fox asked.

'John's pretty well up to speed,' Clarke answered quickly.

'I won't ask whose doing that is.' Fox gave her an arch look. 'Does he know about the field, though?'

'What field?' Rebus enquired.

'The one where the VW Polo sat for the best part of a decade. It was only moved to the gully two or three years back.'

'Around the time Ness sold up to Jeff Sellers,' Clarke clarified. 'Who in short order sold to Brand.'

'It sat in a field?' Rebus didn't sound as if he quite believed it. 'With the body inside?'

'From the condition of the bodywork, Professor Hamilton reckons it had a tarpaulin over it. But nothing underneath, which is why weeds and the like pushed their way up from ground level. They were uprooted when the car was moved, but were still all twisted round the exhaust and had even invaded the interior floor.'

'Sitting in a field and no one noticed?'

She shook her head slowly. 'I know.'

'So now,' Fox said, 'we have to look at farms and fields within a twenty-mile radius of Poretoun, which means asking the NFU for help.'

'You talk like it's your inquiry, Malcolm,' Clarke said.

'I can't help myself.' Fox gave a thin smile, staring at the surface of his drink.

'Almost finished your report?' Rebus asked him.

'A result this time round would help shift the focus from previous failings.'

Rebus nodded. He was thinking back to another bar, another conversation.

'I visited Poretoun,' he began. 'Got talking to a local whose son has a farm there. Guess what that farmer did when he was young?'

'Enlighten us.'

'Acted as an extra in one of Jackie Ness's flicks.'

Clarke stared at him. 'You're winding us up.'

Rebus lifted a hand. 'Cross my heart.'

Fox was busy on his phone. He held it up so they could see the screen. 'Poretoun Glen Farm?' he said.

'Maybe,' Rebus conceded. 'We could all jump in a car and go see.'

'Not without Sutherland's blessing,' Clarke stated.

'And what would we see in the dark anyway?' Fox added.

'Spoilsports,' Rebus said. Then, eyes on Fox: 'Mind if I have a quick word with Siobhan?'

'For her ears only?' Fox nodded his understanding. 'Anyone want another?'

They shook their heads, but he went and stood by the bar anyway, half-filled glass in hand. Clarke moved a little closer to Rebus.

'I think,' Rebus explained in an undertone, 'I've got just about enough for us to take to Dallas Meikle.'

'You know why Ellis did it?' Her eyes had widened a fraction.

'Why it happened, yes.'

'So tell me!'

But he was shaking his head. 'There's something I have to do first.'

'What?'

'Go see Ellis again.' She looked to him for an explanation, but he shook his head again. 'Later,' he said. 'Meantime, Cafferty dropped me a name — Graeme with an e. That's who sold the tainted dope to those ODs.'

'Graeme was a sole trader?'

'According to Cafferty. Seems he got out of Dodge when Cafferty started looking for him.'

'But only as far as Jackie Ness's film set, by which time he was Gram?'

Rebus shrugged. Fox was looking impatient. 'If it turns out to be useful,' Rebus told Clarke quietly, 'just remember that you didn't get it from me.'

'Because that would mean admitting Cafferty confides in you?'

'That's not what he does — he plays games, some of them long-term.'

'You think he's still playing one that started in 2006?'

'Maybe.'

Fox was nearing the table. 'Finished gossiping about me?'

'I was just telling Siobhan it's good news Cafferty is cooperating with the inquiry.'

'He is?'

'Steele won't know any different when you tell him.'

'Why would I tell him when it's not true?'

'To shake the kaleidoscope,' Rebus said with a smile.

'The two of them know one another?'

'Cafferty used him as muscle on at least one occasion, that occasion being a meeting with Irish gangster Conor Maloney.'

'Why are we only hearing this now?' Clarke asked.

'Because — surprise, surprise — everyone concerned will doubtless deny it.'

'So how come *you* know?' Fox asked.

'Grant Edwards got drunk and mouthy one night, couldn't help telling me. I think he thought I'd be peeved Cafferty hadn't picked me for the job.'

'And what does this achieve, kaleidoscope aside?' Fox wanted to know. It was Clarke who answered.

'Driving a wedge between Steele and Edwards?' she guessed.

'The start of one maybe,' Rebus acknowledged. 'Now, if anyone's hungry, I'm in the mood for a curry.'

Fox shook his head. 'I'm supposed to be meeting someone for a drink,' he apologised. His eyes met Clarke's. Her look confirmed that she hadn't told Rebus about Tess Leighton.

'How about you, Shiv?'

'Sorry, John. I've got an appointment too.'

'I'm being stood up,' Rebus said, trying to sound as if he could hardly believe it. 'Don't think I won't remember this when you two are old and on your lonesome.'

'We can't help it if we're young and in demand,' Clarke said, finishing her drink and rising to leave.

47

A second-floor flat in a tenement on Comely Bank Avenue. Dougal Kelly and Derek Shankley were waiting for Clarke at the main door. Kelly slid the key into the lock and they entered the stairwell. It was well maintained, a couple of children's bikes chained to the bottom rail of the stone stairs. Clarke had noticed that the name BLOOM was still on one of the buzzers beside the main door. Having climbed the two flights, they stopped at a red-painted door. Just below the spyhole was a brass plaque, again with the name BLOOM on it. It had been polished in recent memory. Derek Shankley ran a finger across it.

'Catherine?' Clarke asked Kelly. The journalist nodded.

'She comes fortnightly,' he explained, unlocking the door and ushering them into the flat.

'Thanks for doing this,' Clarke said, trying not to sound too grudging. Kelly just shrugged.

Derek Shankley stood with his palms to his cheeks. 'It's exactly the same,' he whispered, studying the hallway.

Clarke flicked a switch and the lights came on.

'Bills get paid on time,' Kelly confirmed.

'Explains why the place is warm.' Clarke touched a radiator.

'Heating's on a timer, an hour each day.'

'That must still add up — never mind the

council tax and what have you.'

'Martin's tried more than once to convince her to sell.' Kelly offered a shrug. They had moved from the hall into the living room. Shankley's palms were still pressed to his cheeks as he took it all in. Books on shelves; a venerable typewriter in a carrying case; a hi-fi with CDs stacked next to it; newspapers and current affairs magazines dating back to 2005 and 2006.

'It's a time capsule,' Clarke said.

'Or maybe a mausoleum.'

She looked at Kelly. 'And once the burial's got the go-ahead . . . ?'

'I doubt it'll change anything. She'll still want to be able to visit. She sits on his bed, I think she even talks to him.'

Shankley had settled on an arm of the sofa, removing his hands from his face and using a finger to wipe a single tear from his eye.

'The door was repaired after the break-in?' Clarke asked.

'Must have been,' Shankley said. Clarke looked to Kelly.

'You knew about it?'

'Not until Derek told me. Catherine confirmed it, though, and yes, she had the door fixed afterwards.'

Clarke studied the room. 'Where would the papers have been?' she asked. 'The ones taken from the safe?'

Shankley didn't seem sure. 'On his writing desk maybe,' he offered.

The desk itself was a dining table with just the one leaf unfolded. It had been positioned near the room's bay window, where there was plenty of natural light.

'He always took his laptop with him?' Clarke asked.

'Always.'

She had noticed a camera case sitting on one of the bookshelves. It was a Canon.

'This was here when the place got turned over?' She watched as Shankley nodded.

'Odd kind of break-in,' Kelly agreed. 'TV left behind; camera equipment and hi-fi untouched; ditto Stuart's passport and cheque-book.'

'Have you got a theory?' Clarke asked him.

'They got exactly what they wanted or else they left empty-handed.'

She nodded her agreement and watched as Shankley left the room, crossing the hall.

'Bedroom,' Kelly explained.

'He feels the family have written him out of Stuart's story,' Clarke said quietly.

'He's not wrong about that. Catherine doesn't want him at the funeral either.'

'Seems unnecessarily cruel.'

'I don't disagree.' He had walked to within a few feet of Clarke. 'How are things with you?'

'Your chums Steele and Edwards are determined to have me for dinner.'

'How about your boss and his team?'

'I'll cope.'

'A drink when we're finished here?'

'Not tonight.' She looked at him, all business. 'The break-in at Brand's office — you've not given it to the media?'

He shook his head. 'I convinced Catherine it

432

was in nobody's interest.'

Clarke nodded, showing she understood. She studied the room again.

'You think it's weird,' he asked, 'them keeping this place as it is?'

'I think I can understand it.' They heard muffled sobbing from the room across the hall. 'Should we . . . ?'

Kelly shook his head again. 'Derek had a hell of a time of it, you know — from the very start, I mean. Dad a big macho copper in big macho Glasgow. He lived a lie for a long time; coming out was hard.'

'How did his dad take it?'

'Denial to start with. Then whisky and shouting. Just the two of them in the house, hardly speaking, the one hoping and praying the other would start to understand.'

'Nicely put,' Clarke said. 'I hope he does make it into your story — it's probably the least he deserves.'

Kelly nodded distractedly, watching the doorway as Derek Shankley appeared there.

'I don't think I can stay any longer,' Shankley said, voice trembling. 'I thought it'd be okay, but it's really not. I'll wait outside till you're done.'

When he was gone, Kelly looked towards Clarke, wondering if she'd seen enough. In answer, she checked the bedroom, kitchen and shower room, lingering in none of them. The bed had been made up, a slight indentation where Shankley had rested for a moment. Clarke brushed the surface flat, so Catherine Bloom wouldn't suspect.

433

'Good thinking,' Kelly said from the doorway, ready to lead her back to the outside world.

Friday

48

When Clarke brought her car to a halt in the farmyard next morning, she saw that another car and a van were already there. Three men in pristine wellington boots were studying what looked to Clarke like architectural plans as they pointed in the direction of the nearest fields, fields that currently were occupied by a herd of untroubled cows.

Clarke had brought Crowther with her. Fox had pleaded his case, but Sutherland had reminded him that he was attached to the investigation only tangentially and for a specific reason.

'In fact, I've had Jennifer Lyon on the phone; she reckons you must be about ready to wind everything up. Says there's plenty of work waiting for you at Gartcosh.'

Fox had slouched from the room without saying another word.

'Puts hairs on your chest,' Crowther said, sucking in a lungful of the pungent air. 'That's what my dad used to tell me.'

Clarke was walking towards the group of men.

'You the civil engineer?' one of them asked.

'I'm a detective.' She showed her warrant card. 'I'm looking for Andrew Carlton.'

'Join the queue.'

'Can I ask what you're doing here?'

'We're in the process of buying this land. It's

going to be a village in miniature. Sixty to seventy new-builds, mostly detached.'

Clarke had noticed the word Brand on the side of the van. 'You work for Sir Adrian?'

All three nodded.

'He's bought the farm?'

'Taken him a good few years to persuade Carlton and shred all the red tape, but Sir Adrian's not a man to give up without a fight.'

'Not unless he's caught napping by a bloody film producer,' another of the three said, pretending to throw a punch. Laughing to themselves, the men moved off, holding the site plans between them as they walked.

Turning around, Clarke saw that Crowther was checking the outbuildings. A large empty byre; a milking shed full of gleaming equipment; a silo half filled with manure; a barn with more machinery, a well-stocked workshop situated in a lean-to attached to it. The farmhouse was a modest two-storey affair, its door locked. Through the windows Clarke could make out breakfast detritus on the kitchen table — just the one plate, knife and mug — and a living room that looked like no one used it much.

Crowther gave a shrug and they continued their search. A muddy track behind the barn led to a ramshackle gate, beyond which stood a churned, steeply sloping field. Crowther gestured towards the field's furthest corner. It had become a dumping ground for unwanted machines and implements.

'What do you think?' she asked. It was Clarke's turn to shrug.

They opened the gate and headed in, slipping and sliding until they adjusted to the ground beneath them. As they got closer, Clarke could make out a baler (she thought), and other bits and pieces that could be attached to a tractor. There were a couple of old trailers, their wood mostly turned to pulp. A small van was missing all four wheels and had begun to sink into the mire. There were also coils of fencing, dangerous-looking collections of rusting barbed wire, and the remains of a fridge freezer and washing machine. Even a venerable-looking toilet and blackened cast-iron bath.

The two detectives' interest, however, had quickly shifted to a gap between one of the trailers and the van. The ground here was a slightly different colour. What weeds and plants had pushed through the soil weren't quite as well established as those nearby.

'Something's been moved,' Crowther commented.

Clarke turned and peered into the front of the van. 'There's a tarpaulin in here.'

'Get on to the SOCOs or a chat with the farmer first?'

'SOCOs. If nothing else, their presence might throw Mr Carlton off balance. I wonder where the hell he is.'

It was then that Clarke heard a tractor in the middle distance. She climbed on to the bonnet of the van for a better look. The tractor was trundling along, the best part of one field over. It stopped suddenly, a figure half emerging on to the running board, facing her. Clarke waved, then watched as the figure leapt down from the cab and stood there for a moment before turning and running in the opposite direction.

'Hell's he up to?' Crowther asked.

'Back to the car!' Clarke called out, jumping from the bonnet of the van and trying as best she could to hurry through the morass.

They called it in as they drove. Crowther had the sat nav up. Poretoun was the only village around. Not many roads, most of them little more than country lanes and farm tracks. They retraced their route towards the main road and took a left. Eventually they caught sight of the abandoned tractor. The lane was lined with hedgerows, with gaps here and there allowing occasional glimpses of the fields and woods beyond.

'See him?' Clarke said from between gritted teeth. Her boots were slick with mud, threatening to slip from the pedals.

'No,' Crowther admitted.

'Get up on the roof.' Clarke brought the car to a stop.

'You sure?'

'Just do it.'

Crowther got out, clambering on to the bonnet first and then the roof. Clarke slid her window down.

'He can't be far,' she called out.

'Unless he's not on foot. Maybe there was a car . . . '

'How long did they say for the cavalry?'

'Fifteen minutes, maybe twenty. Dalkeith and Penicuik are the nearest stations.'

'But not always manned?' Clarke guessed.

'Any chance of a helicopter?'

'Yeah, sure. When we might not even be able to rouse a patrol car.'

Crowther slid back down the windscreen on to the bonnet and half rolled until her feet hit the ground. 'Only asking,' she said, getting back in.

Clarke pressed the accelerator, eyes scanning left to right. A figure darted from the undergrowth before she could brake. The impact threw him forward, spinning. He hit the roadway shoulder first, head next, and lay there, either unconscious or . . .

'Dead?' Crowther asked, jaw refusing to close once the word was out.

Clarke pulled on the handbrake and pushed open the door. She crouched in front of the farmer. Below his blue overalls, his chest rose and fell, rose and fell.

'Ambulance?' Crowther asked from the passenger seat.

'Ambulance,' Clarke confirmed with relief.

49

'What did you do?' Ellis Meikle asked Rebus. They were back in HMP Saughton's visiting hall, same table as before.

'They moved you?' Rebus asked.

'Not yet, but someone's had a word. I'm being treated like I'm not to be messed with.'

'I spoke to someone in here who has a bit of clout.'

'Who?'

Rebus shook his head. 'Best you don't get too close. Had any other visitors?'

'No.'

'Want to know why I came here in the first place?' Rebus watched Meikle shrug.

'You said it was down to Uncle Dallas.'

'A friend of mine, she was the cop in charge of your case.'

'Clarke?'

'That's the one. She started getting prank calls. Being a detective, it took her about ten minutes to unmask the culprit — your uncle Dallas. He'd been given her number and home address by a couple of other cops she'd had some bother with. Being thick and malicious, they decided to offer her up to your uncle. She wants payback but Uncle Dallas wouldn't help unless she took another look at your case. He thinks you're innocent, Ellis. He *believes* in you.'

'He shouldn't.'

'Thing is, though, I'm going to have to tell him he's right. It took me a while to make up my mind — I had your dad in the frame but it didn't quite work. He may have fancied Kristen — he seems to have a thing for women younger than your mum — but like I say, it didn't quite work. So I'm going to have to tell Uncle Dallas about Billie.' Rebus paused to let his words sink in. Colour was creeping up Ellis Meikle's neck.

'No,' the young man said, voice suddenly hoarse.

'What else can I do?' Rebus reasoned. 'You're in here for a crime you didn't commit.' He leaned forward on his elbows. 'Started to dawn on me when I told you I'd been talking to some of the kids who knew you in Restalrig. Remember? I told you they'd said she made you do it, and straight away you asked if they meant Kristen. Afterwards, I began to wonder — who else if not your girlfriend?' He paused, giving his words time to sink in.

'Billie was at your house that day; your focus was on the game you were playing — easy for her to send a text from your phone. And that would have been that, if you hadn't gone out and bumped into one of Kristen's pals, wondering why you weren't at the bunker. You knew straight off who must have sent the text — unlikely it was one of your mates. So you hightailed it, but too late. Billie had already done the deed. You took the knife from her, made sure to wipe her prints and add your own, then threw it where it wouldn't be too hard to find. Got your sister out of there, maybe covering up any blood on her

443

clothes by sticking your own jacket over her. And that was that.' He lifted his elbows off the table and leaned back in his chair. 'Something else you said on my first visit: 'What else was I going to do?' You didn't mean killing Kristen; you meant taking the blame.'

'You can't prove anything.'

'Means, motive and opportunity,' Rebus said. 'The holy trinity of any investigation. Opportunity — well, we've already ticked that box. Motive — I'm guessing if we got some IT experts in or questioned the right pupils at Billie's old school, we might find concrete proof that she was being bullied by Kristen. You'd heard the stories too, I dare say — Kristen trying to get to your dad through you.' The young man looked ready to lash out, so Rebus held up a hand. 'Just stories, Ellis. I'm not saying they're true. But these days with the internet and mobile phones and things like WhatsApp and Snapchat — I'll be honest with you, I don't really know what those are; I just hear about them. What I do know is, they make bullying a 24/7 reality. I've had someone who knows more about them than me take a look. Billie's friends — in the real world and online — were being targeted by Kristen's coterie and told to 'unfriend' her. Billie was a lot happier, more settled, once she was away from her old school, the school where she couldn't help but see Kristen every day. But that wouldn't necessarily stop the taunts and the teasing and all the rest. Besides which, Billie was the woman of the house now your parents had separated; she felt she had to look after your dad.

444

Maybe she'd even started to believe the stories . . . ' He paused again. 'Which only leaves us the means.'

'I'll deny everything.' Teeth bared, Meikle jabbed at the table with a finger. 'This is where I need to be.'

'Why?' Rebus asked, genuinely interested.

'Because out there I'm a nobody. No job, no future. In here, I can be something else.' He took a deep breath. 'Dad and me, we never really . . . He only had time for Billie. But now I've got him and Dallas paying me attention. I get fan mail, you know — women writing to me from all over. And meantime Billie is where *she* belongs, getting smarter and growing up. She got all the brains and all the love. This is where I need to be.'

'But not where you deserve to be.'

Meikle stared across the table. 'Who are you to say that? What do you know about me, about any of us?' His shoulders relaxed a little. 'Go ahead and tell Uncle Dallas anything you like. You want to help your friend — I'm okay with that. But when he asks me, I'll say you're lying. I'll say you've no evidence and you're not even a proper cop.'

'No evidence?' Rebus's mouth twitched. 'Aye, maybe.' He started to get to his feet, leaning across the table, lowering his voice. 'We never did get to means, did we?' He looked ready to make his exit, but stopped and turned back, eyes meeting Meikle's. 'Tell Billie there's a knife missing from the set in her kitchen, the ones in the wooden block. If she wants you serving her

445

sentence for her, she'd better get rid of that block. Only a matter of time before her dad notices — always supposing he hasn't already.'

'I used to visit them!' Meikle was calling across the room as Rebus walked away. 'I could have taken it!'

'Tell your uncle to help my friend,' Rebus called back. 'Tell him to do the right thing.'

The same warder as before was waiting for Rebus in the corridor, arms folded, one foot crossed over the other as he leaned against the wall opposite the library's closed door. He was smiling at Rebus's approach.

'Darryl wants another word,' he said.

Rebus stopped in front of him, their faces only a couple of inches apart. 'You're a fucking disgrace,' he told him, his jaw tight.

'Makes two of us then. He told me you were Cafferty's man.'

'I'm nobody's fucking man,' Rebus spat, so close now that their chests were touching. Then he turned and walked away. Before he'd reached the end of the corridor, he heard the door to the library open. Christie had probably been just the other side of it, listening. Rebus kept walking, not bothering with so much as a backwards glance, even when he heard his name being called.

50

Clarke and Crowther were seated in A&E when Sutherland and Reid arrived. Clarke explained what had happened.

'SOCOs headed to the farm?' Sutherland asked.

'Haj Atwal's already there,' Crowther assured him.

'As of right now, it's all speculative,' Sutherland cautioned.

'Does look good, though,' Reid commented. 'Not least because he tried to run.'

Sutherland nodded. 'Is he in there?' He gestured behind the reception desk towards a large room filled with curtained cubicles.

'They think he may have one broken rib, maybe a shoulder fracture. They're strapping him up.'

'If they give him any medication, might be a while till we can question him.'

'During which time the SOCOs can make their report, maybe get the lab to run a quick check of the tarpaulin in case it left its mark on the Polo . . . '

'Plus,' Sutherland added, 'we can find out as much as possible about Mr Carlton.'

'One thing we already know,' Clarke went on, 'is that he's selling the farm for housing. Brand's been after it for a few years.'

'As good a reason as any to move the Polo

elsewhere.' Sutherland nodded again. 'This is really great work, Siobhan. Christ alone knows how long it would have taken us to search every bloody farm on the NFU list.'

'We've got John Rebus to thank,' Clarke commented. 'Plus Emily's keen eyes.'

'There'll still be a few questions to answer, mind. Bosses will want your version of the accident.'

'It wasn't deliberate, Graham,' Clarke assured him.

'Car's not even dented,' Crowther added. 'Couldn't have been doing more than twenty.'

A doctor in a white coat was heading in their direction. 'You're here with Andrew Carlton?' he asked. 'Good news is, he's fine. The bruising will be extensive and he'll be in pain for some time.'

'What have you given him?' Sutherland enquired.

'Painkillers, you mean? He refused them.'

'He's awake?'

'Pretty much ready to be discharged. If you'll follow me . . .'

All four followed the doctor to one of the cubicles. He parted the curtain and they saw the farmer lying there, stripped to the waist, chest and left shoulder tightly bandaged.

'Quite a welcome party,' he said, studying their faces. 'Am I under arrest?'

'We've got a few questions, Mr Carlton,' Sutherland said. 'Best asked down at the station.'

'I need to speak to Gerry first.'

'Who's Gerry?'

448

'Farmhand. He'll be wondering where the hell I am.'

'He already knows,' Clarke said. 'The scene-of-crime team met up with him.'

'He doesn't know anything,' Carlton said quickly.

'About the Polo, you mean?'

The farmer's face tightened. 'Do I get a lawyer?' he asked.

'We can sort all that out,' Sutherland told him. 'Are you okay to move? Should we fetch a wheelchair?'

'I think I'm all right. Could do with some clothes, though.' He looked down at his chest and shoulder. 'Shirt won't go on, but maybe the overalls will.' His eyes met Clarke's, recognition dawning. 'It was you, wasn't it? Behind the wheel? You need to be more careful on country roads.'

★ ★ ★

It had taken a while to manoeuvre Carlton into the back of Reid's car, and almost as long to get him out again at the other end. He was kept in the interview room while a duty solicitor was fetched. Leighton and Yeats had been busy at their computers and on their phones, digging up as much as they could about the farmer. Carlton had neither wife nor current girlfriend, and asked them not to notify his parents, despite being told it wasn't the sort of thing that would stay secret for long. He was thirty-eight years old and had been born and raised in Poretoun,

449

coming to farming comparatively late after a university degree in accountancy and jobs in insurance companies and banks. The farm had been his uncle's, the man desperate that it should stay in the family if at all possible. On his uncle's death, Carlton had secured a large enough loan for the purchase of the farm, all of this happening towards the end of 2005, just a few months prior to Stuart Bloom's disappearance.

The farming had been fine for a few years, but things got progressively tougher until he knew he had to sell. There had always been offers — it was commuting distance to Edinburgh and housing was always needed. Nobody wanted the land for farming, Brand eventually convincing the relevant bodies that it could be re-zoned — green belt no longer. Carlton's loans and interest would be repaid, and he'd even have a bit left over, though it meant letting down Gerry and the various part-time farm labourers, plus his uncle's memory.

All of this they had learned by the time the flustered-looking solicitor arrived. Her name was Sian Grant. Clarke didn't know her. She looked young — still in her twenties — and inexperienced. But she would also be idealistic and hungry; Clarke knew they couldn't afford to underestimate her. Sutherland had decided that Clarke and Crowther should be the first ones to question Carlton — as a reward, and because they knew as much as anyone, if not more. Crowther got the equipment ready after Carlton had had ten minutes with his lawyer. Teas were fetched, the farmer trying hard not to grimace when he lifted the mug.

'Sure you're up to this?' Grant asked him.

'It's going to happen anyway, isn't it? If not now, then later?' He watched Clarke give a pleasant nod. 'Let's get on with it then.'

The three women shifted in their seats, composing themselves. Carlton's overalls hadn't been done up quite right, his left arm across his strapped chest preventing buttoning. He seemed self-conscious about it. Whenever his good hand wasn't holding the mug, he tugged at the blue cotton, trying to pull the garment closed.

'Cold?' his lawyer asked.

He shook his head, and they began. Clarke got him to fill in some of his biography, leading up to the purchase of the farm.

'Whole family thought I was bonkers,' he admitted. 'Maybe I was, but I'd been going to my uncle's since I was a toddler. Always took school pals there, especially in the summer break. It was a giant adventure playground. Never looked like hard work to me. Long hours, but I didn't mind that.'

'We're interested,' Clarke eventually said, 'in how Stuart Bloom's Volkswagen Polo ended up in a corner of one of your fields.'

'Lot of stuff got left there.'

'Sorry,' the lawyer broke in. 'Do you have evidence that the car in question was at my client's farm?'

'We're pretty confident.'

'But until you can prove it, it remains supposition, yes? And he's just told you that things got dumped in his fields — fly-tipping is a perennial problem in the countryside.'

'Actually,' Crowther corrected her, 'the word he used was 'left' rather than 'dumped'.'

'Left under a tarpaulin,' Clarke added, 'so no one would see what was inside. But you must have known, Mr Carlton?'

He looked to his solicitor. She shook her head.

'Our theory is,' Clarke continued, 'that the car and its contents had to be moved when discussions started about selling the land to a developer. It couldn't be left there for others to find. Must have had a hell of a job getting it out of that quagmire, but I suppose a tractor and tow chain would come in handy.'

'We'll have the scene-of-crime and forensic lab report within the next few hours,' Crowther added. 'They've logged all the vegetation that had grown through the Polo's chassis. They have soil samples that these days are as good as fingerprints. Chances are there'll even be a few threads from the tarpaulin stuck to the Polo. Trust me, a few threads are all they need.'

'But as of right now,' Grant countered, 'you don't have any of that, DC Crowther.'

'We have your client fleeing the scene,' Clarke told the lawyer, 'soon as he saw someone next to where the Polo had been. A woman perched on the bonnet of an old van, waving — scare easily, do you, Mr Carlton?'

'Not something I expected to see,' he muttered by way of explanation.

'Actually, that word 'scare' reminds me of

something.' Clarke pretended to be finding some information in the folder in front of her. 'You acted in some zombie films for Jackie Ness, didn't you?'

The question seemed to catch Carlton off guard. 'Just in the background.'

Clarke showed him a still from *Bravehearts*. 'This is you, yes? Next to your friend Gram?'

'If you say so.'

'I'm asking you what *you* say.'

'Could be anyone,' Grant prompted.

'Could be anyone,' Carlton duly parroted.

'But you did play an extra in that film? And in others, too?'

'Loads of us from the village did. It was a good laugh.'

'You didn't get paid, did you, or fed and watered come to that?'

'Wasn't why we did it.'

'Plenty of drugs, though, eh? To keep the spirits up?'

'I'm not sure what you're . . . ' Grant began, but Clarke's words rolled right over her.

'Drugs brought along by your good friend Gram. Your good friend Gram who also managed to supply a pair of handcuffs when one scene demanded them, handcuffs identical to the ones found around a murdered man's ankles in a car that was parked on your land for almost a decade.' Clarke broke off, giving time for her words to take effect. 'All of which makes you an accessory, at the very least. Unless you helped murder Stuart Bloom as well as disposing of his body.'

Grant had swivelled her whole body towards her client, demanding his full attention.

'None of this is proven at this point. It's a fishing expedition, Andrew, that's all. The allegations are serious, which is why you shouldn't have to deal with them until your mind is lucid and free from pain.' Then to Clarke: 'You hit him full-on with your car, Inspector. Concussion may be the least of it.'

Clarke ignored the lawyer. Her focus remained on Andrew Carlton, just as his eyes stayed fixed to hers. When he said something, Clarke didn't quite catch it, masked as it was by Grant's continuing remonstration.

'Sorry, Andrew,' she said, gesturing for the lawyer to be quiet, 'what was that?'

Carlton's eyes dropped but his voice was strong and steady. 'Graeme was his real name. Not Gram. Graeme.'

'And his surname?'

'Hatch.'

Clarke watched Crowther scratch the name on her pad in large capital letters. 'And what happened to Graeme?' she asked.

'I don't know.'

'I think you do. I don't suppose he still looks like this?' Clarke held up the still from the film. The farmer managed a rueful smile.

'We can trace him, you know,' Crowther said. 'Better for you to cooperate and not be found out later to have held anything back.'

'He moved away for a while,' Carlton conceded. 'Changed his name, changed *every-thing* . . . ' He was lost in thought for a moment.

454

'I didn't know what was in the car. Nothing was in it when he brought it, nothing I could see.'

'Bloom's body was in the boot,' Clarke stated quietly. Tears were welling up in Carlton's eyes.

'I need five minutes with my client,' Sian Grant demanded.

'Where's Graeme now?' Clarke asked the farmer. 'A weight's about to lift from you when you tell us.'

Carlton was shaking his head, sniffing and angling his head so no tears would escape. Clarke turned her attention to the lawyer.

'You need to make your client understand that helping us is the smart thing to do.' She began getting to her feet, gesturing for Crowther to switch off the recording equipment.

'Interview suspended,' Crowther said into the machine, checking her watch and adding the time. Then she followed Clarke from the room.

⋆ ⋆ ⋆

They made their report in front of Sutherland's desk while Malcolm Fox brewed fresh mugs of tea. Phil Yeats had been sent to keep watch on the interview room. When Clarke had finished speaking, she checked with Crowther that she hadn't left anything out.

'We've definitely got him,' was all Crowther said.

Clarke turned back to Sutherland. 'Forensics?' she asked.

'No sign on the Polo's bodywork of any fibres

455

matching the tarp. The tarp itself, however, is another story. We think we have flecks of paintwork; probably flaked off as the bodywork started to corrode around the wheel arches. Might not get an exact match, but we'll be able to say what make of car was wrapped up. Add to that the patch of land where the car sat — it's been measured and is a near-perfect fit for a Polo. Less luck with the vegetation, but the soil will be checked by Professor Inglis and she's promised not to take so long this time.'

'All of which adds up to what?' George Gamble asked. 'Is this farmer our killer?'

'I don't think that for a minute,' Clarke said. 'His pal Gram or Graeme is the one I think we want.'

'Internet isn't giving me much,' Tess Leighton interrupted, peering at her screen. 'There are a few Graeme Hatches listed, but no Poretoun or central Scotland connection.'

'If need be,' Sutherland said, 'we hit Register House, try for a birth certificate. Plus we go ask everyone in and around Poretoun.' He looked at Clarke. 'He was local, right?'

'As far as we know.'

'And dealing a bit of dope,' Crowther added. 'Someone's bound to remember him.'

'Did someone say dope?' John Rebus was standing in the doorway.

'You can't be here,' Sutherland stated. 'We've a suspect and his solicitor along the hall; if she gets wind that anyone can just walk in off the street . . .'

Rebus held up a hand to say he understood.

'Just wanted a word with Siobhan and she's not been picking up messages.'

'I've been a bit busy, John. Can it wait?'

'Only take five minutes,' Rebus persisted.

'Outside then,' she eventually conceded.

They headed downstairs in silence, through the reception area and on to the pavement. Clarke sucked some air into her lungs, shaking her head at Rebus's offer of gum.

'You've got someone?' he asked. 'The farmer I put you on to?'

She nodded and sketched the morning out for him.

'In which case,' he said, 'my news can wait.'

'You sure?'

He nodded.

'It's about Ellis Meikle, though?'

Another nod.

'And is it good news?'

'I suppose so.'

'You don't sound very certain.'

'I was going to say we should go have a chat with the uncle, but it might be best if I did that myself. You're up to your eyes as it is.'

'I don't need to be there?' She watched him shake his head. 'Did you at least manage to have a bit of fun, John?'

'Fun?'

'Playing detective again, I mean.'

'All the fun in the world, Siobhan.' Rebus stretched out an arm. 'It's just one huge amusement park out there, happy families everywhere you look.'

She looked like she was struggling to think

457

what to say, so Rebus patted her on the arm and told her to get back inside. She started to obey, but paused.

'Remember that still centre you told me about?' she said. 'That's how the interview room feels to me right now.'

Rebus nodded slowly before crossing the road to his waiting car. Instead of turning the ignition, he just sat there chewing, staring into space.

'Families, eh?' he muttered to himself. He was thinking of the Meikles, but of cops, too. One big unhappy, dysfunctional family. Steele had told him that it was ugly when cops ratted on fellow officers, because it was like a betrayal of family. Certainly that was the way it had been in Rebus's day. You covered up for the faults and foibles of your colleagues. Many a time a patrol car or van had come to the Oxford Bar to take him home. He'd wake up on his bed fully dressed, no idea who had got him up the two flights of stairs or how they'd managed it. Nothing was ever said — that was just how it was with families. Ellis Meikle reckoned he was where he needed to be. His father meantime was working hard at providing Billie with a settled home life. What right did Rebus have to interfere? A result had been achieved, and it seemed to suit everyone — with the possible exception of Dallas Meikle.

Yes, Dallas Meikle.

The next person Rebus needed to speak with.

★ ★ ★

Sian Grant was in the corridor between the interview room and the MIT office, Phil Yeats alongside her. Clarke came to a stop in front of them.

'My client has a name he'd like to give you,' the lawyer said.

'Go ahead.'

'On the understanding that you acknowledge you are receiving his full cooperation and that this will be taken into account in any future proceedings.'

'It will.' Clarke was almost holding her breath. The lawyer handed over a scrap of paper. Clarke looked at the name written on it. 'Phil,' she said, 'take Ms Grant back to her client. The interview will restart in a couple of minutes.' Then she walked into the MIT office and over to Sutherland's desk, holding the scrap of paper in front of her. Sutherland looked up from the call he was making to the fiscal's office.

'Glenn Hazard,' she said. 'Aka Graeme Hatch.'

'Brand's PR guy?' Sutherland had lifted the phone away from his face.

'Brand's PR guy,' Siobhan Clarke confirmed. 'We need to let DCS Mollison know.'

Sutherland nodded thoughtfully. 'You do it,' he told her. 'Explain to him how the dots got joined. Try not to talk down your own role.'

Their eyes met as Clarke smiled.

'Thank you,' she said.

'Doesn't mean you're off the hook with ACU, mind.'

'Oh, I've got a few plans of my own for them,' Clarke said, turning away to make the call.

51

'I'm due at work in an hour,' Dallas Meikle said, recognising the figure on his doorstep.

'This won't take that long,' Rebus assured him. 'Is Ellis's mum home?'

'Aye.'

'Then maybe we could talk somewhere else.' He tugged on Brillo's lead, confident that, even untethered, Dallas Meikle would follow.

Rebus was on the bench in the play park by the time Meikle caught up. He offered him gum but Meikle shook his head and gave Brillo's head a firm rub. Then, having decided that neither man nor dog was about to bite, he eased himself down next to Rebus.

'I've done what I can,' Rebus began, staring out across the park. 'I've re-read everything in the files, talked to a few people, visited Saughton twice.'

'And?'

'And in doing so, Siobhan Clarke has kept her side of the bargain.'

'So what have you found?'

Rebus shook his head slowly. 'That's between Ellis and me. He'll tell you if he wants to; maybe one day that'll happen.'

'You got the truth from him, though?'

'I got most of the story, I think.'

'But you won't tell me?'

'I don't remember that being part of your deal

with DI Clarke.' Rebus turned his gaze to Dallas Meikle. 'You wanted the case re-examined and that's what I've done. Some would have skimmed the evidence and court transcripts — I did a lot more than that. Some of the stuff I found out, you probably don't want to know — might make things a bit difficult between you and Ellis's mum.' He paused, expecting Meikle to say something. When he didn't, Rebus angled his head slightly. 'Except maybe she's already let you in on at least one of her secrets. Aye, probably after I called her out on it. How does it feel, knowing Billie's own mum was bullying her online?' Meikle's expression darkened but he kept his mouth shut. 'Fair enough,' Rebus eventually said, 'but now you need to do the right thing.' He paused again. 'And remember this — Siobhan could have reported you. If she had, you'd be in the middle of becoming a court transcript yourself.'

'That'll happen anyway, won't it? By handing over those two cops, I'm condemning myself.'

'Not if you say you took it straight to the authorities; not if you say you'd never got round to making any anonymous calls.'

'Making it my word against theirs.'

'How did they get her mobile number and home address to you?'

'Walked into the bar and handed them over.'

'Still got the bit of paper?' Rebus watched the man nod. 'CCTV in the pub?' A further nod. 'Suddenly it's not just your word against theirs. Idiots even told you who they were.'

'Told me not to use a traceable phone

— suggested one of the call boxes near the pub. Told me not to say anything during the calls. But they wanted to know when she started sounding rattled. And if I didn't think it was working, I could always pay her a visit.'

'So you had to have some way of contacting them . . . ?'

Meikle dug a business card from his back pocket, DS Brian Steele's name on it along with his address at ACU and the Police Scotland crest, with the force's motto beneath — *Semper Vigilo*, 'Always Vigilant'.

'Know what those words mean?' Rebus asked, pointing them out to Meikle.

'Not much cop at languages.'

'Ask Billie sometime; she might have the answer.'

'So that's it? That's as much as I'm getting?'

Rebus was rising to his feet. 'Keep visiting Ellis. Make sure Billie goes too — he's her brother after all; it's the least she can do.'

★ ★ ★

Rebus drove Brillo back to Arden Street and deposited the dog in its basket in the kitchen. For the duration of the drive, he'd been thinking some more about the Meikles, which had led to memories of his own upbringing. His mother had died young, his father raising two sons — Rebus and his brother Michael — as best he could. But he had worked a lot of evenings and weekends, sleeping the day through and with occasional trips away. With the boys left to their

462

own devices, they'd grown feral. John had left school at the first opportunity and joined the army, while Michael went on to sell drugs, do time and die young himself. The word 'dysfunctional' might not have existed back then, but Rebus reckoned his family would have ticked all the boxes.

He decided to call his daughter in Tongue, way up on the north coast of Scotland, where she was hard to visit. He got her answering service so left a brief message to say he was thinking of her and asking after his granddaughter Carrie. He boiled the kettle and made a herbal tea, before pouring it down the sink and reaching into the fridge for a low-alcohol beer instead. His breathing was just about back to normal after climbing the two flights. He sent Clarke a text and waited to see if she'd get back to him. A drug dealer called Gram; a farmer from Poretoun; the Polo left undisturbed for years and years, right under the very noses of the police and local population. He tried to imagine the scenario. At first it's a panicky stopgap of a measure. But nothing happens, it seems to have worked. So you leave it a bit longer, and a bit longer still, until it becomes part of the scenery — you've almost forgotten it's there, or what it means.

He sent Clarke another text and sipped on the beer, beer that had had all the joy sucked out of it. He'd asked his doctor during his last check-up: would a few pints or shorts really hurt?

'Your funeral,' the doctor had replied.

'I'm going to put it in my will that I don't

want any sober pall-bearers.'

The next text he sent was to Malcolm Fox, who called him straight back.

'Nice to hear a friendly voice,' Rebus told him.

'Jennifer Lyon has as good as ordered me back to Gartcosh. She thinks I'm malingering.'

'And are you?'

'I can't leave, John — it's just started to heat up.'

'Yes, Siobhan told me about the farmer.'

'He gave us a name.'

'For his friend Gram?'

'He was Graeme Hatch before. After Bloom's murder he left town and changed it. He's Glenn Hazard.'

'The PR guy?'

'Yes!'

'So it was all Adrian Brand's doing?'

'Hazard didn't start working in PR till a few years ago. There's nothing to show he knew Brand in any way back in 2006. He would have known Jackie Ness, though. He hung around the film set, selling wherever he could.'

'Have you brought him in for questioning?'

'Under caution.'

'He's there now?' An idea was forming in Rebus's mind.

'There's only the one interview room, so they've seconded my office. That's where Carlton is. Someone's fetching some more recording gear from St Leonard's. Meantime, DCS Mollison has arrived and the press are back outside.'

'Fun and games — I can see why you're

464

staying put.' Rebus paused. 'So what'll be in your actual report, Malcolm? Do I get a sneak preview?'

'I know what you did, if that's what you're asking.'

'And what did I do?'

'On top of all the drinking on the job? And landing a reporter in a heap of trouble with Cafferty?'

'There's more?'

'I also know you did your damnedest to cover up the fact that Mary Skelton's affair was with your boss, Bill Rawlston. Same afternoons she was supposedly visiting her sick mother, he tended to be at non-existent meetings at Fettes. You were the one who told people why he wasn't around. You even had him in your notes as being with you when you interviewed Jackie Ness. Problem is, Rawlston's own diary has him at a meeting at Fettes. Different meeting; exact same time.'

'Whoops.'

'Whoops is right.'

'Thing you need to appreciate, Malcolm, is that families always lie — and that's what we were. In and around the Big House, we lied to each other and sometimes to ourselves. And now there's just the one Big House — Gartcosh — and guess what?'

'Nothing's changed?' Fox guessed.

'Everyone still covers their own arse, stabs mates in the back, and tries to look busy when there's nothing going on — ring any bells, DI Fox?'

'You think that excuses what happened in the past?'

'Maybe, maybe not. But thank goodness it all pales into insignificance in comparison with a murder, eh?'

'Nothing is insignificant, John. Poretoun Glen Farm was visited, you know. By Steele and Edwards, as it happens. They talked to the present owner's uncle. He was very frail, housebound really, and very thankful his nephew was taking over the reins. Whatever else you say about Steele, he gets the detail down. Left his card so either of them — farmer or nephew — could get back to him if they heard or remembered anything.'

'Some habits never leave you,' Rebus said with a thin smile.

'How do you mean?'

'*Semper vigilo*, Malc. I'll catch up with you soon.'

Fox must have heard something in Rebus's voice. 'How soon?' he asked.

'Depends on the traffic,' Rebus said, ending the call.

52

He parked at Leith Links — it was the closest he could get. Media vans, a couple with satellite dishes on their roofs pointed skywards, had taken all the spaces nearer the police station. Rebus watched from the corner. He'd caught the local news on his Saab's radio, so knew reporters had also been dispatched to Poretoun Glen Farm.

Eventually, DCS Mark Mollison emerged and was immediately mobbed. He had a statement to make, but couldn't start until everyone had calmed down. Rebus made his move, squeezing past the scrum around Mollison and entering the station. A uniform stood just inside the door, ready to eject unwanted visitors. Rebus held up both hands.

'I'm not press,' he said. He didn't recognise the officer behind the desk so asked to see Detective Inspector Fox.

'He's busy — they all are, if you hadn't noticed.'

'I'm an ex-cop myself,' Rebus explained. 'I've been helping on a case and I need a word with Fox or DI Clarke.'

'I stopped listening after 'ex',' the officer said, turning away. Rebus was aware of the uniform at his shoulder, ready to usher him out with a firm touch. He got out his phone and sent a text upstairs.

'One minute,' he told the uniform. 'If nobody comes down, I'll go.'

'I've already started counting,' the uniform warned him.

Fifty seconds later, Fox arrived, pushing open the inner door. He didn't look exactly welcoming.

'Okay?' the uniform asked.

Eventually, Fox nodded stiffly. Before he could change his mind, Rebus crossed the threshold with a muttered 'Thanks.'

As they climbed the stairs, Fox asked if anyone had spotted him.

'Feeding frenzy around Mollison — I'm not daft.' Rebus stopped, turning to face Fox. 'Look, there's something you need to know. Rawlston's not a well man. A few more months and he won't be here.'

'You're asking me to censor my report? Turn it into fake news?'

'I'm asking you to take your time finalising it. Tell your boss you need to track down a few more people for interview. You're being thorough, that's all.' Fox started climbing again, Rebus breathing heavily at his heels. 'Fuck's sake, Malcolm, nobody's building a pyre around you. It would be a kindness, that's all. I'm not even asking you to lie.' Rebus caught Fox glaring at him. 'Okay, a white lie to your boss maybe. Will you at least think about it?'

They had reached the first-floor landing, where a grim-faced Siobhan Clarke was waiting. 'Just had a text from Laura,' she said, holding up her phone, 'asking what John

Rebus is doing here.'

Fox turned towards Rebus, who was busying himself with his inhaler. 'Not daft, I believe you were saying.'

'So what the hell *are* you doing here, John?'

'Being nosy,' Rebus eventually replied. 'Promise I won't get in the way.'

Clarke turned to Fox. 'And I thought I heard that you'd been recalled to Gartcosh?'

'Just packing up my things,' Fox told her.

'What things?'

'Whatever they are, it's taking me a little bit longer than anticipated.'

Clarke rolled her eyes and turned away, disappearing into the MIT room before re-emerging.

'Malcolm,' she said, 'I'm putting you in charge of John. Try not to let him slip his collar.'

Fox nodded and led Rebus to the cramped room that had been his office for the past week.

'I thought the farmer was in here,' Rebus said.

'He's been released,' Fox said. 'With conditions.'

'Meaning not enough evidence to charge him?'

'Oh, he'll definitely face charges — we're just not sure yet what they'll be, and meantime we want him to keep cooperating.'

'So what's he spilled so far?' Rebus accepted the chair Fox offered him. He picked up a sheaf of paper — all relating to the 2006 inquiry.

'Please don't do that,' Fox said. 'Anyone walks in and sees you here . . . '

'Don't worry, I won't breathe a word about

you inviting me up here to help you massage your report.'

'You ever thought about stand-up?'

Rebus put the sheets back. 'You were about to tell me about the farmer,' he prompted.

'He was friends with Graeme Hatch, had been since school. Then Hatch went off to college. Flunked first year and came home to Poretoun, but he'd picked up a new skill while away.'

'Selling dope?'

'Not massively, according to Carlton, but enough to make a living. Pubs and clubs around Edinburgh, plus the village and others like it. When a film was being made, that was always a good market.'

'And all of this under Cafferty's nose?'

'We did ask Carlton if Hatch was working for anyone, but he reckons he was all on his own.'

'Must have got the stuff somewhere.'

'The internet apparently.'

'You're kidding.'

'Ordered from China and elsewhere via the Dark Web.'

'Was Carlton a client as well as a user?' Rebus asked.

'Just a few uppers to keep the party going.'

Rebus grew thoughtful. 'Interesting phrase, Malcolm.'

Fox's brow furrowed. 'Is it? Why?'

'That spate of overdoses — the connection with Rogues. Cafferty says it was all down to a seller called Graeme.' Rebus paused. 'So what does Carlton say about the car?'

'Just that Hatch turned up with it one night

470

and said he needed to leave it there.'

'Did he ask why?'

'Says he joked about it being stolen. Hatch was adamant — no questions. They took it to the corner of the field, made sure it was surrounded by junk, and draped a tarpaulin over it. He says the interior looked empty. Hatch had a bag with him; Bloom's laptop and phone could have been inside.'

'Plus the papers from Brand's safe?' Rebus guessed. Fox just shrugged.

'We know Stuart Bloom's body was kept in the boot. It's feasible the farmer never took a peek.'

'Hatch isn't saying?'

'He's still being questioned, not twenty feet from here.'

'Lawyered up?'

'Oh yes.'

'The car was moved two or three years back?'

Fox nodded. 'Around the time Carlton told his old pal he was considering selling the farm. They towed it out of the field, jump-started the battery and put a bit of air in the tyres.'

'It was still working after all those years?'

'German engineering,' Fox agreed. Hazard drove off in it and that was the last Carlton heard of it.'

'He knew, though, right? Knew who it belonged to?'

'I'd say so, or else why panic when he saw Siobhan?'

'But what does *he* say?'

'He denies it. Never watched the news, so was

only vaguely aware someone had gone missing.'

'He must be lying.'

'Of course he's lying.'

'So his old pal turns up again a few years later having added a bit of weight and with a new haircut, new attitude. And they never talk about the car? Carlton never goes near it?'

'Allegedly.'

'And when it turns up again in Poretoun Woods with Stuart Bloom's remains inside . . . ?'

'He still doesn't watch the news.'

'Aye, right.' Rebus gave a snort.

'That's his story.'

'Well, it stinks worse than a freshly laid cowpat. And cooperation or no cooperation, if he knew what he was doing, he's headed jail-wards.'

'Which is why he'll keep denying it.'

Rebus nodded in agreement. 'So now you just have to play him off against Hazard.'

'Exactly. Though there is just the one problem . . . '

Rebus nodded again. 'Why did Hazard do it?'

'Any thoughts on that?'

'Put me in a room with him for five minutes and I might be able to help.' Rebus watched as Fox gave a wry smile. 'I'm serious, Malcolm,' he said. 'Deadly serious.'

53

They could hold Hazard for twenty-four hours without charging him. They were using that time to search his home and office, his computers and phone records. They were interviewing people from his past as well as his present. His lawyer meantime was making a bit of noise. What was it with MIT and unproven allegations? First the break-in and now a long-unsolved murder.

Sutherland had stared hard at the solicitor. His name was Francis Dean. He didn't work at the same firm as Kelvin Brodie, but word had obviously got around.

Hazard's fingerprints had been taken and he'd been swabbed for a DNA sample. They'd be re-examining the handcuffs, the Polo's steering wheel and door handles, the tarpaulin and the various vehicles and bits of equipment surrounding the space where the Polo had lain. They'd asked Carlton, but his memory was that Hazard had worn gloves when they were getting the Polo going again. And Carlton himself? No gloves that he could remember. His prints and a cheek swab had been taken, too. The lab at Howdenhall had been told to pull an all-nighter if necessary. Sutherland had already arranged for a delivery of pizzas and soft drinks.

Eventually tiredness got the better of them. Glenn Hazard was taken to a cell at St Leonard's, and Sutherland's team were told to try and get a bit of rest. Not too much, though — the clock was ticking and they had plenty to do to convince the fiscal's office that a murder charge was in order. Rooms had been found in a B&B on the links. Clarke had turned down the offer, insisting that her own flat was only a five-minute drive. Fox asked if he could take the sofa, and she agreed.

'So that's a chair for me,' Rebus said, 'unless you're offering this exhausted old man your bed?'

Clarke stared at him. 'What's wrong with your own place?'

'You might forget to call me if there's a break in the case.'

'And Brillo?'

'Good point . . . '

Rebus drove to Marchmont to fetch Brillo. Meanwhile, Fox had been dropped off at a chip shop near the top of Broughton Street. By the time Rebus reached Clarke's flat, his fish supper was tepid at best. But the kettle had been boiled and tea brewed, and Fox had brought a battered sausage for the dog.

'He'd better not sick that back up,' Clarke cautioned.

'Me or Brillo?' Rebus enquired, stuffing vinegary chips into his mouth.

They were seated in the living room. Fox had added cans of cola and Irn-Bru to his purchases, Rebus opening one of the latter.

'Caffeine's probably the last thing I need,' Clarke said, sticking to the peppermint tea she'd made. Having eaten from the wrappings, she dropped them to the floor, leaned her head against the back of her armchair and closed her eyes.

'You won't sleep,' Rebus told her. 'This is the cops' equivalent of Christmas Eve.'

'What if the lab comes up short? Right now it's just Carlton's word against Hazard's. If the farmer's prints and DNA are all we find on the car . . .'

'Jesus, you're cheery. I thought I was supposed to be the cynical one.'

'Shiv's right, though,' Fox said. 'The car was on Carlton's land; Carlton and Bloom were both extras in one of Jackie Ness's films so maybe knew each other better than Carlton says.'

'You saying the farmer's a closet gay and that's why he killed Bloom?'

'Bloom spots him at Rogues. Maybe they even have a snog. Bumps into him again during filming. Carlton's — '

'So embarrassed he kills him?' Rebus said, not bothering to hide his disbelief. 'I don't see that at all.' Brillo had climbed on to his lap and was dozing, Rebus rubbing him behind his ears.

'So why did Hazard do it then? A drug deal gone wrong? Money owed?'

Rebus held up one hand, fingers splayed, his meaning clear to Fox: *five minutes with him* . . .

'Doesn't matter why it happened,' Clarke said sleepily, eyelids still closed. 'We just have to show that one or the other of them *did* do it.' She seemed to remember something, rousing herself a little, eyes suddenly on Rebus.

'You had news for me, John.'

He nodded. 'Ellis Meikle is covering for his sister.'

'Billie?'

'I probably couldn't prove it in a court of law, but I know that's what happened.'

'What will you tell the uncle?'

'We've already spoken.'

'He'll give us Steele and Edwards?'

'Well, to be precise, he'll make a complaint to PIRC, leaving you out of it as far as possible.'

'Meaning what?'

'Meaning he never acted on the Chuggabugs' suggestion that he use your mobile number — a number they handed him — to harass you.'

'His word against theirs?'

'Not quite.'

'You reckon they might not worm their way out of this one?'

'Steele's going down for *something*, Shiv, trust me.'

She stared at him. 'What do you know that I don't?'

'Well for one thing, I can name every Rolling Stones B-side from the 1960s.'

'Would you put money on it, though?' Fox asked.

Rebus started counting on his fingers. ''I Want to Be Loved', 'Stoned', 'Little by Little' . . . '

'Don't encourage him,' Clarke said to Fox. 'It's just his way of ducking the question.'

'She knows me too well,' Rebus agreed with a shrug in Fox's direction. Then, to Clarke: 'Has Hazard said anything at all that gets us closer to knowing what happened?'

'He didn't know Stuart Bloom, never met Stuart Bloom, never sold drugs, didn't move away and change his identity because he was fleeing any sort of crime, has no idea why Andrew Carlton would concoct such a story — except that farmers everywhere are feeling the economic strain and maybe the balance of his mind has become disturbed.'

'That last sounds like a lawyer talking.'

'Most of what I've just said came from the lawyer. Hazard just sits there like he's made of granite.'

'He's not, though, which means we can get to him.'

'How?'

'John here,' Fox interrupted, 'wants a bit of time alone with the suspect.'

'Well *that's* not going to happen,' Clarke stated, closing her eyes again.

'Not necessarily alone,' Rebus reasoned. 'One of you could come along for the ride.'

'Hazard's legal team would have a field day. This isn't Miss Marple, John. You don't get to walk all over the inquiry.'

'I got a lot wrong last time, Siobhan. I'd just like the chance to make up for that.'

'You can't always get what you want.'

He stared at her, then at Fox. 'B-side of 'Honky Tonk Women',' he intoned. 'Still want to take that bet?'

54

Just before midnight, having made up his mind, Rebus asked to be excused for an hour. Brillo's ears pricked up, but Rebus shook his head. He left the flat on his own and headed for his car. It was a quick drive, the city quiet, lit by sodium and illuminated shop windows. A few drinkers were huddled outside their favoured bars, sharing cigarettes and stories. Rebus wished for a moment that he were among them. Instead of which, he switched one piece of gum for another and kept driving.

The tenement door was locked, so he pushed the buzzer. This time of night, he'd probably be taken for a passing prankster, so he pressed it again. At the third time of trying, the intercom crackled into life.

'Wrong fucking flat,' Charles Meikle said.

'It's John Rebus. I need a quick word.'

'At this time of night?'

'Thought it best to wait till Billie was asleep.'

There was silence for a moment, then a buzzing as Meikle unlocked the door. Rebus took his time climbing the stairs. Even so, he was breathing heavily as he reached Meikle's floor.

'You about to peg out on me?' the man asked from the open doorway.

Rebus shook his head. 'I could do with a glass of water, though.'

'So long as you promise to keep your voice down.'

Rebus nodded and followed Meikle into the kitchen. He didn't think he'd woken the man. Meikle was still fully dressed and fully alert. He turned from the sink with a half-filled glass. Rebus took it from him, but instead of taking a sip, he placed it on the worktop.

'Last time I was here,' he said, 'this is where you rested your fists. I remember thinking it was a bit odd. You had your palms raised when you did it, like you were trying to hide something.' He gestured towards the worktop. 'I see you got rid of it.'

'Rid of what?'

'The knife block with the one blade missing.'

'Says who?'

Rebus ignored this. He finally lifted the glass and sipped from it. 'Know what that told me? It told me you knew. Well of course you did — where else was Ellis going to take Billie afterwards? She was spattered with blood. He needed to get her back and into clean clothes.' He paused. 'All of which makes you an accessory.'

'None of which you can prove.'

'Maybe not.'

'How do you mean?'

'Let's say I were to talk to Billie herself . . . '

The look the man gave him, Rebus suspected that if the knife block had still been there, he'd have snatched another blade from it.

Rebus held up a hand. 'Thing is, I'm not sure I need to. She's smart and she's sensitive. No

479

way she's going to be able to put it behind her. It's like a shadow she'll always carry, meaning you're always going to be on edge, wondering if and when she'll crack. Same goes for her brother. Whole family's under a life sentence, not just Ellis.' He raised his voice a notch. 'Isn't that right, Billie?'

She emerged from the darkened hall into the doorway, looking pale and fragile in her full-length nightgown.

'It's all right, petal,' her father told her. 'That was a promise then and it's a promise now.' Then, to Rebus, his voice taking on a threatening tone. 'You should bugger off now. Come round here again, I swear I'll wring your neck.'

'I don't doubt it.' Rebus turned towards Billie. 'Some dad you've got there. But it's one thing to talk about it — or even think about it. Carrying it through, though . . . ' He eased past her on his way to the front door. 'That's cold, Billie — something your dad and Ellis might start to appreciate some day.'

He let himself out and stood on the landing. If words were being spoken inside, he couldn't hear them. As he descended the stairs, he began to hum a tune. It was only when he got to the bottom that he realised what it was.

R. Dean Taylor, 'There's a Ghost in My House'. He hadn't heard that one in a while . . .

Saturday

55

6.30 a.m., still dark outside, weekend workers just beginning to trek into town, quarter-filled buses, windows misted with condensation, and a few pedestrians seeking out early-opening shops or those that stayed open round the clock. Clarke had made them coffee, Rebus asking if the newsagent's would be open. Fox had argued that there'd be nothing in the papers that hadn't already been reported online.

'Ever tried reading the racing pages on a phone?' Rebus had countered.

They'd then split up — Clarke and Fox heading to Leith, while Rebus took Brillo for a Meadows pit stop before the Arden Street flat.

'Normal service will be resumed,' he promised the dog, turning to leave.

Just the one journalist outside Leith police station. He looked junior and cold. He asked Rebus what time they'd be bringing Hazard back.

'Soon,' Rebus answered, taking pity on him. The young man took his phone out, ready to alert his colleagues. Rebus realised the same question would have been asked of Clarke and Fox, but they'd stonewalled.

Some short straw, that, he argued to himself as he headed indoors; like stakeouts in the old days, bum going numb and nowhere to pee . . . The desk officer recognised him this time, waved him through.

Sutherland was waiting at the top of the stairs, flanked by Clarke and Fox. The DCI was as well dressed as ever but pallid and tense. He pointed at Rebus.

'Out you go,' he commanded.

'Listen, I think I might be able . . . '

But Sutherland was already striding into the MIT room. He half turned, eyes on Clarke. 'He's still here in thirty seconds, you're off the team.'

The arm Clarke stretched to her side could either have been apologetic or a gesture of dismissal.

'Tell him I can help,' Rebus said.

'If all else fails,' Clarke agreed with a nod.

'I'll sit in my car.' He fixed her with a stare. 'Keep me posted unless you want me causing a scene in front of the press.'

She gave a slow nod, which he only half believed.

★ ★ ★

In MIT, Sutherland was being briefed by Reid and Crowther. The others had yet to arrive. Not much of use from the lab, but the soil sample had proved a ninety per cent match, which, Professor Hamilton had indicated, was good enough for a courtroom.

'No prints on the tarp?' Fox asked.

'Just the farmer's,' Reid said. 'And a bit of paint from a car the same colour and age as the Polo. They couldn't give us a definitive match.'

'Hazard's prints aren't on the cuffs?'

484

'He was savvy enough to wear gloves when they moved the car. Maybe he's always been clever that way.'

'He wore gloves when he attacked Bloom?'

'*If* he attacked Bloom,' Sutherland felt it necessary to qualify.

'You're having doubts, sir?' Clarke asked.

'Right now it's Carlton's word against his. Even if those handcuffs had at some point in the past been in Hazard's possession, all he has to tell a court is that he lost them. Maybe his farming friend picked them up or stole them from him.' He met Clarke's eyes. 'Who was it ran from you? Who was it had the car on his land until selling that land meant he needed to move it?'

'Everything points towards Carlton rather than Hazard,' Reid agreed.

'Except,' Clarke argued, 'Carlton didn't do a runner after the crime and change his identity, change his whole life. And he didn't know the victim.'

'We don't know that Hazard knew him either.'

'Hazard hung around whenever a film was being made, which puts him next to Jackie Ness, and Bloom was working for Ness as well as appearing as an extra in his films.'

'We're going round in circles,' Sutherland said, not bothering to conceal his frustration. 'And pretty soon we're going to have to release Hazard from custody.'

'Or charge him,' Clarke commented.

'With no evidence? His lawyer will boot that out of the park.'

'The farmer's statement is fairly compelling,' Crowther interrupted.

'I doubt Francis Dean will see it that way,' Sutherland told her.

'And we've dug up nothing from Hazard's past? None of his old friends, contacts, clients?'

Reid handed the paperwork to Clarke. 'Look for yourself. Seems he stopped dealing, started applying himself, found his metier in public relations . . . '

'All of which happened straight after Bloom's disappearance,' Clarke muttered.

'We've gone through his flat, his email accounts. We've dug up old girlfriends, people he shared digs with during his years in Glasgow. No police record, not so much as a speeding fine or parking ticket.'

'A man who couldn't risk getting into trouble,' Crowther stated.

Sutherland was checking a message on his phone. 'And on his way here as we speak. His solicitor's probably downstairs waiting.' He turned to Reid. 'Can you try to rouse our sleeping beauties?'

Just as he finished speaking, Leighton and Yeats appeared in the doorway, Gamble toiling behind them. All three looked breathless as they offered their apologies.

'Don't bother getting comfortable,' Sutherland said. 'George and Phil, I want you at the forensic lab, make sure they did all the tests known to man, woman and the beasts of the field. The car, the tarpaulin, the handcuffs. The lab have got DNA for Glenn Hazard. If he left a drop of sweat, a strand of hair, or spittle from a cough, I want it. Understood? The rest of you are going to comb through everything we've compiled on Hazard thus far. Plenty gaps in his life story; we might have missed something crucial. Malcolm and Tess, one last dig through the original case files — is he lurking somewhere in there?' He nodded towards Reid. 'Callum, you're with me in the interview room.' Then, to the room at large: 'I want us lining the corridor when Hazard gets here. A combination of hundred-yard stares and a gleam in the eye that tells him we know we've got him.' He clapped his hands. 'We need a result, folks, and that means getting busy. Think you've put in some tough shifts? Today's going to be a brand-new definition of hard work. Let's get started . . . '

56

Rebus saw the van arrive and emerged from his Saab to watch the circus. The press had been alerted and were ready to pounce. There was no rear entrance to the police station, no alleyway where the van could deposit its cargo. Reporters and cameras surrounded Glenn Hazard as he was led across the pavement to the police station's door. He looked bemused, the very picture of innocence. His lawyer was waiting at the steps, ready for battle, his freshly shaved face roseate and gleaming. Rebus didn't know him, but he knew the type — tailored like a shop-window mannequin and spritzed all over by an aerosol called privilege. The escorts eventually got Hazard indoors and the scrum began to thin out, as cameras and phones were checked, updates sent to news desks and social media outlets. Laura Smith approached Rebus with a smile that was trying not to seem overly professional.

'No comment, Laura,' Rebus told her.

'Strictly off the record, John, with you being a civilian and all . . . '

'Go on then.'

'Is there enough in the tank?'

'To charge him?' Rebus waited for her to nod. 'Like you say, I'm a civilian.'

'Yet you're sticking to this case like glue. I hear you turned up here earlier not long after Fox and Siobhan.'

'I'm impressed.' Rebus was seeking out the young reporter who'd been acting as nightwatchman.

'He's on a well-earned break,' Smith said. 'He might be young, but he prides himself on knowing faces and the names that come with them.' She paused. 'If someone were to mention in print your involvement, that might jeopardise any eventual prosecution, no?'

'What is it you want, Laura?'

'A heads-up.'

'Siobhan's the one you should be asking.'

'But I don't seem to have any leverage over Siobhan.'

'If you interfere and the case goes tits up, you might as well delete her from your contacts.'

'I just need to be an hour ahead of the competition, John.'

'Right now, I can't help you.' He gestured towards the paving slabs they were standing on. 'I'm out in the cold, same as you.'

'But . . . ?'

'Time's almost up. If MIT don't want to have to spring Hazard, they're going to need a bit of help.'

'Help from you, you mean?'

'So maybe stick around another hour or two and see what happens.'

'I've not got my car, though.' She peered over his shoulder towards the Saab. 'Any chance I can sit in the warm with you?'

'No.'

'Are you afraid my superbly honed skills would get the better of you and you'd end up letting something slip?'

'Aye, right.' Rebus's mouth twitched.

'Then why not put that confidence to the test? How else are you going to pass the time?'

'I thought I might take up a foreign language.'

She nodded. 'Conversation's always the best way to learn. I can offer you French, German, a smattering of Italian . . . '

Rebus felt his resistance melt a little. 'All right then, but tell me something first — and no lying.'

'Sure.'

'Are you really here without a car?'

'Really, yes.'

'And how many streets over did you leave it?'

She drew in her lips for a moment. 'Two,' she eventually confessed.

Rebus nodded and turned back to the Saab, knowing she was following. 'Then be prepared for a numb posterior and no facilities.'

57

Graham Sutherland emerged from his toilet break to find Clarke in the corridor. She gestured towards the stairs, pausing halfway down and waiting for him.

'Your face,' she began, 'tells me there's been no breakthrough. Nothing from the lab or anywhere else. It's still all hearsay, with no corroboration. We both know what the fiscal will say to that.'

'This isn't exactly balm to the soul, Siobhan — what's your point?'

'I think John knows something, something that could help.'

'And what exactly does he know?'

'He'll only say it to Glenn Hazard's face.'

'Not possible.'

'Why not? You'll be there and so will Hazard's lawyer. It'll all be recorded. I don't see that it necessarily blunts our case.'

'You've no inkling what Rebus would say in there?' He watched as she shook her head. 'Then it's too risky.'

'I don't think so, not when there are other bodies in the room who can call a halt if necessary.' Clarke was holding out her phone. 'Talk to him. What harm can it do to just listen? If we have to let Hazard go, who's to say he won't do another vanishing act?'

Sutherland hesitated, then snatched the phone

from her, only to have to hand it back so she could find Rebus's number and ring it. He took it from her again, more gently this time.

'Rebus,' the voice said.

'It's DCI Sutherland, John. Siobhan tells me you might have information that could help us with Glenn Hazard.'

'I think so.'

'Could you tell me what it is?'

'I need to tell him myself.'

'I don't think that's a good idea. His lawyer — '

'I'm not fussed about his lawyer. But there might be things *you* don't want to hear.'

'A police officer needs to be present.'

'So be it.' Silence on the line. 'Do you want me or not?'

'I'll need to clear it with Francis Dean first.'

'He's the lawyer?'

'Yes.'

'I'll be there in two minutes. Make sure they let me past the front desk.'

Rebus ended the call. Sutherland handed the phone back to its owner.

'I take it that's a yes then?' Clarke said.

'It's a maybe,' Sutherland replied, starting back up the stairs.

★　★　★

When Rebus walked into the interview room, Callum Reid left with a glower he'd spent some time preparing. Hazard sat with arms folded, alongside his solicitor. The room was stuffy and

Dean had removed his jacket but kept his waistcoat on. It boasted a fob watch on a gold chain, just when Rebus thought he couldn't dislike lawyers more than he already did.

Sutherland was making sure he could work the recording equipment. Rebus took the chair next to him, still warm from Reid's posterior. Hazard had demolished one mug of tea and been brought another.

'Do you two know one another?' the lawyer asked. Rebus looked to Hazard and shook his head.

'Never met,' he said.

'We can put it on record that you've never met or spoken with my client until this day?'

'We can,' Rebus confirmed.

'And can we also agree that this is highly unusual practice and that any conversation may be inadmissible in future proceedings?'

But Rebus's focus was on Hazard now. 'You should tell your lawyer to leave,' he said.

'That's not going to happen,' Dean stated. Rebus ignored him, locking eyes with Hazard.

'We're going to be talking about Rogues nightclub, almost exactly two months before Stuart Bloom died. But I want to do it without a stuffed shirt in the room.'

Hazard just stared, but Rebus had been in plenty of these contests before. He tried to look bored, folded his arms even, and arched his head as if the ceiling had suddenly become extraordinarily interesting to him.

'Look, DCI Sutherland,' Dean began, colour rising to his already ruddy cheeks, 'I'm not sure what game you think you're playing here, but this has stopped being highly irregular and entered the realm of the absurd.'

Sutherland was looking to Rebus for an explanation, but it was Hazard who spoke. 'Does your guy leave too?'

'I told him he should, but he's adamant.'

Dean had turned towards his client. 'In which case, it would be rash in the extreme for you to sit here without any counsel being present.'

Hazard nodded and leaned back a little in his chair. 'Off you go, Francis, but not too far — just outside the door will do.'

'I'll only need five or ten minutes,' Rebus said.

'Glenn, I urge you to reconsider — '

'Just fuck off, will you, Francis? Don't worry, the money meter keeps ticking over.' Hazard lifted his mug and drained it. The lawyer's face was almost puce as he gathered his papers, grabbed his jacket and shouldered open the door. Once he was gone, Rebus leaned across Sutherland and stopped the recording.

'Wait a moment,' Sutherland began to complain.

'You're free to leave,' Rebus said with a new steeliness, knowing the man wouldn't budge. He met Hazard's gaze again.

'You were a dealer back then,' Rebus began. 'Small-time. You had to keep dodging and weaving, so as not to appear on the radar of the bigger players — people like Morris Gerald Cafferty.' He paused. 'You know the name?'

Hazard nodded.

'Cafferty even came to the film set,' Rebus

went on. 'I'm guessing you made yourself scarce that day.'

'Can I just ask,' Hazard interrupted, 'what proof you have of any of this?'

'Precious little,' Rebus admitted. 'But I *know* you were dealing and I know you sold the dope that put six kids in hospital. I was a cop at the time and I remember it well. Cafferty was the only dealer we knew; even so, we were shocked. His stuff had never been tainted before. Suddenly there are six overdoses in a single night, six admissions to Accident and Emergency. And only five survived — Jamie Spowart didn't make it. Don't suppose it meant much to you, but his parents were devastated and probably still are.

'After that, you had to make yourself scarce. You left Edinburgh, but you kept dealing — on film sets and probably in the towns and villages south of the city. I'm guessing you changed supplier — you didn't want anyone else snuffing it on your watch. But meantime, we were all over Cafferty like a rash. Which put a dent in his business for a while and also put a black mark beside his name as far as other men of his persuasion were concerned. He'd been wooing an Irish thug called Conor Maloney — name mean anything to you?' Rebus received a shrug by way of response. 'I'm pretty sure you knew Stuart Bloom's name, though. He was a regular at Rogues, maybe even bought a bit from you. Then the kid dies and suddenly you're off the scene. Few months later, he's an extra in one of Jackie Ness's films and spots you, remembers you. So now you have a problem. What happens next, I can only guess. He tried blackmailing you? He was going to go to the police? Maybe you only feared he would do one or the other. So you met up with him, killed him, and dumped the body on your pal's farm.' He paused. 'How does that sound so far, Mr Hazard?'

'I'm still waiting to hear anything that isn't a theory.'

'Theory's all I have.'

'And you think I'm suddenly going to throw up my arms and confess?' Hazard's eyes had widened.

Rebus was slowly shaking his head. 'What I think is this: I'm going to leave this room, your lawyer's going to come back in, DCI Sutherland's going to fire the apparatus back up, and you're going to offer him your full and frank admission of guilt.'

'Is that right?'

'See, you're absolutely correct when you say I've no proof, and that's a problem.'

'You better believe it.'

'You misunderstand.' Rebus leaned across the table. 'It's not a problem for me, it's a problem for *you*.'

Hazard laughed and gestured towards Sutherland. 'Are you hearing this? You've brought a certified nutjob in here.'

Sutherland seemed about to say something, but Rebus waved a hand to stop him. His attention was still on Hazard.

'In about half an hour from now, we're letting you go, as is required by law. But I'll have been on the blower well before then, giving the story to Cafferty. See, Cafferty has a long memory, especially when it comes to vendettas. You cost him a lot of money and a big chunk of his reputation, which it took him years to recover. He's wanted you since 2006, Glenn. Twelve years he's festered.' Rebus paused. 'But now he's going to get you. From the moment you walk out of here, you're a marked man.'

'Are you hearing this?' Hazard told Sutherland, a slight but noticeable quaver entering his voice. 'Your man's threatening to feed me to the wolves.'

'Wolves are doubtful,' Rebus said, 'though Cafferty does own a pig farm in Fife. We can show you evidence of all the men he's tortured and murdered down the years. We only put him behind bars once or twice — that's because he's good at getting away with it. A lot of those victims vanished into thin air, just like Stuart Bloom. But you're not quite as capable as Cafferty; Bloom popped up again.'

'Say I didn't kill anyone, you'd be sending an innocent man to — '

'Oh, but we know you did. And that's what you'll confess to, so as not to become one of Cafferty's victims. And in exchange, we can offer you a deal.'

Hazard seemed to calm a little. 'What sort of deal?'

'Better than you deserve. After your trial, we'll ensure you go to HMP Saughton. Why? Because there's a guy called Darryl Christie in there, a powerful guy who hates Cafferty as much as

Cafferty hates the person who sold that overdose. Christie won't want Cafferty getting to you. In point of fact, he'll make damned sure he doesn't. You staying alive will be a thorn in Cafferty's paw, an irritant that'll always be there. That's worth a lot to Darryl Christie, trust me.'

It was Rebus's turn to lean back in his chair.

'You've got about twenty minutes to decide,' Sutherland said with renewed vigour.

'No he hasn't,' Rebus corrected him. 'Because when I leave this room, if we've not got a deal, I'm straight on to Cafferty.' He buttoned his suit jacket and rose to his feet. 'Oh, and DCI Sutherland? Bring in Clarke rather than Reid when I've gone — she's every bit as good as you think she is.'

'Wait a sec,' Hazard said. He was rubbing at his forehead, as if that would help him come to a decision.

'Time for games is over,' Rebus told him, making for the door. He paused to remove his phone from a pocket, then placed his hand around the door handle.

'Please,' Hazard said, half out of his chair. 'I need one fucking minute.'

Which was exactly how long Rebus gave him, his eyes on his wristwatch.

'Okay,' Hazard said as Rebus pushed the door open. Rebus pulled it closed again and turned to face the room.

'Okay?' he echoed, receiving a nod in reply. 'In which case, I only have one more question for you.' He approached the table and folded his arms. 'Who gave you the handcuffs? Was it Brian

Steele? Word was, he used to do a bit of coke back then.'

'I knew him,' Hazard conceded.

'You also knew Ness needed handcuffs for his film and you wanted to keep in his good books, so you went to Steele . . . '

But Hazard was shaking his head. 'Not Steele,' he said.

Rebus tried not to let his dismay show. 'Who then?'

'His partner.'

Rebus's eyes narrowed. 'Grant Edwards?' He watched Hazard start to nod. 'Another of your clients?' Hazard kept nodding. Sutherland was looking at Rebus, but Rebus could only shrug. He pushed open the door again. Francis Dean was waiting across the corridor.

'He's all yours,' Rebus said.

Clarke and Fox were standing in the MIT doorway. Rebus kept his face impassive as he headed for the stairs. As he descended, he heard Sutherland's voice summoning Clarke to the interview room.

⋆ ⋆ ⋆

Laura Smith was waiting in the Saab, catching up on emails on her phone.

'You don't even have a USB port,' she complained.

'Told you vintage cars lack a few amenities.'

'It's not vintage, it's just old. How did it go in there?'

'Let's give it half an hour.'

'They'll have had to release him by then.'

'Wait and see,' Rebus said, turning on the Brian Eno CD. 'No more talking for a while,' he told Smith. 'I need to do a bit of thinking.'

*   *   *

'Time's up,' Smith commented, checking her phone.

'So it is,' Rebus agreed.

'And he's still in there — meaning he's talking?'

'Looks like.' Rebus allowed himself a small smile.

'So when do I get the story.'

'After I get the call. Speaking of which . . . ' Rebus picked up his vibrating phone and answered it.

'There were things I heard in there,' Graham Sutherland said in an undertone, 'that I probably shouldn't have.'

'Which is why I didn't want you in the room.'

'Yes, I can see that now.'

'He's talking?'

'Fairly freely, despite the best efforts of his increasingly flustered solicitor.'

'Has he said why he did it?'

'We've not quite got to that yet, though if I were to guess, I'd say you weren't far off the mark. I've taken a break so Siobhan and Callum can have a go at him. Dean's furious that you were allowed in; says it taints whatever story his client spins us.'

'I doubt that'll sway a jury.'

'The fiscal, meantime, is highly delighted. I might owe you a drink, John.'

'Not while I'm on duty, sir.' A weak enough joke, but Sutherland laughed anyway.

'I sort of wish you were still on the force.'

'Aye, me too,' Rebus confessed.

'Do you really have any sway with this Christie character?'

Rebus pondered for a moment. 'Maybe,' he eventually concluded. 'Though I'm hardly likely to waste it on a turd like Glenn Hazard.'

'So he's on his own then?' Sutherland paused. 'And Cafferty?'

'Will know about it sooner or later.'

'I really wish I hadn't stayed in that bloody room . . .'

'You going to report me?'

'Of course not.'

'Tell Siobhan to call me at end of play.'

'I will. And thanks again.'

The line went dead. Smith had leaned across so far in her seat that her head was practically in Rebus's lap.

'Catch any of that?' Rebus asked.

'No.'

'Just as well.'

'But he's confessing to the murder?'

'Seems like.'

'Bloody hell, John — what did you say to him?'

'Whatever was said stays in the confessional.'

'You're hardly anyone's idea of a priest.'

'I used to drink with one, though, a long time back — maybe he taught me a few tricks.'

501

58

Mid-evening at the Oxford Bar. Rebus, Clarke and Fox had requisitioned the back room. The three of them sat around the table nearest the fire as Clarke filled in the blanks.

'Hazard's story is he didn't know Bloom was dead. He hit him with the corner of his mobile phone. Just wanted him unconscious. The plan was to take him to the farm, tie him up in the byre and persuade him not to go ahead with his plan.'

'His plan being?' Fox asked.

'Bloom had spotted Hazard on the film set. Knew who he was and why he'd suddenly stopped being a presence on the clubbing scene.'

'The ODs?'

Clarke nodded. 'Hazard thought he was selling ketamine sourced from China, but the batch was a mix of ketamine and MDMA — in too strong a dose.' She took a sip from her glass. 'If Hazard didn't do what Bloom wanted, he was going to start talking — either to us or to Cafferty.'

Rebus watched her from above the rim of his own glass. 'And what *did* Bloom want?'

'He'd already broken into Brand's office. He reckoned that if you could take something, it would be just as easy to leave something.'

'He was going to plant drugs there?'

'Either in the office or more likely the house. Then he'd tip off the police or the press and

502

Brand would no longer be a threat to Jackie Ness's ambitions.'

'Why the handcuffs?'

'As I say, Hazard swears he thought Bloom was knocked out. They were to stop him trying to run off when he woke up — much more effective than round the wrists.'

'And they stayed on because . . . ?'

Clarke gave a faint smile. 'Guess.'

'He'd lost the key?'

'He'd lost the key,' she confirmed. 'When he gets to the farm, he opens the boot and starts to get a bad feeling.'

'Where's Andrew Carlton in all of this?'

'I think Hazard thought he might help put the frighteners on Bloom, but once he saw Bloom was dead, Hazard panicked. Went and got Carlton and told him he just had a car that needed stashing somewhere.'

'You buy that?'

Clarke considered for a moment, then shrugged. 'I'm not sure it greatly matters. Carlton's an accomplice at best. Hazard isn't saying he was there when he met with Bloom and smacked him.'

'Where was this meeting anyway?'

'On the edge of Poretoun Woods — Bloom's idea, apparently.'

They sat quietly for almost a minute, digesting the story. Rebus was trying to make his IPA last, gripping the glass without drinking from it.

'Anybody want anything?'

They looked up and saw that Grant Edwards had arrived, his bulk filling the doorway.

'We're fine, I think,' Clarke told him. He disappeared to the bar, coming back with a well-watered whisky. He drew out the chair next to Clarke and sat, taking a sip without bothering to offer a toast.

'Thanks for coming,' Rebus said.

'Was I ever going to do anything else?'

Rebus realised the man wasn't smiling. He wore a heavy woollen coat and showed no sign that he'd be taking it off.

'On a scale of one to ten,' Edwards enquired, 'how fucked am I?'

'Eleven,' Rebus said.

'Depends on what you've got to say,' Clarke qualified.

'You know we had a word with Dallas Meikle?'

'That's pretty old news,' Clarke told him.

'And dealt with,' Rebus added. 'Dallas Meikle is our guy now.'

'This won't be any use to you then.' Edwards had dug his phone out of his pocket. He gave it a few taps and held it up so they could hear the recording. It was rough, but audible. They recognised Steele's voice.

'*Phone her often enough and I promise you it'll get to her. But if it doesn't, or you think she deserves worse, you've always got her address.*'

'*Let's see what happens,*' Dallas Meikle said.

'*Keep me posted — once she's riled, I want to know.*'

Edwards switched the recording off and slid the phone back into his pocket.

'Steele always said you were smarter than anyone gave you credit for,' Rebus commented.

'Bit of insurance never goes amiss,' Edwards agreed.

'You've known for a while it might all go belly up?' Clarke asked.

'Insurance, like I say.'

'What did you think,' Rebus broke in, 'when Bloom turned up handcuffed?'

'At first, not much. Then when they turned out to be police issue . . . '

'You recalled the pair you'd given to your dealer?'

'He was Brian's dealer too — we couldn't risk buying from Cafferty's lot. It would have given the big man something *he* could have used as insurance.'

'You knew, though, right? When those kids overdosed, you knew who was responsible?'

'Brian warned Gram to get out of town for a while.'

'But not too far, eh? So you'd still be assured of a supply?' Rebus paused. 'When did it dawn on you the cuffs might have been yours?'

'Didn't really make any odds — Gram had dropped off our radar years back.'

'And when he did a runner, just at the time Stuart Bloom vanished off the face of the earth, you didn't connect the two?'

'I can't speak for Brian.' Edwards swirled his drink, not raising his eyes from it. 'So what does it all add up to, everything you've got so far?'

'Enough,' Clarke stated. 'I doubt Hazard is going to stop talking.' She glanced in Rebus's direction. 'He's got too much to lose.'

'What have you offered him?'

'Never you mind,' Rebus said stonily. 'All that should be concerning you is how much of your own sorry career you can hang on to.'

'I've worked hard for my pension. I've got it earmarked for a motorbike dealership.'

'That's nice,' Rebus said, his tone suggesting the exact opposite.

Edwards looked at each of the three of them in turn. 'What do I have to do to save it?'

It was Fox who answered. 'Sit in a room with Professional Standards and PIRC and anyone else who needs to hear your story. Don't hold anything back. Everything needs to come out.'

'Including Cafferty?'

Rebus leaned forward into the ensuing silence. 'Talk to me,' he said.

'Him and Brian go back a ways. Lot of gen has passed between them, and it's always been a two-way street.'

Rebus gestured towards Edwards's pocket. 'Any of their wee chats feature on that phone of yours?'

'They might,' Edwards conceded. 'All depends whether I'm going to get hit by kid gloves or a knuckleduster.'

'That won't be up to us,' Clarke said.

'None of this is up to us,' Edwards spat back. 'We're just the ones they send down the sewers with a shovel and bucket and a torch that's low on juice.'

'That what you've told yourself all these years?' Rebus said. 'A fairy tale to help you drift off at night?'

'I sleep fine, thanks for asking. How about

you, Rebus? All the stuff you've covered up over the years — and don't tell me you've never traded with your good friend Cafferty.' Edwards turned to Clarke. 'And you with your journalist pal — we knew damned well who'd been talking to her . . . ' He broke off as he saw a quick look pass between Clarke and Fox. 'Oh,' he said, drawing the vowel out. 'Seems we maybe got that one wrong.'

'Which didn't stop you setting Dallas Meikle on DI Clarke,' Rebus snarled.

'Brian's idea — I told him it wasn't one of his best. He was too into it, though.'

'How come?'

Edwards fixed Rebus with a look. 'Because we could never get to you. You were Cafferty's creature.' He saw that Rebus was about to interrupt. 'Insofar as Cafferty enjoyed playing with you too much. We'd have spoilt that if we'd taken you down.' He turned his attention towards Clarke without saying anything.

'Because you saw *me* as John's creature? You couldn't have him, so you'd have me instead?'

Edwards offered a shrug. 'That was Brian's way of thinking.'

'Maybe he was jealous, no?' Fox offered. 'He wanted to be the one Cafferty took an interest in?'

Another shrug from within the overcoat.

'This all needs to come out,' Fox went on. 'I'll put you in touch with Professional Standards. Best if *you* go to *them* — keeping us out of it.' He waited until Edwards had nodded.

'Then we're just about done here,' Rebus

stated. He gestured towards the whisky glass. 'But not before I get you a refill.'

As he returned from the bar, he had to squeeze past Fox and Clarke, who were already on their way. 'Catch you up in a second,' he said.

Edwards sat ruefully at the vacated table, draining his drink. Rebus placed the fresh one in front of him. But as Edwards reached for it, Rebus grabbed him by the wrist. Edwards was strong, but Rebus was on his feet, which helped give him more purchase over the seated figure.

Plus, no point denying it, his dander was up.

By the time Edwards did rise from his chair, his wrist was already held to the table leg by the handcuffs.

'Same ones you used on me,' Rebus said, backing away until he was out of range. Edwards had upended the table, the glasses flying. He studied the table leg and saw that it was connected to the others by a crosspiece. He couldn't release himself by simply sliding the cuff down the length of the leg.

'Seem to have lost the key,' Rebus said with a shrug of his own, turning to leave.

Clarke and Fox were waiting for him outside. They began to walk along Young Street, towards North Castle Street where they'd parked their cars.

'Is Edwards going to get off with this?' Clarke asked.

'Ever hear the story of Burke and Hare?' Rebus answered, breathing heavily.

'Killers who sold their victims to medical people for use in dissections,' Fox stated.

Rebus nodded. 'Hare turned king's evidence — grassed his compadre up, in other words. He was let go, which sounds outrageous but apparently that was the deal. Didn't help him much — he fled south but was recognised. Someone blinded him and left him like that. Ended his days begging.' Having reached his Saab, Rebus paused. 'Nobody ever quite gets away with it.'

'Not even Billie Meikle?' Clarke asked.

'I suppose there may be exceptions,' Rebus conceded. 'Though even then, I'm not sure. Doesn't mean you should feel guilty about any of it.'

'I doubt that'll stop me,' she replied, shoulders hunched, head down as she headed to her own car.

★ ★ ★

Edwards was still wrestling with the table when he spotted a figure in the doorway.

'A bit of help here,' he said.

'Well, well.'

Edwards froze momentarily as Brian Steele walked in. Steele had his hands in his pockets but removed them as he bent at the knees, the better to study his colleague's predicament.

'You go shooting your mouth off and this is the thanks you get, eh?' He shook his head in mock sympathy.

'Fuck you, Brian. Just give me a hand here.'

'Here it is, Grant.'

The slap was like whiplash. Edwards tried

lunging at Steele, but the table prevented it. Instead, Steele got him in a headlock, his forearm pressing hard on his partner's throat. Edwards made a choking sound, eyes bulging, teeth gritted.

'Been watching you for a while, lad,' Steele hissed into his ear. 'Wondering if and when you'd crack. Seems I have my answer.'

Edwards's free hand clamped itself around Steele's fingers and prised at one of them, bending it back until it threatened to snap. Steele gasped in pain, the pressure lessening on Edwards's larynx. Edwards wrestled himself free and stamped hard on the table's wooden crosspiece, snapping it and freeing the handcuffs. He turned towards Steele just as the punch connected, catching him square on the nose. Blood began to flow, his eyes filling with tears. Blindly he threw his whole weight at Steele, the two of them colliding with one of the other tables. Edwards had his hands around his old friend's throat as the few regulars from the front bar finally plucked up the nerve to intervene. There were just enough of them to wrestle the two men apart. When Steele tried throwing another punch, he found himself restrained by the bar staff. Snarling and spitting, he was manoeuvred out of the room, down the steps and into the night.

The barman pointed at Edwards. 'Take it outside if you want,' he said, 'but first you're paying for the damage.'

'It was Rebus did this,' Edwards roared, shaking the handcuff in the barman's face. 'Get him to pay!'

'If that's the way you want it.' The barman took out his phone. 'We'll let the police handle it.'

'I *am* the police!' Edwards went quiet as he got his breathing under control. 'I am the police,' he repeated quietly, though with a little less certainty than before.

59

Back home, Rebus fed Brillo and took him out to the Meadows for a run. He looked across the expanse of grass towards Quartermile. He knew which windows belonged to Cafferty's duplex. One of them had its lights on. He took out his phone and made the call.

'You have reached the Samaritans,' Cafferty growled. 'How can we help you tonight?'

'I think you might be about to lose your friendly face at ACU.'

Silence on the line for a moment. Then: 'Plenty more where that came from.'

'Maybe so, but not many you'll have nurtured for so many years.'

'Well, thanks for the warning. I'm guessing there's a favour you want in return.'

Rebus watched Brillo, wishing he had even a fraction of the dog's energy. 'What can you tell me about the break-in at Brand's office?'

'It was a set-up,' Cafferty explained. 'The paperwork was fake, the intention being to wrong-foot Ness if he ever got hold of it.'

'And you know this because . . . ?'

'Stuart Bloom made a note to that effect. Didn't even bother showing any of it to Ness. He knew as soon as he read through it.'

'You broke into his flat?'

'In point of fact, a nurtured and friendly face did that for me.'

Steele . . .

'And afterwards?'

'When Bloom disappeared, I ditched everything.'

'You must have been gutted the papers didn't give you the leverage you wanted with Conor Maloney.'

'Water under the bridge, John.' Cafferty paused to sip from a glass, making sure Rebus could hear him. He gave a noisy exhalation. 'I hear Siobhan got someone for Bloom's murder, though.'

'That dealer, the one who used to be Graeme Hatch. Reinvented himself as Glenn Hazard.'

'The PR guy?'

'Bloom was threatening to hand him over to you.'

'Really?'

'I'm guessing it'll come out at the trial.'

'All of it?'

'Maybe not quite all,' Rebus conceded. Brillo had started barking at another dog. Rebus told him to sit, then clipped the lead back on to his collar.

'You're at the Meadows with your mutt? I can't quite see you.'

Rebus turned to peer at the lit window. 'I can see you, though, clear as day.'

'Pop by for a drink. Wine's supposed to be good for the blood pressure.'

'Maybe so, but I doubt *you'd* be good for mine.'

'Remember to congratulate Siobhan for me, John. And don't be a stranger.'

'One last thing . . . '

'Yes?'

'Steele and Edwards, they knew Graeme Hatch back in the day. All the time you were looking for him, they protected him so they could keep buying what he was selling.'

Silence on the line while Cafferty digested this. Then he made a snuffling sound. 'I hope you're not just spinning me a line.'

'I'm not.'

'In which case, I might have to have words with them.'

'I wouldn't put it off. They'll be in custody before too long. Fair warning, though — I want to hang on to Edwards.'

Rebus ended the call and watched the silhouette retreat from the penthouse window. Brillo was straining at the leash.

'Time to go home, son,' Rebus told him.

★   ★   ★

The call came at 3 a.m. Number withheld. When Cafferty lifted the phone, he noticed that there was a text on the second phone lying next to it. It was from the lovely Rebecca. He had messaged her earlier, advising her to dump Brian Steele before the shit storm arrived. Her reply consisted of a heart and a thumbs-up. Cafferty allowed himself a thin smile as he answered the call.

'What's so fucking urgent?' Conor Maloney snarled.

'Bit of news to report — they got Stuart

514

Bloom's killer. It was the dealer who sold the bad stuff to those kids.'

'Oh aye? So it wasn't me, then?'

'And the dealer definitely didn't work for me. So . . . '

'Truce?'

'We've maligned and mistrusted one another for far too long. Time we got out the pipe of peace, don't you think?'

'Depends what's in it for each of us.'

'Plenty of opportunities, Conor. Brexit's going to be a gold mine for disaster capitalists.'

'Is that what we are?'

'I imagine you've been eyeing up the dotted line between south and north, wondering what a hard Irish border might mean.'

'Where did you hear that?'

'An educated guess. I was able to make it because you and me think the same way. Seems that everywhere people are burning bridges or building walls. I want the opposite to happen with us.'

'I suppose we could bounce a few ideas around.'

'Not on the phone, though. I can come to you or you can come to me. Some pretty nice hotels in Scotland — even if I don't own any of them yet.'

'Eyeball to eyeball, eh?'

Cafferty had picked up the other phone. The screen still showed Rebecca's message. 'Sometimes,' he said softly, 'the old ways are the best.'

Epilogue

A bright Sunday afternoon. John Rebus and Deborah Quant walked hand in hand to Bruntsfield Links. Brillo's leash was in Rebus's free hand, the dog leading the way. They soon caught sight of Clarke and Sutherland. Both were wrapped up against the east wind. Both carried a putter and a nine iron. Malcolm Fox gave a wave of greeting as Rebus and Quant approached.

'You the referee?' Rebus asked.

'There'd be rampant cheating otherwise. Three holes played. Graham's not showing much mercy. You heard the news?'

'What news is that?'

'Steele seems to have gone AWOL.'

'Is that right? Vacancy for you at ACU then, always supposing you want it.'

Fox gave him an appraising look. 'Sounds like you think he's not coming back.'

The gesture Rebus made with his shoulders could have been a shrug or a shiver. They watched as Clarke took her tee shot, missing the ball completely with her first swing, then sending it rolling and bouncing along the turf with her second.

'Shouldn't there be slightly more elevation?' Quant asked.

'She'd be better off just using the putter,' Rebus added.

They watched as Sutherland connected cleanly, sending his ball up into the air and landing it on the edge of the green.

'Turning into a massacre,' Fox commented. They joined the players as they walked towards their next shot.

'Twenty quid says Siobhan wins this hole,' Rebus called out to Sutherland.

'Are you serious?'

'Never more so.'

'You're on,' Sutherland said with a grin. Clarke took her shot and almost reached the green.

'Not a bad lie,' Rebus stated. Sutherland started lining up his putt. Rebus reached down and unhooked Brillo's leash.

'Go fetch,' he said. Brillo didn't need telling twice. He bounded across the fairway and scooped up Sutherland's ball in his mouth. Rebus turned to Fox.

'The hole's forfeit, wouldn't you say, ref?'

Deborah Quant was squeezing his arm. 'You're a bad, bad man, John.'

'But we've all known worse in our time, right?' Rebus pecked her on the cheek and tried not to glance in the direction of Quartermile.

We do hope that you have enjoyed reading this large print book.

Did you know that all of our titles are available for purchase?

We publish a wide range of high quality large print books including:
Romances, Mysteries, Classics
General Fiction
Non Fiction and Westerns

Special interest titles available in large print are:
The Little Oxford Dictionary
Music Book
Song Book
Hymn Book
Service Book

Also available from us courtesy of Oxford University Press:
Young Readers' Dictionary
(large print edition)
Young Readers' Thesaurus
(large print edition)

For further information or a free brochure, please contact us at:
Ulverscroft Large Print Books Ltd.,
The Green, Bradgate Road, Anstey,
Leicester, LE7 7FU, England.
Tel: (00 44) 0116 236 4325
Fax: (00 44) 0116 234 0205

Other titles published by Ulverscroft:

RATHER BE THE DEVIL

Ian Rankin

Some cases never leave you. For John Rebus, forty years have passed, but the death of beautiful, promiscuous Maria Turquand still preys on his mind. Murdered in her hotel room on the night a famous rock star and his entourage were staying there, Maria's killer has never been found. Meanwhile, the dark heart of Edinburgh remains up for grabs. A young pretender, Darryl Christie, may have staked his claim, but a vicious attack leaves him weakened and vulnerable, and an inquiry into a major money laundering scheme threatens his position. Has old-time crime boss Big Ger Cafferty really given up the ghost, or is he biding his time until Edinburgh is once more ripe for the picking?